The Book of Marie

MERCER
UNIVERSITY PRESS

Endowed by
TOM WATSON BROWN
and
THE WATSON-BROWN FOUNDATION, INC.

Also by Terry Kay

The Book of Marie

A Novel

Terry Kay

Mercer University Press
Macon, Georgia

MUP/

Published by
Mercer University Press
1400 Coleman Avenue
Macon, Georgia 31207

First Edition.

Books published by Mercer University Press are printed on acid
free paper that meets the requirements of American National
Standard for Information Sciences—Permanence of Paper for
Printed Library Materials.

Library of Congress Cataloging-in-Publication Data

Kay, Terry.
The book of Marie : a novel / Terry Kay. -- 1st ed.
p. cm.
ISBN-13: 978-0-88146-082-7 (alk. paper)
ISBN-10: 0-88146-082-6 (alk. paper)
1. Civil rights workers—Fiction. 2. Race relations—Fiction. 3. Class
reunions—Fiction. 4. Atlanta (Ga.)—Fiction. I. Title.
PS3561.A885B66 2007
813'.54—dc22
2007021868

A Note on Style

This book is presented in both first person and third person perspective—a technique I have never before employed. To maintain focus while writing, I decided to use quotation marks in the first person dialogue and to eliminate them in the third person. It was, for me, a sensible and helpful exercise and I have elected—with the publisher's consent—to continue the style in print. I hope it does not create a distraction for the reader.

Terry Kay

The words of this book are dedicated to my eight grandchildren—Brooks, Jordan, Cheyenne, Tommie, Winn, Casual, Brandon, and Wyatt. My wish is for them to find peace in the giving and taking of the lives they choose to follow, and to be as blessed by the miracle of caring as their Papa has been blessed by them.

Author's Note

Many years ago, I wrote a novel that I titled *A Prayer for Dreamers*. My intention was to examine the sweep of social change in the American south from post-World War II to the mid-1990s, as reflected in the civil rights movement.

The story focused on two characters, a young white boy and a young black boy, born in the same Georgia community on the same day in the same hour.

Originally, there were three parts to the book—the boys' friendship in their childhood years, their separation by the circumstance of time and cultural tradition, and, finally, a half-century later, their eventual reuniting.

Only part one was published. It was called *The Runaway*. For reasons I have never understood, the publisher shied away from the complete story. (I do know, of course, that writing is a business and the romantic notion of putting words on paper, for whatever purpose, gets a wink and a smile when it comes to making business decisions.)

Still, rejection stings and writers of all genres understand what it means to back up and begin again, to delete (or file away) and to toy with new directions guided by different points of view. That is what I did after my original manuscript was edited (or truncated). I began again. And again. And again. I rewrote the unpublished portions from several perspectives over a number of years, until I realized the story was so close to my personal history, it hindered the efforts. (Nothing blinds a writer as much as the glare of reflection.)

Although that personal history no longer clutters *The Book of Marie* as it once did, it does remain embedded in the story. I could not have written it otherwise. I was a child—a white child—of the segregated south. As a young man, I witnessed the confrontations and the promise of desegregation, earned in events of high drama. As a mature adult, I have been elated, and saddened, by the good and bad efforts to assimilate hyphenated cultures into something worthy of that eloquent prayer spoken by Martin Luther King, Jr. on August 28, 1963, in front of the Lincoln Memorial in Washington, D.C.

Unhappily, I have accepted that Dr. King's dream is still mostly a dream, with one glad exception: the relationship of one person with another person works, as it always has, and it does not matter what the hyphen separates or binds together—Irish-American, African-American, Polish-American, Japanese-American, et cetera. There is no hyphen in caring or in friendship.

Eventually, that is what I found in this book —a story of people embracing other people one-to-one, a love story. The theme of social change is still present, but more as background than as issue.

For those familiar with *The Runaway*, a caution: this is not a sequel to that story. (A follow-up, perhaps, but not a sequel.) I changed names of characters, placed them in different situations and watched as they began to express different personalities. Events I had not previously considered appeared magically, and that is the true joy of writing: you are not telling a story; you are discovering one.

I hope readers find elements of their own heritage in *The Book of Marie*. I hope they know, or knew, a Marie Fitzpatrick. I hope they know, or knew, a Moses Elder and an Art Crews and a Littlejohn Curry and an Alyse Lewis and a Tanya Berry and a Jovita and a Lamar and a Hugh and a Wormy and a Sally and a Toby and an Amy and a Rachel, and all the others who peeked up from the word-machine I use for writing. They were there for me because, over time, I have known each of them, or fragments of them. In great part, they are the make-up of my life.

The Book of Marie

Prologue

1962

She heard the fire before seeing it—the sound of it crawling in the walls like a playful scurrying of mice. And then she heard pounding at the front door—far off, it seemed—and with the pounding, a man's voice shouting, Get out!, shouting, Fire! Fire!

All of it happened in the bewilderment of a groggy awakening, each moment piling hard against the moment in front of it—the sound of crawling fire and the pounding at the door and the shouting, and then the heavy smell of smoke, and through the window above her she could see the jerky dancing of flames on the outside weatherboarding, and from across the room she heard the whimpering of a voice—Littlejohn's voice—calling for her, saying, *Mama, Mama, Mama.*

The flames broke through the inside wall near her bed. A thin orange tongue of fire licked against the ceiling. Smoke swirled. She could smell the scent of singed hair and heart-of-pine wood and gasoline. She tried to move, but could not, her muscles as useless as a person paralyzed by polio, the weight of the smoke pinning her to the bed. She thought of sleep, of how good sleep would be, and the thought caused her to close her eyes. Then, as if by magic, she sensed herself rising from the bed until she was suspended against the ceiling, swirling with the smoke in a boneless smoke body. She peered down on the bed below her and she watched a man—she knew him to be Doke Wansley, a drinker and a no-good—lifting her from the mattress, shouldering her like a sack of grain. She saw Doke Wansley turning, bulling his way across the room to a door.

She heard again, *Mama, Mama.* The words were screamed. And then she lost consciousness.

≈

In the years that followed, she would go often to the memory of the fire. It was never long-lasting, appearing mostly in fragments of flashing pictures, and sometimes she wondered if thinking of it was more a habit of her brain than something sealed inside her soul. It could be that, she reasoned, for she remembered it always in the same manner—awakening to the fire around her, unable to move, being carried from the house, Littlejohn's cry for her, fainting on Doke Wansley's shoulder. She remembered being revived by neighbors bringing water to her face with the palms of their hands, their hysterical cries coming as loud as the sirens of fire trucks and police cars. She remembered the heat of the fire and the bright colors of flames playing leapfrog across the roof ridge of the house. She remembered her children crowding around her, all but Littlejohn. Burned, they had said of Littlejohn. Had tried to go back into the house to find her, but the smoke had choked him down. Doke Wansley had dragged him out and he had been taken to the doctor's house. She remembered the sickness of terror. And then, in the way of incident leaping time, she remembered all the moments after the fire when she saw the crinkled skin of burn-scars on the right side of Littlejohn's neck and face and also the disfigured ear. The marking of fire on Littlejohn's face and neck and ear kept the story alive in the lore of Overton long after the gossip of it had become as age-wrinkled as those who remembered it.

The gossip had been mostly about the fire-setter—guessed-at names said whisper-light for fear of reprisal. She had been asked hundreds of times if she knew the truth of it. She did not, she had replied with honesty. She knew—or believed she knew—the reason the match was struck, but she kept the thought to herself. There had been enough talk about her and about the young white girl, the outsider, and also about the boy, coming back the day after the fire as he did, causing such bitter talk so soon after the picture of him showed up in the newspaper.

The reason for the fire was in all of it, yet she did not offer her opinion. Not then. Not ever.

In the early 60s, many things were best left alone if you were colored.

Time would even things out, she believed.

Maybe not in my life, but someday, she said to those who still listened to her, nodding placating nods out of the kindness of friendship. Among themselves they had talked in a more pitying manner, saying the answer had been around since the beginning, saying if the sheriff had paid any attention to Doke Wansley, the name of the fire-setter would have been known before the smoke cleared.

Yet, after almost half a century, the truth of the fire would matter very little, for the ash of it had long blown away and weeds and scrub trees had taken root where the house had been.

The land had healed.

Doke Wansley had died.

The sheriff, whose name was Julian Overstreet, had also died.

Doke had said he saw the fire-setter. The sheriff had said Doke was half-drunk when it happened—which, by all accounts, was true—and he was not about to take the word of a half-drunk. A half-drunk's word in court was as wobbly as his step.

Doke had said the fire-setter was running away carrying a gasoline can with him, running so fast a man would think the Devil was close behind.

White or colored? Julian Overstreet had asked Doke.

White, Doke had said too quickly.

How you know that? the sheriff had demanded. You that close up on him?

Not real close, Doke had answered cautiously.

Then you don't know for sure, the sheriff had insisted, using a voice that made Doke rethink his words.

Uh, nossir, I guess not, Doke had confessed.

How I know you didn't set that house on fire, Doke? Julian Overstreet had asked. You could of gone over there and pissed on the back porch and lit it with a kitchen match and it would of caught fire like a kerosene log from all that rot-gut you been drinking. How I know it weren't you?

Those who were there, watching, listening—some who would be chief among the gossipers in the following years—had said they saw Doke go scared, saw him take a backward step and duck his head. Had said they remembered hearing him mumble, Nossir, it weren't me. I was just coming down the road, going home, when I seen it.

Was it burning hard? the sheriff had pressed.

Just a little bit when I first seen it, Doke had mumbled. Then it pick up, real fast. I could hear it. Sound like the wind when the wind whip up out of nowhere. And I could smell it, too. Smell the gasoline.

That when you saw the man running?

Uh-huh. Yessir. That's when.

Going which way?

That way, Doke had answered, pointing east on the road, where the road took a sharp turn to the left behind a stand of pine trees, leaving Milltown.

Had a gas can with him?

Uh-huh. Yessir.

You didn't see nobody else?

Nossir.

Didn't see no car?

Nossir, but they could have been one. Thought I heard a car door slam.

You didn't go look?

Nossir. I went down to the house and started knocking on the door, trying to get everybody out. Weren't no time to do nothing else.

That when you kick down the door?

Yessir.

Anybody see you around there? the sheriff had asked, and a number of people—neighbors—had answered for Doke, saying, Yessir, he's telling you right. He went in the house and started running out the children and then he got out Jovita and the littlest boy. Yessir, they be dead now except for Doke.

And Julian Overstreet had left it at that, knowing it would be touchy to make a great fuss over some burned-down colored house in Milltown. It was 1962. With all the bellowing about the colored going to school with whites, putting doubt on the fire-setter being a white man was as far as he needed to take it.

Besides, the day had been full enough with talk about the Bishop boy having his picture plastered on the front page of every newspaper from Atlanta to Hong Kong. It was a shame, the way that boy had changed, but everybody knew it was the girl's doing, the girl putting nonsense in his head. Her kind would be the ruin of the country if she had her way about things.

Goddamn agitators.

ONE

2004

On the evening before the letter arrived, he had hosted a surprise birthday party in his home for Grace Webster, using the ruse of a faculty committee meeting to review plans for a summer literary tour of Ireland—Dublin to Donegal.

The meeting would not take long, he had promised Grace with apology. A matter of dotting i's and crossing t's. Admittedly an aggravation, yet something needed to be done before Christmas holidays.

The party had been childish. Guests pouring out of back rooms wearing party hats, yelping. Grace in shock, covering her mouth with her hands to hold back squeals. A dinner of southern food, demanded by the party-planners, saying it was it his duty since he and Grace were the only southerners in the department. Giving in, he had prepared fried chicken and ham-hock turnip greens, black-eyed peas covered with tomato gravy, butter-soaked grits, cornbread sticks, a sweet potato soufflé, and iced tea heavily sweetened with sugar.

The food had caused laughter and jesting, as he expected it would. In Vermont, much of the food was as foreign as escargot would have been at the dining table of his parents' home in Georgia.

After the dinner, gifts had been presented. Books. Music on compact disks. A scarf. Gloves. A basket of products from the fields and woods of Vermont. And, last, skimpy lingerie pulled from a box having no giver's name on it, making a moment of awkwardness, a tittering of nervous giggles, leaving the guests to wonder and to speculate, most of them believing the lingerie was from Gere Contrada—Gere's sexual orientation being suspect and Grace being young and seductively pretty. Grace saying, *Oh, goodness...* in her soft Tennessee voice, her voice as blushed as her face.

And then the playing of the party games, designed by Gere. In the games was the tease, the warning, that would be found in the letter.

The games had been intentionally adolescent, the sort played by children on the cusp of being adults, and he had suspected it was Gere's way of jesting with Grace over her age. Just a baby, Gere had cooed.

One game had required each guest to write a fortune in the manner of those found in Chinese fortune cookies, and to place it in a box. Grace had to do the drawing, reading each fortune aloud, then assigning each fortune to one of the partiers. We'll see how well you know us, Gere Contrada had said.

The fortune Grace Webster had assigned to him was: *The destination you seek is waiting for you at the start of your journey.*

Gere Contrada had laughed. My God, Cole, do you even remember where that is?

He had answered, Barely.

The next day, the letter arrived.

The way his name was handwritten on the envelope—graceful, looping letters—told him it had been addressed by a woman.

The postmark was from Overton.

The return address was 151 Franklin Street.

Inside the envelope was an announcement of the fiftieth reunion of the class of 1955, Overton High School. It read, in centered print:

For those of us
Who made it this far,
Now is the time
To see who we are.
So make your plans
To include this date
And be prepared
To tell us your fate.

The date advertised was April 16, 2005. The place was DeWitt Kilmer's Recreation Hall. A parenthetical held the word Restored.

A note, also handwritten in graceful, looping letters, was included. It read:

Cole,

Your sister Amy gave me your address. All of us hope you can make it to the reunion. It's been 50 years. Can you believe it? Maybe you don't know, but I married a man named Jody Pendleton from Ila. He died three years ago of a heart attack. I still miss him, but I have our children (3 of them, 2 boys and a girl) and 5 grandchildren, and they keep me believing I'm young, even if the mirror won't let me hide from the truth. I've worked at the library for 22 years now. It's something I enjoy, and it's taught me the pleasure of reading. As I recall, you were our reader during our school years. I wish I had started younger. A lot has happened to all of us and I'm sure most of us never believed our lives would have turned out the way they have. We're all proud of you, so please, please make plans to come, and bring any mementoes you may have saved—from report cards to letter jackets. We want to make a table display.

The letter was signed:
With affection,
Alyse
There was a P.S.

By the way, do you know how to reach Marie Fitzpatrick? She may have been different, but she was a member of our class and we want to make sure she gets an invitation. If you know anything about her, please let me know, or you could just ask her about coming. Are you freezing up there in Vermont? It snowed here last week, almost two inches deep. It was pretty, but I couldn't take being knee-deep in it. And thinking of snow reminds me: Merry Christmas.

And there it was: the name.
Marie Fitzpatrick.
The name caused him to lean back in his chair, to sit for a long time, holding the letter from Alyse Pendleton.

And then he pushed himself from his chair and went into his office, to a rolltop desk. He took a small key from a polished mahogany box once used to hold cuff links and then he opened a drawer filled with letters, neatly arranged. He removed one at random and opened it, reading it again, reading the words, though he knew most of them from memory.

Dearest Cole Bishop,

I think I am a little tipsy, my beloved fool-friend. I wish you were here with me. We could be tipsy together, and we could celebrate my new life. Oh, yes, Cole, there is a new Marie. I have decided to abandon my ambition of becoming the world's grandest surgeon to become the world's grandest attorney.

I can see you now, as you read this—mouth flapping open, eyes blank and staring at the page, your little one-cylinder mind churning away with some feeble argument about my erratic behavior. It doesn't matter, Cole; your argument would be useless, as always. And, no, my decision has nothing to do with failing grades. The truth is, I'm teaching about half of the classes I'm taking, but I've lost the passion, Cole—that wonderful burning that has always made me do things. Also, I've been having visions lately, visions of standing before a judge in some severe courtroom, locked in mental combat with a shyster from a multi-trillion dollar law firm, and I am kicking him in the balls, Cole. I am defending some good, but helpless person (like you), who doesn't have a snowball's chance in hell of beating the system. But I beat it. I tear it asunder. I destroy it.

Isn't that also a noble calling, Cole? Isn't it? I mean, what good is a healthy heart if the hope flowing through it is being devoured by the cancer of The Takers? And I've seen it, Cole. Too many times. I have seen the great masses—you may remember them; you used to think of them as your audience—wandering lost, trying to do things the right way, but being squashed by power-hungry men believing they are God.

I want to see people win who have never won. I want to win for them.

Wouldn't you like this new Marie, Cole? Wouldn't you want to stand beside her? Wouldn't you want her to have your children?

Oh, God, I miss you so much at times. How can I enjoy grandiose dreams without you, my fool-friend, the Jester of Dreams?

But I do warn you: I will not represent you pro bono when you are sued for alienation of affection by some moon-eyed little coed who falls for your smooth talk. Even I cannot defend inane bullshit.

Ain't life wonderful, Cole Bishop? Don't you love me?

She had written the letter when she was a senior at Harvard. Two days later, he had received another letter from her, informing him she must have been drugged by someone. She would never be an attorney. Attorneys were asses. She hated attorneys.

If I frightened you, or made you glad, Cole, I apologize. The fact is, I was destined to be a doctor. I guess my actions prove you were right with that silly drivel you used to quote: Look before you leap. Well, I'll remember it now. You should too.

He had responded with a bellowing of triumph, telling her he was pleased she had finally learned something he knew all too well. She had returned the letter, with his boasting underlined and a single, over-sized word written in the margin with the wide tip of an ink pen. The word was *Ha!*

❧

The letter he wrote to Alyse Pendleton, saying he would attend the reunion, contained one carefully worded reference to Marie Fitzpatrick: *I'm afraid I can't help in the search for Marie.*

It was a statement of part-truth, part-lie—the hedging of not-saying and, to Cole, the employment of good sense. From their first meeting, Marie Jean Fitzpatrick had had power over him, much the same as a wizard casting spells in some children's story, and it did not matter that he had last seen her the night of their graduation from Overton High School. She had vowed she would be peering forever over his shoulder, always at unexpected times, taunting him with her wisdom, and for a half-century, it had seemed that way, appearing as she did from memory-codes as distant as the music of their youth or as immediate as a stranger's face—usually a new student—having her features.

Now she had returned in a letter from Alyse Pendleton, and he knew she would not easily leave him.

He was right.

That night she appeared in a dream, wearing her white high school robe of graduation, sitting in a child's swing, swinging high in the air, so high she touched stars with her toes. And then she was standing near him, her face tucked against his chest, and she was saying, I do love you, Cole Bishop.

The dream ended and he awoke exhausted, a coating of perspiration across the top of his chest.

He thought, My God, where did that come from?

He looked at the digital clock on the bed stand and saw the time was closing in on midnight.

He said aloud, Go away, Marie. It was gently spoken, with some weariness in his voice.

From somewhere in the room, deep in his imagination, he heard her snicker.

He lay in his bed, listening, believing the dream of her was from the melancholy of the season of Christmas, being alone as he was. Mind tricks brought on by age. One minute in childhood, the next minute bone-weary by too many years too quickly lived. Age leaving its calling card—faint, tell-tale wrinkle-scarring on his skin, the beginning of a sag on his chin line under his beard, small brown liver dots, like freckles, on the back of his hands, a slight loss of hearing. Age playing with his mind, also, and he knew it, knew he was a tick slow in his reasoning and in the repartee that had served him well among colleagues and students. In the last year or so, he had jokingly been called a curmudgeon, had been teased over memory lapses that struck him like strobes of white light. There were many questions about his retirement plans, some in jest, some serious.

Putting all of it together—being alone as he was in the melancholy of the season of Christmas with age playing its tricks—it was not a surprise to him that Marie Jean Fitzpatrick had come calling in the middle of sleep, keeping her promise to peer over his shoulder at unexpected times.

She would find delight in Alyse Pendleton being a medium for her appearance, having found Alyse tediously predictable in their youth.

Patience, he thought. He would have to practice patience.

Her presence would eventually disappear.

It always had, given time.

Again, he heard her laugh. Almost real. Real enough to have an echo.

He pushed back the covering and rolled off the bed and made his way into his office and went to a bookcase and eased a worn book from the top shelf and opened it to a page marked by a small Christmas card shaped in the face of a Santa Claus laughing a jolly laugh.

On the page, he saw the word and the word caused a smile.

He had celebrated only one Christmas with Marie during the period of the blithe charade they had called dating. On Christmas Eve 1954, alone in the living room of her home, beside a Christmas tree lavishly decorated, he had given her a bracelet engraved with her initials and a small bottle of perfume that Amy, his sister, had selected.

I think you should kiss me, too, Cole Bishop, she had said softly, but if you do, I'll cry. A moist film had filled her eyes. It's the first time a boy's ever given me anything.

It didn't cost much, he had replied stupidly.

It did to me, she had cooed. To me, it cost a million dollars. She had hugged him quickly, then stepped away and looked at the bracelet on her wrist. I'll wear it forever. I won't ever take it off.

Really, it's not expensive, he had insisted. It'll probably turn your skin green.

And the perfume, she had said excitedly. The next time we have a date, I'll wear it, and I'll tell everybody that it's called Passion On Hold, and that you gave it to me to keep until our wedding night, but I took out a drop just to remind me of you.

Don't go overboard, he had warned.

I bet you think I didn't get you anything, she had countered.

If you did, you didn't have to. I mean, it's not like we're really going steady, or anything like that, no matter what people think we're doing.

Well, I did. I got you something you need.

What?

She had reached beneath the Christmas tree and removed a package. He knew it was a book by the shape of it and it was—a thesaurus.

Do you like it? she had asked hopefully.

Uh, sure, he had answered.

No, you don't. I can tell by your face.

Sure, I do, he had insisted. I just sort of thought it would be a novel.

You can get novels anytime, but you need this. It'll help broaden that pitifully limited vocabulary of yours.

My vocabulary's as good as yours, he had argued.

No, it's not, Cole. It's all right, but it's not as good as mine.

Merry Christmas to you too.

Quit acting hurt, Cole. All right, your vocabulary's great. I mean it. You can talk to me, and I understand you, don't I?

Thanks a lot, Marie.

She had taken the book from him and had opened it to a page marked by the Santa Claus Christmas card signed, *Fondly, Marie.* I underlined a word for you, she had said.

The word was *escape.*

What's that supposed to mean? he had demanded.

Memorize it, Cole, she had answered. Years from now, without me to protect you, you'll need to know all the words you can about escaping.

From what?

From everything you can't handle.

He had looked at her closely. She was smiling, but there was sorrow in her eyes.

You know, you're strange, he had said.

I know, Cole, she had whispered. Merry Christmas.

Some of the synonyms for escape were: *avoidance, elusion, shunning, flight, lam, slip, eschewal.*

Over the years, he had used them all.

He closed the book and placed it back on the shelf and went into his kitchen and took a container of orange juice from his refrigerator and a glass from the cabinet. He stood for a moment, holding the orange juice, then reconsidered his desire for it and put it back into the refrigerator. He realized he had begun to do such things, and for some reason the refrigerator seemed part of it, the same as a plot-reference in a mystery novel. How many times had he opened the door to the refrigerator lately when wanting to use the microwave? Or how many times had he discovered the salt and pepper shakers near the milk? Often. Too often. And it was not the only time he had taken orange juice from the refrigerator, not really wanting it. Three nights earlier—the night of the party for Grace Webster—he had done the same. He thought of Tanya Berry. Tanya would razz him mercilessly. Tanya would turn the unwanted orange juice into a metaphor the equal of Jesus turning well water into wine, and if not that, she would compare the refrigerator to Pandora's Box, or to some mausoleum filled with the icy spirit of demons.

He shook his head, chuckled hard enough over his meandering thinking to make sound rise from his throat, and he wondered why Tanya Berry had leapt into his mind. She had been one of his most cherished friends for twenty years, a sister-like colleague at Raemar University, yet he knew there was more than friendship at play in the moment. Tanya was also a brilliant clinical psychologist, a woman who had earned her liberation from a middle-class Philadelphia neighborhood by being assertive and blunt, using a sailor's language when the occasion invited it. She had long teased that one day, due to his bouts with boredom or from the emptiness of his day-dreaming ways, he would come begging for her professional services. Someday, she badgered. You wait. Someday, you'll come crawling. Someday you'll understand you can't find all your answers in books.

And maybe that time had come, he thought. Maybe with the letter from Alyse Pendleton and with the dream-presence of Marie Fitzpatrick still hovering in his home, he had reached the tell-all stage of his life and talking about it to Tanya Berry would clear away some of the confusion. It had worked for other people that he knew—or so they had claimed.

Yet, Tanya was wrong about one thing: he would not go crawling. There would be no trembling, no begging for help, no howling cries of need.

He was not a crazy person.

Aging, perhaps, but not crazy.

ॐ

At five o'clock, he awoke again from a weighty sleep. He was again lathered in perspiration, again heard the voice of Marie Fitzpatrick in the room with him, the voice saying, Do you think you can hide from me, Cole Bishop?

He licked his lips and realized his mouth was dry. In the dark of the room, he could sense her watching him. A great chill struck his body, causing him to convulse violently in the tangle of his bedcovering.

At eight o'clock, he called Tanya Berry.

I think I need you, he said weakly.

The call surprised her. She could hear quaking in his voice. She said, Cole, this isn't one of your jokes, is it?

No, he replied, his voice dropping to a whisper. No, he repeated.

All right, she told him. Nine o'clock. My office.

TWO

He would write about the way Marie Fitzpatrick came into his life because Tanya Berry insisted he do so, telling him it would help set the memories straight, and if he had the memories straight, he would be able to follow them back to some understanding.

Do it little by little, she said. Begin at the beginning. Each day, write something. You're on sabbatical next semester, aren't you? It shouldn't be difficult for you. You're a teacher.

Of literature, not of writing, he protested.

Excuse me, she said. I believe you won the National Book Award for biography, did you not?

A fluke, he mumbled. And it was fifteen years ago—or longer.

I hear it was good stuff, she countered. One of these days, I'll have to read it.

He smiled, knowing she had celebrated his award by using portions of it in her counseling. She had even quoted lines to turn the tables on him in their harmless arguments.

Don't quibble with me, she added. Words are words are words. Start at the beginning and for God's sake, don't think of it as an essay you're writing for some tight-assed literary journal. Just write, Cole. Just do it. Forget the rules. If I see anything that even resembles iambic bullshit, I'll rip your heart out. Just write.

And so he did.

On Sunday, two days following his counsel with Tanya Berry—having no other purpose to occupy his time and needing something to assuage the trembling that struck him unexpectedly at unexpected times—he went into his office and opened the laptop computer on his desk. He keyed in a new folder that he titled, without reason, MARIE, and having written her name, a sentence came into his mind: This is how I remember meeting Marie Jean Fitzpatrick.

He began to write.

December19, morning
This is how I remember meeting Marie Jean Fitzpatrick.

I am dressed in a purple short-sleeved shirt that is rolled once at the sleeves, the collar turned up to scrub against the feathers of my ducktail haircut. The beltless blue jeans I am wearing, fitting snug on my hips, are starched and the legs ironed in the blade of a crease. A pair of white athletic socks dangle from one back pocket like a flag. My new loafers, still glittering from the oil of the leather, click sharply on the wood flooring. The spearmint taste of chewing gum is in my mouth. After shave lotion—too powerful and unnecessary—surrounds me. A smile, proud and smug, worms across my face.

Perfect.

It is near-autumn 1954, and my life is perfect.

Dreamy, yes, but perfect.

I have waited two years to be where I am—in the epicenter of the wad of bodies that move in a swagger along the corridor of Overton High School. My eyes wander over the awed faces of students who are swept against the walls of the corridor by the tide force of those bodies that surround me. I do not hear anyone speak, but I am certain I know what they are saying.

Whispers.

"There he is," the whispers are saying. "That's Cole Bishop. He's the quarterback."

I can see the gaze of girls giddy with dreams of adolescent passion, can hear their sighs, their muted giggles of excitement.

I do not believe any of my teammates understand it, but the march of the Overton High School Purple Panthers through the hallways of Overton High School on the first day of school, 1954, is as ritualistic as ancient warriors conquering a city. Attila the Hun, Alexander the Great, Napoleon Bonaparte. All of them had made such marches, surrounded by men who would protect them. Still, I am not foolish enough to make an issue of it with my teammates since they likely have never heard of Attila or Alexander or

Napoleon, but, to me, there is little difference between a General and a quarterback.

A half-dozen boys scamper through the opened door of a classroom, and Lamar McDowell, who marches in front of me, his wide body moving like the bow of a ship, growls at them. "Cockroaches," Lamar says.

We move on, our footsteps echoing in gunshots of hard-rubber heels on wood.

"Go Panthers," a voice calls from one of the rooms. Lamar flips a stubby-fingered bird toward the room. A giggle wings back toward us. Lamar's gesture is like a blessing. It will be talked about for weeks, for years. In small schools, small moments are memorable.

We are nearing the end of the corridor, approaching the stairwell leading to the second-floor library. English classes were conducted in the library, and by agreement with Marilyn Pender, the football team always met as a group, always during first period. Marilyn Pender had long surrendered in her efforts to teach English to football players. She met us at the door of the library and distributed magazines. Reading skills, Marilyn Pender contended, were as important as writing skills. She had one rule for anyone who played football: never interrupt the regular class. It was a rule I broke daily. I had a love, and a knack, for all things related to English.

I see three young boys rush up the stairwell, see one pause, turn back and lean over the railing. The boy calls out: "You better move."

A girl stands in the middle of the corridor, perfectly calm, gazing arrogantly at the stampede approaching her. The new girl, I reason. Supposedly bright, supposedly strange. Recently moved to Overton from Washington, DC. She looks different enough—glasses, long hair braided in a single pony-tail, no makeup, dressed in a brown ankle-length skirt and a man's over-sized white oxford shirt, white socks on her feet and her feet tucked into sandals. She is holding a large notebook filled with note paper. She could have been nude and not have looked as out-of-place.

"You better move," the boy on the stairwell shouts again.

The girl does not move.

"Yeah, you better move," Lamar growls.

"Go to hell," the girl says calmly.

The Purple Panthers of Overton High School stop in mid-step unison, stop as though slapped, or jerked back by a tethering rope.

"What'd you say?" Lamar mumbles after a confused moment.

"I said you could go to hell," the girl hisses, stepping toward Lamar. "Just who do you think you are, anyway?" She is only inches from Lamar's blood-blushed face.

"We're the Panthers," Lamar says.

"So?" the girl snarls.

"Ah, we're the football team," I say, pushing forward to stand beside Lamar. In the romantic way of youth, I believe such a response is expected of me. A quarterback always speaks for his team.

The girl's face relaxes. She looks at me, and then her eyes wander over the team. A smile cracks on her mouth.

"We're headed for English class," I tell her pleasantly.

The girl snickers. "This is the football team?" she says. "The big team? The number one team?"

I nod foolishly.

"Oh, my God," she says. She turns and begins walking away, toward the stairs. She is still snickering.

"Now, just a damn minute," Lamar sputters.

The girl does not turn back. She waves a hand over her shoulder and continues up the stairwell. Her giggles grow into a laugh.

"Who the hell was that?" Art Crews says bitterly. Art plays right tackle. His hair cut makes him appear bald.

"The new girl, I guess," I say. "She's from Washington, DC, or somewhere like that. I hear she's a little strange."

"Well, shit, Cole, so are you," Art mutters. A smile cuts across his broad, red face. "But at least you one of us, boy."

By the end of the day, I knew that Marie Jean Fitzpatrick, daughter of George and Laura Mullen Fitzpatrick, was the smartest person who had ever attended Overton High School. I sat in astonishment through English, biology, history, geometry and typing and watched her commandeer each class. There was not a single teacher who was her equal. In a classroom, she was immediately obsessed, her large, peering eyes darting wildly from textbook to teacher. She squirmed restlessly in her seat, muttered caustically about inane comments the teachers made, corrected them without fear. She seemed emotionally brittle, afflicted by some demonic presence that swelled inside her, pressuring against her brain, tearing at the membrane coating it.

At football practice that afternoon, Art Crews declared her to be certifiably crazy. I remember he looked at me and said, "Damned if she don't make you sound normal, Cole."

I remember countering, "She's just smart." But I knew she was more than smart; she was brilliant. And scary.

I remember, too, that Art mused, "Wonder what her titties look like? Couldn't tell with that shirt she was wearing."

I remember Lamar saying, "She ain't got nothing. Nothing. She probably makes Cole look like a woman."

I remember laughing, as I always did when Lamar attempted humor.

Still, I had a sense—a premonition—that the presence of Marie Fitzpatrick would change all of us.

That afternoon the premonition began to take shape.

Bell's Drugstore was on the corner of Main and Cameron. In Overton, it was where the teenage in-crowd met on after-school afternoons to drink cherry colas and to eat potato chips and pimento cheese or ham sandwiches. And to be seen. Especially to be seen. It was, in many ways, a ritualistic gathering, where posturing for notoriety was learned with far more interest and far more insight than the conjugation of verbs in Marilyn Pender's first-period English class.

In my memory of it, Bell's had three high-back booths against one wall. There were two glass-topped eating tables in front of the soda fountain with stool seats that swiveled from each wrought iron leg. By custom, the booths were reserved for those who dated, giving them a chance to nuzzle close, swapping erotic touches in leg rubs and flashing fingers. The booths had a name: the Temperature Zone. Even the three, long-bladed overhead fans could not cool the Temperature Zone.

Traditionally, the in-crowd consisted first of athletes and cheerleaders, and that, too, was part of the learning: with position comes privilege. The others of the in-crowd were usually children of merchants and leading citizens. They had money and money dressed them well, made them enticingly bold, gave them an air that seemed to border on boredom, and somehow they knew that boredom played well, could be as alluring as a forty-yard pass for a touchdown on the muddy plain of Overton High School's football field.

It was a mix of snobs and hangers-on, the same mix as in every small town in America in 1954—the in-crowd, the clique.

And it was that mix that gathered in Bell's on the Monday afternoon of the first day of school, the football team arriving late, scrubbed clean from soapy showers, our faces flushed from the aftermath of exercise.

Art Crews paused at the door, his arms raised, his voice thundering, "Where's my baby?" Art was always first through the door at Bell's, always announcing himself loudly. It, too, was part of the ritual. Waiting in one of the Temperature Zone booths, Sally Dylan sighed and rolled her eyes as she always did—ritual added to ritual. Sally and Art had dated for three years. Art bragged openly to the football team about the size of her breasts, which was needless boasting. The size of Sally Dylan's breasts had been obvious to all of us for years.

Thinking of it now, I am profoundly astonished by the power of our ritual. Day following day. Year following year. Bell's was like a half-way house for half-way adults and the lessons learned there were learned through the monotony of repetition.

Yet, I have a mental motion picture of that particular day, one that rewinds itself after each viewing. When it plays, I see us taking our places in the store, filling it with laughter and with the babble of voices telling stories suggestively edged with double entendre, but short of vulgarity. Stood against the language of young people today, 1954 was the Age of Piety.

I remember we talked about Cone Bailey, our coach, and how his behavior had taken a turn for the worse. Cone Bailey had returned from the African campaign of World War II with a Purple Heart for being wounded by shrapnel from an exploding grenade. There were whispers that the grenade also had affected his ability to reason. Shell shock, the whisperers said. It was common. A lot of men returned from war in a muddled condition.

Lamar was delivering a funny, rambling theory that Cone Bailey's problem would be solved if he could find a mindless, loose woman for off-the-field companionship when the door of Bell's opened and Marie Fitzpatrick entered.

The laughter and the talk stopped abruptly. A gasp, as involuntary as a sneeze, flew from one of the booths. To this day, I believe the gasp came from Art, though he would later deny it.

Marie was dressed in unironed shorts and a T-shirt that must have belonged to her father. She wore her sandals, but without socks. Art's curiosity about her breasts was answered in the expression of awe on the face of every male in the store. Marie Fitzpatrick was beautifully, fully, proudly endowed. It was obvious she was not wearing a brassierre.

She tossed a glance at the numbed crowd, scanned her eyes over me and locked on Lamar, who was sitting on one of the swiveling stools.

"Oh, the team," she said easily. Then: "Rah, rah."

"Well, rah, rah to you, too," Lamar answered in a haughty voice. He looked around for approval. No one responded. "You lost?" he said.

Marie smiled sweetly. "That's so kind of you to ask," she cooed. "I am. Maybe you could help me."

Lamar shifted on his stool. He rolled his massive shoulders, let his eyes wander over Marie's breasts. "You come to the right man," he said, grinning arrogantly.

"I need to buy some Kotex," Marie purred. "Do you know where they keep it?"

 è.

Tanya Berry laughed over the telephone, saying she loved what he had emailed to her.

A good beginning, she said. I like this girl.

So do I, he said.

It seems as though you're having some fun with this, Tanya said. Are you?

I don't know, he replied.

Cole, it's all right to have fun, she advised gently. Don't make the mistake of believing that what you're doing is exorcism. Maybe it's just the opposite. Maybe it's discovery.

I didn't think about it one way or the other, he told her.

A question, then, she said.

Sure. Ask away.

Did you laugh at all when you were writing?

Once or twice, he admitted after a pause. The Kotex episode was funny. Was then, still is.

I thought it was hilarious, Tanya said. This girl reminds me of someone I'm very fond of.

Who? he asked.

Why, me, of course, she said. Now go back to work.

THREE

December 20, mid-afternoon

Day Two of this—this going back to Marie Jean Fitzpatrick. After reading what I have already written, I realize I am taking great liberties. No one can remember conversations from fifty years in the past, yet, I am not conscious of putting words into mouths. It is as though what I remember is occurring as I remember it. The voices are clear to me. I hear the slang we used, the profanity. I hear the slow, unmistakable tinting of the Southerner's drawl. I see the faces, the gestures, the exaggerations of smirks turning into smiles. In some way that is magical, or at least mystic, the players of my past have crowded into my office like a traveling band of troubadours and are performing scenes memorized from our history together.

Now, today, as I write, I still see the look on Lamar's face in Bell's after Marie embarrassed him with her question about the location of Kotex. His face faded to ash, then colored crimson. No one spoke, no one laughed. After a moment, Marie turned and wandered toward the back of the store. Lamar stood and walked out. He did not look at anyone. And then Art snickered and the snicker rippled throughout the store, picked up giggles along the way, then turned into a roar of laughter.

Before the week was over, Lamar had received enough Kotex to open a black market. The thick white pads were left in his car, shoved into his locker, stuffed into his football helmet, mailed to him in bulky envelopes. He was called The Kotex King and Marie the Kotex Queen. The taunting stopped only after Lamar bolted the door to the locker room before football practice on Thursday afternoon and made an announcement: "Next time I see one of them things, I'm gonna whip everybody's ass in here, and that, by God, is a promise."

Lamar was very large, very strong, and no one ever doubted the sincerity of one of his promises.

But Lamar was not the only person who suffered from meeting Marie Fitzpatrick. In the days that followed, she overwhelmed Overton High School, and everyone, from lunchroom attendants to O. J. Mayfield, the principal, believed she was possessed. Teachers were terrified of her, and none objected when, in the middle of a classroom discussion, she would abruptly leave and wander to the playground of the elementary school and swing in the swings. "Well, that's Marie," the teachers would say nervously. "She must be bored again. She's very smart, you know."

Thinking of it now, from the far distance of a half-century, I believe the attitude of everyone at Overton High School toward Marie Fitzpatrick was philosophically pronounced by Sally Dylan following the Kotex incident in Bell's Drugstore: "She's a joke. As long as she don't bother me, I'm not about to bother her."

It was an unspoken truce that lasted until a Wednesday afternoon in mid-September, a still-warm afternoon, late summer by temperature, but with the color and scent of autumn lingering invisibly in curled tree leaves and sun-dried grass. On the dirt surface of the Overton High School football field, the team was jogging through our version of wind sprints before straggling off to the field house.

This is how I remember what happened, and it surprises me that I am still able to hear the words. Perhaps it is because the words of youth are as melodic as poetry, even in the crudity of their use.

"Well, by God," whispered Bobby Matthews, slowing to a stop. Bobby had the nickname of Wormy. He played fullback and middle linebacker. He had a body like a small weight lifter and he loved to inflict pain. He was staring toward the school. He repeated, "Well, by God."

We turned to look in the direction Wormy was gazing.

Marie Fitzpatrick was striding toward us.

"Well, damn," muttered Lamar.

"Maybe she's run out of—them things," Art suggested, smiling.

"I'll whip your ass, Art," Lamar said matter-of-factly. "You may be my best friend, but I made a promise, and I meant it."

"Cole made me say it," Art replied quickly.

"Cole ain't that stupid," Lamar countered.

Marie continued toward us. Her breasts rolled seductively under the tight green sweater she wore.

I could hear a low moan from Art.

She stopped at the sideline and glared at us. "Cole Bishop, I want to see you," she said evenly.

"Me?" I asked.

"Yes. You."

"Well, shoot, Cole, don't let us keep you," Wormy mumbled, giggling.

"Yeah, Cole," Art said in a low voice. "Ask her if you can use them things as shoulder pads." A snicker skimmed across the field.

I glanced at Lamar with my quarterback look, the pretentious one faking authority, if not threat. Lamar shrugged, then turned and started walking toward the field house. The rest of the team followed. I could hear them giggle, could hear their low mutterings, and I knew it would be torment when I appeared in the field house. I moved slowly, cautiously toward Marie.

"Good Lord, you look like you're scared to death," she scoffed.

"Just wondering what you want with me," I said.

"I want to see if you're as smart as you're supposed to be," she told me.

"What do you mean by that?" I asked.

"Just what I said. From everything I can gather, you're supposed to be the brains in this school."

I looked away. I saw the team standing outside the field house, shucking shoulder pads, watching me. "I don't know," I said. "I get pretty good grades."

Marie laughed. "In the school I came from, you'd be lucky to get Cs. You do know that, don't you?"

I could feel a rush of anger flooding my face. "No, I don't know that. And you don't, either."

"Ooooh, temper," she teased. "I like that." She paused, studied my face. "Maybe you're right. Maybe I don't know. Maybe you're one of those people who just do what they have to do, no matter where they are."

I did not reply.

"I want you to do something for me," she said.

"What?"

"I want you to come by my house this afternoon, instead of wasting your time in that stupid drugstore."

"What for?"

"You'll see when you get there. Do you know where I live?"

I shook my head.

"In the old Bailey house, on Church Street, down past the Baptist Church. The one with the wraparound porch. You know where it is?"

I nodded. The house was one of the showcases of Overton.

"Good," she said. She turned to leave.

"Wait a minute," I called. "I didn't say I'd come."

She turned back. Her gaze felt like heat on my face. "But you will, won't you?" she said. She pivoted confidently and began to stride away.

When I think of it now, I believe it was the badgering from my teammates that made me turn my parents' car onto Church Street and aim it in the direction of the old Bailey home with the wraparound porch.

The badgering had been ceaseless. Laughter. Mocking. Breast jokes. Towel-slaps. I lied, saying she had asked about a book. The lie meant nothing to my teammates. And I knew their badgering would be worse in Bell's Drugstore. Only a fool would go to Bell's.

I remember slowing the car to a stop in front of Marie's home, wondering why I was there.

I remember listening to the clicking idle of the car motor—can hear it even now. Remember peering at the house. Remember thinking, Maybe she's not here.

And then I heard her voice: "You going to sit there, wasting gas, or are you going to get out?"

She was standing in the shadows of a large pecan tree, wearing a straw hat, with her hair pulled under it, an over-sized T-shirt and denim overalls. She looked like a boy.

I turned off the engine and opened the door of the car and pulled myself out slowly.

I remember looking down the road, remember her asking, "Think somebody's spying on you?"

I remember blushing.

"Come on," she said. "I was beginning to think you had chickened out. You should have been here an hour ago."

I did not move. "What's this about?" I asked.

"If you can manage to put one foot in front of the other, I'll show you," she answered irritably. She started toward the garage.

She's crazy, I thought. Just like everybody thinks. I looked again down the road and then followed her.

I could hear voices in the garage before we reached it. Small voices, the voices of children. They were laughing over something one of them had said. Marie glanced back at me, then stepped inside the open door of the garage.

The voices fell silent when I entered.

"This is what I'm talking about," she said.

I stood, gazing in bewilderment at four black children, two girls, two boys, small to pre-teens, who were sitting on makeshift benches before a table cluttered with books and papers.

"You could say hello," she said.

"Hi," I mumbled.

The children whispered a reply I could not understand.

"Say it out loud," she commanded easily. "Say, 'Hello, Cole.'"

The children spoke in unison: "Hello, Cole."

"Do you know who Cole is?" she said.

The children shook their heads. They stared in wonder.

"This is Cole Bishop," she explained. "He goes to school with me. He's supposed to be a big football star and all the teachers think he's smart because he talks all the time." She smiled at me. "Of course, he's not as smart as I am, but he doesn't know that."

Grins waved over the faces of the children.

"He your boyfriend?" one of the girls asked.

The other children giggled.

"My boyfriend? Good heavens, no," Marie said. "I wouldn't be caught dead with somebody like him for a boyfriend. He's too ugly."

"He ain't ugly," the girl said.

The children giggled again.

"Well, he is to me. He's ugly enough to win a Mr. Ugly contest, but that's not why he's here," Marie said.

The children exchanged glances that held laughter.

I remember clearing my throat and crossing my arms in front of my chest. I made a sound. Not a word. A sound.

"Oh, you wonder who they are," Marie said lightly. She smiled proudly. "They're my students, Cole. The Curry children." She pointed to the giggling boy. "That's Alfred." Her finger moved to the girl sitting beside Alfred. "That's Sarah." Her finger moved again, again to a girl, the one who had asked if I were her boyfriend, "That's Seba, and—" she turned to the last child, a small boy, no older than three or four—"and this is Littlejohn." She looked back at me. "That's his real name. Don't you love it? He was named after Little John in Robin Hood."

Littlejohn slipped closer to Seba and took her hand. He ducked his head, then looked up at me and grinned shyly and ducked his head again.

"Remember what I told you about reading?" Marie said quietly to the children. "If you can read, you can do just about anything you want to. Cole Bishop's read hundreds of books."

"How many's that?" asked Alfred.

"It's a lot," she answered. She looked at me.

"Yeah, a lot," I said.

"Cole Bishop's read more books than anybody in Overton County, except for me," she added. "And I just wanted you to see him. If Cole Bishop can read books, so can you." She looked again at me.

"Yeah, that's—right," I said.

"He read us a book?" asked Alfred.

"Maybe he will, someday," she said. "But it took him so long to get here it's time for you to go. Your mama will be waiting for you. I'll see you tomorrow afternoon, all right?"

The children nodded and slid from their benches and left the garage, their gazes holding on me. Outside, they sprinted across the yard toward the house.

"What was that all about?" I asked after a moment.

"That's a dumb question," she said. "What do you think it was about? Exactly what I said. They needed to see somebody in person who reads, somebody they wouldn't think about, and you fit that description."

"Don't get mad at me," I said. "I don't even know what's going on."

She sat on one of the benches and pulled the straw hat from her head. Her hair fell across her shoulders. She gazed out of the garage door as a tall black woman came from the house, surrounded by the children.

"That's what's going on," she said at last. "Their mother works for us. Her name's Jovita." She paused. "I like that name. I really do." She sailed her hat toward the table, missing it. "Anyway, I found out that none of Jovita's children could read. Seems like their school system is even sorrier than the one we attend, if you can believe it. So I decided to teach them. They're great."

"Why didn't their mother teach them?" I asked.

She laughed sarcastically. "Damn, Cole, sometimes you're as dumb as everybody else around here."

"And not everybody's as arrogant as you are," I said, hearing the anger in my voice.

The smile fell from her face. She looked up at me. "I deserve that," she said. "You're right. I am arrogant. I love being arrogant. It's so easy, especially around here. Tell you what, Cole, I'll make you feel better. In the last school I attended, I was about as average as a loaf of stale bread. So, you see, arrogance is a new experience for me. Down here, I can't help it. What we're studying in the twelfth grade, I studied in the seventh. You'd be arrogant, too, if you were in the same situation."

"Well, I'm not," I said. Then: "I got to go."

"Cole."

"What?"

"The reason Jovita didn't teach her children how to read is because she doesn't know how to read herself."

I looked away, toward the street. I could see Jovita and her children walking on the sidewalk. The children were dancing around their mother, jabbering gladly, their high, shrill voices playing like wind chimes. I do not think I had ever felt so uncomfortable. After a moment, I asked, "How did you know I'd read a lot of books?"

"It's kind of obvious," she answered. "You're the only person in school that ever has an answer more than three sentences long, but the real reason I know is because I asked."

"Asked? Where?"

"At the library. You're a legend in there, Cole Bishop. A legend. It's a wonder they don't name the library after you."

I remember blushing, shuffling my feet. "I got to go," I mumbled.

"Cole?"

"Yeah."

"Wasn't this better than wasting time at the drugstore?"

I shrugged. "It was all right."

"Cole?"

"Yeah."

"You want to help me teach them?"

"I don't know how to teach," I said.

"Sure you do. You'd be a great teacher."

"I wouldn't even know where to start," I protested.

"You don't want to do it, do you?"

"I didn't say that."

"Sure, you did. You just didn't use the words. Is it because they're black?"

"That's got nothing to do with it," I countered.

"You're lying, but you don't know it."

"What're you talking about?" I asked irritably.

"You're from the South and it's nineteen fifty-four, that's enough to know," she answered. "Do you really ever read anything besides comic books? It's in the papers every day and on television every night. Turn the schools into private schools. That's what they're trying to do, just to keep Jovita's kids from sitting down beside somebody's little white girl or little white boy. Do you think they care that those kids out there can't read? They don't. They don't give a damn, and that's what I'm talking about."

"Excuse me," I said, "but I do read, and if I'm not mistaken, the same thing's been going on in Washington, DC, which you seem to believe is holy ground."

"They settled that," she shot back.

"No they didn't," I said. "They just compromised."

"At least they did that," she snapped.

I took a step toward the garage door, then turned back to her. "It must be great being perfect," I said curtly.

She did not answer for a long moment, then she whispered, "No. Not all the time." She stood. "Get out of here, Cole. Leave me alone."

"What did I do?" I asked.

"Good God," she sighed. "I feel sorry for you." She walked past me, toward her house.

ə̰

It was after ten o'clock when he finished the writing about going to Marie Fitzpatrick's home and meeting the children of a maid named Jovita, and the muscles of his back and shoulders ached from sitting so long in front of his computer, his only break coming for a cheese sandwich at the dinner hour. Still, he was not sleepy. He did a printout and went into his kitchen and made a cup of hot chai tea, sweetened with honey, and he sat at his kitchen table and read what he had written, thinking how ancient the event was, yet how fresh it seemed in the reading. His mind-pictures were clear. Marie, boyishly dressed as she had been. Littlejohn. Alfred. Sarah. Seba. It was a miracle that he remembered their names, remembered their asking Marie if he was her boyfriend, remembered her answer. It was a question he would ask Tanya: Is the mind capable of such recall, or was he merely inventing memory?

He took his tea and returned to his office and emailed the writing to her. It was a compromise, the emailing. Tanya had wanted him to read it aloud. I want to hear you say it, she had told him. The way you say it matters. He had balked at the request, insisting that he would find reading aloud awkward, and she had laughed at him, saying, You're like every teacher I know, Cole. You've got scholaritis.

You've been around academia so long, you've lost all your imagination, but if you want to be stubborn about it, then do it your way.

I will, he had answered, hearing irritation in his voice.

He struck the keys to cause sleep in his laptop, and then he opened the drawer containing Marie Fitzpatrick's letters, again selecting one at random.

Dear Cole:

You may now address me as Doctor Fitzpatrick. I am, after all these years, a legitimate sawbones, as they used to say in the old west. I am pleased to announce to you that I will be moving to Columbus, Ohio, to begin practice. Why Columbus? God, I don't know. They made a pitch for me and it sounded so earnest, so pleading, that I had a momentary meltdown of good sense and agreed to become Goddess of the Scalpel among Ohioans. If you had asked me three months ago where I wanted to live, it would have been in any state in the nation other than Ohio. I even would have chosen Georgia, for crying out loud, and you know how I despise Georgia.

Maybe I need whatever humbling I'm certain to encounter, and that should make you happy. You've always been unbearably rude about my God-given superiority. Maybe, in Columbus, I'll meet another Cole Bishop and after the lobotomy I perform on him, he will play the same role in my life that you have played—being the irritant that forms the pearl in my soul—but he will be mute. I'll see to that.

And maybe I'll only stay a couple of weeks. Maybe I'll go to work one morning and someone will say something so sugary sweet, I'll throw up, turn in my stethoscope, and strike out for parts unknown. Maybe I'll even wind up in that miserable little Vermont town you're in. (No, I wouldn't do that. I'd have the unhappy accident of bumping into you in a food market.)

Isn't it strange, Cole, that we've never visited in all these years?

Why is that? (Other than our agreement, I mean.)

Are we so afraid of one another?

Oh, God, I'm beginning to feel sentimental. That tiny, uncontollable part of me—the one I would exorcise in a heartbeat if I could—misses you. I wanted you to be here to celebrate with me.

Excuse me, I think I'm going to stop writing now and go into my bedroom and close the door and throw myself across the bed and cry you out of my system. It's what I get for revealing myself.

Never reveal yourself, Cole. Never. You may discover who you are.

I hate you.

ôâ

In sleep, he dreamed of Tanya Berry.

An erotic dream.

In the dream, she said to him, This is your healing.

The dream was still locked in his senses the following morning when she called. The timing of it—of memory matching call—invited a smile.

You were up late, she said.

I was, he admitted. He added, As you should know.

It was worth it, she told him. What you wrote was fascinating. No wonder this woman has bothered you all these years. She's remarkable. Did that really happen—about teaching black kids?

It did, he said.

He could hear her sigh over the phone, a sound of awe. It must have caused a row back then, she said.

That's a kind way of putting it, he told her.

Write it for me, Cole, she urged. I want to read that part.

For a moment he did not speak, then he said, That part won't be easy.

Who said it would be? she countered. But does it matter? You've started and you won't be able to stop it until it's over.

Probably not, he admitted.

Did you dream about her last night? she asked.

He laughed softly, remembering his dream. No, he said.

That surprises me, she replied.

I don't think I'd better talk about my dreams with you, he told her.

Why not? she asked.

I don't want your ridicule, he said.

Fine, she conceded. Keep your dreams to yourself. You'll tell them when they lace you up in a straitjacket. Now, are you still coming to Christmas dinner at my place?

Sure, he answered. If it's not an intrusion.

She laughed. You just can't scrub that last little bit of the South out of you, can you? No, damn it, it's not an intrusion, and don't ask what you can bring because the answer is nothing. Just your handsome, regal self and your willingness to put up with my husband's blithering about football.

I like your husband and I like football, he told her.

How wonderful, she said pretentiously. Why don't you regale Mark with your heorics? I'm sure he'll be impressed. I'm sure everyone there will be also.

You're cute, he said.

I know, she replied.

FOUR

Mid-morning, after a shower and his third cup of coffee, he took his Overton High School yearbook—the *Panther*—and leafed through it. He had not opened it in many years and reading it again was like discovering events from the history of strangers. Names he recognized, but it was not easy to put names with faces, unless the name and the face appeared togther. He found himself smiling out of many pages—in uniforms of sport and in the groupings of clubs—and in each photograph he seemed to be acting the fool, the same look most of his classmates wore. All except Marie. The one photograph of Marie, in the alphabetized senior class lisitng, was a non-smiling gaze. Under the photograph, she was identified as:

Marie Jean Fitzpatrick
Valedictorian
Class Prophecy: Surgeon General of the United States

Reading the prophecy caused a smile. It was intended as a joke, the kind of hyperbole teenagers always found clever, yet he believed there had been a jittery uncertainty among the writers of the class prophecies: it would not have been a great surprise for Marie Jean Fitzpatrick to become Surgeon General or even to preside over the United Nations. She had the brains and the intiminating nerve for the job.

His own prophecy had been: Oscar-winning Actor.

And that, too, caused a smile, bringing the memory of the set falling around him during the senior class play, and how he had shrugged and continued with his lines while the audience howled in laughter.

Perhaps the prophecy had been correct, he thought—minus the Oscar. Perhaps he was merely an actor. Someone who had found his stage in a classroom. The photograph of him standing proud in his football uniform, his hands resting on his hips, certainly had the look of an actor. An amateur, of course, but still an actor.

Yet, it was not what Marie Jean Fitzpatrick had predicted.

After the late hour of the night before, he surrendered to a morning nap and then had an early lunch of black bean soup before he sat again at his laptop computer and began to write.

December 21, afternoon

I am at my work-desk, with my high school annual open near me. On the page is a photograph of me as a seventeen-year-old boy wearing a football uniform. In truth, it is a silly picture—a skinny boy believing he was a giant. Still, I occasionally visit those boyish moments as a make-believe athlete with great pleasure. Given the distance of time, it is easy to become increasingly heroic, yet such is the joy of memory. I am sure Art and Wormy and Lamar and Corey and Hugh and all of my other teammates have felt the same. In memory, we were gods of war, those of us who wore the uniforms of sport and threw our bodies against one another in tender boy-man years.

I know now that we did not play for the moment; we played for the memory.

And for me, Marie is there, in the memory.

There was a game—it was the seventh of our season—that we won. I do not remember the team we beat, though I know the score was 13-7 and the winning touchdown came in the fourth quarter on a thirty-yard pass to Hugh Cooper, who played left end. I remember also that it was a rough game. Corey Johnson broke his arm and I was twice carried bodily from the field after being knocked breathless. A cut was over the bridge of my nose and blood was caked to my right leg from a scrape caused by a rock on the field.

(As I write, I am realizing that it must be necessary for heroes to be wounded warriors, blood being the color of bravery. In truth, the cut on the bridge of my nose was probably a scratch and the red on my leg nothing more than mud from the field. Truth does not always work for heroes.)

The first person to reach me after the game was my brother, Toby. He said, "Mama wanted me to make sure you were alive."

"I'm not sure," I told him.

"Well, by God, that last pass you threw was dead on the money," he enthused. "What's that make y'all now, four and three?"

"Yeah," I muttered.

"Damn," he exclaimed. "That's close to the best record this school's ever had." He added, "You going to the dance?"

"I don't know. Tell you the truth, I'm worn out," I answered honestly.

Toby laughed and threw his arm around my neck. He whispered, "Aw, horseshit, boy, ain't nothing wrong with you that rubbing up against one of them cheerleaders won't cure." He slipped his car keys from his pocket and handed them to me. "I'll ride home with Daddy and Mama," he said. "Go have some fun. Just don't go messing up my backseat." He laughed again, then looked warmly at me. "Hey, boy, I'm proud of you. For somebody that's worthless as a tit on a boar hog trying to do farm work, you all right. You know that?"

I smiled and flicked a weak jab toward him. There were times when I loved Toby to the point of tears.

"You better get something on that cut," Toby advised.

"Yeah, I will," I said.

I watched Toby fold back into a dance of bodies do-si-do-ing around the team. Sally Dylan rushed to me, threw her arms around me, squealed in my ear, then slipped from me and dashed for Art. Brenda Davis and Jennifer Mobley hugged me. Kenny Williamson, who had had to quit football because of asthma, shook my hand and said something I did not understand, but smiled as though I did, and then I started a limp-walk toward the field house.

"Great game, Cole," someone yodeled from the bleachers. I glanced toward the voice. It was Gervis Morgan, who had played quarterback two years earlier. He was wearing his letter jacket. I threw up a hand in acknowledgment.

And then I heard an unmistakable call: "Rah, rah."

Marie Fitzpatrick was standing near the bleachers. I stopped walking and looked at her. I had never seen her at a game.

"Yeah," I said wearily.

She walked onto the field and crossed to me.

"Where are you going?" she asked.

"To get out of this uniform," I told her.

"Let me walk with you a few feet," she said.

"Why?"

"To make my mother and father believe I've got friends," she said lightly. "Don't look, but they're up there in the stands, checking you out."

"Why me?"

"You wouldn't know it, but my father played football in college. He thinks you're a shining star of some sort. I told him we were great buddies."

"Well, I'm glad you think so," I said.

"They made me come to the game tonight," she continued. "They said I'm missing out on life, not being with all the young people of Overton. You think I'm missing out on life, Cole?"

"It's not my life," I said.

"Are you hurt?" she asked.

"Not bad."

"I thought they'd killed you. I thought we'd see flags at half-mast tomorrow."

"A couple of times I thought so, myself," I admitted.

Marie laughed. "That was funny, Cole." She stopped walking and turned to me. "I think they'll believe me now." She paused. "I hope you're all right," she added. "That cut looks pretty bad."

"It'll heal."

"I'm sure it will," she said. "Anyway, thanks for the walk. I'll see you."

She turned and moved quickly away. I watched her. She waved across the field to a crowd still dancing around Hugh Cooper. It was a wave meant for her mother and father. No one waved back.

Torment is as much a part of being young as hormones playing chemical tricks on the body. As a teacher, I have long observed that young people who know how to weave in and out of torment are the ones less troubled.

For a reason I still do not understand, I handled torment well during my teenage years. Perhaps it was because I learned early that humor could deflect words dipped in the poison of meanness—intended or unintended. Laugh at yourself and others tended to laugh with you, not at you.

I knew there would be torment after the game we won on the night Marie Jean Fitzpatrick walked onto the field to speak to me in a show intended to please her parents. It began in the mugging and the giggling and the silliness of my teammates as we showered and dressed for the after-game dance at Kilmer's Recreation Hall. Little comments. Winks. Kisses blown my way. Art straddling a towel, making it look like a giant Kotex, saying, "Anybody know who this is?"

I laughed and everyone laughed with me.

"Watch out, boy," Art bellowed.

In the melodrama of those autumn nights of football, I danced only the last dance at the after-game party at Kilmer's Recreation Hall. It was a trick I had learned as a sophomore, watching Gervis Morgan. Even when he had played an entire game without being tackled, Gervis would enter Kilmer's with a pronounced limp and little dabs of iodine on his face. He would sit heavily in a chair on the edge of the dance floor and accept praise and sympathy like a bored king enduring gifts from peasants. When the last dance was announced, Gervis would pull himself painfully from his chair, drag his aching body onto the dance floor, and slump against any willing girl with pillows for breasts.

I too played the role of the injured, as Gervis had played the role, but after the game we won 13-7 there was no pretending. My face and leg were bandaged. The knotting of nerves at the base of my skull had splintered off into my left arm and I could not lift the arm above my shoulder. There was a ringing in my ears.

I did not sit near the dance floor in my usual chair (the one Gervis had occupied), but at a back table, and watched the festivities. I remember thinking there were only three more games to play and I would be able to skin myself out of the football uniform I wore and would never again duck my head through a pair of shoulder pads or into an ill-fitting helmet. Glory was overrated. Glory hurt like hell.

Now, seeing it from the telescope of fifty years, maybe it would have been different at another school, with better equipment and better players, or with a coach who was not drifting aimlessly in a cloud of confusion. There was no question that Cone Bailey was deteriorating, and what happened that night was proof of it. It remains one of the oddest moments of my memory, yet, now, when I think of it, I cannot stop the smile that grows across my face.

At halftime of the game, trailing 6-7, Cone Bailey commanded a hush from the team, and he strolled among us, rubbing the palms of his hands together, a slobbering, wild grin etched in his face. He said nothing about the game, or about football. He spoke instead of the quiet ones. "I'll guarantee you, boys, it's the quiet ones that's getting it all. All you boys going around bragging about it, y'all ain't getting nothing. Nothing. Old Lamar, there. He ain't getting nothing. He ain't getting his finger wet, unless he's picking his nose, but to hear him tell it, he's got women lined up from here to Athens. But you take old Sidney, there, he's getting so much, he's wasting away. Anybody ever hear Sidney talking about it? Anybody ever hear Sidney talking about anything? I'm telling you, boys, you can take a lesson from old Sidney." Sidney was Sidney Witherspoon, a shy junior who stuttered and who played football only because his father, who was the Presbyterian minister, forced him to play.

It was a speech that left all of us stunned. I believe it was Lamar who whispered, "We got to get that man laid."

I remember glancing around the dimly lighted dance floor, searching for Sidney Witherspoon, but I did not see him. I remember thinking it would be a good thing to go to the Presbyterian Church on Sunday and to sit with Sidney through one of his father's monotone sermons. I remember pledging to talk to Lamar, knowing that Lamar would make Sidney a target of his ruthless ribbing.

Sitting alone, listening to the music, watching the dancing—bodies against bodies—I thought of Marie and I knew the kidding I had received in the locker room was not over.

I was right. Near the end of the night, Wormy made his way to the table where I was sitting. He asked in an easy fashion, "What's with you and the crazy girl?"

"What crazy girl?" I said.

"You know. Marie. The Kotex Queen."

"Nothing," I replied.

"I saw you walking off the field with her."

"No, she was walking off with me," I said.

"Same thing."

"Not in my book."

"Looks like she's after you," he said.

"Good Lord," I sighed. "You ever heard of the word impossible, Wormy?"

"Yeah, sure have," he replied. "All my life, I've heard it was impossible to run a mile in under four minutes, but it happened, didn't it? This year. Maybe this is the year nothing's impossible. Hell's bells, we may win six games. We do, they'll have statues of us in the middle of town."

"I can't wait," I said.

"Fate, boy, fate," he teased. "You can't fight fate."

The music to *Ebb Tide* ebbed away and there was a shuffling of feet as dancers moved across the floor.

Alyse Lewis—the writer of the letter I received about the reunion—called out: "Last dance, last dance." Her voice was forced cheerfulness. Alyse was captain of the cheerleaders. She was pretty and friendly and caring. She repeated, "Last dance, everyone. Last dance." A look of sadness swept across her face and I thought of the whispered news that Alyse and Corey had agreed to stop dating one another. Interference from her parents, the whispers said.

The opening strains of *Stranger in Paradise* cried mournfully from the jukebox.

"Com'on, Cole, let's go find a woman," Wormy said.

"I think I'll sit this one out," I told him.

"You hurt that much?"

"I do," I admitted.

"See you," Wormy said, walking away in his affected last-dance limp.

I watched as couples floated together on the dance floor, slow-moving to the music, and then I pulled himself from my chair and started toward the door, where Alyse stood.

"You leaving, Cole?" she asked.

"Yeah," I said.

"It's the last dance and you haven't been on the floor all night," she said. "I've been watching you."

"I'm a little too sore to do much of anything but walk," I told her.

"I'll bet you are," she said tenderly. She looked longingly at the dancers nudging against one another, faces against faces, arms wrapped around bodies, and then she turned back to me. "Can I walk you to your car?"

"Sure," I answered.

Outside, the night was cool. A half-moon lounged against a cushion of murky white clouds. Alyse slipped her hand under my arm and we walked slowly across the parking lot toward Toby's car. I could smell the scent of perfume from her neck. Moonlight gathered like blond smoke in her blond hair. *Stranger in Paradise* drifted from Dewitt Kilmer's recreation room.

"You seem a little down," I said.

She sighed. "I'm all right."

"You don't sound like you are," I said.

"Oh, I guess I'm just lonely."

"Thinking about Corey?"

"Maybe. I'm sorry he got hurt."

"Why did you break up?"

She did not answer for a moment. Then: "We just did."

We were at Toby's car.

"Thanks for walking out with me," I said.

She looked up at me. "Can I have a hug, Cole?"

"Sure," I replied. I folded my arms around her and I could feel her nestle into me. She tilted her head to gaze up at me.

"Please kiss me," she said softly. She pushed up on tiptoe, ran her hand behind my neck and pulled me to her. The kiss was warm, moist. Her tongue flicked over my lips, parted them, slipped into my mouth. Her fingers kneaded the back of my neck and her body shuddered against me. And then she pulled back. "Oh, God," she whispered. "I've wanted to do that for a long time." She released me, turned and hurried away, without looking back.

I could still taste the peppermint of Alyse Lewis's kiss as I turned Toby's car onto Church Street.

There was one light on in Marie Fitzpatrick's home. Her room, I guessed. I imagined her propped against a mound of pillows in her bed, reading.

And there, in Toby's car, after a football game that left me aching but momentarily happy, I had a sudden and overwhelming sensation of sadness for the girl everyone considered crazy, the girl all of us ignored, the girl of our locker room jokes. She had walked onto a football field among people who would never speak to her, and she had forced herself to stand near me, pretending to belong—simply because she needed to perform the shameful role of being popular to bring comfort to her parents.

I had never known anyone who was so alone.

FIVE

It was six o'clock when he stopped writing. He struck the keys to email the words to Tanya, and then he dressed in his heavy winter clothing and went outside in the faded light of day. A fine snow was falling and the wind blew it like a dust storm, stinging his face. The cold of winter had been a great adjustment for him, coming to Vermont from the South. In his first year, he had dreamed of freezing—from cold and from loneliness—and then the spring had unfolded in its splendor of green, exhilarating him, and gradually, year by year, he had learned to accept the snow and the bone-chilling that came with it. Alyse Pendleton's mention of two inches of snow had amused him, yet he understood it. Once in his youth, it had snowed in Overton County on Christmas day and the sight of it was still a great thing in his memory—Christmas cards made of weather. His mother had called it a miracle.

He drove from his home to the campus of Raemar University, parked in his assigned parking space, and walked across campus to the Epps Fine Arts Building, where his office was located.

It had been thirty-four years since he first arrived on the campus to interview for a position as a teacher of Southern literature, bringing with him the reputation of an able researcher and an energetic lecturer. And though he could cover the sacred grounds of Faulkner and Wolfe and Welty and O'Connor and most of the others who were considered icons of the Southern expression, he had concentrated his study on the life of Joel Chandler Harris, creator of the Uncle Remus stories. His biography, *Briar Patch*, had won the National Book Award and was considered a definitive accounting of the life of Harris. It was a pleasing honor, yet pragmatically he understood the limits of it. No one studied Joel Chandler Harris any longer, not in the reigning environment of politically correctness.

He had not intended to stay in Vermont longer than three years, enough time by his judgment to hone his craft and to concentrate on his biography of Harris, and then he would return to the South, hopefully to the classrooms of Upton University in Atlanta, his alma mater. Yet, he had lingered year after year, his life becoming rooted in the small town of Raemar and in the comfortable familiarity of the university. It was an institution with demanding academic standards, annually challenging schools of the Ivy League for excellence. Among its graduates were diplomats and politicians of national influence, business leaders of great wealth, scientists who had distinguished themselves in break-through research. And pleasing to Cole, there had been a number of published writers—novelists and poets and playwrights and screenwriters—emerging from the department of English. One, a woman named Ginger Kennedy, had won the Pulitzer Prize for playwriting.

Yet, to Cole, the joy of being at Raemar University was in the setting—the dazzling beauty of Vermont. The town and the campus was his universe and he had never lost the thrill of discovering it each day. It did not matter if it was the blazing of autumn or the echoing laughter of students, something about it exhilarated him with each sunrise.

On campus there was a quadrangle with a statue in the exact center of the enclosure. The statue was of a man chiseled from a monolith of marble. Only the face and shoulders of the man had been shaped and polished. A benefactor of great wealth, a recluse, had placed the statue on the campus. On the day of its unveiling, he supposedly made the only public statement of his life. He said, I don't know if that man's rising up out of that rock, or if he's sinking down into it. It's something to think about. And then he sat down. For years, the students of Raemar had argued the possibilities. They had even named the statue (UN)BOUND.

Once he thought it was a ridiculous name, that it would be far more dignified to choose something from mythology, something as romantic as Pegasus or Odysseus, something that had the sound of poetry and mystery. Now, after more than thirty years of experiencing it daily, he believed (UN)BOUND was the world's most appropriate name for an object.

On days crackling with energy, days of joy and excitement, days of such promise he could feel the power of regeneration churning in his chest, (UN)BOUND whispered to him as he walked pass it: *Rising up, rising up, rising up....* And he would fantasize that the man embedded there was about to shatter the marble and stand full-bodied on legs chistled by the magic of his own will.

On days of sour moods, of schedules off track, of contentious exchanges with colleagues or students, (UN)BOUND whispered: *Sinking down, sinking down, sinking down....* And he would wonder if the marble body was receding like a man gradually drowning in the thick soup of quicksand.

Only an oracle of great wisdom could make such accurate pronouncements, whispering from stone lips, he believed.

And on the day of going to his office after his writing of Marie Jean Fitzpatrick, he thought he heard the voice of (UN)BOUND saying, *Rising up, rising up, rising up....* A voice made of wind and snow.

The campus was mostly deserted, a ghost village caused by the Christmas holidays. The few who greeted him were professors doing the same as he: checking for mail or messages or working on their own papers for publication. The silence of the building was both comforting and eerie.

There were several letters announcing conferences and twelve Christmas cards sent to him by former students, all giving him updates of their lives—their work, their spouses, their children—and all thanking him for his influence. One, a girl he had known as Olivia DeFoor, wrote: *You showed me the beauty of words. I want you to know that I am almost finished with a novel and if it is ever published, it will be dedicated to you.* He remembered the girl as vivacious and dreamy, a child of wealth, and one of the rare students who had surprised him with her insight. He had guessed she would marry a man of means, have her children, spend her time in social clubs, and perhaps, one day, would become a generous benefactor of Raemar. Her catch-up note proved him wrong. She was a teacher of underprivileged students in a Pittsburgh ghetto, her husband a software programmer for the government.

Her note made him think of something Marie Fitzpatrick had said to him in one of her letters: *Never judge me, Cole Bishop. You have no idea who I am.*

On impulse, he called Tanya Berry.

Where are you? she asked. I tried calling you at your home a few minutes ago.

He told her he was on campus. Checking on things, he said. Did you get what I sent?

That's why I was calling, she replied. I think I know your problem.

And what's that? he asked.

You're in love this woman. Always have been.

I'm not sure you'd call it that, he said.

That's because you're a man, she insisted. What men know about love, you could put in a thimble.

Is that a professional remark? he asked.

Are you paying me? she replied.

I hope not, he answered.

Then I can say whatever I damn well please, can't I? she said.

Good point, he told her.

So, here's what I think, she said. Personally, I mean. I think I now know why your marriage to Holly failed. My God, compared to Marie Fitzpatrick, Holly was a mannequin. Her only worth was to pose in semi-expensive and sometimes-tacky clothing.

He laughed easily. Another good point, he said.

Now hang up the phone, she ordered. Go home. Get back to work. I want to get to the part where you make love to the woman.

He laughed again.

At his home, with Tanya's remark about his former wife still fresh in mind, he searched through the letters from Marie, selected one, opened it and read:

Dear Mr. Bishop,

Let me review the letter I received from you today. You say you have become engaged, at the age of 37, to a woman named Holly, described by you

*as being pretty, lively, intelligent and, most important, patient. You want
my blessing, out of friendship, for this glorious event in your life.*

*Are you an idiot? You want my blessing to marry someone with the
ridiculous name of Holly? I can see her now. She looks exactly like Barbie,
and she's just as dumb, regardless of your fawning description of her
spectacular intellect. How many years will it take for you to realize that I
am the only woman—and, yes, damn it, I am a woman—who could possibly
enhance your miserable life? Here's what's in store for you, big boy: you will
amble along year after year, bending to Holly's inane blithering, until you
become nothing more than an echo of who you used to be, or could become.
And then—surprise, surprise—she will kick your highly educated but sorry
ass out the door and run away with some street bum packing muscle and
wearing a face like Burt Reynolds. Just do me a favor: don't ever mention
her name again, unless it's to tell me you're divorced. My God, Cole, when
will you ever learn anything about women? Don't you understand there's
always danger behind slow blinking eyes and puckered lips? Do you not know
the cooing sound a woman makes in her throat is as lethal as poison? No.
No, you don't. You live by a code that makes you want to be a gentleman, an
innocent. What you don't understand is how vulnerable that makes you.
Holy God in heaven, sweet Mary, mother of Jesus, I feel sorry for you. I
wish I had never met you.*

He closed the letter, held it between his fingers.

He could feel the smile resting on his face, and with the smile, a
stinging of his eyes. Of his litany of regrets, his failed marriage
carried great pain, yet he had been relieved when it ended. Still, it
puzzled him how something begun in joy and passion could become
so lifeless and bitter.

The death of tenderness was a lingering death.

SIX

That night, at nine o'clock, he resumed his writing.

December 21, night

I have had a satisfying dinner of a single hotdog folded into loafbread and covered with a chili concoction from a can. Hot tea with it. A bachelor's dinner. An eccentric's dinner. Tonight is the night for the Christmas cantata at the United Methodist Church. I had promised to attend, but remembered it too late. Yet, even if I had not forgot it, I likely would have stayed at home. A big-flake snow is falling, the kind that seems to make whispers on its way to the ground. And the truth is, I want to stay with this writing of Marie Fitzpatrick. It is becoming a mild obsession, which should not surprise me. Tanya Berry warned that such a possibility was likely. I am eager to rush ahead, to get to those moments that changed me—or branded me—yet Tanya has urged me to take small, cautious steps rather than a blind leap.

"You need to remember the details," she said. "The details matter."

I know she is right. It was something I had to consider in writing about Joel Chandler Harris.

Football practice on Monday afternoon was little more than jogging and bragging about winning the game that had left me bruised and Corey Johnson with his arm in a cast. Corey watched us from the bleachers, with Alyse Lewis sitting beside him. From first period English, the sweet taste of gossip at Overton High School had been about Corey and Alyse making up on Saturday. Alyse had looked at me only once during the day. It was a look of pleading, and I had nodded imperceptibly, telling her that our kiss was held in secrecy. A smile, like the nervous flicker of a bird's wings, had thanked me.

After practice, Corey appeared in the field house.

"Hey, Cole," he said, "I hear you're making a move on the Kotex Queen."

I laughed, pulled my practice jersey over my head and began unlacing my shoulder pads.

"Naw, I'm serious," Corey continued. "Wormy was telling me about it. Said she walked off the field with you after the game."

"Yeah," I said. "She wanted to know how bad you were hurt. She's been lusting after you."

"Don't blame her," Corey countered, "but I got all the lust I can handle."

I remembered Alyse's kiss and the thought of it caused a smile.

"Got a deal for you, Cole," Corey said.

"What's that?" I asked.

"Ask her out for a date."

"Are you crazy?" I said.

Corey grinned and motioned with his head for Art and Lamar and Wormy to crowd around him.

"We been talking about it. You take her out, Cole, and we'll put twenty bucks in the pot," Corey said smugly.

I laughed again.

"Twenty-five bucks," Lamar offered.

I shook my head and threw my shoulder pads into my open locker.

"Thirty," Corey said. He added, "And that's it."

"Cole, I'd date a three-legged duck for thirty bucks," Lamar said. "Good God, I'd date Wormy and I'd wear the dress."

"Com'on, Cole, she ain't that bad looking," Art said. "Everybody knows she's got great tits, and if she ever put on some makeup and dressed like a normal girl, you might even be able to take her out in public."

The Dare, I thought. The Great Dare. It was like standing on a mountain cliff and having someone urge you to nudge closer to the edge. The Great Dare was always electric with fear. Always.

"Well, Cole?" Wormy pressured. "Thirty bucks."

I sat on a bench and began to unlace my cleats, knowing the only way to stop the badgering was to forestall it and to hope it would simply vanish. "I'm still too sore to think about it," I said after a moment.

"Maybe? You saying, maybe?" asked Corey.

I made a small shrug with my shoulders, a habit I had when wanting to avoid answering a question.

"He's saying, maybe," Art exclaimed. "That's good enough for me. Tomorrow, boy. You got to tomorrow, but here's some advice: you turn us down, no telling what sort of grief you got in store." A deep grin cut across his mouth, showing the dimples that Sally Dylan found irresistible. "No sir. No telling." He turned and walked away.

I did not know if it was the money or the dare, or if the money and the dare had simply given me an excuse, yet that afternoon, driving home from school, I turned my parents' car suddenly, impulsively, onto Church Street.

Better to ask her at her home than at school, I thought.

I slowed the car to a crawl, asked aloud, "What am I doing? I'll never live it down. Never."

I glanced at my watch. It was almost five.

I wondered if she was in the garage, teaching her class. A cool caking of perspiration was on my forehead.

"I'm an idiot," I said.

I pushed my foot against the accelerator and moved past her house, glancing at the yard. I saw no one.

I remember turning right on Candler Street, then right again on Howard Street to Beggs Street, and from Beggs Street back again on Church Street. The car was barely moving.

I thought, What am I afraid of? She's just a girl.

And then I saw them. Marie walking from the garage toward the house with a tall black boy trailing her. The children were tugging to him, chattering.

I braked the car to a stop and glanced in the rearview mirror, checking for traffic, saw nothing. My hand flicked to the gear shift and I shoved the gear in reverse and began to back the car down the street. At a driveway, I cut the wheel sharply, felt the rear of the car rise up. My hand yanked the gear shift down and the car shot forward, turning left.

I wondered who the black boy was, wondered if Marie had learned about him from the maid who worked for her mother. I guessed the boy was fifteen, maybe older. It was hard to tell. I wondered if Marie had talked about me, saying I had refused to help teach her afternoon-children. It wasn't true. I had not refused. She had not given me a chance to consider it.

I would have helped.

I was certain I would have.

This is what I thought: whoever the boy was, he would be terrified of Marie Fitzpatrick. Talking to Marie Fitzpatrick would be like talking to a foreigner, or an outer-space alien. She would rule him, pound him senseless with her words and with her arrogance.

I felt sorry for the boy.

I did not know it then, not clearly, but I do now, at this age: It was not the dare or the money that persuaded me to ask Marie for a date, though I would hide protectively behind that ruse, knowing it provided me with a fall-back of acceptance from my teammates.

I decided to ask Marie for a date because I could not forget my sadness over how we treated her.

It happened on the following Monday, after a morning of aggravation from Corey and Art and Lamar and Wormy. At lunch I told them I agreed to their terms.

"But the minute she accepts, I want half the money up front, non-refundable. When the date's over, I want the other half," I said.

"You got it," Wormy replied eagerly. "When you gonna do it?"

"Now. But when none of you are anywhere in sight," I answered. "Otherwise, the deal's off."

A magician could not have made my teammates disappear as quickly as my threat.

It was thirty minutes before typing class.

I knew Marie would be on the elementary school playground, swinging in the swings, or she would be in the library, reading. The playground, I decided. The day was too bright, too autumn warm, to be inside.

I knew also that I was being watched by teammates from behind cars and the corners of buildings as I strolled across the schoolyard, but I could not see them.

Get it over with, I thought.

I saw her from the fence that surrounded the playground. She was alone at the swing set, twisting the ropes of a swing into a coil and then, lifting her feet from the ground, lazily uncoiling. She seemed oblivious to the yelping of first graders playing a game of tag near her. I glanced back over my shoulder, thought I saw Wormy duck behind a tree, then I started down the slope of the playground.

Marie looked up as I approached. "This is my territory," she said. "I don't allow squatters."

"You can have it," I told her. Then I said: "Why do you come down here, anyway? This is where the first-graders play."

"They're the smartest people in the school," she answered.

"Yeah, sure," I said.

"They are," she countered. "They don't know things; they imagine." She looked at me curiously. "I'll bet you were a great first-grader, Cole Bishop. I'll bet you imagined everybody insane."

I thought of the stories I had told as a boy, outrageous tales cobbled from books I had read. To the men of Dodd's General Store in Crossover, the community of my childhood, I had been called a marvel. "Rather listen to that boy than go see a moving picture show," the men had said with laughter.

"I don't know," I said after a moment. "That was a long time ago."

"What happened? Where did you lose it?" she said.

"Who said I'd lost it?"

"I did. It's plain as day. You're just like everybody else now. You're just a dreamer and a talker. Imagining is more than dreaming and talking. Imagining is being."

"Sometimes you have to change," I mumbled weakly.

Marie laughed cynically. "Oh, God," she sighed. She gazed at me. "Were you looking for me, or did you come down to sign autographs for future little Panthers?"

"I was looking for you."

"Why?"

I could feel a chill spill down my shoulders. "I wondered if you'd like to go out sometime."

"All right," she said casually. She pushed out of the swing and started walking toward the school.

"Wait a minute," I called. "Don't you want to know when?"

"Whenever you want," she said without stopping, without looking back.

"Saturday night," I said. "About six."

"Fine with me."

Strange. As I was typing the above I remembered something Marie later confessed to me about that day. She did not return to school for the afternoon session. There was no reason. Typing class was a waste of time, especially since she could type eighty-five words a minute, and no class in school bored her as much as history, which, to her, was little more than a celebration of the Civil War. She found it amazing that so many heroes had been created out of so much disaster.

Still, she told me in a rare expression of admitting to a foolish act that it was not her dislike of typing or history that caused her to walk away from Overton High School and to stroll aimlessly along the streets of Overton.

I was the reason.

Asking her for a date.

She knew it was a set-up, of course, rightly assuming a boyish dare was involved, something initiated by my teammates—idiots, she called them. Something that would involve money.

At first, it angered her, and then she found amusement in it. As long as she knew what it was—the nonsense of fools—she was not bothered, for she knew we were no match for her.

In her telling of it she found herself that afternoon in front of Hendley's Department Store, gazing at a window display of dresses and skirts and blouses. The dresses and skirts and blouses were draped over headless body forms, leaving the impression—for her, at least—that only a headless, mindless person would be interested in them. She told me she thought of listening to the chirping of the girls of Overton High School, making their squeals over some new garment worn by one of them. So much chirping, it had the sound of excited parrots in a pet store she had often visited in Washington.

She opened the door to Hendley's and walked inside, and from the back of the store she heard the singing voice of Sheila Hendley, "Be right there."

"It's all right," she called back. "I'm just looking."

"Looking is the first step to finding," Sheila trilled.

I remember her saying to me in a laughing way, "That woman could have talked the snake into eating the apple."

Meaning, she bought an outfit.

At home, she closed and locked the door to her room and then she undressed and took the skirt and blouse from the Hendley Department Store shopping bag and fit herself into them. She said she stood for a long time before the mirror of her dresser, gazing at herself. Sheila Hendley had praised the soft yellow of the blouse and the forest green of the skirt, saying it was her favorite blend of colors, saying it in such a whisper it sounded like the confession of a tender secret. And maybe that was why she had purchased the skirt and blouse, she reasoned—Sheila Hendley's praise, her words giddy, a faint cigarette scent hiding in them like a delicious sin. To Marie, if no one else in Overton had found his or her place in life, Sheila Hendley had.

She also admitted that she had wondered if I would be shocked if she wore the skirt and blouse for our set-up date.

"And then it struck me that you weren't worth a new skirt and blouse," she told me. "If you wanted to date a mindless body form from a department store window, you could date Sally Dylan."

It was one o'clock, morning of December 22, when he stopped writing and emailed the words to Tanya Berry.

SEVEN

He was still asleep when Tanya called.

What time is it? he asked.

Almost ten, she said. Get up. I'm coming over.

Why?

I want to talk to you.

Now?

Yes, now, she said irritably.

Give me thirty minutes at least, he told her.

Make some coffee, she ordered.

She had with her a printout of what he had written the night before, and by the expression on her face—fresh, alert—he knew she had found something in the words that intrigued her.

I want you to tell me if you considered her vulnerable, she said, stirring cream into her coffee.

Then? he replied. No, not then. Now? Yes, I can see that. Why?

She leaned forward in her chair, her elbows on the table, a girlish way of sitting. She said, What you wrote about her buying the outfit, I thought it was odd that you remembered it. Where did that come from?

I'm not the counselor, you are, he answered. You tell me.

Counselors don't tell, she countered. Counselors ask. But I've already settled that with you, haven't I? You're not paying me, so the rules don't count. This is person-to-person. You and me. Besides, it has nothing to do with you or Marie Fitzpatrick.

Then who? he asked.

Me, she said bluntly. She paused, drank from her coffee. Then she turned to gaze out of the window at the deep covering of snow resting on his lawn and the silhouette of her face against the window was like a cameo carved from ivory. He had always considered her a striking woman. Even in her early fifties, she had a classic look—long brunette hair, a slender face, the comma of a slight scar trailing off her left eye. He thought of his dream of her, the erotic dream. Felt a rush of energy and then a blush of embarrassment.

You? he said. I don't understand.

She held her gaze out of the window. After a moment, she said, I told you this girl reminded me of me. I read what you wrote—about the dress—and I remembered something very similar happened to me when I was young. I never thought of it as being vulnerable, but that's what it was. I was so damn vulnerable, I punished myself for years and I had no idea that's what I was doing.

You want to tell me about it? he asked.

She turned back to look at him. Her eyes, dark against her pale skin, had a shine in them. He was my first lover, Cole, she said evenly. I thought he would never leave me. But he did. Packed his bags, got in his car and drove away without so much as a look-back. She inhaled suddenly, swallowed, then pushed a smile into her face. Live and learn, right? she whispered. I know you'll write about it sooner or later, but I want to know the answer now. Did you make love to her?

No, he said quietly. I did not.

She picked up her coffee, held it. The smile softened. I didn't think so, she said. That's one of the things I love about you, Cole. You do have a modicum of respectability.

Thank you. One of the things I love about you is the confusion you toss about like confetti, he told her.

She laughed easily. It goes with the territory, she said. They teach it in graduate school, but I'm glad to know you have affection for me in some small way.

Go home, Tanya, he said.

She reached across the table and gently touched his face. Don't forget Christmas dinner, she said.

I won't, he promised. But let me bring—

Oh, Jesus, not again, she moaned. Please. Enough of this, Colonel Sanders. She stood. Go take a shower and get back to work, she said.

In an hour, he was again sitting in front of his laptop, inspired by the visit from Tanya. He could feel energy rippling in his fingers as he touched the soft pads of the keys. He wrote:

December 22, morning

I am now in my late sixties, a fine age, I think. Look-backs over time are mostly enjoyable and some of them are remarkably clear—especially those that became important in odd ways. My first date with Marie Jean Fitzpatrick was one of them. Maybe the most important.

Late Saturday, in the dimming of sunlight, I drove to Marie's home. She was sitting on the front porch, dressed in her denim overalls and one of her father's shirts. She had a green shawl draped around her shoulders. She did not wait for me to get out of the car. She opened the passenger door and slipped inside and closed the door. She did not look at me.

"I would have gotten out," I said.

"Let's go," she ordered.

"Uh—do your parents know you're going out?" I asked, knowing it was her first date in Overton.

"I told them I was. I don't think they believed me. I guess they think I'm making it up."

"Why?"

"I told them who I was going with."

"What's that supposed to mean?" I asked.

She cut her eyes to me and sighed. "Why, Cole," she said in a southern accent that mocked Sally Dylan, "it means they simply can't believe it. Plain, little old me, going out with Cole Terrific. Football hero. Quarterback. Town talker."

"Ah—"

"Daddy said you lost the football game last night."

"Me?" I said.

"No, fool, the team. He said you were spectacular. His word, not mine. He only uses it if he's taking about football."

"You didn't come to the game?" I asked.

"I was in such a dither about our date, I had to stay home," she cooed. "You know, go through my wardrobe."

I glanced at her. Dear God, I thought, don't let us be seen. "We almost won," I said. "We were on the one-yard line when the game ended, and—"

"You lost, and that's that, now let's go," she interrupted.

I started the car. "Where to?"

She turned again to look at me. "Wherever you go to park and make out."

"What?" I asked in astonishment.

"You heard me."

"Ah—I don't do that," I told her.

"And don't get it in your empty head that you're going to start tonight," she said. She let a pause, a beat, pass, then added, "I just wanted you to think I was like everybody else around here."

"You hungry?" I asked.

"No."

"You don't want to drive to Dixie Top and get a hamburger?"

"My God, no."

"Why not?"

"Because that's where every idiot you call a friend will be, making sure they're getting their money's worth?"

"What are you talking about?" I asked.

"They're paying you to do this, aren't they?" she said irritably.

"What—what makes you think that?"

She turned in the seat to face me. "Damn it, Cole Bishop. I'm not blind, or deaf. And I'm a lot smarter than that whole football team put together, including you. I've watched it all week, listened to it. 'Cole, Cole, you really going to do it, Cole? Maybe she'll give you some, Cole. Get her in the backseat, Cole. Maybe she'll let you have it.'"

I stared at her incredulously. Plainly, there was a mad woman beside me. I drove quickly away from the house, down the back streets of Overton. Marie sat comfortably against the door. She looked out of the door window at the blur of scenery, humming tonelessly, seemingly oblivious to my presence.

"Where do you live?" she asked after a few moments.

"A few miles from here. In the country. A little community called Crossover," I told her.

"Let's go there."

"Fine," I said.

"You don't have to stop at your home and introduce me or anything. I just want to see where you live."

"All right."

"Tell me about your family," she said. "Your siblings."

"I've got two sisters, Amy and Rachel," I answered. "Amy lives in Arizona, Rachel lives in Atlanta. My brother Toby lives at home and helps my father on the farm."

"Do you like them?"

"Yes, I do."

"I think you were spoiled," she said.

"I probably was," I admitted.

She did not say anything for a few moments and then she asked, "Can you drive with one hand?"

I looked at her. The look carried the question I did not ask.

"Good God, Cole, I'm not asking you to put your arm around me or feel me up, or anything like that," she said. Then she laughed softly. "I just want to look at your right palm."

"Why?"

"Because I read palms. I want to read yours."

I extended my hand to her. She took it, turned it palm up, and began to gaze at it.

"Where'd you learn to do that?" I asked uncomfortably.

"From books, fool," she answered. "Where I learn everything—just like you. Now shut up, so I can concentrate."

I remember the awkwardness of that moment—my hand being held by her hands, the curious, hard-stroking of my heart against my chest, telling me I was in a place, a moment, I did not understand. I thought of the day I went to her home and met the children of a black maid named Jovita.

I remember thinking it could have been interesting helping her teach, if the teaching could have been kept private. If it got out that we were teaching black children in a garage, there'd be talk, and there already was enough talk about blacks and whites mixing in schools, with the Supreme Court deciding that segregation by color was unconstitutional. That had already caused a stir at Overton High

School—a big one—and the *Overton Weekly Press* had carried an editorial by Ben Colquitt, the publisher, calling for impeachment of the justices of the Supreme Court.

Yet, what Marie was doing was harmless, I reasoned. She was playing school. It was like babysitting. Games. Nothing more than games. If children—black or white or yellow or red or Mars green—learned to read while playing games, then the game was good. Besides, she wasn't mixing the races. The children she taught—babysat, played games with—were black. There wasn't a white or yellow or red or Mars green among them.

Marie brushed her fingers over my palm. She said, "You're sweating. Are you hot and bothered because I'm touching you?"

I pulled my hand from her grip and wiped it across the leg of the blue jeans I wore.

"Give it back," she commanded.

I obeyed.

Marie giggled. "I love the way you take orders."

"What did you want me to do?" I asked in exasperation.

She pushed my hand away from her. "Just testing," she said. "Actually, I've finished."

I did not speak for a moment, then I said, "What did you see?"

"Wonderful things, Cole Bishop. Wonderful things."

"What?"

"I'm not sure I should tell you."

"Why not?"

"Because you won't think they're wonderful."

"What does that mean?"

She leaned against the door and gazed at me.

"What?" I insisted.

"You're going to be very famous, Cole. Very famous."

"Doing what?"

"Many things. A teacher, I think. You're also going to be in some kind of spotlight, but you won't understand it. You're not that smart."

I closed my hand, rubbed my fingers over my palm. "None of that makes any sense at all," I said forcibly. "In the first place, I'm not going to be a teacher, unless I have to do some courses as part of the job. I'm going to be a football coach."

She giggled and looked away, then giggled again. "You may be a teacher in some little school that stays on academic probation, but you'd be a jerk as a football coach."

"Why?"I asked.

"Because the boys you'd coach would want to hear something other than once-upon-a-time stories they quit thinking about when they discovered why they wake up in the morning with erections."

"Good God," I muttered.

"Did I embarrass you?" she asked casually.

"You're damn right, you did," I sputtered. "Girls don't talk like that."

"But I'm going to be a doctor," she protested. "I need to know such things. An erection's nothing but lots of blood filling up the penis."

"My God," I whispered.

She laughed easily. "Actually, I think you're going to make a great teacher, Cole. Sometimes you surprise me. You remember when you got to raving about reading that Erskine Caldwell book, *The Sacrilege of Alan Kent*? I'd never heard of it, and you'd read it. I skipped the rest of my classes that day and went to the library and checked it out and read it that afternoon." She paused. "I just thought you should know."

We were nearing my home. I drove with both hands on the steering wheel, my body pulled up close to it, my eyes focused on the road. Marie began to hum again, tonelessly. She sounded like someone I'd read about—an insane person in an asylum who stared at a brick wall with peeling paint and made guttural noises in her throat. I tried to think of the name of the book, but couldn't.

I saw my home in the distance.

"That's where I live," I told her, nodding.

She sat up, peered through the car window at the house. "It's pretty," she said softly.

"Just a farm," I mumbled.

I drove past the turn-off, hoping I would not be seen by my parents or Toby. Marie settled back in her seat.

"You ready to take me home?" she asked.

"No," I said. "Why'd you ask that?"

"Because you don't know what to do with me."

"You're right about that," I told her.

"Is there a cemetery around here?" she asked.

"There's one back toward town," I answered. "Goes back before the Civil War. Why?"

"Let's go there. I like cemeteries."

You would, I thought.

The cemetery was on the crest of a hill, under a cluster of pine and oak. Briars and underbrush covered the borders. I stopped the car near it. There was just enough light left from the day to watch darkness fold around the stones. Marie pulled the shawl around her neck.

"You cold?" I asked.

"No," she told me. "Let's get out."

She opened the car door and stepped outside and began to wander among the tombstones. After a moment, I followed her.

"It's beautiful," she said in a soft voice. "What's the name of it?"

"People call it the Breedlove Cemetery," I answered. "Used to be a lot of Breedloves around here, my mama said."

She kneeled to examine one of the leaning markers, read in a whisper, "Daniel Breedlove, age three. Now resting on the bosom of God." She paused. "Do you think he is, Cole Bishop?"

"Is what?" I asked.

"Resting with God."

"I do," I said. "He was just three. Wasn't old enough to do any wrong."

She stood, looked around, a sad, pensive expression on her face. "Do you know what I learned from Jovita?" she asked.

"No. What?" I said.

"In a lot of cemeteries, blacks were buried in the woods around white cemeteries," she replied. She looked at me. "Did you know that?"

"No," I replied.

She did a slow, full turn, her eyes moving over the stones as though memorizing them. "All right," she said. "I'm getting cold now."

In the car, she said, "Would you have helped me—teach, I mean. If I had given you time, would you have helped?"

The question stunned me. It was as though my thoughts of Jovita's children had traveled from my brain, down my arm to my hand and she had seen them puddle in my palm. "Maybe," I answered. Then: "I guess I could still do it, if you want me to."

"I'm not doing it anymore," she said solemnly.

"Why not?" I asked.

"We're in the South," she answered. "Jovita won't let her kids come any more. She's afraid of trouble."

"What kind of trouble?"

"God, Cole, how would I know that? You're from here. You tell me. It's the South. What good are little Negroes when the cotton's been picked and the turnip greens are boiling? Or whatever it is all you rednecks say."

"I'm—I'm sorry," I stammered, not knowing what to say.

"Can you tell me something?" she said.

"What?" I asked.

"I never see a single one of you around a black person," she said. "I never hear any of you ever talk about anybody who's black, unless it's some sickening joke. Why is that, Cole?"

I wanted to tell her something profound and understandable, but I had no words to offer, other than the feeble excuse of "It's just that way." I knew Marie would rip such words apart with the keen blade of her tongue, scatter them in sarcastic laughter, so I kept them to myself. How do you admit to someone that you have fallen lock-step in the march of behavior of your own Lilliputian world? She would not have had patience to hear of childhood friendships with blacks, of the long days of play and field work, and she would not have accepted the excuse that, as we grew older, we simply separated, went our own way following our own color, losing ourselves in the preening of whoever we thought we were. In that time—in the 50s—with the rubble of wars still cluttering much of the world and with the rumor of change waiting around every corner of our imagination, we seemed to have time only for ourselves. We were, I suppose, too busy filling the space of our smallness to think of anything larger than the moment we were in.

When I did not answer her, Marie said, "It's all right. I learned something."

"What?" I asked.

"I learned this is not where I want to be, not where there's so much wrong, so much to be afraid of. How can you be yourself when all you've ever been taught is to be like everybody else?"

I did not respond to her. She was right. It was what everyone I knew had been taught—to be like everyone else. It had always been that way. Always.

"Cole?" she said.

"Yes."

"Can we be friends? I'd really like that. We could turn that school upside down, the two of us. We could have a great time, just playing games. It'd keep us from being bored to death. You wouldn't know it, but I'm a great actress—like my mother. She used to work with an amateur theater in Washington. She loved playing those pitiful southern women that Tennessee Williams writes about. If you ever listen to her, she still sounds like she's on stage. Her favorite word is mendacity. It's in one of his plays." She paused and looked at me. "Do you even know what that word means, Cole Bishop?"

I admitted I had never heard of it.

"It's the state of being mendacious, and mendacious means deceit, or falsehoods, but not always intended as deceit or falsehoods," she recited as though from a dictionary. She smiled. "People who run on at the mouth, telling such outlandish tales other people don't know whether to believe them or not. You, Cole Bishop. You're just full of mendacity."

"Well, I'm glad to know somebody's finally got me all figured out," I said.

"Want to play that game, Cole?"

The thought of it caused a smile to grow unexpectedly. "I don't know," I said.

She leaned her head back on the headrest of the seat. "I think it would be fun."

"You mad at me?" I asked.

"About what?"

"The talk. The dare."

"Why should I be?" she said. "I'm out with the prize, the catch of this poor backward county. I don't care what you say about it. Tell them anything you want. I'll have my own story to tell and, Cole, they're going to love what I have to say. Believe me, by next Monday afternoon, I'm going to be the most popular girl at Overton High School. They'll be wanting to rename the drugstore after me. Talk about mendacity, I'm going to be spreading it like the plague." She whirled in the seat and pulled close to me. "Don't you know? I'm crazy. Everybody says so."

"Are you?" I asked. "Crazy, I mean?"

Marie laughed. Her eyes brightened. "Oh, God, no," she exclaimed. "I'm smart, Cole Bishop. Smarter than you. And a lot braver."

"And what's that supposed to mean?"

"It means I know what I'm doing, which is more than I can say for you. That's why I'm always talking to myself in class. Why I get up and walk out. Everybody thinks it's just crazy little Marie. Everybody else stays in those God-awful classes and thinks I'm crazy. But I'm not. I'm outside, swinging, enjoying myself. Who's crazy, Cole Bishop?"

"You putting me on?" I asked.

"No," she replied. She pushed back against her seat. "And that's honest. It really is. Sometimes being the odd person has great advantages."

I looked at her. "Well, you're odd. I'll give you that," I said after a moment.

She smiled happily. "You're going to be very famous, Cole Bishop. I know that and you don't. God, you need me. You'll always need me. I think we should start planning our wedding."

"And I think I should take you home," I said.

EIGHT

In his years of marriage, he had developed an interest in cooking, realizing early that Holly, his wife, had no liking for the kitchen. It was, to him, a pleasant escape from the classroom and from the demands of administration expected of him as chairman of the department of English. A cookbook was not complicated. Read the recipe, follow it with patience and, remarkably, something eatable would likely come of the effort. He did not understand it until his divorce, but the cooking was also a way of avoiding conflict. Sautéed shrimp with roasted asparagus was a better way of muting disagreement than the unbearable weight of silence.

The dinner he prepared for himself after a day of writing was simple: an omelet of mushrooms and bell peppers. Grits, also, since he had purchased a package for Grace Webster's surprise birthday party. His guests had laughed, had tasted them tentatively, and then had pushed them aside. His guests had asked if grits were made of sawdust.

After eating, he took his cup of coffee, brewed purposely strong, and opened his front door and stood on his porch, taking in the cold and the scent of snow. It was the first time he had been outside all day and the realization startled him. He could not remember when he had stayed inside for a full day.

He went back into the house. He had turned on his radio for the presence of sound while eating his omelet and grits and the music was of Christmas, of angels singing of a newborn King, of a holy night with stars brightly shining, of a drummer boy with his rum-a-tum-tum, and he realized there was nothing of Christmas in his home—no tree, no blinking lights, no ornaments, no miniature manger scene with hand-carved shepherds and wise men and animals crowding around the hand-carved family of Joseph and Mary and the child named Jesus.

A great sense of melancholy struck him. It was two days until Christmas, yet there was no sign of it in his home. Tomorrow, he thought. Tomorrow, I will buy a tree and put it up.

The melancholy followed him to his office, guided him to his desk and to the drawer of letters from Marie Fitzpatrick. He pulled one from the stack, opened it, read:

Dearest Cole Bishop,

Well, I did it, my poor, backward friend. It. You know. The sex thing. The deed. Yes, I did. It's 1958, and I am 20 years old, and I did it. His name is Noel. He's still in my bed, sleeping the sleep of exhaustion, wearing a silly, little-boy smile. (Do you smile after sex, Cole? I think you must. I know you would if you were with me. I would make sure you did.)

We met two days ago in a bookstore, where he works. I thought at first he was you, the way he was making a fool of himself with customers. It made me want to see you.

I won't go into what happened at the store, but you should know that I put him in his place, smashed his arrogance like cheap crystal, and he was so impressed he asked me for a date. I wouldn't have agreed, but he's from England (Bath, which is a city and not the Saturday night scrubbing you used to give yourself), and he has this accent that has more power than musk. I knew we would make love, and I've never wanted to make love to anyone but you and Burt Lancaster. (You didn't know about Burt, did you?)

I liked it, Cole. I liked the feel of his body and I liked touching his (don't blush) erection. I liked the way it swept against my body—blunt and hot and fleshy. It did hurt slightly when he penetrated me, but the kind of hurt that is both pleasure and pain. I could easily get used to it, or obsessed by it. Mostly, I liked his tenderness. (He didn't ask, but I'm sure he knew it was my first time.) He held me gently after we finished, then he went to sleep. I couldn't, of course—couldn't sleep. Being there, in bed with him, with his arm across me, I began to think of you, and that was as pleasant as the sex had been. I pried myself from Noel and came here, to the kitchen. I wanted to call you, but that would have been unfair to Noel. Me, in the middle of the night, trying to find an old boyfriend. (You were that in truth, weren't you, Cole? You were my boyfriend. I couldn't stand it if you thought we were just friend-friends, just classroom showoffs.)

Are you jealous? Just a little, I hope.

Making love to Noel also made me realize how much I would like to be a mother. Problem is, I don't really care to be married. I think being married was what turned my mother into Greta Garbo. I've thought about this before, as you would suspect, and it makes perfect sense to me to have a baby, but not marry. Especially someone like Noel. What in the name of God could a man who works in a bookstore offer me? That's why I would never marry you, even if you flew to Boston tonight and begged me from your knees. What in the name of God could a man who believes in dreaming offer me?

But I do love you, Cole Bishop. I do. In a good way.

By the way, can you tell me: What happens next? Is it dangerous, this getting involved? Should I pull him from the bed and insist that he dress and take his British accent out the door and out of my life?

There are some answers I don't have, Cole.

But, then, I don't think you do, either.

Go dream, my lovely, dear friend.

Go dream of me.

Believe you are Noel.

At his desk, he checked his incoming email, found one from Tanya. *I didn't get anything from you. Why? Did you waste the day? And, no, you can't bring anything for Christmas.*

He answered: *I decided to wait until I have more to send. Maybe tonight, maybe not. Tomorrow, I'm going to find a Christmas tree, a small one. This place seems drab and I'm beginning to feel Scrooge-ish. Also, I plan to start roasting a goose for your Christmas dinner. Otherwise I know we'll be served bologna sandwiches.*

He switched off the internet connection and opened the document he had titled MARIE, and he began to write.

December 22, night

I did not try to stop the talk about my date with Marie. It would have been impossible, like trying to swat back a tidal wave with a tennis racquet. The talk was a hailstorm of words that pummeled both of us on Monday, and Marie, to everyone's surprise, seemed to glow in the heat of the gossip. She even appeared at school dressed as though she had spent the day shopping with Sally Dylan—penny loafers, a skirt with crinolines, a cardigan sweater over a white button-up blouse. I could see the girls inching closer to her with each class, surrounding her like insects, timidly asking questions, and I knew that Marie's answers pleased them from the way their faces brightened into blushes.

I did not want to know what she said.

I had my own questions to endure, questions I chose to answer with a crooked smile—the look that mischievous boys learn to use in defense. I was fascinated that those who asked about the date—mostly my teammates—shook their head in wonder, as though they understood every syllable of the silence.

In typing class, Marie whispered to me, "Just enjoy it."

"Guess we should," I told her.

Marie had been right, of course. Together, we had the power to manipulate Overton High School as smoothly as magicians pulling rabbits from empty top hats, and before the day was over, we were playing to on-lookers like vaudevillians strolling under spotlights.

"A few more dates, Cole, and we'll have them bowing at our feet," she predicted.

"Could be," I said.

That week, Marie and I were seen together constantly, not hand-holding as other couples, but together still. We perfected the impression that we were joyously happy. Marie's behavior in class changed. She seldom argued, seldom volunteered to answer even the simplest of questions. She did not leave class abruptly. She sat, gazing at me, pretending to blush when I looked at her, and I learned quickly that she was far more clever than I. Our dates that week—for she insisted we needed to be seen as inseparable—were alleged dates, for we never left her home, and at her home we studied from a curriculum she had prepared as attentively as she had prepared her reading exercises for Jovita's children. I was stunned by her knowledge and by my own yearning to discover what she knew.

Yet, we both understood that our court of on-lookers at Overton High School wanted adventure, mystery, visions of night-covered passion, and Marie provided it with remarkably inventive suggestions, telling whispered stories of my tenderness and passion, pledging her awed listeners to absolute secrecy.

"Of course," her listeners said.

"Promise."

"Cross my heart."

"Trust us."

Those vows of secrecy were shattered like dropped crystal within minutes of the telling, and the stories spewed in wildfire speed and in wildfire heat throughout Overton High School, tumbled into Bell's Drugstore for afternoon tittle-tattle, circled the dance floor at Kilmer's Recreation Hall on Friday nights, and eventually made their way to me in a flapping of tongues. I merely smiled when asked about them, and my smile became confirmation.

In those small daily dramas of imagination, with a chorus of whispering, unsuspecting players richly adding to the comedic splendor of our theatrics, the ad-libbed performances Marie and I offered were as grand as any story I had ever read. And, surprisingly, there was no torture from the football team or from anyone else. Everyone believed I had provided a balance for Marie's delicately unpredictable nature, that my presence calmed her, and they believed also that Marie was making a realist of me. Teachers blushed with pride: the two brightest students in Overton High School were together, and that was good. Marie's essay on the South, a deliberate propaganda piece written with the acid pen of sarcasm about an outsider being captivated by the grandeur of her new surroundings, won a competition sponsored by the newspaper. I recognized the sarcasm, found it deadly. My own entry, a humorous account of the culture of high school football, won second place. Only Marie recognized the humor.

"As principal, I predict great things from both these fine students," O. J. Mayfield said in an assembly program before the entire high school. "Yes, I do."

Marie and I ruled, commanded.

And every day was a day of possibility, a day of daring.

One morning, before class, she said to me, "Let's do something spectacular today."

"Let me think about it," I told her.

During English, a dragging, tiresome discussion about Shakespeare's *Romeo and Juliet*, I committed the most foolish, childish act of my life, and as I think of it now, I believe it is a good account of how juvenile we were in those days.

It was a scene that could have been on the television program of the 1970s and early 1980s called *Happy Days*, the one with Ron Howard as Richie and with Henry Winkler playing the Fonz.

I asked Marilyn Pender if I could make an announcement.

"Why, of course, Cole," she said sweetly.

I stood and walked to Marie's desk. A hollow silence fell over the room.

"I just got to thinking about it, listening to Mrs. Pender talk about Shakespeare," I said. I paused for the drama of the pause, cleared my throat. "That night we went out for the first time—when we were driving—I looked over at you, and I remembered that line out of *Romeo and Juliet*, the one about the light and Juliet being the sun."

Sally, who was sitting behind Marie, giggled. Wormy whispered, "You idiot. What're you doing?"

"Wormy, be quiet," Marilyn Pender warned. "Go on, Cole."

I reached for Marie's hand and tugged her from her seat. She stood close to me, gazing tenderly into my eyes.

"Everybody's got to have their sun, I think," I said. "You're mine. I want to give you this."

I slipped my class ring from my finger and presented it to Marie. She held it in the palm of her hand, staring at it. Tears welled in her eyes. She lifted her face and kissed me tenderly on the cheek, then she turned and ran from the classroom. I could hear Marilyn Pender sigh.

"Cole, you fool," Wormy whispered.

The class applauded.

That night, when I appeared at her house to study, Marie danced gleefully around me.

"That was great, Cole, great," she cried. "Better than anything I've ever thought of. Did you listen? They didn't make a sound when you gave me your ring. Not one. They didn't even breathe. God, I thought old lady Pender was going to faint, or start crying, or have an orgasm or something. You were great. Maybe you should be an actor."

"You weren't bad yourself," I told her.

"Did you like the tears?" she asked.

"Good touch."

"I can do that anytime I want to. Always could," she said triumphantly.

"Where's my ring?" I asked.

"Here," she said. She touched a soft spot on her sweater, low between her breasts. "It's on a chain. I've got to keep it for a while, you know." She smiled and cooed, "It's in a safe place, Cole. A nice, warm place. But anytime you want it, all you've got to do is reach in and get it."

"Come on, Marie, stop that," I said irritably. "All right, you can keep it, but just for a few weeks."

She laughed and dropped to the floor of her living room, in a circle of books and papers. "I'll bet we could make the breaking up even better," she said.

As absurd as we must have seemed in public, Marie and I were mostly quiet when we were alone, like library patrons pausing in long spells of reading for whispered questions across a desk. To me, Marie was the first person to give advice I wanted to hear, wanted to think about, wanted to heed. She believed absolutely in the power of a person to accomplish whatever that person wanted to accomplish, provided he or she had the discipline to work for it and the good sense to understand limitations. Everything else was foolish, a kind of hopscotch exercise of spending time. It amused Marie that people believed the stories she told of our relationship. Such people were as playable as paper dolls.

"Do you know, Cole Bishop, we'll never meet such people again," she said to me on Thursday night before the final football game of the season. "Nobody will ever eat out of our hands like this, and, God, I'll miss that. Anytime I want to make Sally Dylan green with envy, I just drop a hint that you and I may have been talking about getting married."

We were sitting in the kitchen at Marie's house, drinking hot sassafras-root tea sweetened with honey, a brew taken from Jovita. The sound of television played dully from the living room, and an occasional muffled laugh could be heard from Marie's parents. I glanced in horror toward the closed door. "Look," I said fretfully, "you can't go around saying that. There'll be all kinds of talk. My mama and daddy would have a fit if they heard that."

"Oh, Cole, it's just a game. Sally stuffs toilet paper in her bras. She likes things like that."

"Like what?"

"Like us getting married."

"But it's not true."

"Cole, of course not. But Sally will never have anything in her narrow little world of lipstick and stuffed bras that even comes close to as much excitement as I'm giving her. Let her enjoy it, Cole. Let her talk about it when she's fifty and fat and her hair's dyed orange and she can't get over being fifteen. She'll need something, Cole. God knows, there'll be nothing else. Maybe some snot-nosed grandkids. I feel sorry for her. She'll need to remember us."

"You don't like anything about this place, do you?" I asked.

Marie tilted her head and thought about the question. She said lightly, "No, no I don't. It's amusing, but I don't like it. If I didn't have you around, I'd be bored to death."

"Wait a minute," I complained. "You're talking about me like I'm Sally Dylan."

"Cole Bishop, that's not what I mean and you know it," she said angrily. "You've got some promise. Or you better have. I don't like wasting my time. But you've got more faults than almost anybody I know."

"Like what?" I asked.

"Like not knowing who you are."

"What does that mean?"

"It means you've been pretending to be somebody else so long, you get it all mixed up. Every book you read, you believe you're the person you're reading about. If you ever have to be just you, you're going to be lost. That's one big fault."

"What else?" I asked.

"You trust people."

"What's wrong with that?"

"Nothing, if they're the right people. But you trust everybody, and that's crazy. Don't ever trust anyone who's smarter than you."

"That doesn't make sense," I argued. "Everybody's smarter than other people in some things."

"God in heaven, you make me mad," she snapped. "Do you know that? I keep trying to help you and you don't listen to a word I say. I told you: someday you'll be famous, you'll be somebody. You won't be Cole Bishop, high school fool. You'll be Cole Bishop, somebody. Except you'll never completely lose the fool part of you. Every bum who comes along, no matter if he's dressed in a pair of overalls or a three-piece suit, you'll take him at his word, and if you're not careful you're going to be fall flat on your little quarterback ass."

"Don't talk like that," I said.

"Like what?"

"Why don't you try to be a lady?"

"Is that what you want?" she said. "A lady?"

"I want you to be one."

"I can't," she countered. "You ruined me."

"How?"

"By getting me in the backseat of your car all those times. The girls keep asking me how you are on that backseat. I tell them that's our secret."

"For God's sake, Marie, don't say that," I whined.

"Am I any good?" she purred.

"How would I know?" I snapped.

"You want to know?"

"No."

She smiled coyly. She glanced toward the door leading to the living room. A peel of muffled laughter rose and died from the television. She could hear her father cackle. "Tomorrow night, after the game," she teased. "We'll call it a celebration."

"No," I said again in exasperation.

"Why not?" she whispered. "I'm beautiful. I'm as beautiful as anybody in school. You'll see when we show up at the prom together next spring. I've got the biggest breasts in our class. It'd take a whole box of tissues for Sally to be as big as me, no matter what that ridiculous Art Crews tells you."

"Stop it, Marie," I warned. "You're just doing that to aggravate me."

"Want to see my breasts, Cole?" she whispered.

"No, Marie, I don't. I definitely do not want to see your breasts," I answered in a hushed voice.

"Don't you trust me?" she said.

"Yes," I told her.

"You're a fool, Cole Bishop. You'll never change."

NINE

On Thursday morning, December 23, he drove to the First United Methodist Church of Raemar and selected a six-foot Christmas tree, a spruce, sold in a fund-raiser by the youth fellowship, and then he returned home and placed it in a metal stand in his living room, far enough from the stone fireplace for safety, and he decorated it with ornaments he had acquired after his divorce, having lost the finer collection to Holly. He did not string lights. It seemed useless.

Still, with a new-blaze fire in the fireplace, there was a cheerful spirit to the room, and a scent of cedar. Once he had gone into the woods to cut his Christmas tree, but the romance of such a tradition had long been lost to the drudgery of labor. Now, he only went into the woods in winter to visit the harvesting of maple sap on the farm of Dexter Williams, a friend he had met during his first year at Raemar. Dexter operated a nursery and had a small facility for making maple syrup. He was also a reader, a lover of the stories of Southern writers, and his time with Cole was spent in prying for information. On the day Larry Brown, the Mississippi writer, died, Dexter had called, saying, My God, we've lost one of the good ones. He could have been a giant.

At lunch, Cole called his sister, Amy, telling her he was sorry he had elected to stay in Vermont for the holidays. Next year, I'll be there, he promised. But since I'm coming down in April, I thought it would be best to stay here.

Amy wanted to know how he was spending the holidays.

I'm doing a little writing, he said.

Poetry? she asked.

He chuckled, answered, No. I guess you could call it faction.

What's that?

Some fact, some fiction, he told her. A friend of mine calls it a word brew.

And what is this faction about? she asked.

Growing up, he said.

She laughed the laugh she used when teasing him. If it's about you, I think you'd better let me and Rachel read it, she said. You do have a way of gilding the truth.

No, he replied, I have a way of dignifying the truth, unlike my two sisters, who believe gossip is the holy word of God. You forget, dear one, I am a man of letters, trained to be compassionate and, at the same time, detached. I am, modestly speaking, something of a genius at it.

She laughed again and there was happiness in her voice. I do miss you, Cole. I miss your stories, she said softly.

And I miss telling them, he replied, also softly.

Are you going to be alone on Christmas? she asked.

No, he told her. I'm having dinner with Tanya and Mark Berry. You met them when you were here. She's a psychologist.

The pretty one? she said.

She is, yes, he admitted. And very bright and, like you, she enjoys irritating me.

Good, Amy said. I feel better knowing you'll be in the kind of company that knows how to handle you.

&

It was mid-afternoon when he resumed his writing, feeling invigorated from his decoration and his conversation with his sister and from a short walk he had taken.

December 23, afternoon

I have been doing this for so many days now I have to resist beginning each session by writing, Dear Diary. There are moments when it feels as though I am composing a journal fifty years after the fact. And perhaps it is that, with a slight difference: I am not searching for memories; I am letting memories come to me. Surprisingly, they seem eager to show themselves, their behavior being a little like men in a sports bar bellowing about a weekend game, each needing to out-do the other.

See? I will take the bellowing about a game as an omen.

The Overton High School Purple Panthers won the last football game of the season, defeating the Maryville Owls, 18-14. It was an upset. Maryville had won eight games. All three of our touchdowns were scored by Wormy. We (or I) failed on each extra point, all on attempted quarterback sneaks. Still, we won, ending the year with a record of six victories, four losses, the best in school history.

After the game, Marie stood away from the mob that rushed the field to gather around Wormy, and then she strolled casually toward me.

"Who won?" she asked in a bored voice.

"Yeah, sure," I said, laughing.

"Am I supposed to hug you?" she cooed.

"Why not?" I told her. "Give everybody a thrill."

She wrapped her arms around my neck and squealed.

"Jesus!" I said. "That's my ear."

"That's what Connie did," she said. "I saw her."

"She didn't bust my eardrum doing it."

She giggled and released me. "Now, what do we do?"

"Go to the dance, I guess," I said.

"Do I have to dance?"

"Yeah. Once, at least."

"I'm not very good at it. I even got expelled from a ballet class in Washington."

"There's nothing to it. You just stand there and sway."

"In your arms?"

"Yeah."

"My God, that sounds juvenile."

"It is," I said. "Come on."

"Oh, I have to walk off the field with you?" she asked in a sugary voice.

"I'm a hero. You're my woman," I told her. "Besides, everybody's looking." I put my arm around her waist and we began to stroll away.

An orchestra of sound—voices with the tongues of trumpets and violins and drums—blared in unrelenting profusion across the field. Bodies sprang up and down on pogo legs, pirouetting in a dance of glory. Hands clawed the air for mystic souvenirs of the moment. Flashbulbs sizzled, spitting shots of heat into the cool air.

Marie caught my arm with both hands and held it tightly. "Good God," she screamed, "these people are crazy. I feel like I'm in the middle of a Roman orgy."

"Close to it," I said. I ducked under the wingspread of an arm aimed for my neck, and pulled Marie around a pile of bodies wallowing on the ground. In a moment, we were free of the frenzy.

"You love it, don't you?" she said.

"Yeah, I do," I answered honestly. "But it's over."

"No, Cole. It's just started. You're going to be famous."

The dance was noisy, the night intoxicated with energy. I was muscle-sore, but happy. Marie, who had protested that she did not know how to dance, was spectacular on the hardwood floor of Kilmer's Recreation Hall. "Cole," she said in a bored voice, "I lied to you about being expelled from that ballet class. I was great at it. This is nothing."

I did not arrive home until one o'clock. To my surprise, my parents were sitting in the kitchen, drinking coffee

I asked why they were still awake.

"Just talking," my mother said.

"Kind of late for old people," I joked.

"Kind of late for young people," my father said soberly.

"Well, we had the dance, and a bunch of us just got to talking, and—"

"You don't have to tell us," my mother said gently. She reached for my hand and stroked it. "We're very proud of you. You played a good game."

"We were lucky," I said.

"Sometimes things happen you don't expect," my father said. I could feel his eyes boring into me.

"Oh, honey, we noticed that same little girl walking off the field with you," my mother said cheerfully. "What's her name again?"

"Marie," I answered. "Marie Fitzpatrick." I added, "We're just friends."

My father cleared his throat and looked away.

"Is anything wrong?" I asked.

"Of course not,"my mother answered. "We just heard some, well, talk."

A queasiness swept over me, filled my mouth. "Talk?" I said.

"You know how people are, honey," my mother said. "They can twist the truth until it looks like a plateful of spaghetti."

"I don't know what you're talking about," I told her.

"What your mama's saying is that people are talking around that you're about to get married to that girl," my father said sternly.

I laughed, unexpectedly, inappropriately.

"You think that's funny?" my father demanded.

I sat in a chair and wiped my fingers over my mouth to control the laughter. "Daddy," I said, "that's just a joke. I promise you. Marie's, well, she's different."

"What I hear tell, she's crazy," my father growled.

"No, she's not crazy, Daddy," I said, trying to be firm but not argumentative. "She's the smartest person I've ever met, and when she came here, everybody treated her like she had leprosy. All she's doing is toying with some of the girls at school."

"You're sure, honey?" my mother asked in a begging voice. "You're not about to throw away your chance at life, are you?"

"No, Mama. No," I said. "I like Marie. She's a good friend. But I'd rather spend the rest of my life farming with Toby than be married to her. She's too smart. She'd drive me nuts."

"Oh," my mother said.

"You be careful," my father advised. "Hot blood's got no brains."

I did not inform Marie of my parents' concern about our relationship until years later, in a letter meant to comfort her over a breakup with a boyfriend. I remember one line from her reply: *Oh, my God, were we that accomplished in our little game, Cole?*

Considering it now, from such a distance, yes. Yes, we were.

The rumor of our impending marriage—shrewdly manipulated by Marie—blew through Overton High School like a bawdy joke told in school-ground huddles. It was laughed at, shrugged off, but not forgotten. For the rest of the school year, occasional reminders of the rumor appeared with the regularity and familiarity of an old standard punched up on a jukebox. In its harmless, settled-in way, it became part of the culture of the class of 1954–1955. As fall turned to winter and winter surrendered to spring, Marie attended basketball and baseball games to cheer lustily for me. She wore my football letter jacket like a cape belonging to royalty. We were called Mr. And *Mrs.* Overton High School. For a tease, she often could be found dreamily gazing at wedding dresses in women's magazines. *The Wedding March* was included the Glee Club's Winter Concert, disguised in the program as a selection from Richard Wagner's *Lohengrin*. Everyone in the audience knew why. Everyone laughed.

It was because of the way we reveled in the ribbing that it continued.

"Let them have their fun," Marie said. "They don't know it, but the best is yet to come."

"What does that mean?" I asked suspiciously.

"The Junior-Senior Prom, fool. We're going to make their eyeballs spin at the prom. I told you, I'm going to be beautiful. No, ravishing. The most spectacular sight this sad little town has ever seen. Every boy—and man—in the place will spend the night picking his chin up off the floor. Before the night's over, Art Crews will be throwing bricks at Sally Dylan, and Sally will hate me. They'll all hate me. Every girl—and woman—there will hate me. If you look halfway decent, they'll be talking about us into the next century."

"Don't over-do it," I warned.

"Oh, but I will, Cole," she promised. "I'm going to over-do it in ways that your celebrated, but listless, little imagination could never comprehend."

"What does that mean?" I asked, and I could hear the worry in my voice.

"I'm going to be a woman, Cole."

There was both fear and anticipation in my vision of how Marie would appear at the prom. I knew only that she and her mother had driven to Atlanta one weekend to shop for a gown. When I asked about it on the following Monday, she fluttered her eyes and sighed seductively, and a sinking feeling, followed by warm joy, shimmered through me.

That afternoon, I purchased from Hendley's Department Store a double-breasted soft-gray wool suit, a pale lavender shirt with French cuff sleeves and wide lapels curled open by flexible stays, a dark burgundy silk tie, and cordovan-red wingtip shoes. Harry Hendley pronounced my selections as "...top of the line." To show his enthusiasm, Harry contributed a handkerchief to my attire. The handkerchief had been monogrammed in a small, cursive thread script with the letter H. "H for Hendley. Just for our appreciative customers," Harry whispered.

After buying the suit, I crossed the street to the New Bloom Flower Shop and placed an order for a wrist-band orchid. Because I could not describe Marie's dress, it was decided the orchid would be the color of lavender, matching my shirt.

In the coming-of-age acts that all young people experience, I believe the purchase of that suit for the prom and the selection of the orchid for Marie was the beginning of my independence.

Yet, after these many years, I am still coming-of-age.

TEN

He did not email what he had written to Tanya. It was incomplete and he wanted to finish it—to tell of the prom and what happened there and afterward. He needed clear thinking for it, and he knew he was exhausted from the day and from the lateness of the hour.

Yet there were two letters from Marie he wanted to read again.

The first had been written in 1976. On a trip from Columbs, Ohio, to Charleston, South Carolina, to attend a medical convention, she had impulsively driven through Overton.

Dear Cole,

On the day that I left Overton, I did not believe I would ever return to it, yet I did. Or maybe it couldn't be called a return. I did not stop in the town, afraid that someone would remember me and escort me to a lynching tree. If it has changed, Cole, I didn't see it. Well, a few things. Bell's is now a jewelry store, which made me wonder where the young and privileged of today waste their time, or where young ladies purchase their Kotex. I drove by our old home with its wraparound porch (and that I did like from those ancient days), and I drove to the school, except it isn't a high school any longer. There was a sign: Overton Middle School. The swings were gone from the playground, Cole. Gone. I almost cried. Damn them. Why can't people leave the swings of children alone? Do they forget about the joy of swings? I think that is why I raced away, even running a signal light. I had thought of finding Jovita, but I couldn't make myself stop the car and ask about her, and I had forgotten where she lived. I simply couldn't. I have never felt so sad, so in need of you.

The only place I stopped was at Breedlove's Cemetery—out of town and out of sight. I picked wildflowers and put them on the grave of Daniel Breedlove.

Do you know what's strange to me, Cole Bishop? It's strange that you are always the first person I think about when I get desperately lonely.

Maybe if I had given in to one of those drunken marriage proposals that I've received over the years, I could put you away like a winter sweater I have worn for the last time. Just forget you. But I'm now thirty-eight years old and, for me, that's old age. Why didn't you come and rescue me, Cole? Why did you have to marry that horrible woman who has a name like a Christmas wreath? Holly. God. Cole and Holly. It doesn't sound nearly as wonderful as Cole and Marie, or, better still, Marie and Cole. I'm glad I've never seen pictures of the two of you. (And I hope she reads this letter. She needs to know I despise her.)

Forgive me. I shouldn't speak ill of someone I've never met. I'm sure she's a saint. She'd have to be to endure you. Holly has nothing to do with my irritibility. It's the drive through Overton. Forgive me also for being negative about your hometown, Cole. Maybe I'm jealous because I don't have one. We moved around too much. If I had a hometown, I think I might enjoy visiting it. Going home must be wonderful.

But I'm glad I have my memories of you, and of those special moments we shared when we were playing our game. If you were a landscape, a piece of geography, I would think of you as my home. There are times when I wish we had not made the pledge to refrain from sending photographs to one another. (But that was my doing, wasn't it? I think of it as the Period of My Rebellion. Dear God, how did you ever tolerate me?)

Love to you.

The second letter had been included in her Christmas card for 1974. In early December of that year, shortly after they had begun dating, he had taken a train trip with Holly to New York City to do Christmas shopping and to attend offerings of the theater.

One of the plays they saw, at the Greenwich Village Theater, was *The Fantastics*. Ironically, Marie had been at the same performance, yet neither knew the other was there—not then, not on that night.

Her letter read:

Dearest Cole,

I have just returned from New York, one of the most glorious weeks I've had in years. Joined some friends from the Harvard days (and, no, there wasn't an old lover among them—damn it). Just girls. We shopped and dined in the most wonderfully snobbish and expensive restaurants we could find, and in honor of my dear mother—who is fifty-eight now and managing poorly after my father's death—I went to the theater on Friday night to see a production of "The Fantastics." It was as grand and as silly as I knew it would be, and I thought of you, especially when they sang "Try to Remember." I wished you were with me. As sentimental as you are, you would have been putty in my hands. (Curiously, as we were leaving, I saw a man across the lobby who reminded me of you. He even looked the way I imagine you must now look—a grown-up, bearded version of that little testosterone-afflicted boy who used to tag after me on the school ground of Overton High School, drooling with passion. I even thought of elbowing my way through the crowd to speak to him, but he was with a gaudy woman wearing fake fur and the most ridiculous red hat I've ever seen.)

Someday, Cole, we really should have a reunion. We should mark a day on the calendar and declare it the annual Marie-Cole holiday. We could meet in exotic locations—New York, Paris, Rome, London (for me), Chattanooga, Birmingham, Memphis (for you)—and spend the day having wild, uninhibited sex and telling outrageous lies to one another, like that couple did in the play "Same Time, Next Year." I think that would be lovely, don't you? Don't you believe we deserve at least one day a year? We could make it happen, if we tried, you know. As they say, timing is everything.

Merry Christmas, my famous friend.

He never shared with Marie that he was the man she had seen in the lobby of the theater. He couldn't. It would have been cruel. On that night, he had proposed to Holly sitting in a coffee shop. She had nodded yes under her red hat.

❧

He awoke early and it surprised him, surprised him also that he felt vigorous. He reasoned it was from the soundness of his sleep, one without dreaming—or if he had dreamed, he could not remember it. He showered and dressed and then left to have breakfast at Arnie's Place of Gathering, where a group of men met daily to discuss the affairs of the world during the twenty-four hours bridging their last get-together. The men jokingly called themselves The Superior Court. He liked them. They were hail-to-you friendly and they always motioned him to sit with them, pulling him into their back-and-forth opinions. They called him Doc, saying it in a respectful way.

Among them was a pharmacist, two retired attorneys, the owner of a heating-and-air business, an insurance salesman, a real estate agent, and the proprietor of an antique shop having more junk than antiques. The owner of the shop—called the House of History—was Wilber Etz. He was their leader, only because he was the natural talker among them, a gift that carried over into his business. If he could not verify the history of an item—from armoires to spoons of thread—he would simply make it up. It had taken Cole many years to realize Wilber Etz was a master storyteller.

Arnie's Place of Gathering was small and as rustic as a log cabin—which, in part, it was: the inside back wall. It was decorated in scenes and objects of Vermont's Green Mountains, and it had the odor of oven-baked bread and tableclothes that had been starched and steam-ironed. In daytime it was bright and cheerful and noisy. At night, Arnie kept the lighting dim. Candles flickered on tables. Instrumental music, as subdued as the candle flames, played from hidden speakers at low, barely audible volume. For people who wished to carry on dinner conversations, it was as inviting as any restaurant in the world.

The men of the Superior Court met in Arnie's because it was located in the center of Raemar, on the corner of the two main roads crossing in the middle of town, and they could sit at the up-front window table and watch the comings and goings of townspeople. To Cole, Raemar had the look and the feel of Overton. Small, personal, neighborly. On the surface, a good place to live. Still, in the backrooms of politics and business greed, the town had its villainy, its darkness. And there were drug-pushers and drug-takers causing tragedy, and petty crime and assaults rising from temper and the dragging-down of poverty or addictions.

And fear. There was also fear. Fear of change. The same as in Overton.

Yet, on Friday, December 24, 2004, the meeting of the Superior Court was festive, as merry as the greetings of the season. As he had his breakfast—eggs benedict and coffee—Cole listened to the men's banter. The presidential election was still contentious among them, the war in Iraq a head-shaking worry. And then there was the quarrel over having a Nativity scene on the courthouse square in a town in Minnesota, with Wilber suggesting that all of them—if they were real men—should load up in their automobiles and head to Minnesota to join the protests against the three or four radicals spouting off about separation of church and state.

They need horse-whipping, said Elton Dewberry, the heating and air man. Any son of a bitch that wants to keep Jesus out of Christmas, after the way this country was founded, needs his ass kicked.

They asked Cole's opinion on the subject. He said, I'll be glad to lend a boot, and the men laughed.

Wilber said, Doc, what'd you get us for Christmas?

He answered, That's why I came in this morning. I'm picking up the check. Merry Christmas.

Well, be damned, said Wilber.

The breakfast with the Superior Court invigorated him and also reminded him that he had not purchased a gift for Tanya and Mark, though Tanya had warned him against doing such.

In Paige's Jewelry and Gift Shoppe, he selected a yellow silk tie for Mark, knowing Mark's pride in his public appearance, and for Tanya, a cameo. He would not tell her the reason for the gift, still it pleased him that it was more personal than he could admit. The memory of her sitting at his kitchen table, gazing outside at the show, her face lovely in profile, warmed him. He wondered if it was lust, or simply the gladness of having her as a friend. Both, maybe. But if was lust, it was as much for her presence as her sensuality.

He left Paige's and made a leisurely drive through the town, to the neighborhoods surrounding it. Snow quilted the yards, sculpted plants. Christmas decorations dangled from porches, some lighted in small white lights, like glowing snowflakes. Wreathes marked doors in large green Os, the bows of wide red ribbon dressing them.

He needed to get his camera and take photographs and send them to Amy and Rachel, he thought. Once, years earlier, they had visited him during Christmas, tugging their husbands with them, and they had been in awe at the sights.

The drive back to his house left him jittery with energy.

For lunch, he had a turkey pot pie taken from his freezer and baked in his oven. He considered it emergency food, knowing its contents were too calorie-and-fat rich, yet he liked the taste of it.

After eating, he returned to his office and turned on his computer and checked his email messages, finding only one—from Tanya. *I assume you're still alive and still writing. I'm sorry I asked you about making love to Marie. Knowing the answer dulls my anticipation. I wanted something so steamy it would send shivers through me. My fault for being nosey. Remember tomorrow. And screw your goose. We're having leg of lamb.*

He laughed, returned a message: *My goose is offended. See you tomorrow.*

He opened the MARIE document, read his last entry, then began writing. He would not move from his chair for many hours.

December 24, Christmas Eve day, afternoon

It is true that aging toys with memory. Inexplicably, some moments, completely unimportant, remain vivid while others, far more significant, are forgotten. One of the vivid moments for me was dressing for the prom. Perhaps it was because of what happened that night, or because proms are seminal events in the lives of young people—as much ritual as party, the ritual celebrating some mark of growth, somewhat like the pencil line on a door showing height year to year.

I remember wondering if the orchid I had chosen was too small, too pallid for the quaint, erratic girl who had become a surprising fixture in my life.

I remember this, also: pulling a trough in the burgundy silk tie, under the knot. Remember standing in front of the dresser mirror, thinking myself as decently handsome as clothing could make me. The soft-gray suit seemed tailored. The lavender shirt was the color of early morning when the sun first dims the clouds—if the clouds are right. I remember admiring my new wing-tip shoes, remember lifting one foot, wiping the face of the shoe across the back of the pants on my opposite leg, and then lifting the other, repeating the motion.

In the kitchen, my mother's eyes filled with delight. She hugged me, declared me more striking than movie stars and princes, then made me do a full turn as she checked for price tags. Even my father seemed pleased. "I had a suit almost like that one time, son," he said. "Courted your mother in it."

Toby, my brother, was amused. "That's a trouble suit," he advised.

"What's that supposed to mean?" I asked.

"Means it's gonna get you in trouble," Toby answered. He winked at me. "Wish you was big enough to be a real man. I'd borrow it from you."

"Leave him alone, Toby," my mother admonished. Then, to me: "Make sure you tell Mrs. Fitzpatrick that you want a couple of the pictures she takes. You need to send one to Rachel and Amy."

"Yes ma'am."

I knew Marie would not be ready to leave when I arrived at her home. My mother had advised that being late, staying in their bedroom for the final fussing over the final, out-of-place hair, was part of the Junior-Senior Prom ritual for girls. For boys, it meant small talk with fathers. Awkward, throat-clearing small talk. Or it meant the irritating gawking and giggling of younger siblings, believing that a Junior-Senior Prom was little more than an occasion akin to Halloween. And they were not far from the truth. Photographs would prove it. Photographs that, years later, would look childish and humorous. I had watched my sisters, Rachel and Amy, through their prom nights, doing the expected gawking and giggling. Girls turned into girl-women, their dates turned into boy-men. There was little difference between a four year old appearing from the bedroom in her mother's high heels, baggy dress, swallowing hat, her face smeared in lipstick, than in a teenage girl dressed in a gown. Both were pretending.

The small talk with George Fitzpatrick was about football. George had played for the University of Maryland. Offensive left guard and linebacker. Once he had intercepted a pass against Clemson and had returned it for a touchdown. "Greatest moment of my life," he assured me.

"You thought about playing college ball?" he asked.

"No sir," I said politely. "I don't think I'm big enough."

"Lot of good small colleges around," he advised. "You're fast. Got a good arm. I think you could make it."

"I've thought some about it," I said. It was a lie. After my last football game, I had rejoiced secretly that I would never again have to play football. The boasting I had made to Marie about being a football coach had been nothing but that—boasting.

The small talk about football ended with a nodding from George Fitzpatrick. He cleared his throat, glanced at his watch, cut his eyes toward the door leading from the living room to the bedrooms.

"Girls," he said. "Never on time, are they? My Laura was the same way. Still is. I can get ready to go somewhere, and I have to sit around half the day, waiting." He glanced at his watch again. "Why don't I go back there and hurry them along?"

"Yes sir," I said, then wondered if I had answered too quickly. "But I'm fine," I added. "We've got plenty of time."

"I'll just check on them," he said. He left the room in a rush.

I remember the moment as one without equal, a sensation that chilled me then and does still with each memory-visit I have of it.

I was standing in the living room of the rented home of George and Laura Mullen Fitzpatrick, the home with the wraparound porch, and I was looking out of the window at the lights of early night glistening on the waxed hood of my parents' Chevrolet, and I knew that someone was gazing at me. I could feel it, like people who feel the paralyzing presence of ghosts.

I turned.

Marie was standing in the doorway leading to the dining room.

She had not lied.

She was astonishing.

Not girl-pretty.

Woman-beautiful.

Her long hair had been cut and was swept like the break of a dark wave to one side of her head. She had never worn makeup. Now, she did. And the makeup—tan from the magic of liquid and powder—was flawless. Eyeshadow of lavender, the orchid's color, barely visible over eyes that seemed also lavender. Lips of pale, melon-red gloss. The gown she wore was a brilliant white, riding low on her breasts and fitting snug over her body to her knees, and then yawning open in the mouth of a short train that was edged in lace. The dress was topped in a matching, but more delicate lace cloak, a netting that fastened with three pearl buttons at her throat. Her neck and the rising slopes of her breasts teased beneath the netting. She wore white pearl earrings. The orchid was clinging to her wrist like a remarkable piece of jewelry.

"Do you like it?" she asked softly.

I could not speak. I remember that, remember being speechless. I think I nodded.

"Do you know what it is, Cole?"

Still, I did not answer.

"It's a wedding dress," she said.

I blushed.

"Am I beautiful?" she asked softly.

"Yes," I told her. "You are."

"Am I the most beautiful woman in Overton?"

"Yes."

She smiled prettily. "I told you, Cole Bishop."

George and Laura Fitzpatrick appeared in the doorway behind her. George waved a camera in the air.

"All right, young people, get to posing," George cried happily. "I've got a whole roll to shoot."

We were an hour late arriving at Kilmer's Recreation Hall, which had been decorated by the junior class in purple and white balloons and streamers and dimly lighted with colored gels clothespinned to the hoods of small spotlights. Some of the sophomores, dressed as waiters, strolled the dance floor, blowing soap bubbles from small bottles of liquid soap. The bubbles floated in the air, took the color of the gels, popped on the heads of dancers. The song playing from DeWitt Kilmer's jukebox was *Three Coins in a Fountain*.

"Behave yourself," I whispered at the door.

"Not a chance," Marie said.

We entered the room to a gasp that rippled across the room. The dancing stopped and the dancers parted, shuffled back, gazing in awe at Marie Jean Fitzpatrick. She stood under the canopy of one of the spots, a soft straw color that covered her like mist from the moon. Straw-colored bubbles rolled like delicate, transparent planets around her face.

I heard Lamar mutter, "Damn," in an astonished voice.

"Make it mine, make it mine, make it mine..." the jukebox serenaded.

She had said it not as a prediction, but as a warning, and I understood immediately that Marie had known exactly the reaction she would receive at the Junior-Senior Prom of Overton High School.

The boys—the men—were like whimpering servants around her.

The girls—the women—hated her.

Or envied her.

I could hear them hissing, could hear their snarling, their bickering, their sniping. All of it in whisper.

"Art Crews, you remember who you're with!"

"Pull your eyes back in your head, Hugh. You've got all you can handle."

"If you think those things are real, you're crazy. She's just got them pushed up."

"My God, that's a wedding dress. That joke's a little old."

"I wonder who did her makeup—a house painter?"

"I swear she dyed her hair."

If any of the boys—the men—listened, they did not show it. Their eyes feasted on Marie, undressed her, danced naked with her, stroked her body with their hands and with their mouths.

"I'm gonna dance with that woman before the night's over," Art confided to me at the punch bowl. "And I don't give a damn if Sally kicks me in the nuts for doing it."

"She's taken," I said proudly.

"You ever tried dancing with both legs broken?" Art snarled. "I hear it ain't easy to do."

"You have a point," I admitted. "You care if I dance with Sally?"

Art stared at me in disbelief. "Cole, I'll trade you on the spot, and throw in my Ford to boot and even give you the bottle of vodka I've got in the trunk."

It was a funny, almost-desperate line and I laughed, took two cups of punch from the table, and turned back to look at Marie. Wormy and Hugh Cooper and Jody Turner surrounded her. Cone Bailey was standing behind her, leering, tugging subconsciously at his trousers. He did not have the look of a chaperone. Marilyn Pender stood beside him, an expression of awe frozen in her face.

"No trade," I said, "but if she wants to dance with you, that's her business."

"I'll kiss you flat on the lips if she does," Art moaned. He hurried away toward a glaring Sally, the punch sloshing over the glass rims.

An hour later, I had danced with Marie only once, a close-fitting, barely moving slow dance to the music of *Hey, There*. Those who watched us believed she was murmuring love sighs into my ear. She was not.

"Oh, my God, Cole," she whispered, "do you see them? I told you. They're all talking about us."

"Not us," I corrected. "You. And, to be honest, I think you're better ease off a little. You've got Sally nipping at Art's bottle of vodka."

Marie giggled, nestled her face against my neck.

"That's her problem," she said. "Personally, I think she's jealous because I'm with you. I saw you dancing with her. A lot of rubbing, Cole. A lot of rubbing."

"I told you. She's a little drunk," I warned. "Do me a favor, okay?"

"What?"

"Don't dance with Art again."

"Why?"

"I don't want any trouble," I said. "He's my friend."

We turned, bumped against Lamar and a girl named Peggy Colquitt, who was the daughter of Ben Colquitt, the newspaper editor. Lamar grinned, blushed, looked away, forced Peggy into a spin. He gazed over Peggy's shoulder at Marie, rolled his eyes to me.

"All right," Marie said.

"Thanks," I told her.

"You're not mad at me for dancing with other people, are you?"

"No."

"I'm with you, you know. There's no one else here I'd be seen dead with."

"I'm not mad," I assured her.

"Do you really like this dress?"

"Yes."

"I'm going to save it for our wedding."

"Good," I said.

"You don't believe we're going to get married, do you?"

"I do not."

She laughed, snuggled against me, tilted her head, blew softly over my ear.

"Stop it," I said, using my annoyed voice.

Marie broke her promise about not dancing again with Art, but I knew it was not her fault. Art had cut in on Sidney Witherspoon and Marie, nudging Sidney aside with a powerful sweep of his elbow.

"Well, pissant, looks like you're losing your woman," Cone Bailey whispered in an evil snicker.

Cone Bailey had made his way across the room to stand with me. A heavy air of cologne swam around his face.

"Naw," I said easily. "Art's just aggravating Sally."

"Doing a good job of it," Cone Bailey said. "She's been ducking outside to the car. Probably got a bottle."

"Don't know," I lied. I also had watched Sally leave the hall and return a few minutes later. I had danced with her. The faint, hiding odor of vodka was on her breath and in the fire that blazed in her eyes.

"You getting that, Cole?" Cone Bailey asked.

"Sir?"

"Shoot, Cole, it's me you're talking to," Cone Bailey said. "Coach and quarterback. Coaches and quarterbacks got to be up front with one another." He snickered again, reached into his pocket and drug out his handkerchief and wiped the perspiration from his forehead. "It was me, I'd be on that like white on rice."

"We're just friends," I said.

Cone Bailey nodded his head and pushed his handkerchief back into his pocket. "You never had none, have you, Cole?"

"Sir?"

"You talk too much. It's the quiet ones that's getting it all."

"I guess you've got me there," I told him.

Cone Bailey clucked his tongue. His eyes closed to half-lid. He stroked his mouth, his chin. "Take my advice, boy, start out being a Southern gentleman," he said after a moment.

"Sir?"

"You ain't a Southern gentleman until you have you some colored stuff," Cone Bailey said. He nodded again. "Uh-huh. You should of seen me in Africa in the war. I went from being a Southern gentleman to being a Confederate Colonel." He snorted happily.

The music stopped.

"You better go get her before old Art drags her off to the woods," Cone Bailey advised.

"I guess so," I said.

The familiar sound of Hank Williams singing *Your Cheatin' Heart* began to blare from the juke box.

I reached Marie at the same time as Sally Dylan, who jerked at Art and pushed him aside. She glared at Marie.

"You got a date," Sally snapped. Anger trembled in her lips. "Why don't you leave mine alone?"

Marie did not reply. She smiled patiently.

"Jesus, Sally, I'm the one dancing with her," Art protested. "I cut in on Sidney."

Sally whirled to Art. "Is that right? Well, do you know who you're dancing with?"

"Come on, Sally," I said gently. "They were just dancing."

"She teaches little niggers," Sally hissed.

Hank Williams sang, *"When tears come down like fallin' rain…"*

"What?" Art said, a look of confusion curling across his face.

"She teaches a bunch of little pickaninnies after school," Sally repeated triumphantly.

"Where'd you hear that?" Art asked.

"Our maid, Lois, knows all about it," Sally said.

Art turned to look at me. A puzzled, dumb look. He said, "Cole?"

"It's not true," I said. "She—"

Marie touched my arm. "Don't," she urged quietly. She looked at Sally, smiled softly, sadly. "It's been such a lovely evening, hasn't it?" She turned to look at Art. "Thank you for the dance." She slipped her hand under my elbow. "I think we should be leaving now."

"Now?" I said.

"Now," she repeated.

"But—"

"Your cheatin' heaaart will tell on you…"

"Good night," she said to Sally. She stepped back, pulled on my arm, turned me gently.

"Maybe you ought to go to the colored prom," Sally hissed.

I could feel Marie's body tensing. She raised her chin, forced a smile, and began walking away, pulling me with her.

We had driven for several minutes without speaking before Marie said, "I love my orchid, Cole."

"Thanks," I told her. "I'm glad."

"You look very handsome tonight. I can't wait to see the pictures."

"Yeah. Me, too."

"If they turn out well, I'm going to frame one," she said. "I may never look this beautiful again."

"You look the same way you do every day to me," I said.

She smiled and pulled close to me, leaning her head against my shoulder. "That's the sweetest thing you've ever said to me, Cole Bishop. In fact, that's the sweetest thing anyone has ever said to me."

"I mean it," I insisted.

"Of course you don't. You're a great liar."

I remember taking her hand and feeling her fingers lace into mine. Oddly, it was the first time in all of our game-playing that we had held hands.

"You want to talk about it?" I asked.

"About what? Sally? No. I don't want to be sad, Cole. Not tonight. I don't want to talk about anything that's sad."

"I just wanted you to know—"

"It's all right," she said. Then she added, "But do you know what I would like to do?"

"What's that?"

"I want to go see Jovita."

"Who?"

"Jovita. The woman who works for us. You saw her at my house."

"Sure. I remember."

"I want to go see her."

"Now?"

"Now. She wanted to see me in my dress, but she had to go home early. Littlejohn was sick. Do you remember him? Littlejohn?"

"I do, yes," I said. "But it's kind of late, don't you think?"

"If the lights aren't on, we won't stop."

"All right," I told her.

The lights were still on in Jovita's home.

It was a small house, located on Freeman Street in a neighborhood known as Milltown. Once, the homes had belonged to white mill workers who worked long, solemn hours and lived short, solemn lives, enduring the taunting of being called lintheads. Cole remembered his mother talking about the workers, calling them beat-down. Don't ever make fun of people like them, she had warned. It's sad, what they have to put up with. If they didn't have some pride, they'd have nothing at all.

And then the mills had moved to another location and another mill village had been constructed for whites, and blacks had taken over their old, abandoned homes on working arrangements that gave them shelter in exhange for the same kind of menial labor that had enslaved their forefathers. After that, Milltown had become, for many, Niggertown.

I could see a face staring out of a window as I turned off the lights to the car.

"You want to wait out here?" asked Marie.

"No. I'll go with you," I said.

The door to Jovita's house opened as we reached the porch steps.

"Miss Marie?" Jovita said from under the door arch.

"Marie," Marie corrected.

"Yes ma'am," Jovita said. An edge of worry was in her voice.

"I wanted you to see my dress," Marie told her.

Jovita stepped onto the porch. She put her hands together, palm to palm, and drew her hands to her chin. Her eyes covered Marie. "Oh, my," she whispered. She repeated, "Oh, my."

"You like it?" Marie asked.

"Child, you look like a picture. You the prettiest thing I ever saw."

Marie giggled. "Can I show the children?" she asked.

"Honey, they all asleep, but Littlejohn."

"Can I show him?"

Jovita looked at me, hesitated.

"You remember Cole Bishop," Marie said. "He's the lucky man who gets to date me."

Jovita nodded, smiled nervously.

"How are you?" I said.

"Fine," Jovita answered cautiously. Then, to Marie: "Honey, y'all come on in. But the place is a mess. I been taking care of Littlejohn."

"Is he feeling better?" I asked.

"He's fine now. Had him a little cold, but he's been sleeping so much he don't want to go to bed," Jovita said.

"Well, I'm glad," Marie said. "And don't you say another word about your place being a mess. You see my room all the time, and you know what that looks like."

Jovita laughed lightly. "Come on," she said.

We followed Jovita into the house. The room was small, but immaculately clean. I could smell the lingering odor of the cooked and finished dinner, the almost-sweet scent of biscuits, of chicken that had been pan fried, of greens that had bubbled in hot water. It had the same scent of my mother's kitchen.

Littlejohn was curled in a worn armchair near a lamp. He was coloring on a sheet of tablet paper.

"Look who's here, honey," Jovita said.

Littlejohn looked up, saw Marie. His eyes flared open in an amazed stare.

"Hi," Marie said. "What're you doing?"

Littlejohn did not answer. He seemed mesmerized.

"Say hello, honey," Jovita said.

"Cat got your tongue?" Marie teased.

"Somebody done turn you to a princess," Littlejohn whispered.

Marie smiled, knelt before Littlejohn and embraced him. "Thank you," she purred.

"Say hello to Mr. Cole," Jovita urged gently.

"It's just Cole," Marie said. She pulled away and stood beside me.

Littlejohn grinned.

"How you doing, Littlejohn?" I said.

"I been drawing," Littlejohn told me.

"Can I see it?" I asked.

Littlejohn nodded, handed the sheet of paper to me. The drawing was of a turtle with an orange shell.

"Hey, I like this," I said. "This is a great turtle. Looks a lot like Brer Turtle to me."

"What's a Brer Turtle?" he asked.

"Why, he's my friend," I said. "I see him all the time."

Littlejohn's grin spread. His eyes flashed.

"You started it," Marie said. "You finish it."

"Honey, they ain't got time to talk about no turtles to you," Jovita said softly.

"Of course we do," Marie countered. "In fact, I want to hear this myself."

"Well," I said, "the first time I saw Brer Turtle, he was sitting on a log down by the creek where I live."

Littlejohn laughed.

"I'd never seen an orange turtle, and I'd never heard a turtle that could talk, but Brer Turtle could."

Littlejohn's eyes stayed on me like bright beams.

"First thing he said to me was, 'I'm losing my orange.' Now, that surprised me, of course. I said, 'How come?' And Brer Turtle, he said, 'Too much sun. The sun's making me fade.'"

"Uh-uh," Littlejohn whispered in amazement. "Ain't so."

"That's what he told me," I said seriously. "He said the sun was so hot it was making the orange on his shell just fade away. So I said to him, 'Well, why don't you just get out of the sun? Crawl over under the shade somewhere?' That made Brer Turtle laugh. 'In case you didn't notice, I'm a turtle. I'm too slow,' he said."

Littlejohn put his hand to his mouth and giggled.

"I told him I'd sure like to help him out, but I didn't know what to do," I continued. Then I reached over Littlejohn and picked up the short stick of orange crayon.

"You know what Brer Turtle said to me?"

Littlejohn shook his head.

"He said, 'Does your daddy have any orange paint?' and I said, 'Well, now, I think he does.' And Brer Turtle said, 'I sure could use a paint job.' So I ran to the house and found my daddy's bucket of orange paint and an old paint brush, and then I ran back down to the creek."

I began scrubbing the orange crayon over Littlejohn's drawing, making it brighter.

"And I painted Brer Turtle until he looked like the sun just before it turns red and goes down, and he was so happy, he crawled down to the creek and looked at himself in the water."

I handed the crayon and the drawing to Littlejohn.

"And since that time, we've been great friends. I talk to him all the time. He's the one who told me I should ask Marie to go to the prom. He said I wouldn't believe how pretty she would be."

Littlejohn laughed again. He tucked the drawing to his chest.

I turned to Marie. I saw tears rolling over her cheeks.

"Was it that bad?" I asked.

Marie stepped to me. She touched my arm. "It was beautiful," she whispered.

I do not know if I have ever felt as grand as in that moment.

Yet there is a bitter memory of the night. As we were leaving Jovita's house a police car from the city of Overton stopped us and the policeman—a man named Julian Overstreet, who would later become the county sheriff—demanded to know what we were doing in the neighborhood.

"Visiting a friend," I told him.

His face took on a hard, suspicious look. "In Niggertown?" he said incredously.

"In Milltown," I replied.

"You Cole Bishop, ain't you?" he said. "On the football team."

"Yes sir, I am," I answered.

"Boy, don't you know better than to come down here at night?" he snarled.

Marie leaned forward, said, "Are we breaking any laws?"

"Was I saying anything to you?" Julian Overstreet snapped.

I could see Marie's face flaring in anger.

"It's all right," I said to her. Then to Julian Overstreet: "But I guess it's a good question, sir. Are we? Breaking any laws, I mean."

"I don't need your lip, boy," he said. "Who was it you was seeing?"

I hesitated before answering. "A woman named Jovita Curry. She works for Marie's parents. Marie wanted her to see her prom dress."

Julian Overstreet leaned close to the car window, aimed his flashlight at Marie. He said in a low voice, "You get this car out of here and don't let me catch you back down this way at night. You understand me?"

I could feel the thundering of my heart, not from fear, but from the same anger Marie wore on her face, and I remembered all she had said about the South, about its inequities, its mentality of power over blacks and poor whites.

Still, I knew what needed to be said, and I said it: "Yes sir."

I had never felt awkward standing at Marie's front door at the end of a date. Our dates had always ended with laughter, with a fencing match of words, with a feeling of comfort.

Now, it was awkward.

"Don't worry about that policeman," I told her. "That's just the way he is. He likes the power."

"No, Cole," she said softly. "That's the way *it* is. I don't know how anyone lives in this kind of world." She paused. "I really don't understand it."

"I'm sorry," I said.

She touched my lips with her fingertips. "Don't be. We wouldn't have seen Jovita and Littlejohn if things hadn't happened the way they did, and seeing them was the best part of the night."

"It was nice," I said.

"You liked telling that story, didn't you?"

"Yes, " I admitted. "Yes, I did."

"You're going to make a great teacher."

"You believe that, don't you?" I said.

"Yes, I do. You're going to be a teacher."

"You may be right."

A pause settled between us, and then she leaned forward and moved her lips over mine. Not a kiss. A touch. Then she stepped away and opened the screened door.

"I'll see you," I said.

She nodded, smiled, reached for the inside door, turned back to me.

"Cole, don't get mad at me if you think I start acting strange."

"What do you mean?"

She shook her head. "Promise me. The person you've been with tonight is the person I've always wanted to be, but it's not the person I am. Promise me."

"All right," I said. "I promise."

She lifted her wrist to her face, inhaled the perfume of the orchid. "Thank you for this, for tonight."

"No," I said. "Thank you."

ELEVEN

At three o'clock, he awoke with the queasy feeling of illness—a sourness in his stomach and the unmistakable heat of fever on his face. By morning, he was barely able to stand, yet he forced himself to go to his kitchen and to make tea, knowing he was dehydrated from the perspiration that soaked his pajamas and bedding. The tea was good, though he only wanted a sip of it.

He sat in his reading chair—large, cushiony, comfortable—wearing his robe, drained of energy, the tea on a sidetable beside the chair, and he wondered if the sickness was from food he had eaten the day before, or from fatigue of the writing. Possibly both. The tenderness of his body reminded him of an episode of food poisoning he had had years earlier, yet the writing had also taken its toll. In all of his experience, he had never worked with such speed or obsession. It was as though he had fallen into a swift-moving river and had been swept downstream over rapids hurling through a funnel of rocks. His body had the feel of such punishment.

He thought of his commitment to have dinner with Tanya and Mark Berry, knew it was impossible, and he made his way to the telephone and punched their number. Tanya knew immediately that he was not well.

My God, Cole, what's wrong? she asked.

Don't know, he told her. Just sick.

I'll be right over.

No, no , no, he protested. I just wanted to apologize for today.

Unlock the front door, Cole, and then go to bed, she said. I mean it.

Tanya—

Damn it, Cole, quit being so noble. Do what I tell you, she ordered.

He had drifted into sleep and hearing his name, softly spoken, jarred him awake. Tanya was sitting on the side of his bed, her hand touching his throat.

Jesus, she said, you're burning up.

He nodded weakly.

I think we need to get you to the hospital, she added.

He shook his head, said, No.

Damn it, Cole, you do aggravate me, she mumbled. She stood, walked away. He could hear water running in the bathroom. In a few moments she returned with a cool bathcloth. She sat again on the bed and began to wipe his face with it.

Go home, he whispered hoarsely. It's Christmas.

So? she countered.

You've got guests coming, he said.

Tonight, she replied. Besides, Mark does the cooking. You know that. And before you start with that ridiculous Southern-gentleman modesty act, you should know he insisted that I come over. He knows I love you, but he also knows you're too feeble to attack me. Anyway, I've given up sex, except to dream about it. I like it that way. I'm always twenty-three and my lover is always twenty-five. My skin's as tight as a rubber glove and nothing droops, and he has muscles made of hot marble. So, unless you can offer me that, Dr. Bishop, I would advise you to keep quiet and do as I say.

He closed his eyes in surrender.

That's better, she said. She folded the cloth in a rectangle and placed it across his forehead. I'm going to make you some soup, she added.

He nodded.

Out of a can, she said. Assuming you've got some. If not, I'll go home and get it.

In the pantry, he whispered.

Chicken? she asked.

He nodded again.

He submitted to being spoon-fed. The broth of the soup—chicken and rice—was good. Even the sound of Tanya's voice, chiding him for his disregard of health, was comforting. It was also a new experience for him. In his marriage, Holly's reaction to his occasional illnesses had always had the aura of disgust and complaint. He had accepted it, knowing she was squeamish.

After the feeding, she gave him aspirin and then ran lukewarm water in the bathtub, adding baking soda to it, instructing him to soak in it. She threatened to strip him of his clothing and to drag him bodily to the tub if he resisted. In her way of goading him, she said, I hope you do. I hope you put up a fight. I need a good laugh.

You have no shame, or dignity, he told her.

She smiled. If you think it'd embarrass me, you're whistling Dixie, as they say in that backward region of your upbringing. You don't have anything I haven't seen many times. She paused, smiled, leaned to him and whispered, On many men.

Go home, he said again. You're evil.

Not yet, she replied. Where's your laptop?

In my office, he told her.

She went into his office and returned with it, demanding that he open the MARIE file.

I don't want you to read anything else, not now, he protested.

And you're sick and can't stop me, so open it, she said.

He did as she ordered, not wanting to listen to her badgering.

The bath temporarily revived him, or left him with the illusion of being revived. At least the water washed away the coating of perspiration and the baking soda left his skin with a cool, silky feeling. He vowed to remember the remedy, or trick.

When he came out of the bathroom, dressed in clean pajamas and wearing his robe, he found her in the kitchen, at the table, reading from his laptop. The expression on her face was soft, almost pained.

She looked up. Feel better? she asked.

Some, he said. At least cleaner.

I found your tea and made a cup for myself, she told him. Can I make one for you?

Please, he replied.

He moved to the table and sat and watched as she prepared the tea and talked of what he had written.

She said she had read it twice, once quickly and once slowly, and both times she had the quaint sensation that two different people had done the reading. The quick reader wanted the adventure of the words; the slow reader wanted to savor them, to wonder about them.

I wish I had grown up with her, she said in her admiration of Marie. As God is my witness, Cole, you can't believe how much I was like that. Still am, I think. And I don't mean the prom, not that. I didn't even go to the damn thing, but now I wish I had. I wish I had been that bold.

She laughed and gave him the tea. I wish I'd been that beautiful, she added.

I'm sure you were, he said.

She reached to touch his forehead. I think you've cooled off, she told him. Then: No, Cole, I wasn't beautiful. I was as homely as a girl can be. I didn't begin to blossom until my sophomore year in college, and that was after the embarrassment of braces and a nose job. Amazing, isn't it, what a little surgery can do?

She did a turn, like a model. I even had breast enhancement, she added. Can you tell it?

He offered a smile, too weak to make it a chuckle. Shook his head.

Do you think I'm like her? she asked.

He took a swallow of his tea, thought of how Marie had been and how Tanya was. In many ways—their aggressiveness, their language, their stubbornness—they were so alike they could have been twins.

Yes, he said. In spirit. And you bully me as much as she did.

He expected a sharp-edged retort, something sassy. Instead, she said in a soft voice, Maybe that's the only way we can tell you we love you.

There was a pause, uncomfortable, awkward.

She sat opposite him at the table. Did I just frighten you, Cole? she asked.

No, he answered after a moment.

Don't misread me, she said. I do love you, but it's not a dangerous thing. Believe me. I don't yearn for you like a teenager with overactive glands, and in case you wonder, yes, I do love my husband, even if we sometimes act as though we barely know one another. Someone once told me that the perfect marriage is when two people don't actually need one another, yet stay together because the other one is there. I believe there's some truth in that. Or maybe it's not truth. Maybe it's comfort. I don't have to worry about Mark. If I were with you, I would be as much mother as lover. You need that. You need mothering. That's what Marie saw in you.

You may be right, he admitted.

I'm not going to ask you anything else about her, she said. I don't want to know until I read it. But I don't want you to try to write today. I want you to go back to bed. I'll check on you later. Maybe Mark and I can drive over after dinner.

You don't have to do that, he said. If I need you, I'll call.

She stood, walked around the table, leaned to kiss him on top of the head. Merry Christmas, she whispered.

Merry Christmas, he replied. Then, remembering the gifts he had bought, but had not wrapped, said, That shopping bag on the counter, the one from Paige's. Take it. It's for you and Mark.

Damn it, Cole, I told you—

I'm sick, he said. Don't raise your voice to me.

She went to the counter and took the bag and opened it and removed the tie and the cameo. He saw her pull the cameo to her face, saw her press it gently against her cheek, saw her smile.

Before he returned to bed, he went into his office and selected another of the letters from Marie. He stood at his desk and read it, saying the words aloud, but in a voice so subdued he could not hear himself.

Cole,

I know I am supposed to understand dying. It is part of my profession, still it is a mystery to me. Two weeks ago, a young woman came into our hospital with mild discomfort. The discomfort was advanced ovarian cancer and it was necessary to operate on her.

I couldn't save her, Cole. I couldn't. I tried, but I failed. I saw her die, saw the last faint pulsebeat that pumped through her body. Saw her muscles give up whatever energy the cancer had left in her. Maybe you don't know it, but when a person dies, their muscles want to keep trying. There's a scientific reason for it, of course, but you would never understand it, and, to be truthful, I think there's more to it than that. The muscles are in the habit of living. They don't know how to give up, and they can't, until the heart quits feeding them.

I believed I saw her soul rise up out of her, up from the steam of the blood.

I believed I felt it slither coolly pass my face. I even looked up to see if I could watch it escaping the room.

I believed I was that woman, or maybe it was nothing more than sensing that she reached out to touch me as her soul left her. What was it, Cole? A touch of forgiveness, or a kind of ethereal tag? Did she say in that touch, "Now you have it?" It being the cancer.

I know I will see other people die. I'm not God.

But I will never forget her. Never. She was an indigent, as helpless as anyone I have ever known. I was her last hope, and I failed her as everyone else had failed her.

This is what one of the nurses said to me later: "She's better off."

Is she, Cole?

Maybe.

Maybe the dying of the past is relief.

Send me a letter. Tell me the dying is not my fault. Tell me you care for me.

He had written to her immediately, saying the dying was not her fault, saying he cared for her, saying he had wept at her words.

&.

There were demons in his dreams, in the fever of his sleep. Swimming, grotesque faces, cackling voices making mockery. In the heat of the fever, the images swirled, danced wildly, rushed up to him, spun away. And then a snow fell over his sleep-seeing, blinding white, and out of the snow he saw the faces of his brother Toby and of his father and mother. Their faces were like bubbles of colorful lights floating in the snow, falling to the ground, disappearing. And from the snow, a flame appeared, grew rapidly into an inferno, but it did not melt the snow.

In the leap of dreams, he was in a room having nothing but a bed in it. A child, a black child, was on the bed, not moving, and around him there was a gathering of adults, moaning, their faces carrying pain. He could hear a woman's mournful whisper—*He gone, he gone…*—and then he saw an old man—his dark skin leathery, his hair white, his yellowed eyes watery—reach out his hand to touch the boy's face, could hear the old man say, *Jesus be here, Jesus be in my hand. Jesus touching him. Jesus be bringing him back.* And the chest of the boy moved. A great cry went up from the gathering. *Praise Jesus!* a man shouted.

His eyes snapped open. He could feel his heart thundering in his chest. His body was again lathered in perspiration. He pulled himself up to sit on the side of the bed. His mind seemed electrified, and then the memory began to speak to him.

Marie.

Marie telling him about the tall black boy he had seen on the day he drove to her house, following the dare by his teammates.

His name was Moses, Marie had said. He had been raised from the dead.

Weeks into their friendship, after becoming comfortable in her presence, he had confessed about the drive-by and of seeing the boy, of wondering who he was, of speeding away.

Marie had been greatly amused. She had asked, Were you jealous?

He had replied, Jealous? Of what? I was just curious.

Now, sitting on his bedside, the story flooded back to him, the same as his dream, only clearer: the dying child, the family, the old preacher man—there to fling prayers around because it was his duty, what he was good at doing, or so it seemed. Still, there was something different about the old man. He had not said a prayer; he had made a declaration, and the boy had begun breathing again.

In the hazy window-light of the room—reflections of moon on snow—he thought again of Marie and of Moses.

Marie had learned of Moses because she wanted to a do an essay about Jovita's children for a contest offering a scholarship. Jovita had balked, saying she did not want anything written about her children, or about her.

He remembered Marie saying, So I asked her to tell me the best story she knew, the one thing she remembered more than all others. She was ironing one of my father's shirts and for the longest time, she didn't say anything, but I knew she was thinking. I could see it in her eyes. And then she said, Moses being raised from the dead. I asked her what she was talking about and she told me. It was when Moses was a small boy and became ill and the doctor said he would probably die, so they called the family together and also had the preacher there. As they were waiting around his bed, he stopped breathing and the mother began to cry out that he was dead. But the preacher put his hand on Moses' face and said, *Jesus be here, Jesus be in my hand. Jesus touching him. Jesus be bringing him back.*

Marie had vowed those were the exact words used in Jovita's description of it, the same words he had heard in his dream. She had vowed also that Moses had started breathing again.

He had thought it was a made-up story, one of Marie's cruel exaggerations about the South. He remembered chiding her for making fun of Jovita, remembered also that Marie had become incensed over his accusation, remembered her response: Damn it, Cole Bishop, don't you ever say anything like that to me again. I would never insult her, not in an eternity of time. I was just telling you something I thought you would understand, but I'm wrong. You're a redneck. You know nothing about the wonder of things, and you never will.

It had taken an hour to calm her, to guide her back to the story of Moses.

She wanted to meet him, she had finally admitted, and Jovita had explained that he went to the school for blacks and worked part-time at a black funeral home named Higginbottom's.

Marie had gone to the funeral home, had met Moses, had somehow talked him into helping her teach Jovita's children.

That's what he was doing with me when you saw us, she had said. It was a great afternoon. He's smart, Cole. Smarter than you. Maybe even smarter than me. He just hasn't had the same chances we've had. The kids loved him. But that was the only time he was there. Jovita stopped letting her children come to my class, and I had to tell him. It was one of the hardest things I've ever done. He didn't say anything. He just turned around and walked away, back into the funeral home.

He looked at the clock on his bedside stand. A digital blink made the time 7:33, and it confused him. He did not know he had slept so long. He wondered if Tanya—or his sisters—had tried to call him. He had not heard a ringing, but he had had hearing loss over the past five years and it was possible his sleep had been too deep to be jarred awake.

He pushed himself from his bed and went into his bathroom and cupped cold water in his hands and rubbed it over his face and eyes, and then he went into his kitchen and checked his answering machine. He had been right about sleeping through the ringing of the telephone. There were two calls—one from Amy, one from Rachel. Both wished him a Merry Christmas. Both teased about not answering their call, both suggested he must be having Christmas dinner with some lonely and desperate woman. Both ended their call with the same warning, as though they had rehearsed it: Remember your age.

There was no call from Tanya, but it was not a surprise. She had guests, was probably serving the dinner of leg of lamb. It would be good to be there, enjoying the noise of merriment. His own house was as quiet as a wake and without lights on his sparsely decorated tree, it had a somber, depressing mood.

Next year, he would have lights, he thought.

He made a single piece of toast and reheated the soup Tanya had prepared, leaving the leftover in a plastic container in the refrigerator. It was not lamb, but it satisfied his taste, and, he guessed, was good for him. The fever that had overwhelmed him in the morning seemed to have cooled slightly and he was not as exhausted as he had been. The sleep, he decided. Even with the wildness of the dreams, the sleep had helped.

After eating, he went into his office and awoke his dozing laptop and read what he had written the day before, and the memory of the prom and of the visit with Jovita and Littlejohn and of the warning from the policeman named Julian Overstreet played again in fifty-year-old images. It puzzled him that he remembered Julian Overstreet's name. Over the past few years, he had had trouble remembering the names of students who had spent four years in his classroom.

He wanted to continue the writing, but knew it would tire him. Instead, he took another of Marie's letters and read it:

Dear Dr. Bishop,

I have good news, Cole. Good news from that place you used to call home and that place I so despised—except for you and Jovita and Jovita's children. Littlejohn is a college graduate. Think of that, Cole. That little boy who believed your wonderfully silly story about an orange turtle, is now an educated young man. He's going to be an artist and a teacher. I've never shared it with you, but after I left Overton, I wrote to Jovita and the children regularly. It was my way of forcing them to learn to read and write. And it worked, Cole. Little by little, I began to get letters back from Jovita. You would have scoffed at the writing, but I thought it was great literature, far better than Shakespeare. And then Littlejohn started writing. Sometimes he would send me something he had drawn and I knew he had talent. I could see it, year by year. I have a whole collection of his drawings and paintings. They're framed. They hang in my bedroom. It's too bad you'll never see them. Even if you did visit me, I would not permit you in my bedroom. That's another thing you don't know, do you? I've decided to deny any and all sexual pleasures. I'm going to be as chaste as a nun. That's what you've done to me, Cole Bishop. I hope you're happy. Oh, one other thing about Littlejohn's education: I paid for it. Every penny. Of course, Littlejohn doesn't know it was me. I did it anonymously, a special scholarship. Is it boasting to tell you that, Cole? I hope not. I'm proud of it. Are you surprised? Of course you are. Everything that happens to you, or around you, is a surprise to you. You never see anything. It's a wonder that you've managed to survive.

Okay, I'm lying. I do that sometimes when I have this insane compulsion to write to you.

But it was only part-lie.

I do not know about Littlejohn. What I wrote was from a dream I had years ago after treating a young boy who reminded me of him. But I did write to Jovita and the children. And Jovita did write back a few times, or Sarah wrote for her. And I do have some drawings from Littlejohn sent along in the letters, but as far as I know, he never made it beyond high school—if he made it that far.

But I would have paid for his education. I would have. I'm sorry I didn't find a way to make it happen. He was a bright little boy. And beautiful. Wasn't he, Cole? Wasn't he beautiful?

I'm sorry I quit writing to Jovita. After a time, I was unable to take the guilt of being so well-off while she was still struggling. I wonder if she has had her homegoing. (Do you know about homegoings, Cole? It's a word I learned from Moses when I was asking him about the funeral home business. He said black people referred to death as a homegoing. Isn't that a great word? I think so. I think it's the most poetic word I've ever heard. Homegoing to God. I like that.)

Oh, I also lied about denying sexual pleasures. If my damnable schedule provided me some free time, I would be as chaste as a nymphomaniac. Yep, my fine friend, my great innocent, I have to admit it: I do love sex and I indulge every chance I have, even with patients too drugged to know what I am doing to them. Last week, I took my pleasure with a football player who had been hospitalized with a knee injury. A football player, Cole. One of the rah-rah boys. Does that take you back?

Okay, I just lied again. You know that, don't you? You know I would never violate something I consider sacred.

Sometimes, Cole, I really like aggravating you (or amusing you). Sometimes, I believe the game we played in high school is the only thing in my life that is worth remembering.

Damn you.

Tonight I miss you. Happily, tomorrow I'll be too busy to think about it.

Your Juliet.

Because of all that had happened, the letter always brought sadness and the damp blur of tears.

TWELVE

The call from Tanya came at 9:30. In the background, he could hear voices and laughter.

They won't go home, she said in an irritated whisper. How are you?

Better, he told her. I think it was just a twenty-four-hour bug.

Good, she said. I'm not sure when I can get away.

I don't want you to, he insisted. Stay there. I made a fire and I'm just sitting here, reading. I'm going to bed in a few minutes.

Are you sure? she asked.

I'm sure, he replied. Go back to your guests.

I'd much rather be there, she muttered. Things are getting out of control over here. I swear it's the last time I'm serving alcohol, or even having a Christmas party. It's not even my holiday, for crying out loud.

What do you mean? he asked.

I've never told you, Cole, but I'm Jewish, she answered.

Sure, you are, he said. And while we're making confessions, I think it's time you knew that I'm really a Buddhist.

He had expected a laugh, but did not get one. She said, No, Cole, I am. It's something Mark and I have kept private. I converted to Christianity before we married, but it was just an act, something to make his parents happy. I go to church, yes, but I'm an agnostic, if I'm anything.

I don't believe it, he said.

And I don't give a rat's ass if you do or not, she told him. It's the truth. Since I've been reading about your private life, I just thought you should know, but you're to keep it to yourself. If you don't, I'll have you up before the administration on a sexual harassment charge.

He did not reply.

After a moment, she added, All right, not that. No one would believe it anyway, but I'll think of something.

Of course I'll keep it private, he said earnestly. But I do want to talk to you about it someday.

Someday, she replied. But not now. I've got to get back to the madness. I'll call you in the morning

All right, he told her. Then, without thinking: Merry Christmas.

Happy Hanukkah, she said.

He could hear a peal of laughter in the background, then the click of the hang-up.

In his chair, sitting before the fireplace, watching the flames lick across the birch logs provided by Dexter Williams, he thought of Tanya Berry's admission about being Jewish. He was stunned she had hidden it so well and wondered if the secrecy of it had brought shame to her, or to her family. She had never spoken of religion to him, not in a serious way. Once he had made a reference to the small United Methodist church of his childhood, how it had been a place of solace, and she had said, My grandfather taught me something. He told me that religion was like playing with a paper doll. You could dress it up to look a thousand different ways, but you put all those dresses on the same doll.

A good way of considering it, he thought.

And maybe Tanya Berry's story about being Jewish was only a tease. Maybe she was as Presbyterian as her husband, born into the heritage of the Church of Predestination, as his United Methodist teachers had called it.

Maybe Tanya was simply feeling frisky from dinner wine and wanted to toy with him, the same way Marie Fitzpatrick had toyed with him. He was gullible enough for it, and he had begun to believe there was more of Marie in Tanya than he had realized.

It was possible, he reasoned.

Maybe even predestined.

He slept for only a short time, yet it was a good sleep. There were no visits from demons, no floating bubbles of familiar faces, no fire-burning drifts of snow, no child being raised from the dead. No dreams at all.

At 2:11 by his digital bedside clock, he awoke hungry and went into his kitchen with an odd craving for cheese grits, leaving him to wonder if the writing of his boyhood had caused a chemical memory to take place. Still, he wanted the grits and he made them, crumbling feta cheese into them, eating them with buttered toast and jelly. The fever that had invaded him had slipped out of his body and he could feel his energy building. He made hot tea, sweetened it with honey, and went into his office and turned on his laptop.

He wrote:

December 26, early morning

After the night of the prom, Marie did not return to school until the following Thursday. I tried calling her but was told she was not at home, or was resting. I knew by Jovita's voice, and by Laura Fitzpatrick's voice, that they were lying. Or maybe not lying. Maybe they were merely protecting her.

I believed her absence from school and her refusal to talk to me had to do with Sally Dylan's anger and with the hammering, insidious gossip she thought would swirl throughout Overton High School.

Oddly, there had not been any gossip. Not about Marie teaching black children in her garage.

The gossip had been about Sally Dylan and Art Crews. They had been stopped by the county sheriff on the highway leading from Kilmer's Recreation Hall. Sally had been inebriated and sick, incensed by Art's attention to Marie. In her ranting after Marie and I left the prom, she supposedly announced that she was pregnant. The sheriff had driven her home, with Art following. The next day, Art and Sally had become engaged to be married after graduation.

It was the kind of gossip that filled mouths and minds, overwhelming everything else, even the sensuous appearance of Marie Fitzpatrick at the Junior-Senior Prom.

I had expected to be kidded about her, but was, instead, avoided, shunned, somehow held accountable for what had happened at the prom. Yet, it was not open hostility. The boys who had been my teammates simply stopped talking to me, or if they did say something, it was edged in the kind of harshness that I received one afternoon from Wormy. He looked at me with a hard glare and said, "You a nigger-lover, Cole?" I asked what he was talking about. He replied, "Word is, you went to see some nigger after the prom. That right?" I walked away without answering him. It was the wrong thing to do. To Wormy, and to others, it was confirmation, and I now believe that the only thing preventing ugliness was the history we had shared. The goodness of history between people is powerful.

When she did return to school, Marie was different. Quiet, timid. She wore an expression of sadness, like someone who lived alone, at ease only in the company of shadows. She avoided me, and I knew intuitively not to pressure her. She had asked for my promise of understanding; I had given it. She would sit in classrooms, gazing out of the window, not responding even when her name was called. At lunch break, she would wander to the elementary school playground and sit in the swings, or hide herself behind trees.

I remember that Marilyn Pender asked me if she was all right.

"She's fine," I said. "She's just got a lot on her mind, I guess. You know how she is."

It was an answer Marilyn Pender, and everyone else, understood. No one had forgotten Marie's first few weeks at Overton High School. Everyone knew how she was, or had been, or could be.

It was best not to bother her.

A week later, also on Thursday, the last day of classes for seniors, I discovered an envelope under the windshield wiper blade of my parents' car. I tore open the flap and pulled out a single sheet of paper written in Marie's careful cursive.

Cole, you'll understand everything soon enough. I miss you.

She had drawn a small, orange-colored turtle at the bottom of the page.

She's about to do something, I thought. Something no one could stop.

I was right.

It had always been believed by my classmates that I would be the valedictorian of Overton High School's class of 1955.

Until Marie Fitzpatrick appeared.

After that, it was not a contest.

I was named salutatorian, Marie valedictorian.

And it was Marie who delivered the valedictorian's address during graduation ceremonies in the school auditorium.

The memory of that night and of her speech is as clear and as significant to me as any experience I have ever had. Her speech was short and stunning and as deliberate as a suicide.

She offered no greeting to school officials, or to her classmates, or to the attending audience after her introduction by O. J. Mayfield.

She stood in her cap and gown, her face clean of makeup, her body appearing small and weak. Stood gazing at the sheets of paper she had placed on the podium in front of her. Stood waiting for something to invade her. Stood long enough for a jittery movement to begin among our classmates, long enough for Wormy to begin patting his leg with his hand, long enough for O. J. Mayfield to clear his throat and cough.

And then she looked up and inhaled and her body seemed to lift, to grow behind the podium. "I came to this school," she began in a strong, sure voice, "believing it offered an inferior education. I leave it affirmed in that fact.

"You are good people," she continued, "but good people are often timid people, and timid people are always afraid of change."

She paused, looked over the audience, caught my eye, then glanced back at the typed paper on the podium in front of her.

"One of the first things I learned about the history of this town was of the tornado that struck in 1932. Many of you remember it. Many of you had family killed in the destruction. I want to tell you that you are in the path of another tornado, a tornado of change that is gathering strength all around you. It is a tornado that will destroy every tradition you own, sweep away every belief that props you up, assault you like invisible armies. You cannot survive it as you are.

"You will be confused and angry. You will fight back with words and threats. You will vow to stand strong and resist. You will ask yourself, 'Why is all of this necessary, when things are fine the way they are?'

"But things are not fine.

"When I first came here, I learned of four small black children who could not read, and decided to teach them. Their mother stopped my teaching. She was afraid. Afraid of what the good white people of Overton County would think, afraid for the safety of her own children and afraid for my safety. She was afraid of being considered an agitator. Better that her children grow up illiterate than to be thought of as trouble-makers.

"When I first came here, I sat in classrooms filled with students who simply wanted to last through the day, and then the month, and then the year, until, finally, they could gather here tonight to receive a sheet of paper that lies to them about their education.

"When I finished my last class here, it was the same. Nothing had changed.

"But it will. It will change because so many of my classmates will struggle to make a living, and, years from now, they will look about at the rubble left by the tornado of change and they will say, 'Yes, I failed. Yes, I must do better by my children.'

"In twenty years, nothing will be the same.

"You will not work at the same jobs in the same way.

"You will be invaded by people from other nations, looking for jobs, for a chance to be free, and they will teach you things you have never imagined.

"You will sit numb in front of your television sets and watch wars play like cartoons.

"Your children will sit in classrooms with red children, yellow children, black children, and you will cry in anguish because you won't understand what is happening.

"And the answer is so simple: you cannot exist without change."

Marie paused again, staring at the sheet of paper. She touched it tenderly with her fingers, then looked up. I thought I saw tears.

"When I came to your town, to your school, I was considered an outsider. And I was. And I am. I cried for weeks when my parents told me we were moving here. Surely, I thought, there must be a reason. Something. Anything.

"I now know the answer to that.

"I came here to warn you, to make you angry.

"And I have done both. And I am at peace."

She stood silently, let her eyes flicker over the audience, then she said, "To my mother and father, I want to say that I'm sorry. I know I've embarrassed you."

She picked up her paper, stepped back from the podium, looked once at me, then walked off the stage and out of the auditorium.

I thought I would hear grumbling, hissing, loud objections, but no one spoke after Marie left. I could feel my face covered with a blush, could feel eyes turning to stare at me. From behind me, in the section reserved for parents, I finally heard a single whisper: "She's crazy." I turned to see Laura and George Fitzpatrick stand and wiggle their way along the row of seats and rush up the aisle to the door, their heads down.

O. J. Mayfield stood from his seat on stage and ambled to the podium. "Let's see now," he stammered. "Where are we?" He studied the program. "Uh-huh, uh-huh," he said. "Time to pass out the diplomas."

After the ceremony of graduation, with its jubilation muted by Marie's speech, I slipped away from my parents and from Toby and Amy and Rachel and went to the playground of the elementary school. Marie was there, swinging lazily, the heels of her dress shoes skimming the soft belly of dirt beneath the swing path.

"Marie, why'd you do that?" I asked in exasperation.

"Because it was the right thing to do," she said nonchalantly. She did not stop swinging. "And, as you've surely learned by now, I'm not afraid of the truth."

"The truth? Is that what you call it?" I snapped. "I felt like an idiot sitting in there, watching you walk out."

"You?" she said. "Cole Bishop? Did I embarrass you, too, Cole?"

"You damned right you did," I told her. "We're supposed to be friends. Everybody knows that. It's been the talk of the year—all that stuff about being engaged, all those stories—and we've played it for all it's worth. Friends don't make other friends feel like idiots."

Marie drug her feet in the dirt, slowing the swing to a stop. She looked at me curiously, tilting her head. She said, "Are we, Cole? Are we friends? Really?"

"Of course we are," I argued. "What about all those nights of sitting around your house, studying and listening to records and talking? What about the day I gave you my ring and all the other things we did? Nobody was paying me to do that. I just made thirty-five dollars the first time we went out, and I gave that back."

Marie giggled. "You did?" she said in an astonished voice. "You gave it back? Oh, my God, Cole Bishop, you are the grandest fool I've ever known."

"I'm glad you think so," I said coolly.

"Sit in the swing next to me," she said.

"No."

"Sit down, Cole. How long has it been since you sat in a swing and pushed it up in the air?"

"Not since I was little."

"Maybe that's your problem," she said. "You stopped being little."

"I'm sure there's some deep meaning to all of that," I said. "But I'm also sure that only you understand it."

She laughed easily. "You just grew up, like everyone else, that's what it means. I think—no, I believe—that you were a great kid, a great one, Cole. I believe you had an imagination that aggravated everyone around you. I believe you were so unique that nobody understood you, and then you grew up and you became just like everyone else around here."

I said to her, "Look, Marie, you're not from the South. Some things you just can't understand. You don't know how it is."

"Oh, really?" she snapped. "You know who you sound like? You sound like one of those stupid, tobacco-chewing rednecks at Earl Cartwright's gas station. I don't know how it is? What's that supposed to mean?"

"I don't know how to explain it," I answered meekly.

"Try."

I remember that I did not speak for a very long time. I sat in the swing next to her, wedging my body between the ropes.

"I mean there're things you can't understand, and you can't, Marie, no matter how hard you try," I finally said. "What you said in there tonight was right, and maybe everybody knows it deep down inside, but they didn't hear you because they know you don't understand. You can't understand, and I can't explain it, because I don't know how to. Nobody can explain it, and anybody who tries to, they're just pretending."

Marie touched the ground with her toe, pushing the swing. She slipped her hands up the ropes and pulled. Her body began to sway.

"God, I'm glad I wasn't born here," she said. "I can't wait to leave."

"Yeah. Me, too. In a way," I whispered.

"Do you know where I'm going tomorrow, Cole?"

"No," I answered. "I didn't know you were going anywhere, except on the senior class trip."

"The senior class trip?" she said, laughing. "Oh, my God, Cole, do you really think I'd humiliate myself by traveling to New York and Washington with a bunch of giggling idiots? No, Cole, I'm going away. My parents are driving me to Atlanta and then I'm going to catch a train all by myself and I'm going to go to Boston."

I twisted toward her. "What?" I said. "Why?"

"To work," she explained casually. "You think you're the only person going off on a grand adventure, Cole? God knows, you've been talking about it enough. I guess everybody in this backward little Brigadoon knows that Cole Terrific will be working as a lifeguard at a camp in North Carolina this summer, but you're not the only person alive." Her voice had become sing-song, something strangely gay and mock-Southern, something rushed and frantic. "I have a cousin who lives in Boston and she's got jobs for us this summer, and then I'm going to go to school up there. Harvard, Cole, Harvard. Maybe you've heard of it. This is my last night in this town, and I'm never coming back. Not ever. My parents will be moving back to Virginia this summer. Daddy's going to work with the Department of Agriculture. It's been his dream, you know. Get out of fieldwork and into administration. Well, we're both graduating, Cole."

"Quit lying to me," I said firmly.

"Oh, but I'm not lying, Cole. I'm going tomorrow. I just thought I'd let you know."

"Of course, you're lying," I argued. "I'd know it if you were leaving town. I've been with you too much not to know a thing like that."

"I don't tell you everything. Just the unimportant stuff."

"Thanks a lot," I grumbled. "I'm glad to know how you feel."

"But you don't, Cole. You have no idea how I feel."

"I think I'm getting a pretty good clue," I said.

"Oh, Cole, quit sounding so bitter. Why are you mad at me?"

"Well, for one thing, this is one hell of a time to tell me you're leaving Overton," I said. "I mean, I could've done something if I had known."

"What, Cole? Have a party for me? Invite all my dearest friends? Connie and Sally and Alyse and all the others? Made love to me? Now, that would have been nice. After all those nights, me fighting you off, and on our last night together, I finally give in, pull my skirt up and let you paw away."

"My God, Marie."

She became suddenly solemn. She pulled from the swing and walked away to the sliding board and rubbed the slick surface with her hand. She said, "I didn't mean that, Cole. Not the way it sounded. I think I will regret not making love to you. Someday, I will. When I discover what it's about. I think I'll hear about you, or read about you, and I'll miss you and wonder."

She turned to face me. "Thank you for being here for me, Cole Bishop. Please take care of yourself. Please be careful. I won't be there to protect you. You're so blind to so many things."

"What things?"

She crossed to stand in front of me. She reached to touch the ropes of the swing. There was a sadness in her eyes.

"You believe in stories," she said softly. "You believe in stories of dragons and knights and talking rabbits and flying horses and orange turtles. You don't even know what's going on around you. You think you do, but you don't. You think we live in a time when everything's all right. You think the wars are finally over. I don't, Cole. I don't believe in stories. I believe in what is, and what's about to be. Cole, the wars are not over. They're just beginning. I read about what's happening and it scares me. You read stories that end with everybody living happily-ever-after, and you think that's the way it is. You think that's going to happen to you. But it won't. It's not that way. You keep dreaming and you'll just disappear one day. You'll open up a book and fall into it and somebody'll come along and close it, and there won't be a Cole Bishop. Stories always end, Cole. Not everything else does. Some things never end."

"I don't understand you," I told her.

Marie reached for my hands and tugged me from the swing, and embraced me. I could feel her weeping.

"I knew you wouldn't," she whispered. She turned her head on my chest, resting her face against me. "I do care for you," she said. "I will miss you."

"And I'll miss you," I said. "But we'll see each other. Tonight's not the last time we'll be together."

"I guess I love you, Cole Bishop. In a good way, I mean."

"I guess I love you, too. The same way."

"I've got something for you."

"What?" I asked.

She reached behind her neck and unfastened her silver-coated necklace that held my high school ring. She slipped the ring from the necklace and pressed it into my hand.

"Thank you for letting me keep it," she said. "It's the best treasure I've ever had."

"That's—all right," I whispered.

She moved against me. Her hands touched my face. "You're going to be famous. I can see it. It's all over you. Sometimes when I'm close to you, like this, I can even feel it. It's a sweet, cool feeling, Cole. But it scares me."

"I'm just going to be me, Marie. Just me," I said.

"No. You're going to be somebody."

"I feel like you just condemned me," I told her.

"Maybe I did," she said.

"Will I survive whatever it is you know and I don't?"

"Barely, Cole Bishop. Barely."

"Will it ever come to an end?" I asked.

She hesitated. The expression in her eyes was one of sadness. "Yes, Cole," she answered.

"When?"

"You'll know," she said.

She leaned to me, tilted her face to my face, kissed me, held the kiss, letting the electricity of it surge through both of us.

"I do love you, Cole. I truly do," she whispered. "And I'll always be with you—as trite as that sounds. I will, though. I'll be with you, looking over your shoulder. Be still, listen, and you'll hear me. I promise."

Marie left Overton the following afternoon, as she had announced. Three days later, the senior class left for its trip to New York City and Washington, DC. I declined to go, knowing my presence would be uncomfortable to my classmates. For Art and Sally, it was their honeymoon.

Two weeks later, I received a large envelope from Marie—the first of many letters that would sustain me for many years. It was a wonderful, rambling narrative of her train trip and of Boston, and it also included one of the photographs taken of us by her father on the night of the Junior-Senior Prom as well as a copy of her graduation speech. She wrote:

You should be here, my naïve, mendacious friend. I'd like to hide behind trees and in doorways to watch you wandering around. You'd look lost, and you would be. There are things here that your feeble mind could never comprehend because you're a hick and you'll always be a hick. How you'll ever become famous, I have no idea, and if I didn't believe in fate, I'd never believe it could happen. God, I miss you. There's not a fool in this city as gullible, or as grand as you. As to the photograph, I hope you choose to keep it and occasionally take the time to look at it. We were both beautiful that night. But I want us to make an agreement: never send photographs to one another. Even better, never call me, never send me a telegram or a message by carrier pigeon. If you choose to communicate with me, I want it to be by letter. When I think of you, as I often do against my better instincts, I want to open my photo album and remember you from that night, and I want to read your letters and listen to your voice rise up out of your words. If we do have a friendship, let it be that, Cole. A friendship of words, not pictures. That way we'll never age, will we? We can be one of those happy-

ever-after couples you dream about in that Dixie Crystal sugar sweet world you want to live in.

And, yes, I know you may not want the enclosed few pages (a copy of my graduation speech), but I wanted you to have them. Destroy them if you wish. However, it you do, first read them. Read them carefully, without prejudice. I have never felt as sure about anything as I do about those words. Change, Cole, change. It's rolling over us. Don't let it crush you.

I replied to her letter, but did not hear from her again until Christmas. In a card, she enclosed a short note:

I've found my world, Cole. College. I love it. It loves me. I hope you're learning something in that backward little school that finally agreed to accept your enrollment. At least I hope you're not embarrassing yourself. Remember, you're supposed to be famous. Famous as in Fame, my ridiculous friend. That is what resides in that sweaty little palm of yours, somewhere among the masturbation warts. Someday it will happen. Someday.

I still love you.

In the years that followed, I wrote faithfully to Marie and she answered with long, exquisite letters that somehow trapped her voice and her laughter inside the envelopes—the way she had imagined hearing me.

We never exchanged photographs. I never tried to call her.

She wrote of school, of infatuations, of love-making, of lectures and concerts that dazzled her, of skip-away trips to New York for a feast of Broadway shows, of funny unexpected encounters with funny unexpected people, of books she had read, of dreams invading her. She wrote with passion, with words that bounced across her life like the ball that bobbed up and down on the lyrics of sing-along television programs. There was no order to her letters, no serene walk along a picturesque garden path. Marie's words raced, leaped fences of thought, lay waste to fields of reason. Her letters were like a child at play in a room filled with toys.

I re-read each letter many times, memorizing lines that made me laugh with gladness or ache with loneliness.

But one letter, each year in the early years, said only one thing.

It arrived always on my birthday.

Are you famous yet?

And each year, I replied: *Not yet, and time keeps ticking away.*

A few days later, I would receive another letter, always with the same response: *Ticking closer, you mean.*

In 1962, the ticking stopped.

In 1962, on the day of the killing, I became famous.

THIRTEEN

He emailed his night's work to Tanya, then napped for an hour, from eight o'clock until nine o'clock, then showered and dressed and stripped his bed and washed his sheets and pillowcases. His breakfast was a hard-boiled egg and hot tea.

Being Sunday, he thought of going to church, but decided against it. He was no longer ill, but he did not trust his body, not after his erratic schedule of sleep. It would not be good to fall into a slumber during the sermon of the Reverend Kenneth Casey, and that was always a possibility. Kenneth Casey spoke in a monotone, only slightly above a whisper. He had been accused of causing the angels of the stained-glass windows to doze, their wings visibly, miraculously drooping around their shoulders like birds at rest. Sadly, the content of his sermons was usually as dull as his voice.

He knew also he would hear from Tanya. Or guessed he would. It would depend on the lateness of the Christmas dinner and the work of the clean-up. If she attended church, she would not call him until the afternoon.

He was wrong. She knocked on his door at ten o'clock, as he was putting his dishes away in the dishwasher.

She was dressed in jeans and snow boots, wearing a dark heavy coat over a blue turtleneck sweater. A matching blue scarf was swirled around her neck. She carried a large bag bearing a design of Santa Claus smiling at a gathering of children with awed expressions, the cheeks of their faces rosy from the winter cold and from innocence.

You must be feeling better, she said.

I am, he told her. What are you doing here?

She held up the bag. Delivering your Christmas dinner, she said. She walked past him into his kitchen, placed the bag on the counter. Actually, it's just a ruse, my way of getting out of the house. I told Mark you'd sent an email, saying you were still feeling poorly. He insisted I check on you while he's at church. She looked up at him and smiled triumphantly. He loves his tie, by the way, even wore it to church. Then she opened the bag and removed the printout of the writing he had completed that morning. I'm here because of this, she added. She looked at him in amazement. Did you make this up?

No, he answered. At least I don't think so. It's the way I remembered it.

She pulled her scarf from her neck, slipped out of her coat, and draped it across a chair at the kitchen table. Do you have coffee? she asked.

Not made, he said. But I'll make some.

Good, she replied. She sat in one of the chairs at the table. I'm exhausted. Make it strong.

She talked as he prepared the coffee, pausing only for the loud, irritating grinding of the beans. She was in disbelief over Marie's graduation speech, saying he must have lived in the most backward town in America if no one jeered her, though it was her guess that no one understood what they were hearing. Or they were in shock. Or they heard it as a final confirmation that Marie was as off-the-wall as they suspected.

If you didn't dream it up, it was one hell of a speech, Cole, she said. Problem is, there's not a hint of reality about it. No one, not even someone like Marie Fitzpatrick, would dare make such remarks in front of the crème de la crème of redneck society.

She did, he said quietly.

For a moment, Tanya did not speak. She held her gaze on him and he believed she was searching for a sign that he had lied—in his writing and to her.

Okay, she finally said. My mind wants to reject it, but my intuition tells me different. She shook her head. My God, she whispered. I've never heard anything like it.

She was different, he said.

I would say so, she replied. She paused, then added, And what happened?

You said you didn't want to know until you read it, he reminded her.

Damn it, Cole, she said. Don't do that to me.

It's your call, he told her.

She stood, crossed to the coffeepot, watched the final dripping, then took a cup and poured coffee into it. All right, she said. I'll wait. She turned to him. But I think you should be aware that I do know something about the killing. I've always known about that. I remember when it happened. I even remember the picture. I was only a child, but I remember it.

He could feel a wave of surprise on his face. You've never mentioned it, he said.

Of course not, she replied. I'm your friend. Maybe you haven't noticed, but no one talks about it up here. At least, not now. Maybe they used to, but not now. We all believe that's why you came here, to get away from it. You've got a lot of people who care about you, Cole.

He sat heavily at the kitchen table.

Coffee? she asked.

He nodded.

She took another cup from the cabinet and poured the coffee and gave it to him. Then she sat across from him.

Let me give you a perspective, she said. I think that experience has haunted you for a long time, but I think it doesn't have as much to do with the picture as people might suspect. There was something else, wasn't there?

Yes, he said after a moment.

Does it have anything to do with Marie? she asked.

He picked up his coffee cup, touched it to his mouth, drank from it, then put it back on the table. In a way, he said. Yes. In a way.

When was the last time you saw the picture, Cole?

It's been years, he answered.

That's right, she said. Years. And the truth is this: once it was a headline, now it's a footnote, and I think there's a simple explanation for its fading into obscurity. You weren't a mover and a shaker, Cole. A lot of other pictures were made after that one and the people in them were movers and shakers. That's what we see today in all those retrospectives.

He settled back in his chair, thought of what she had said. It made sense, and maybe he had always known it was the reason the picture—The Photograph—was no longer as important as it had been.

I don't disagree, he said after a moment.

But you will write about it, won't you? she asked.

It's part of what happened, he answered.

Then you need to put it in words, she said.

He looked at her. Or maybe it's time I stop thinking about it. Maybe it's time for a hobby. I've been considering a bonsai garden. It would be relaxing, I think. What's your opinion?

She laughed.

Now I have a question for you, he said.

Ask, she replied.

Are you really Jewish?

Her laughter turned to merriment. One of the things I've learned in reading about Marie is how easy it is to toy with you, she said. She leaned forward. No, Cole, I'm Presbyterian. I think I'd like to be Jewish. I like their spirit, their sense of pride. I like Jewish women. They're not eaten up with guilt, at least the ones I know aren't.

She stayed until noon, making an early lunch for the two of them from the leftover of Christmas dinner. She said nothing else about the writing, or about Marie, or about the killing. The talk, upbeat, funny, was about the party of the night before—of Mark's anxiety over some football game, of Quentin Hargrove's endless litany of obscene email jokes showered on him by friends, of Janice Spencer drinking too much and making suggestive remarks to David Goodlove while John Spencer, her husband, watched and steamed. The night, she reported, was what she had expected it to be—a disaster performed as a comedy. She told him he had been fortunate, being sick. Next year, I'm going to find my own germ, she vowed.

Before she left, she embraced him gently and said to him, Your friendship means a lot to me, Cole. I want you to think about doing something that could bother you.

What? he asked.

Write to her, she said.

He frowned quizzically.

Marie, she said. Write to Marie.

Where did that come from? he asked.

I think it would help you.

How?

She let her gaze hold on him for a moment, a studying expression. Then she said, Do you know what I say about you to other people?

No, he replied.

I tell them you're a man of many shadings. I tell them that you can be as funny as Billy Crystal when you're relaxed and as serious as Bill Clinton in denial when the occasion calls for it. But I've never said that to you, have I? When I'm talking *to* you, rather than *about* you, the distance between us is closer. It makes me want to tell you things I would never tell anyone else. I believe that's important.

He did not reply.

Will you think about it? she asked gently.

He nodded.

In early afternoon, after a short, dreamless nap, he went again into his office and opened his laptop and read the last segment of his writing. It had been a seminal moment in his life, his last meeting with Marie Fitzpatrick, yet the memory of it—even the writing of it—seemed incomplete. And it was. The other part of the story—the killing—was necessary.

He began to write.

December 26, afternoon

I want this to be right, or as right as my memory of it permits. Even now, before I put the words on paper, I see it happening, hear the voices of it.

My memory of the day of the killing is very much like a recurring dream that never ages, never changes.

It began in Wade Hart's apartment, a shared late breakfast of cold cereal after a night of study. It began in the kind of college-wit bantering that Wade and I often exchanged—light-hearted hyperbole, meaningless, the one-upmanship of young men who are friendly enough to take jabs of insult. In those days, I was good at such repartee. It is something I have lost, or tempered, over the years.

Wade did not believe anyone named Bevo Francis from Rio Grande College had scored one hundred points in a basketball game. He called me ridiculous, said I knew nothing about sports. The only man who ever scored one hundred points in a college basketball game was Frank Selvy from Furman University, he contended confidently.

I challenged him with a ten-dollar wager.

His come-back was: "You're on." He added, with a touch of arrogance, "You may be the golden boy of literature around here, but you don't know the first damn thing about sports."

"I wouldn't be so sure," I said.

Wade cackled a mocking laugh.

"No, I mean it," I added. "You're talking to a former high school quarterback, and a basketball wizard. They used to call me Zippy, after Zippy Morocco at the University of Georgia. We ran the Bishop Offense. It was unstoppable."

"Yeah, and what was that?"

"When we crossed the centerline, I shot the ball," I told him.

"Sounds like you," he scoffed. "Sounds like that school for retards you attended. What classification was it? D? F?"

"It was C," I said. "Poor, but proud. We were humble folk."

He exhaled a great, painful sigh. "Jesus H-for-Holy Christ. Humble? What a word. Especially coming from you. What a great word. How many games did you win?"

"I can't count that high," I answered. "They used to triple-team me, and that's when we were on defense. When we had the ball, they had everybody on me. Sometimes, when we got forty or fifty points ahead, we'd let them play with six or seven guys, and they still couldn't stop me."

"God, Cole, you never let up, do you?" he cried in desperation. "I doubt if you can even dribble a basketball."

I waved away the insult. "Bevo Francis," I said, "actually scored one hundred and thirteen points for Rio Grande. My ten dollars against your ten. The Golden Boy of Literature against the Urine-Stained Jock Strap."

"Let's go to the library," he snapped.

"Bring money," I said.

I liked Wade Hart, liked the give-and-take of our talks, always sharp-bladed and quick, like fencers twirling foils or epees or sabers in ballet steps that made poetry out of slaughter. It was the language of clever college show-offs of the early 1960s, and it fit us perfectly. Wade was a history major and a superb athlete. He was on the Upton University tennis team and played intramural basketball with both fury and finesse. There was a rumor he had rejected an offer to play baseball at Georgia Tech, a rumor Wade would not discuss. He believed that superb athletes did not need to promote themselves—a far cry from the athlete of today. He said only that baseball bored him. Too much standing around, waiting to do something.

In 1962, Wade was in his senior year of undergraduate study at Upton and I was in my final year of the Masters program. We had become friends because we both had apartments in a private boarding facility called Morrow House near the university. Wade was the scion of a prominent and wealthy Atlanta family—his father a doctor, his mother a bank official—and I thought of him as a reluctant blueblood. There was nothing pretentious about him. He was tall and handsome in the fair German way of blonde hair and blue eyes and chiseled chin. He did not own a car, did not want one. He wore neat, but conservative clothing. His room was spare and uninviting. The only thing to suggest that Wade Hart had access to money was an expensive record player and an astonishing collection of records. He favored folk music, loved the Kingston Trio.

Wade also loved argument. It was in his disposition, in his fierce sense of discipline, in his passion to learn. Argument had fashioned our friendship, and always there was a pitying remark about my background. As I believed Wade was a reluctant blueblood, Wade believed I was a dreamer trying to pull myself from the mire of rural poverty.

Our argument over one-hundred point basketball games had begun with a casual conversation of Wilt Chamberlain's hundred-point game earlier that year.

"My favorite one-hundred point man was Bevo Francis," I had said casually. "I like that man's name."

"Who?" he had asked.

"Bevo Francis."

"Okay, Cole, I'll bite," he had said. "Where did you dig up Bevo Francis? And, for God's sake, don't tell me it's out of Shakespeare. Not even Shakespeare would come up with a name like that."

"Bevo Francis was a basketball player for Rio Grande College," I had explained.

"Wait a minute, let me guess," he had countered. "Zane Grey. You got him out of Zane Grey. He was one of those cowboys that massacred Indians and slept with horny horses out on the lonesome trail." He had paused, cocked his head, furrowed his brow in thought. "Or, maybe not. No, I'd say Hemingway. Sounds like Hemingway to me. Bevo. That's the kind of name Hemingway would love, and unless I've misread you, you've been wandering around Paris in that misguided mind you think of as an imagination, sniffing the seat of every bar stool that poor bastard ever sat on."

"I'm telling you, Bevo Francis was a basketball player," I had insisted.

"And you forget who you're talking to, Cole. I'm the jock. You're the bullshit artist. And I'm also the one who's put up with your bullshit for a year. Frankly, it's amusing, as long as you stay out of my field."

"Believe me, Wade, I know what I'm talking about," I had replied.

It was a clean April day—sun-bright, with high, spinning coils of bleached-white clouds, with sweet, honeysuckle air. In Atlanta, the greening of spring had unfolded in a rush, in a blink of pale green leaves pushing from the tips of bare, swollen limbs, in the bowed heads of jonquils raising their yellow faces to light. The blinding white blossoms of dogwoods had exploded like popcorn and purple strands of thrift covered patches of ground like ribbons dropped by small, enchanting girls at play. Azaleas blazed in red and pink and white.

Our bantering continued as we crossed the campus to the library. It is like a song in my memory, one stuck there, somewhere in the gray web of brain matter.

"God, I love this weather," Wade cried. "And I love this place. I love everything about it. Except you, Cole. You're the only blight I know in Camelot."

"Speaking of Camelot," I said, "did you know that one of my ancestors was a knight?"

"Sure," he answered brightly. "I've heard you talk about him. Sir Cockroach. I thought you were lying, so I looked him up. He was a deserter. Took up with the Italians. Ran a whorehouse in Rome. I know about stuff like that, Cole. I'm a history major, you know."

"I'm serious," I said. "Actually, he did get wounded in battle and had to hang up his armor, but he was very famous."

Wade laughed cynically. "And you've never told me about him? There's a redneck hero in your family, and I don't know about it? That's hard to believe."

"It's kind of embarrassing," I said.

"Embarrassing?" he bellowed. "Cole, you're embarrassing. What in the name of God could have happened to an ancestor that would bother you?"

"It was his wound," I confessed.

"His wound?"

"In history, he's regarded as the world's first accidental eunuch. Caught a sword right in the tiara of the family jewels," I said.

He laughed like a child.

"You know what's on the family coat-of-arms?" I asked.

He shook his head, slowed his stride to listen.

"A sword buried to the hilt in the groin," I told him. "Some people have mistakened it for a decorated penis, but it's not; it's the handle of a Roman sword. Now, I ask you, would you go around telling people you descended from a eunuch? In the first place, who'd believe it?"

"Since it's you, I would," he said. "God, you're impossible. You know who you sound like? You sound like that idiot you hang around with. Jack Alewine. The two of you sound exactly alike."

"Thank you," I replied. "Jack's brilliant."

"Where has he been, anyway?" he asked. "I haven't seen him around for a couple of days."

"I don't know where he's been, but I know where he is," I answered. "He went to check on joining the Peace Corps. He's a Kennedy man, through and through."

"He's a fool," Wade mumbled.

"We all are," I said.

Wade stopped walking and turned to me. "Do either of you know what's going on in the world, Cole?" There was no teasing in his voice.

"I think we do," I answered evenly. "We're not Laurel and Hardy, if that's what you mean."

He shrugged. "No, that's not what I mean." He looked across the quadrangle. A small gathering of men dressed in the rough clothing of laborers, their faces hard and unsmiling, mingled near the Administration Building. "Wonder what's going on?" he said. "Looks like some of your kin, Cole."

"Cousins," I said in the fake voice of put-on pride. "They're contributors to Upton. Big contributors. The only man who gives more to old Upton than my cousins is your daddy, and he's just trying to buy you an education. Not my cousins. They give because they love real college men, like me, and they've got it to give, Wade. Lots of it. They probably put on the sidegates of the pickup and loaded it with cash and drove it over."

"Good. Maybe we can get a new gym," he mumbled. Then: "Come on, you've got to prove to me that Bevo Francis is real." He again inhaled deeply from the sweet April air. "God, I love this time of year," he crowed. "Love this place. Love everything about it. Everything but you, Cole. You're a wart on perfection."

I have always been at ease in libraries. In libraries, I discover stories that astonish me, stories that make me want to cry out in exhilaration and to worship the minds of those writers who took words and, like oil drops from the palettes of great painters, created visions so vivid they burn the eye of the reader. I like to walk the rows of bookshelves and run my fingers over the spines of books, brushing them lightly, reverently. I like the smell of books, the musk of paper and bindings, the slightly dusty odor of human touch. To me, libraries are like great restaurants and books are the food of my gluttony.

The library at Upton was far grander than any library I had ever toured. A wealthy man named Donald Byers, in a philanthropic whim prior to his death, had bequeathed millions to the Upton library in a steady, but generous flow, and the library was regarded as one of the finest among the nation's universities. It was the principal reason I had elected to stay at Upton for graduate study. I knew, in the library, I would be happy.

I also knew exactly where to find the fact of Bevo Francis's one hundred and thirteen points—in the *Sports Book of Facts*: Bevo Francis, February 2, 1954, against Hillsdale College. Thirty-eight field goals, thirty-seven free throws.

"Well, I'll be damned," Wade whispered. "For once in your irritating life, you were right. I've never heard of Bevo Francis."

"He was my inspiration," I said, "the reason I was a great basketball player. I was a junior in high school that year."

"Who the hell were they playing?" he grumbled. "Hillsdale? What was it? A girl's team?"

"Wade, I don't care if was a girl's team, a traveling band of midgets, or three blind mice. Bevo Francis scored one hundred and thirteen, and you owe me ten," I said.

"How about a little one-on-one?" he countered. "Double or nothing."

"You're younger than I am," I said seriously. "And you're sensitive and spoiled. You'd be totally crushed. You'd probably drop out of school and become a derelict. Your father would become so despondent he'd wind up a recluse, and withdraw every nickel of support to this place you love so much. I couldn't be responsible for that. I'd never forgive myself."

He pulled his billfold from his pocket and fingered two five-dollar bills from it. "I'd rather pay you than listen to you," he said wearily. He handed me the money. "I need to do some reading for a while. You staying or leaving?"

"Leaving," I told him. "I'm working on a paper back at the house, and Jack's coming back. Said he'd stop at the Varsity and bring some hotdogs."

"See you later," he said.

"Maybe we can shoot some hoops," I suggested.

He smiled. "I can't wait, Cole. Bring money."

"Zippy," I said. "Call me Zippy. And, don't worry, I've got money. Just earned it, in fact."

I saw the marchers nearing the Administration Building as I left the library and I stopped under the umbrella shade of an oak to watch. I estimated there were fifty of them, mostly young, mostly black, with a few whites reluctantly following, trying to blend, but not blending well. They were sing-chanting, but I could not understand the words.

Across from them, the group of men Wade and I had seen earlier were huddled together, like migrant workers looking for pick-up jobs. They were glaring at the marchers.

Near them were three policemen and a few photographers. One of the photographers was Ernie O'Connor, who worked for The *Atlanta Chronicle*. I knew Ernie from my part-time job as a copy editor. Ernie was a throw-back to the journalism of the 1940s and 1950s, a hard-drinker, a hanger-on. There was never anything spectacular about his photographs, and his assignments were mainly for civic clubs or social functions or high school sports events.

The sing-chant rolled across the quadrangle.

I had heard reporters who covered the civil rights movement talking of a possible protest march to the campus, and I had listened to Jack Alewine rage about the absurd policy of segregation rigidly supported by Upton's major contributors, but it had not occurred to me that a march would actually be held, not at Upton. I believed the talk of it was nothing more than newspaper gossip, the guessing game of reporters sniffing the air for a scent of controversy.

The door to the Administration Building opened and Dr. Olin Douglas, the registrar, stepped timidly onto the top step. A campus security officer approached and stood near him.

The marchers moved closer to the building.

Marian Shinholster and Henry Fain, both brilliant students and close friends, came out of the library and stopped near me to watch the gathering crowd.

"What's going on?" Marian asked.

"You've got me," I told her. "It's a protest, I think. I heard there may be one."

"Here?" Marian's voice was edged with surprise.

"We're not exactly overbooked with blacks," I said.

"You think there'll be any trouble?" Henry asked anxiously. Henry was small, with delicate, almost fragile features.

"I doubt it," I answered. "From what I hear, these things are as much show as anything. Some singing, a few speeches, then everybody goes home to wait for the news." I paused and watched the marchers positioning themselves before Olin Douglas. "Look at Dr. Douglas," I added. "Looks like he's about to faint."

"He's a nice man," Marian said absently. "What are they singing?"

"Can't make it out," I said. "Come on, let's go listen."

"Not me," Marian said quickly. "And you shouldn't either, Cole. You could get in trouble."

"How? All I want to do is listen. Come on. It'll be something to tell your grandchildren."

"Not me."

"Count me out, too," Henry said.

"Suit yourself," I said. "But I'm going. Jack would never forgive me if I didn't get close enough to tell him everything that went on."

"He's not one of them?" Marian asked with an edge of cynicism.

"Not today," I told her. "He's downtown, checking on the Peace Corps."

"God help the Peace Corps," Marian sighed. She added, "If you go down there, be careful. I don't like the look of things."

"Yeah, Cole, be careful," Henry urged.

Marian and Henry walked away quickly, hugging their books.

The song-chant was festive.

One, two, three, four.
Teach us how, and we'll count some more.
Five, six, seven, eight.
Open up this big white gate...

Olin Douglas trembled visibly before the singers. His face was pale. Bubbles of perspiration welted across his forehead. He tried to smile.

One of the demonstrators—a young black man with a large, joyful face—raised his hand above the crowd, and the song-chant became a murmur, then it stopped. He said to Olin Douglas, "Are you, sir, a representative of the university?"

Olin Douglas cleared his throat. "I am," he whispered.

"We have some things we want to say to you," the young man continued. He made a slight motion with his hand, like a conductor before a choir. The song-chant began again—softly, rhythmically, a rolling heartbeat of voices.

"All right," Olin Douglas replied nervously.

I moved into the crowd, prying around bodies. I wanted to be closer to the young man confronting Olin Douglas, knowing that Jack Alewine would want to hear about him in exacting detail. His voice. His eyes. His posture. Jack would want to know all of it. To Jack, detail was important. Detail enhanced the moment, gave the moment sinew as well as nuance. Detail made the moment immortal, if the moment deserved immortality.

"Would you tell us your name?" the young man asked pleasantly.

The song-chant of the crowd bubbled quietly. Olin Douglas's face blistered red. He said, "Dr. Olin Douglas. I—" He cleared his throat, swallowed. "I'm the registrar."

I watched the young man. He had a happy, calm face, a smile that promised laughter. Jack would like him, I thought.

"Thank you for coming out to meet with us, Dr. Douglas," the young man said. His smile radiated confidence.

I pushed gently around a young white boy, stopping behind two black girls who stood at the hem of the crowd. They were repeating the song-chant in girlish voices, voices with giggle and excitement. One nudged the other and gestured to the men gathered directly across from where we were standing. The men wore sullen, dangerous expressions. I could see jittery movement among them, like disturbed hornets. Two policemen stood near them.

One, two, three, four.... The song-chant swelled in repetition.

The girl standing directly in front of me laughed and her laughter carried high above us. She turned and smiled at me. I returned the smile.

The young man lifted his hand again, and the song-chant muted to a whisper.

"We have rights that we want to declare, Dr. Douglas," the young man said in a rising, happy voice. "It's time to open the doors of Upton University to—"

He did not finish the sentence.

There was a cracking sound, like the sharp snapping of a stick, and the laughing girl standing in front of me threw up her hands and fell backward. I caught her instinctively, dropping to my knees, and she rolled into me, nestling into my arms, her neck cradling against the crook of my elbow. I felt her body convulse in hard spasms, and I turned her head to look at her and saw the hole in her neck. I could feel the spurting of warm blood pumping across my face before I knew it was blood.

My memory of what followed is still a blur and is as much a memory of sound as of sight.

There was a stampede of movement around me, the pounding of frantic running. Piercing screams. I shook my head against the blood still spitting over my forehead, and then I was suddenly aware of Ernie O'Connor kneeling before me on one knee, his camera aimed. I heard the sizzle of the bulb as it fried on the battery stroke.

I ducked my head and curled the girl in my arms, wiped my face against her blouse to clear the blood from my eyes, and then I turned and saw two policemen, guns drawn. They knelt to cover me and the girl with their bodies. I struggled to stand.

"Get down, damn it," one of the policemen commanded forcibly.

FOURTEEN

There was no reason for it, other than seeing the Christmas cards he had opened and displayed on his rolltop desk, but he thought of Olivia DeFoor as he took his dinner of stir-fried chicken and brussels sprouts, a quick and easy meal for him.

Her note to him was a pleasant surprise, and he wondered about the book she was writing, wondered, too, how he had influenced her enough to earn its dedication. Perhaps it was the conference he had had with her over an essay she had written on Herman Melville's *Moby Dick* for one of his American literature classes.

She had called it a great book, but one compromised by study, by his classroom presentation of the celebrated symbolic content. He remembered one line from her paper: *I had the sense that I was bending over a cadaver, dissecting it, rather than embracing a body still having life in it.*

He remembered her sitting in his office, her hands playing nervously over books she held in her lap, her always-easy smile twitching in discomfort, her eyes darting from object to object on his desk.

He had asked what she meant by the line about the cadaver.

Her answer had been quick: I'm sorry, Dr. Bishop. I shouldn't have written that. I love your class. I didn't mean it as a criticism of your teaching.

And I didn't take it that way, he had assured her. In fact, it may be the most profound sentence I've ever read from a student.

Her eyes had blinked in surprise.

I mean it, he had told her. It's exactly the way I've felt about many, many books with great reputations. I never really liked them as much as I was supposed to, and it bothered me. I believe you've given me the answer to a question that's baffled me for years. I was dissecting when I should have been embracing.

A blush had come into her face, covering her smile. She had said in a rush of words, I love reading. I do. I always have. But I never read a book for the story, only for the characters. Sometimes, in class—and I don't mean yours, but others—I get the feeling the teacher is only listening for what the writer is supposedly saying. I never read a book that way. I always listen for what the characters are saying. If I were a writer, I wouldn't care if a reader forgot my name, as long as they remembered my characters.

He remembered sitting for a long moment, gazing at her.

He remembered saying to her, Olivia, I don't know what you want to do with your life, but I have some advice for you: never teach. You know too much.

He remembered seeing her face blink in confusion, remembered adding, That was a compliment, Olivia. A poor joke, but a compliment.

Yet, she became a teacher.

A good one, he believed.

And perhaps she did it in search of characters that intrigued her, knowing she would find them in an underprivileged neighborhood in Pittsburgh. It would be a rich lode for discovery, a complex and harrowing environment.

Once Marie had said much the same about Overton. On one of their nights in her home, studying, she had said, If I decided to be a writer, this is where I'd want to live, Cole. You can walk down the street of this town and run into more weird characters than you'd find on Fifth Avenue in New York. The sad thing is, they don't know they're weird.

And that was what was waiting for him at his laptop.

The Overton story.

He did not read, as was his after-dinner habit. Instead, he got into his car and drove, without a destination to guide him. After the killing on Upton University campus, he had done the same, borrowing Jack Alewine's Volkswagen Beetle. Driving somehow relaxed him, helped him clear away the rubble his mind had collected. He did not know why it was so, but it was. One of the reasons he had decided to return to Overton for the reunion of his high school class was the drive he would make to get there, watching the greening of spring as he traveled south. He had never made the trip in autumn, due to his teaching schedule, but he had always wanted to—a leisurely, drifting drive, beginning in Vermont and meandering to Georgia, following the changing of the season. He loved autumn. In autumn, the trees colored themselves like dancers dressed for a festival—flamboyantly costumed in crimson and orange and yellow and gold. In autumn, the colors of the trees could be breathed from the leaves and the odor of the colors was as euphoric as a narcotic.

It had snowed lightly in early morning, then stopped, leaving its dusting to cover the landscape. In his first year at Raemar, his first winter, he had sent dozens of photographs to his mother and she had compared them to postcards touched up by artists. She had said the scenery did not seem real. To his mother, it as though God had spread a white quilt over the land with a flip of his hands, tucking in the land for a long sleep.

It was as apt a description as he had ever read.

He made his drive through Raemar. All stores and shops were closed, the town mostly deserted. He believed a car parked in front of Arnie's Place of Gathering belonged to Wilber Etz, though he could not be sure, snow-covered as it was. Likely had a dead battery and if it belonged to Wilber, he had not bothered to get it charged. Wilber would have offered a discourse of man's dependency on such objects as batteries, and then he would have talked someone into driving him home.

He found himself on Green Hills Drive, the street where Tanya and Mark Berry lived. There were no lights showing from the house, and he wondered if they had already retired to bed or if they had gone somewhere. It was early for bed, not yet being eight o'clock, but after the Christmas party, bed might have been too inviting to ignore. And maybe they weren't sleeping. Maybe they were making love. He smiled. Knowing both of them as well as he did, he imagined their love-making was vigorous and gleeful.

He wondered if she had emailed him, asking for new words.

The thought of it made him want to continue his writing.

In his home, he made a fire, stacked it well with wood to bring the flames high, and then he took his laptop from his office and carried it into his living room and settled into his oversized reading chair, balancing the laptop across his thighs, and he began to write.

December 26, night

I am surprisingly energetic, though I know I should be exhausted after a long day of writing and still sensing the effects of my twenty-four hour sickness and having had very little sleep—almost none, to be honest. Yet, I want to keep working. The iron is hot, as my father would say when it came time for harvesting. Now's the time to strike, he would declare. Not tomorrow. By tomorrow, the iron might be as cold as well water.

After the killing, I had to endure the presence of Jack Alewine.

Jack was a maverick with an intimidating mind and a punishing tongue. Jack did not debate issues. Jack made declarations. The most inconsequential argument was global war, fought with one objective: complete annihilation. In an argument, Wade Hart was stubborn and persistent, but Jack was a madman, an assassin. He did not strike and retreat; he drew blood, crowed over victims, reveled in their agonized surrenders. He was an irritant with a talent for non-conformity, proclaimed with colorful obscenities. On the night we met, Jack said to me, "If you don't like me, you can kiss my royal ass. If you do like me, I may find it in my soul to like you one day, but don't hold your breath. I hate rednecks, and you look like one to me." I thought of the assualts I had endured from Marie Fitzpatrick, and I smiled. I think the smile confused Jack.

Still, we had become friends. It was a friendship constantly tested, and from moments of near-enmity we had developed warning signals that always tempered our encounters. In the unspoken acts of forgiveness to heal disagreement, I learned that Jack was a tender and compassionate man, and his caring was as demonstrative as his insults.

And on the afternoon that a girl—a black girl—died in my arms at a protest on the campus of Upton University, Jack appeared in his Volkswagen at Morrow House. He had with him suitcases and wadded bundles of clothes and books and his typewriter and a table lamp with a damaged bronze shade. The bronze shade, Jack believed, had properties as magical as Aladdin's lamp.

"They're about to cut your nuts off," he announced as he dumped a shouldered load of clothes onto the sofa in my apartment. "And you're gonna need the best man you can get to stand beside you, and that's me, son. They piss around with you, they got to piss around with me, and nobody in his right mind wants to do that."

"What're you talking about?" I asked. "That situation this morning?"

He stared at me incredulously. "That *situation*," he began, punching the word with his voice, "is about to be the biggest thing that's happened in this town since Sherman's little wiener roast incensed Miss Scarlett. You dumb shit, a girl got killed out there today—a black girl, a colored girl, or as they say in your hometown, a nigger girl—and you just happened to have been right there in the middle of it, like somebody with good sense." He ripped a cigarette from its package and lit it quickly and sucked hard from it.

"And?" I said. "I didn't kill her. She fell into me, and I caught her, Jack. That's all. If you were here thirty minutes ago, you could have asked the police. They just left, and they seemed perfectly satisfied with what I just told you—I caught her. And, by the way, that girl has a name—Etta Hemsley."

"Etta Hemsley," he said softly, exhaling a ribbon of blue smoke. "Good name. It's a name to celebrate and, Cole, they'll certainly do that, whether you like it or not."

"I'm sure they will," I replied. "I hope somebody does. I'd hate to think she just died. Jesus, I'm not that callous, you asshole, but no matter what you think, it's got nothing to do with me."

He pushed a stack of books from a chair and collapsed onto it. He said wearily, "You know, Cole, sometimes I think you're one of the smartest people I know, and then I think you're just plain stupid. It's like that idiotic fascination you have with Joel Chandler Harris, of all people. You're out-of-step, Brer Rabbit, and I mean way out-of-step. Christ, my friend, you're the doo-doo and the doo-doo's about to hit the fan, and the fan's running on high."

"Why?" I demanded.

"Try 'because,'" he said dryly. He drew from his cigarette and flicked ashes across the floor. "Cole, Cole, Cole," he muttered. "Come on, help me get the rest of my stuff out of the car." He pulled from the chair. "You had any calls yet?"

"Three or four."

"Who?"

"Some newspapers," I said.

"Don't be an idiot," he replied. "Write down everything, every name. But best of all, quit answering the phone. I'll handle that."

"One of them was a guy I know at the *Chronicle*—Dempsey Rhodes. He just wanted my reaction," I said.

"What'd you tell him?"

"I told him the truth. That I was just there, listening, and the girl fell into me. That's all there was to it. He's a good man. I talk to him a lot. He likes Joel Chandler Harris as much as I do."

"You idiot," he sighed. "How dumb can you be? Everybody and his brother will have it forever fixed in their minds that you were part of it. You were there, Brer Rabbit. Do you honestly think the administration won't hang you out to dry? They don't like agitators, boy, and, right or wrong, they'll think you're an agitator. I know. That's what they think about me."

"All right," I said. "You want to know why I was there? You can ask Marian Shinholster or Henry Fain. I was there because I thought you'd like to know what was going on, because I knew you'd pester me about it until they carried me off in a straitjacket if I couldn't tell you every shady little fact. What would you have done? If you'd been around, you'd have been leading the singing."

He smiled smugly. "You're right. Pisses me off that it was you and not me. You don't deserve it. I do. And I'd know how to handle it. I'd be out there on campus right now, raising hell about Upton's closed-door policy. I'd be on national television. But you, you just sit around with your thumb up your ass. And that's why I'm here, to tell you what to do."

"That's a comfort," I said cynically. "I was getting worried, but not now, not with Jack-the-Quack around."

"You love me and you know it," he said.

"If you stay here, you've got to keep the place clean," I said.

He laughed. "Yeah, sure. You just sit back and relax. And quit talking to people. Let me handle it. The next couple of days, they'll be hanging from the rafters around here, and you're bound to do something so dumb they'll be writing operas about it. But I'm here, boy. I'll tell them I'm Cole Bishop. They won't know the difference." He flicked ashes on the back of the sofa. "You going to work today?"

"No," I answered. "They called me, told me to take the day off."

He cocked his head toward me, took a draw from his cigarette and rolled a smoke ring above his head. "You know what that means, don't you?"

"I guess they thought I wouldn't have my mind on things," I said.

"Of course, that's it," he replied cynically. "Concern in the work place." He gazed sadly at me. "You stupid shit. The reason they don't want you down there is because they don't want to admit you even exist. That ridiculous rag is one of the great jokes of our time, Cole. Do you think there's going to be a single word in that paper about you working for them? Not one, Cole. Not one. Right now they're in one of those high-level editorial meetings, tossing your name around like it's a lit stick of dynamite with a short fuse."

"What makes you think that?" I asked.

He smiled arrogantly. "Did anybody ask you to write a first-person piece?"

"I'm not a writer," I argued. "I'm a copy editor."

"Cole, Cole," he said painfully. "They should have sent a limousine out to pick you up. They should have given you a typewriter with gold keys. They should have hired a naked copy girl who looks like Sophia Loren to massage your shoulders while you were writing. My God, man, they've got the chance to have the story of stories, and they're passing on it. Why? Because they're scared to death of it. The only way they're ever going to cover anything remotely dealing with civil rights is if the whole damn city burns, and even then it'll be handled as a memorandum from the fire department."

"Come on, Jack," I grumbled. "They're not that bad."

"Yes, they are, Cole."

"Well, I can't help it," I said.

He smothered his cigarette in an ashtray that he pulled from his coat pocket. "I know." He looked up at me. "You all right, Brer Rabbit?"

"I'm all right, Jack."

"That's a feeling that ain't gonna last long, my friend. Believe me."

❧

It was after eleven when he paused in the writing and made a save of it. His legs were sore from balancing the laptop, his wrists ached. Scrolling back over what he had written, he was astonished by the number of words. They had jumped from his fingers in such a fever of memory, he wondered if it was a trick, wondered if the fever was physical, if the sickness was making a return. He stood and stretched, noticed the fire had been reduced to embers, but decided to leave it.

In his kitchen, he made a cup of hot tea, then took it, and his laptop, to his office. From his desk, he removed an album of photographs taken during his years at Upton and found a picture of Jack and Wade, both stripped to their waist, both posing as muscle-builders, both laughing like hyenas. He could not remember the occasion of the pose—an impromptu party, he guessed—but the occasion did not matter. Frozen in the expression was youth and exhuberance.

He replaced the album, opened the drawer containing Marie's letters, fingered one from its lodging and opened it and read:

Cole,

    I write with sadness in my soul.

    My father died last week. Ironically, I was at home on a visit, the first I've taken with my parents in three years. He was standing in the doorway, about to go outside to give my car one of his fatherly inspections. His body folded and he fell. It was like watching the implosion of a large, magnificent building being razed for some God-awful new thing. And, metaphorically, that is what happened. Some hidden charge of dynamite with the slow-

burning fuse of age ignited and exploded in his heart. I tired to save him. I did everything I knew, but nothing worked.

I never talked about loving him, did I?

But I did, Cole. I loved him beyond the words I might have used to describe it, regardless of how sweet they would have sounded.

Do you remember when I wore his dress shirts to school (and on our first so-called date)? It wasn't a rebellious fashion statement. It was because I was so frightened of being where I was that I needed him with me. And here's a confession: the shirts I wore were never clean. They were always taken from the clothes hamper on the day after he had worn them. When I left Overton for Boston, I took two of his unwashed shirts with me. I never wore them, but I often went to my closet and touched them.

Is it strange to believe a person's presence stays in, or on, the clothing they wear?

My mother is at the point of collapse, and I am worried about her. I had no idea she was as devoted to my father as she was, and I do not mean that in a callous way. I knew she loved him. I simply did not know he was the core of her life. Watching her is like watching a one-legged amputee trying to stand for long periods of time. They can't do it, Cole. Not for long. They need the missing leg for balance, for strength. I want her to move to Columbus to be with me, but she refuses to talk about it. She will not desert the town where his body is buried.

Is there a prosthesis for the soul, Cole?

My mother needs one.

As do I.

Will you try to make one for each of us? Will you go to your workshop of words and take your alphabet tools and fashion something for us?

We have not exchanged photographs so you have no way of knowing my appearance, so I want you to remember me as you last saw me—the shape of my face, the color of my eyes, the length of my hair—and I want you to picture me sitting at my father's desk as I am writing this.

Do you have that image, Cole?

Can you see what I am wearing?

His shirt. The shirt he was wearing when he fell like a magnificent building from an exploding heart.

You are much in my thoughts. I would like to hold you tonight. No, I would like for you to hold me.

He folded the letter and slipped it back into its envelope and wiggled it into its proper place among the other letters.

He had written a letter of condolence, saying kind words about her father, and he had offered to drive to Columbus to visit her. In his letter, he had said, Please say yes.

She had not replied.

FIFTEEN

He was writing again by nine o'clock, having slept soundly and having taken a breakfast of cheese toast and hot tea. To his surprise, he was eagerly alert and he believed it was because he was still in pursuit of his memories. The thought of it caused him to remember Toby's love of hunting. It did not matter how hard he had worked on the farm, if a hunt was promised, Toby became jittery with energy.

There was much to compare between a hunt for memories and a hunt for fox.

He wrote:

December 27, morning

I am beginning this with some dread, for it brings me closer to what I believe is the most painful experience of my living, other than the deaths of my parents and my brother.

The killing of Etta Hemsley on a bright April day in 1962, was a story that bellowed across the country, another blood-soaked straw heaped brutally upon the fragile back of the camel disguised as civil rights.

The story, written by Al Cahill, a crime beat reporter for the *Atlanta Chronicle*, confirmed that a man named Walter Beasley had been arrested for the murder of Etta Hemsley on the campus of Upton University.

It was a story carefully crafted, lean with facts. The only people quoted were the policemen at the scene. The word allegedly was used seven times. My name was not mentioned by Al Cahill.

Dempsey Rhodes's sidebar, printed on the third page, was more thoughtful and heavy with sorrow. Dempsey did use my name, yet, as Jack had predicted, he did not acknowledge that I was a part-time employee of the *Chronicle*. Dempsey praised Etta Hemsley as a child of change and referred to me as an Upton University student—one of the curious, passive millions who could no longer dodge the blood that was being spilled in the nation's tragic war over equality.

But it was not the stories that made people gasp: it was the photograph Ernie O'Connor had taken from one knee—the open-mouth shock of death frozen on the face of a black girl, blood from her ripped-open neck painting the bewildered face of a white boy. One thick drop, with a comet's tail, was caught dripping from my chin.

The photograph was printed in a five-column shriek across the front page, beneath a banner headline that read:

Girl Killed in Campus Protest

The caption line under the photograph read:

Demonstration at Upton University Ends in Tragedy

Etta Hemsley, a 21-year-old black girl, lies dying in the arms of Upton University student Cole Bishop after a shooting incident during a campus demonstration. Police at the scene arrested Walter Beasley, an automobile mechanic from Clarkston, GA, and charged him with first-degree murder. The incident occurred during a confrontation with university officials over Upton's admission policies.

Compared to Ernie O'Connor's photograph, the stories meant nothing. It was a startling portrait of a savage moment. Before the end of the day, it would appear in newspapers on every continent, and languages I could not read would report indignantly of the new, unending Civil War in America. Over time, the image would become known simply as The Photograph, deserving the capitalizations.

"My God," Jack said in astonishment as he stared at the picture of me holding Etta Hemsley. "It's worse than I thought. I didn't know there was a picture. You'll never shake this, Cole. Never. And I can't help. I thought I could, but I can't. This is going from bad to worse."

Jack was right.

The call came before my first class the following day. It was from Hoagie Carpenter, managing editor of the *Chronicle*. Jack reluctantly handed the phone to me.

"Don't take any shit," he mouthed.

I waved off the warning. "Yes sir," I said into the receiver.

"When can you come in today?" Hoagie asked gruffly.

"Two, I guess," I told him. "My last class is over at one. What's up?"

"Crawford wants to see us," Hoagie said.

Crawford was Ray Crawford, publisher of the *Chronicle*.

"Why?" I asked.

"I guess we'll find out when we get there," Hoagie told me. "Two o'clock. Be here."

"Yes sir," I said.

I remember that Ray Crawford's office was on the third floor, left off the elevator, at the end of the corridor. The rest of the floor was occupied by the accounting department, where serious-faced men and women worked in funereal quietness. It was a place without energy, without laughter, without the newsroom yodel and jabber of people making stories out of the brew of rumor and fact. In the newsroom, wire machines and typewriters clattered against paper like finger castanets in a primitive street band—rhythm out of chaos. The world bobbed on a sea of words that had the power of typhoons. In comparison, the accounting department worked in the burping gurgle of swamp bogs.

As I stood outside the elevator with Hoagie Carpenter, I could hear the slow pecking of one typewriter coming from an office with the door opened. Someone coughed from another office, a single hack.

I remember saying to Hoagie, "Quiet, isn't it?"

I remember Hoagie glaring at me. It was a look of disgust, a look of superiority. He began to stride down the corridor.

A woman I had never seen sat at a receptionist's desk outside Ray Crawford's office. She was pudgy, her hair the dry brown color of dead grass. She wore too much makeup.

"Go on in," she said to Hoagie. "He's waiting." She did not look at me.

Hoagie nodded, sucked air deep into his lungs and walked into Ray Crawford's office. I followed.

Ray Crawford sat behind a large mahogany desk in a high-back leather chair. He was heavy-set, with heavy jowls, heavy folds under his eyes balancing the curve of his wire-rimmed glasses. His combed-back hair had the look of buffed dark steel. His mouth was curled down at the corners. It was a cynical mouth, a cynical face. He did not speak. He nodded toward two leather chairs placed in front of his desk, but several feet from it. He then swiveled in his chair and leaned forward. His hand disappeared under the top drawer of the desk and paused a moment. I sensed he was pushing a button. Behind me, the door closed. I could hear a click locking it.

Ray Crawford wormed his shoulders into the back of his chair, touched his hands together in front of him, fingertips to fingertips. He sat, gazing hard at me. After a moment, he said, "You're a trouble-maker, aren't you?"

"Sir?" I said, surprised.

"Trouble-maker," he repeated. "I think you understand me."

"I don't know what you're talking about, sir."

"I'm talking about that little photo-opportunity you got caught in."

I looked at Hoagie. Hoagie's eyes did not move from Ray Crawford. He did not speak and I knew he would say nothing to defend me.

"I assume you're talking about the picture that ran yesterday," I said. "I've explained that. It was a coincidence, that's all. I just happened to be there."

"It seems that everybody who joins one of those marches just happens to be there," he shot back.

"I don't know, sir," I said quietly. "I'd never seen a protest until two days ago."

"Unless I miss my guess, you're going to tell me you don't know the first damn thing about this paper's stand on getting involved in demonstrations."

"No sir," I replied. "I'm just part-time." It was not a lie.

Ray Crawford sneered. He tapped his fingers together. "This paper encourages staying away from them, unless you've been sent there to do a story." He shifted his eyes to Hoagie. "I've been trying to get my managing editor to put that word out, but it's apparent he didn't get around to everybody."

Hoagie dipped his head.

"I tell you what I've decided to do," he continued. "I've decided to give you a little help for the rest of the school year."

"Sir?" I said.

"I'm going to pay you, but you don't have to come back to work," he said.

"But—"

"I'm not finished," he snapped. His face flushed red. He shifted in his chair, dropped his hands to the armrest. "You get paid for doing nothing. All you have to do is sign an agreement that you'll not mention the name of this newspaper if, and when, you're asked about any involvement you had in that mess out at Upton."

I sat back, numbed. I thought about Jack Alewine, could hear Jack's laughter.

"Well?" he said.

I swallowed hard. My mouth was dry. I could feel my heart pounding. "I, ah, I don't know," I whispered.

"It's simple," he continued. "You sign a paper, you get a check, and you can spend the rest of the quarter chasing women, or swallowing goldfish, or doing whatever the hell it is you guys do these days to amuse yourself."

"I don't know," I said again.

"Listen, boy, have you got any earthly idea what you're letting yourself in for?" he asked. He reached for a sheet of paper on his desk. "I've got your life's story right here. You're from a farm community in north Georgia. You've made it out this far, and from the grades you've been getting, it looks like you're smart enough to make something out of yourself. They even tell me in the newsroom that you're a damn good copy editor, that you might have a career in journalism if you want it. You sign this paper, finish your education, and in a couple of years, we'll see what we've got for you. You keep going the way you're going, and you won't even be able to go back home for a Christmas visit."

"I don't understand," I said.

He spoke slowly, deliberately. "Boy, that little snapshot of you has been in every newspaper in the world that knows how to smear ink and start a press, or it will be before the week is out. I promise you, right now, back in that little one-horse town where you grew up, you're being called everything from a turncoat to a queer to a nigger lover."

I remember thinking of Marie Fitzpatrick and of the speech she had made on our day of graduation from Overton High School, warning us of changes that would overwhelm us. Like a tornado, she had said. And I remember the sudden surge of anger that flew through me. "No," I said quickly.

"What?" Ray Crawford's voice was a growl.

"I can't do that," I told him, and the voice I used surprised me. It was the voice Marie would have used—bold, direct, daring. "You can fire me, and I'm sure you will, but I can't let you bribe me."

He leaned back in his chair. His eyes burned into me. After a moment, he hissed to Hoagie, "Get him out of here. Cut his check up to the last day he worked."

As I was leaving the building, I heard someone call my name. I turned to see Dempsey Rhodes pushing his way through a group of pressmen congregating in the lobby on their break.

"Wait up a minute," Dempsey said.

We walked together up the street, toward the parking lot, Dempsey waddling like a man with a sore back. Dempsey was in his early thirties, but had already been nominated for a Pulitzer Prize. He had an Irishman's disposition, a mix of anger and melancholy. As a young man he had been a boxer. There was rumor he had killed a man in the ring, and had been haunted for years over it.

"I'm glad you did what you did," Dempsey mumbled at last.

"How do you know what I did?" I asked.

He glanced over his shoulder. "It's out."

"Didn't take long, did it?" I said. "All I had to do was wait for my check. Twenty minutes, maybe. That's the fastest I've ever seen news travel in that place."

A smile coated Dempsey's face. "The old man's having a fit," he said. "He reamed Hoagie's ass, and that's something I would've paid to see." He glanced at me. "Hoagie stand up for you?"

"Didn't say a word," I answered.

He spit a laugh. "The spineless bastard. If it makes you feel any better, I've made that same little visit with him. Didn't stand up for me, either." He chuckled. "How'd you like that little door-closing trick?"

"Scared the hell out of me," I admitted.

"What it's supposed to do," he said. "I'd been warned. I thought it was funny."

"What did you do?" I asked.

"To get called on Crawford's carpet?" he replied. "Well, it was a little bit in the same vein as you. I wanted to do a profile on Martin Luther King, Jr., take a ride with the Freedom Riders, see what it was all about from the other side."

"But you're still here," I said.

"Yeah, I am. I'm a patient man. There's more than several ways to skin a cat. I'll have my moment."

"I hope you do," I said.

We were at the parking lot. He stopped beside a blue Plymouth. "You got a car?" he asked.

"I ride the bus," I told him.

"Beats this piece of junk," he said. He looked gently at me. "I hope you weren't upset by the story I wrote. Nothing personal about it. I admire any man who makes a career out of studying Joel Chandler Harris, and for what it's worth, I think you told the absolute truth, but you've been tainted, and you'd better get used to it."

"Your story didn't bother me," I said. "I thought it was a little strange you didn't mention I worked for the paper, but that was all."

"Oh, but I did," he said brightly. "Got axed."

I laughed. "Like me."

"Like you," he said. "Let it be a lesson. Sometimes the best material winds up in the hell box." He opened the door to his car. "Come see me sometime," he added.

When I arrived at my apartment, I found the letter propped against a sugar dish on the kitchen table, placed there by Jack. It was from Marie Fitzpatrick.

Cole,

I saw your picture in the Boston Globe, on the front page. I was stunned, and frightened. Your fame finally found you, but why did it have to be so terrible? You should have married me. We'd be making babies, not headlines. I would have taken care of you. I worry about you. Don't let them get to you. They will, if they can. Poor Cole Bishop. You won't even know what's happening. Go to the library, Cole. Pick out a book, one that begins with "Once upon a time..." Read about fairy Godmothers or laughing elves pulling pranks on cranky old men. Find something that ends happily ever after. We won't, Cole. Not us. You're famous now. And me? I'm just waiting. Did I ever mention it? I read my own palm on the night of our first date—after you dumped me unceremoniously back at my front door, leaving me to wish for erotic dreams of you when I finally fell asleep. I have a short lifeline. I should be afraid, but I'm not. I think it's wonderful to know things before they happen. Please be careful my famous, innocent friend. There are still many things in your path, still many surprises, before this is finished.

I love you.

SIXTEEN

Once, in his childhood, Cole had been with the Darby twins—William and Carl—at the cotton gin in Crossover, and he had watched as they taunted a young black boy named Fremont, telling him they would pay him a nickel to hambone. He had not known what it meant to hambone and he had asked Toby. It's when the colored slap their hands on their legs and chest, making it sound like skin music, Toby had explained in a whisper that made Cole believe Toby was annoyed with the Darby twins.

Fremont had tucked his head shyly, had said, Can't do no hambone. Don't know how.

And William—or Carl, he did not remember which—had sneered, You a nigger. Every nigger on Earth knows how to hambone. You better hambone, or we gonna whip your butt.

Toby had interceded. You boys leave him alone, or it's gonna be me doing the butt-whipping, he had warned. Then, gently to Fremont: You go on and find Mr. Philips and stay with him.

Cole did not know why the memory of the Darby twins came back to him as he prepared his lunch—potato pancakes covered in applesauce and a dollop of sour cream—though he guessed it was because his writing was hurdling him back over time, and the distance from where he was and where he was headed was the same as a lake too large to see across, but one that invited rock-skipping. The memories were like that, like rock-skipping—the rock striking the water's surface, making circles, then striking again farther out. By chance, the rock had struck where the Darby twins were residing in the history of his life.

It also made him think of the years of the Darby twins, when the echo of the second world war was still faintly heard and all about them change was blowing as invisibly as the wind—change they could not see or sense, change Marie Fitzpatrick would later warn about in her graduation speech.

In small farming communities, farmers still packed their wagons high-up with cotton for near-by gins, still hand-pulled corn in autumn. Blacks, and whites, still hired out to do field labor, the way Fremont and his family worked for Doug Philips. Canning plants still operated in season. Electricity was still new enough to cause shivers of excitement. Boys still played pasture baseball and football, still fished creeks, still trapped rabbits and hunted for squirrels with single-shot 22s, still made walks into such nearby towns as Overton on Saturdays, still gave in to dreams standing in front of dime store windows, wishing for the joy of cheap treasures.

The years of the Darby twins had been restless ones for Cole. His dreams were not of dime store trinkets, but of adventures he read about. And he had been an unashamed pretender, a talker, giving way to imagination and earning a reputation of telling tall tales.

The thought of it made him smile, there in his home in Vermont, so far away from the Darby twins and a black boy named Fremont.

He remembered the men at the cotton gin laughing at him, prodding him to re-tell stories that amused them. Remembered them saying, Ain't nobody like that boy.

Then—in that distant time—such talk had left him with a smug feeling.

He wondered what had happened to Fremont and to the Darby twins.

He napped after his lunch, but only for a short time. Tanya Berry woke him with her call, asking about his state of health.

He told her he was regaining his strength.

Are you writing? she asked.

I have been, he answered. I think today will be the last day of it.

What does that mean? she asked.

It means what it means, he replied.

You've got a snappish tone, she said.

I'm speaking to a pushy woman, he countered.

You're speaking to the one person who knows you better than anyone here, she said cheerfully. You're speaking to your spiritual advisor.

Oh? he said. Is that what you are?

Now you understand our relationship, she replied. Want to have dinner tonight? Mark's going out of town for a couple of days.

Sure, he said. If it's all right with Mark.

She laughed. My God, Cole, I don't think it would bother Mark if we curled up nude under a blanket in front the fireplace. He knows about you.

Knows what? he said.

That you're impotent.

Where did you get that tidbit of information? he asked.

I made it up.

Why?

So Mark wouldn't care if we curled up nude under a blanket in front of the fireplace. Now, where do you want to have dinner?

Arnie's, he said.

Good, she replied. Seven o'clock?

Seven, he said.

Awake, he went into his office and sat at his desk and began to write the words that he knew would bother him.

December 27, afternoon

The greatest worry I had following the killing of Etta Hemsley was personal: my family. I knew the news would frighten them, my mother especially. When I called her the night of my firing from the newspaper I learned I had underestimated her reaction. She was more than frightened; she was terrified.

"Why, Cole?" she asked with desperation. "Why would you put yourself in a situation like that, where it could have been you who was killed?"

I tried to explain it was a coincidence, that I had simply wandered into the group out of curosity.

"Has anything else happened?" she asked anxiously.

I thought of telling her about the firing, but decided against it, knowing it would cause grief. It was something that needed said face-to-face, though my pause in answering must have alerted her.

"Something has happened, hasn't?" she said fretfully. "What?"

"Nothing," I told her. "Just talk, a lot of talk."

"Well, if you think it's the talk out there, you should be here," she said. "Ben Colquitt called, nosing around for a story in that sorry excuse of a newspaper he owns, but I told him what you just said—that you just happened to be there. He made some smart remark about how young people were getting crazier by the day, trying to stir up trouble. I told him he'd better not be talking about you. Paper's coming out today. I guess we'll find out."

"How's Daddy?" I asked.

"He's bothered, but he's not saying much," she said. "Toby's the one I'm worried about. He won't take anybody talking about you. And the girls are scared somebody could hurt you."

"Tell them I'm all right," I said. "Tell them to call me."

"I will," my mother replied in a voice of concern. She asked, "When are you coming home?"

"Soon," I told her.

"You stay away from crowds, honey," my mother begged.

"I will," I promised.

I would go home the next morning.

My mother called early. Anguish and anger was in her voice.

"They burned Jovita's house," she said in a painful cry.

I remember feeling stunned and weak. "Who did it?" I asked.

My mother sobbed, fought to control herself. "I don't know," she said after a moment. "It could have been anybody."

"Why?" I said.

"The paper came out yesterday," she answered, her anger rising. "Ben Colquitt said your involvement in what went on in Atlanta started when you were in high school and became friends with that girl."

"Marie?" I said.

"Her, yes," my mother replied bitterly. "He wrote about the speech she made at graduation—the one I told you would cause trouble—and he blamed it on Jovita. He said she was trying to integrate the schools by getting that girl to teach her children."

"My God," I said in astonishment. "There's not a bit of truth in that. She made Marie stop teaching them. Don't you remember that? She said so in her speech."

"It doesn't matter," my mother argued. "All of it led to this."

"Was anyone hurt?" I asked.

There was a pause. I could hear my mother's deep breathing, could hear her swallow a sob.

"One of the boys—the youngest one—was burned," she whispered. "I don't know how bad."

"Littlejohn?" I asked.

"I think that's his name," my mother replied.

I remember the jolt of shock and the sudden wave of nausea that struck me. (Can feel it at this moment, a chill on my arms and across my shoulders.) I could see the face of Littlejohn as he laughed over my telling the story of an orange turtle. (Can see him at this moment, the shine of merriment in his eyes.) I thought of Marie, thought of how she had yearned to perform a miracle in the garage of her parents, and how that miracle had ended because of the power of fear.

"I'll be home in a couple of hours," I told my mother.

"Don't," she said sternly. "It'll just make things worse."

"I'm sorry, Mama, but I have to," I said. "I have to see it." I hung up before she could object.

A small gathering of neighbors were lingering around the smouldering ruins of Jovita's home. They stood, slumped, their heads bowed, and the expression they wore is something I have never forgotten. It was as though their spirit—whatever throbbed in them as life—had disappeared in the spirals of smoke rising up from deep-buried embers. When I saw them, I was reminded of photographs from the war, where stunned survivors of bombings seemed incapable of moving from the heaps of devastation around them. Two of the women were picking through the rubble, carefully pulling out items cool enough to touch. I saw one holding a scorched dress.

Toby was there, waiting for me. He was standing beside a man who seemed vaguely familiar. My age, I thought. Dressed in a suit a size too large for him, leaving the look of a man who has lost weight.

"You remember Moses Elder?" Toby asked quietly.

I thought: Moses. Yes, Moses, that was his name. My mind flashed to seeing him with Marie and the children of Jovita.

"I don't believe we ever met," I said. I offered my hand to Moses. He took it in a weak, uncertain grip.

"No sir, I don't think so," he mumbled.

"Moses works at Higginbottom's Funeral Home," Toby added.

I wanted to tell him that I knew of him from Marie, that I had seen him with her. I did not. I said, instead, "I'm sorry about this. I truly am."

Moses dipped his head in a nod, but did not reply.

"Nothing you can do here," Toby said. "We better go on home."

"How's Jovita?" I asked, directing the question to Moses.

"Doing well as she can," he said. He turned to look at the remains of the house.

"Littlejohn?" I said. "What about him?"

"Don't know about him, yet," Moses answered. "Got burned pretty bad. He was trying to find his mama when his shirt caught on fire."

"Where is he?" I asked.

"At the doctor's house," Moses replied. "Doctor's got a room there."

I remembered there was one black doctor in Overton, remembered hearing my mother speak fretfully of the risky treatment blacks received because there were no real medical facilities for them.

"I'd like to see him," I said.

I saw Moses glance at Toby, saw Toby look away, saw him begin to gnaw subconsciously on his lower lip. For Toby it was sign language, a speech of worry.

"They not letting nobody in but his mama," Moses said quietly, yet firmly.

"We won't be bothering them," Toby offered. "You just tell them we asked about them, tell them we'll be praying for them."

Again, Moses nodded.

"You tell Littlejohn that Brer Turtle is thinking about him," I said.

Moses' face furrowed.

"It's a story I told him," I added. "A long time ago, when he was no more than four or five."

"Yes sir," Moses acknowledged, not asking about the story.

Toby wanted to take the shortcut from Milltown to our home in Crossover, but I needed gasoline for Jack's Volkswagen and told him I would stop at Earl Cartwright's service station.

A dark look settled into his face. He said, "I wouldn't do that, Cole."

"Why not?" I asked.

"There's some hard feelings in town," he replied. "I wouldn't call you the most popular man in Georgia right now."

"Well, damn it, that's nonsense," I said indignantly. "I need gas. When I go back today, I plan to take the cut-through over to 78. If I don't get it now, I'll have to drive back this way later."

"Okay," he said after a moment. "I'll follow you there."

"You don't have to do that," I insisted. "Go on home."

"Look, Cole, you've been away from here for a few years," he said in a low, even voice. "You forgot what it's like. You also forgot that I'm your big brother and not your goddamn servant, and I suspect you forgot that I can snap you like a twig, so either you do this my way or you can push that thing back to Atlanta."

His tone took me by surprise, yet it also warmed me. Toby had always protected me; he was doing it again.

"All right," I said meekly.

I did not know I would need his presence as much as I did.

At the service station, a group of men huddled at the grease rack, talking. They turned their attention to me when I got out of Jack's Volkswagen at the gas pumps.

From the gathering, I heard, "Well, damn. Look who's here."

Another voice said, "He got a colored girl with him?"

Someone laughed.

The men began to drift toward me. One of them was Hugh Cooper, who had caught the touchdown pass to win one of our football games. He had gained weight and had added a hardness to his face.

"What you doing over here?" Hugh asked.

"Just visiting," I told him.

I saw Toby open the door of his truck and step outside the cab.

"I just been reading about you," Hugh said, holding up a copy of the *Overton Weekly Press*. The photograph of me cradling Etta Hemsley was like a billboard over the front page.

"Tell me something, Cole," Hugh added in a brave voice—the kind men use in the company of other men. "This your girlfriend? Word I hear is, you was dating her. That right?"

"Hugh, I didn't even know her," I said. "I had never seen her until that day. All of that was nothing but an accident."

"Not what I hear," Hugh sneered. He looked at the men around him. The men muttered agreement.

"I don't know where you're getting your information," I said.

"It's the word. That's all you need to know," Hugh replied.

"Maybe he just don't want to talk about it," the man standing near Hugh said.

I saw Toby moving toward the men, heard him say, "That's enough." He turned to me. "Get your gas, Cole."

An older man grinned at Toby. "How's it feel to have a nigger-lover as a brother?" he said.

Toby took three quick steps, caught the man by his shirt and jerked him. The man blinked surprise.

"How you think it's gonna feel to have your teeth lying on the ground, asshole?" Toby hissed.

I saw the other men step back involuntarily, then step forward again, saw Toby spin the man he was holding toward them. "You boys want some of me?" he growled. "Well, by God, I'm here for the taking if you think you can do it." The men hesitated.

Earl Cartwright came running from inside his station. "What's going on?" he demanded.

Toby released the man, shoved him backward. "Nothing," he said. "We just getting some gas."

It was a scene—a memory—that will rest with me in my grave. For a moment, no one moved, or spoke. I could see fury in Toby's face. He was breathing hard, like an animal that has been cornered and is ready to die for its freedom. He stood with his legs apart, balanced. His fists were clenched, the muscles of his arms were like ropes.

"All right," Earl said. "I'll pump it."

The men said nothing to Toby, or to me. They drifted away, back to their huddle at the grease rack. Still they watched us, and as we drove away, I could hear a shout from one of them: "Nigger lover!"

I have not entered the town of Overton since that day.

The visit with my parents on that morning was not as tense as I thought it would be, and from the distance of years, I believe it was because they had talked and had made a decision that anger, or lecture, would not help matters. I told them the truth—again: it was a coincidence, nothing more. I reiterated that I was not involved in the civil rights movement—another truth, and one I have regretted over time. I did not tell them of being fired from the *Atlanta Chronicle*. I said simply that I decided to quit working in order to concentrate on my study. It was an explanation coated in the gray of deceit, still it was a tactic I felt necessary at the time. My father gave me one hundred dollars. To help out, he said. My mother promised to keep me informed about Littlejohn and Jovita and the rest of her children.

Before I left to return to Atlanta, I found Toby in the barn, tinkering with his tractor. It was his sanctuary, the place he always went when bothered. I said nothing to him and he said nothing to me. I simply embraced him and turned and walked out of the barn. I could hear the roar of his tractor as I crossed the yard to Jack's Volkswagen.

In the days following my visit to Overton, I left my apartment only to attend classes, or to bury myself in the library. Jack Alewine was partly responsible, insisting that isolation was better than ridicule for someone of my passive nature. Yet, staying to myself was more my decision than Jack's instruction.

On campus, I could not avoid the stares of people—some icy, some pitying, some sympathetic, some suspicious. It was a rainbow of stares. And I could not avoid the posters that seemed to appear on trees like fungus. The posters where reprints of Ernie O'Connor's photograph with a single word running under it: *Why?* By day, the maintenance department of Upton University would rip the posters down. By night, they would magically reappear, even with the campus security office working at double force.

Wade Hart, who visited me daily, always late at night, believed the posters were the work of a small, rebellious band of students from Northern states. He called them radicals, mostly anti-war, adding that the integration issue was also high on their agenda.

"It ought to be a goddamn fraternity," Jack crowed. "I'd join it in a heartbeat."

"I thought you were a Kennedy man," Wade said.

"I am."

"Kennedy's the man who's going to have us in war," Wade argued.

"Bullshit," Jack snapped. "He's got some advisors over there, that's all."

"You wait," Wade warned. "You wait."

And while Wade waited for the war that would flare up in Vietnam, I waited for the memory of Etta Hemsley's death and for the charred remains of Jovita's small home to leave my dreams.

They did not. They were there nightly, reappearing like the posters on the campus of Upton University.

In my communication with my mother, I learned that Littlejohn was recovering slowly from his burns. There would be severe scarring, noticiably on the right side of his neck and face, and on his right ear. Jovita had moved into another small home in Milltown, her furnishings provided by collections from both blacks and whites. I learned also that a sizeable contribution had been deposited in the Overton bank in her name from an anonymous donor living in Atlanta. I never asked, but I was certain it was from Wade Hart's family, because Wade had wept openly when I told him of Littlejohn.

My mother said no one had been arrested for starting the fire.

No one will be, she added bitterly.

I never wrote to Marie of the fire or of Littlejohn's disfiguring from it. And still today, I do not know why. I think it was because of the guilt I carried over what had happened—guilt that has dogged me since the day I stood at the place where Jovita's home had been, and even greater guilt over never again making an attempt to see Littlejohn.

I feel that guilt now, as I write these words.

That guilt tells me I did the obligatory thing and then walked away, and tried not to look back.

I could not admit such weakness to Marie.

But there was a simple poem I sent to her, trying to explain my own confusion:

I believe that when I am drowning,
I will still be searching for a mirage
(Oasis of palm trees and cool blue springs)
Believing my throat is dry,
And sand is on my belly.

A few days later, I received a letter in reply.

Cole,

I dreamed this last night. We were in the Corner Cafe on Prom Night, you in that silly-funny double-breasted suit and I in my wedding gown of white silk (beautiful, as I had promised you), and the waitress (her name was Frankie, or should have been) asked us what we wanted for dinner. You ordered country-fried steak, green beans and mashed potatoes, a side salad with French dressing, iced tea, blackberry cobbler. I had a salad, with vinegar dressing only. I didn't need the oil. There was enough oil in the air of the Corner Cafe to open a service station. But I really wasn't hungry. I wanted to watch you eat. You were a pig, of course. What else could you be?

You are a Southerner. Country-fried steak, green beans, mashed potatoes. And iced tea. Iced tea is the Southerner's liqueur, I think. It's a wonder they don't use it in church for communion wine. Iced tea for the blood of Jesus, cornbread for his body.

Oh, Cole, I do agonize for you.

Please leave.

Be the runaway that is in your heart.

Run away to me. I will hold you, hide you. There will be no pictures of you covered in blood. We will find a new name for you, something out of a book, or from the obituary pages—a name used, but not used up. I will introduce you as a cousin, or a lover (your choice, my wish). You can pretend you are a writer and live in libraries. There are schools here which are wonderful. You could teach. I know you say you do not like to be cold, but the winters here are cold only if you think they are. The winters are beautiful. Nothing on earth makes you as aware of living as snow on your face, or the steam of your breathing. You can see your soul in that steam. That is why I want to die here. I want my soul to leave my body in that puff of steam.

But if you do not come to me, find yourself another place.

Leave, Cole, leave.

Do you know of bagels?

They do not serve bagels in the Corner Cafe. I know. I called them this morning. I think Frankie answered. She said, "What?" I said, "Bagels. Do you have bagels?" She laughed and (I am only supposing this) switched her gum from one side of her mouth to the other. She said, "What's that?" and I told her, "It's like a doughnut, but not sweet." She had a great answer, Cole, a classic, Southern answer: "Lord love a duck, no. We got biscuits."

Find a place where you can order bagels as easily as you would order biscuits in the Corner Cafe.

The poem you wrote to me is beautiful. I thought I could touch you when I read it. Wanted to touch you. I wonder if you know what it means, or did you simply put down words that sounded right? I shared it with a professor. Told him who had written it. Showed him the picture of you and Etta Hemsley. He raved over it, blithered on and on about the metaphor of a drowning man looking for water. I only listened, Cole. If I had told him the truth—that, for you, the oasis of palm trees and cool, blue springs is nothing but a fool's dream—he would have become huffy. (Professors do not like the crystal of their wisdom shattered.)

Or am I wrong, Cole? Do you really understand what you have written? Is your throat dry, your tongue swollen? Can you feel the sand cutting into your belly?

I do love you. In a good way, I do. In the best of ways.

On the June day that I left Upton University, having chosen to pursue a doctorate at the University of North Carolina, Jack Alewine and Wade Hart and Marian Shinholster and Henry Fain prepared dinner for me, and they lifted glasses of wine and Jack said a toast: "To Cole Bishop, celebrity." He swallowed his wine and laughed and embraced me. "You know," he whispered tearfully, "all this has changed you, changed you forever, Brer Rabbit. I miss the old Cole. God, how I miss him. He was such a grand loser."

SEVENTEEN

Old men cry easily.

Sitting at his desk, staring at the screen of his laptop, reading the words he had written, he could feel the sting of tears, and he remembered his father saying it: Old men cry easily.

It had occurred on a visit to his home during a time when his sisters were also there, visiting with their families. At their leaving, with the chatter of grandchildren calling to his father—*Papa! Papa!*—he had watched tears well up in his father's eyes, and he had said to him, Dad, are you all right?

Old men cry easily, his father had answered, and then had turned and walked into his home.

It was the only time he ever saw his father cry.

And now he was doing the same.

Crying. Or part-crying. Moisture, holding in bubbles.

Still, he knew he had been profoundly affected by the memories he had chased for days, and he realized—almost humorously—that he was older than his father had been when his father had said the words: Old men cry easily.

He stood and stretched, feeling the soreness of his muscles in his shoulders and buttocks, and then a sudden wave of dizziness struck him, causing him to reach for the chairback to steady himself. His mouth filled with saliva and he was aware of palpitations of his heart. He sat again in the chair, leaned forward, closed his eyes to wait out the dizziness.

Exhaustion, he thought. Too many hours living on adrenline, his body finally objecting, saying to him, All right, I've got you this far, now it's time to get sensible.

He wondered if it was why he remembered his father's words about old men, a warning taking from a memory fragment.

It was not easy to accept becoming old, and he did not think of himself in that way most of the time. In his mind, he remained young, and the annoying fact that his body did not function as it had thirty years earlier had never bothered him since the changes had been gradual, like an imperceptible erosion. Though he no longer went snow skiing in winter, or jogged or played in the faculty-student softball game, he still felt vigorous, still had a blood-rush in the presence of a beautiful, sensuous woman, still rejoiced over a long walk or the labor of yardwork.

There was a cliché that being around the young was as good an anti-aging medicine as a person could find, and he believed there was something to it, and that it was one of the blessings of teaching. In the company of his students, he could feel the vitality of their spirit, could see the celebration of their youth in auras of bright colors. He was sure there was a rub-off factor at play.

He could feel his heart calming to a steady rhythm. He opened his eyes and lifted his head, then stood cautiously. The dizziness had passed, yet he knew his body had not lied to him. His body was spent, fatigued. His body needed the comfort of his bed and the promise of dark hours.

He thought again of his remorse over turning his back on Littlejohn and the thought caused watering in his eyes and a tightness in his throat.

By the clock on his desk—a gift from a civic club for a speech he had made on elements of Southern literature—he saw that it was a few minutes after six and he remembered his promise of dinner with Tanya Berry. He hoped she was still at home.

She was.

I think this is a first, she said to him over the telephone. A man turning me down for dinner. And on my invitation.

I'm sorry, he told her. I'm really exhausted.

You sound it, she said after a pause. Then: Did you finish?

I don't know, he replied. For now, at least. I think I've gone as far as I want to with it.

Did you send it to me?

Not yet.

Don't. Just print it out. I'm coming over. I'll get a pizza.

I need to go to bed, Tanya.

Then go to bed, she replied. If you don't want the pizza, that's your choice. I want to read what you've written, there, at your place.

Why here?

Because, Cole, that's where you wrote it, she said. I'm among those people who believe the body gives off energy when the soul confronts itself. I want to read it in the presence of that energy.

That sounds like psychobabble, he told her.

It is, she said cheerfully. I just want to get out of the house.

All right, he conceded.

He pushed the print icon on his laptop and watched as the papers slithered out of the printer, landing with a whisper in the plastic cradle of the paperholder. Seeing the words on paper gave his work—and his memories—a sense of permanence. He did not gather up the pages. For some reason he did not want to touch them.

He stood again at his desk. Slowly. He was not dizzy, not as he had been, yet he was aware of being light-headed. Fatigue, he thought.

He left his office and went into his living room. His Christmas tree seemed drooped and he realized he had not watered it. Doesn't matter, he reasoned. It'll come down tomorrow.

Tanya would want a fire, he thought. He could at least do that. He wondered where he had left the long starter matches. The kitchen, maybe.

A sudden, penetrating pain struck across his shoulder, splintered into his neck and arms and lodged in the soft underbelly of his chin. A single strobe of light flashed in his head. He could feel his muscles collapsing.

And then he fell.

❦

When he awoke, he was in a narrow hospital bed. The room's light had the dullness of pre-dawn, a pewter color. He lifted his arm to place it across his chest and he heard movement near him, heard his name called, and then he saw Tanya and Mark leaning over him.

There you are, Tanya said in a relieved voice. Her face was furrowed with worry.

He opened his mouth to speak, wanting to ask what had happened, but he could not make the words.

Don't try to talk, Tanya said. Then, to Mark: Go find the nurse.

He watched Mark nod and rush away, saw Tanya brush her fingers across her eyes. She touched his face and he could feel the moisture of tears on her fingertips. She leaned close to him, whispered, You scared the bejesus out of me, do you know that?

Again, he tried to speak. Again, the words failed him.

You're going to be fine, Tanya said. But, damn it, you're going to have to start taking care of yourself.

He let his eyes float to her, forced a weak smile into his face.

You fainted, she said softly, gently. Your head hit on the coffee table and you got a concussion from it, but the doctor also thinks you've had a mild heart attack. He said you may need a bypass, but he wants to run some more tests before they make that decision. He'll talk to you about it.

He dipped his head against his pillow.

Thank God you had the door unlocked, she continued. When you didn't answer the doorbell I knew something was wrong. I let myself in and there you were on the floor. I thought you were dead, the way you were sprawled out, and there was all that blood from where you hit your head. It's not as bad as I thought it was. The doctor said he didn't think there'd be much of a scar. But you'll have to have a new carpet.

She was talking in a rush, word spilling over word.

Anyway, I called 9-1-1 and then got Mark on his cell phone. He turned around immediately and he's been here with me. And I called your sister—Amy. I had to go through your personal address book to find the number, and I hope you don't mind, but I really don't care if you do. I had to do something. She's coming up—your other sister, too—but they're waiting until I call back.

He blinked his understanding.

She leaned closer, kissed him on his forehead.

I think I might have caused this, she said in anguish.

He shook his head.

No, I think it could be true, she insisted. Having you start the writing, urging you to keep at it. Christ, I should have known it would be stressful, especially during this season. I'm better at my job than that. I'm sorry, Cole, I'm truly sorry.

He struggled to say the word, heard it come out in a whisper: No.

She put her hand across his mouth. Don't talk, she ordered. We'll fight over it later, but right now, I'm going to feel as guilty as I want to. She began to massage his chest, the way a mother would massage a child ill with flu—as though the touch had healing in it.

Half the faculty and townspeople are in the waiting room, she added quietly. The other's have come and gone, including that insane group of men who call themselves the Superior Court. I tried to get them all to leave, but they won't. I think the wrong word got out. I think they believe you're the Pope or some rock star. It wouldn't surprise me if the cheerleading squad showed up. I'm sure they'd already be here if they weren't on Christmas break.

He could feel the smile, or the half-smile, rise again in his face. He licked his lips, said in a hoarse voice, Did you read it?

She lifted her hand from his chest, hestitated. Then she said, Yes. Yes, damn it. I wish I hadn't. I found it last night after I went by your home to make sure I'd locked it. I cried for an hour. What's wrong with you? Why would you keep all of that bottled up? If we weren't here and if you weren't so damned defenseless, you'd get a lecture you'd never forget.

He frowned, asked, How long—?

Have you been here? she said. Two nights. But it's only eight o'clock in the morning, so it hasn't been that long. Now, quit talking and quit thinking. You've got one thing to do now, and that's to get well. If you die on me, I'll never forgive you, Cole. Damn it, we've got a lot to talk about.

All right, he whispered.

❧

He would be hospitalized for more than a week, would have surgery—performed without complications—to insert a stent in a damaged artery, and then he would be cared for at his home by his sisters, Amy and Rachel, with Tanya acting as hostess to them, the same as an interpreter leading strangers through a foreign city.

His doctor would say to him, You shouldn't worry too much about your condition, but you should be aware that what happened was a warning. Your lifestyle is going to change. I don't like saying it, Dr. Bishop, but you're not as young as you used to be.

And there it was again for him. Age.

In his writing, he again had played football and basketball and baseball, and his body had seemed as lean and as strong as it had been at seventeen. It was a trick, the remembering. The remembering had teased him, had made him subconsciously believe he had not changed.

Having his sisters and Tanya around him, guarding him with warnings about over-doing anything from the simple lifting of a fork to the building of a fire in his fireplace, was annoying, even if he knew it was for his own good. He looked forward to being alone.

Finally, it happened. His sisters left him after two weeks and Tanya returned to teaching during the day. She still visited him in afternoons—her acts of charity, she called the visits—yet he had many hours to himself. Blissful hours. Hours for reading, for rest.

To his surprise, and wonder, Tanya did not mention his last entry in the writing of Marie Fitzpatrick—the story of the burning of Jovita's home—until a late afternoon a week after his sisters had departed.

Tell me something, Cole, she said. What you wrote about never going back into the town of Overton since that confrontation at the service station: is that true?

Yes, it is, he answered. When I went home to visit, I always took backroads to the house. It was easy enough to do.

What about the death of your parents and your brother? she asked. Wouldn't they have been at a funeral home?

Not in Overton, he said. After what happened to me, they started going to Elberton for most of their business. There was only a few miles difference between the two towns. A funeral home there handled the arrangements.

You never saw Littlejohn?

No, he replied.

And you don't know what happened to him?

Regretfully, I don't, he said. He paused, added, It was a busy time for me. I was away, working on my doctorate, and then I got the teaching position at Wofford and I was there two years before moving here. To be honest, I was trying to put all of it behind me, and it wasn't easy. Back then, the picture of me holding Etta Hemsley had a life of its own.

As I said before, a lot of people think that's why you came here, she offered.

He did not answer for a moment, and she knew he was taking an inventory of reasons. Finally, he said, It had a lot to do with it, yes.

They were sitting at his kitchen table, drinking hot tea she had made without asking. It was an afternoon ritual for them, one he enjoyed. He liked the way she had gradually taken command of his home, making it part hers, like an hour-a-day wife. She had rearranged cooking utensils and dishware, doing so, she said, because it would be easier for him to get to them. No reason to strain yourself, she had lectured. He knew it had nothing to do with convenience; it had to do with her need to leave her signature on his life.

Marie knew you well, didn't she? she said casually.

He looked at her inquisitively.

In the letter you included, the one from her, she urged you to leave, Tanya added. She said you were a runaway at heart. I loved that letter, by the way.

I suppose you're right, he admitted. She did know me well, but she should have. As much as anyone—no, more than anyone—she influenced everything I've done.

A soft smile eased into Tanya's face. I believe you have just made a confession that's as close to truth as you will ever get, she said. And maybe that's what you needed to learn from the writing. I have colleagues who would call it closure. I think it's just the opposite. I think it's revelation, the great beginning. It's always irritated me the way people look for closure. My God, getting to the truth—as vague as it always is—is an opening-up. It's impossible to completely close out anything that happens to you, but we yammer on and on about it, don't we? It sounds good, Cole, that's all. I hear it constantly, people telling me that, yes, they're reached closure and three months later they're still quaking over it, but they'd never admit it to anyone but me. They've already declared closure. It would be embarrassing to go back on that serene-sounding proclamation. I've done it myself. I told you about that worthless son of a bitch who claimed my virginity and then skipped town. I had closure with him the next time I made love, and all the times after that, and when I became engaged and when I got married—all of it was closure. But guess what, Cole? That miserable bastard still shows up occasionally in a dream. He looks like a Greek warrior caught skinny-dipping and I can't wait for him to rip off my clothes in the backseat of a two-horse chariot. But then I wake up, and I know it will be a good day. It will be a good day because I tell myself that nothing happened, no matter how much he wanted me. I make a game of it. I am wearing a chastity belt made of polished steel.

She paused, inhaled deeply, smiled triumphantly over her lecture. So there, she declared. If you want to know the true definition of closure, it's a chastity belt made of polished steel.

Sometimes you do sound wise, Tanya Berry, he told her.

That's Dr. Berry to you, she sneered. And if you're making fun of me, you can kiss my ass.

Do you use that kind of language with all your clients? he asked.

Not if they pay me, she said. You don't, so I say again, if you're making fun of me, you can kiss my ass.

Fun? he said. No, I wasn't making fun. In fact, I was praising you.

She shrugged, leaned across the table toward him. You're feeling frisky, are you? she said.

I feel completely healed, he told her.

Would you like to make love? she purred, her tongue tipping seductively over her lips, a playful shine in her eyes.

Are you an assassin? he said lightly. You'd kill me.

Cole, I would make you feel like a god, she whispered.

He could feel a blush tinting his face. All right, stop it, he replied.

She leaned back in her chair, picked up her cup of tea. Her gaze stayed on him. Who knows? she said. Someday, it could happen. If it does, I think it will be a splendid thing.

Marie Fitzpatrick whispered in his ear from fifty years past, standing near the swings of a playground: *I think I will regret not making love to you. Someday, I will.*

The blush burned in his face.

Tanya laughed. Cole, my God, you're blushing like a schoolboy. Are you really that shy?

Maybe it's the blush of excitement, he said.

It should be, she replied. Then: All right, talk to me about something.

What?

Going home. I worry about you going home.

Why?

It won't be easy, she said.

Do you know something that I don't? he asked.

She smiled. I know you're going to be looking for something that isn't there anymore, and it's going to bother you. You can call me any time, day or night, and talk about it, but here's what I want you to do: I want you to keep writing. I know you think you don't need to, but you do.

Is that a personal suggestion, or a professional recommendation? he asked.

She did not speak for a moment, then she said, Both, Cole. No matter what kind of nonsense you hear from people in my profession, you can never truly separate the two, even if you think you have. Why do you think counselors resort to counseling? We need it. Now do what I tell you. You're my favorite, non-paying lunatic. I've got a right to be be bossy.

All right, he said quietly.

EIGHTEEN

2005

The return to Overton for the fiftieth reunion of the Overton High School class of 1955, was a trip made of miles and memories. He drove it in a slow fashion, keeping the speed limits, taking time to see the unfolding of spring along the way—early green turning lush as he crossed from Vermont into New York near Ticonderoga, following the Tongue Mountain Range to bypass New York City by going west into Pennsylvania, then wiggling south into Maryland and Virginia and the Carolinas before crossing the Savannah River into Georgia.

He had with him more clothes than he needed, a sign that he had been so long away from the South he did not clearly remember the seasons. And maybe it was also a sign that he was no longer an expatriate in Vermont, but had become a Vermonter.

He had with him his letter jacket from his senior year at Overton High School, faded, yet still intact, the white O dingy against purple wool. In the lie of his imagination, he believed he could still smell the scent of Marie Fitzpatrick's perfume in it.

He had with him his briefcase, and in his briefcase, he had the framed photograph taken on prom night by George Fitzpatrick, the photograph of him standing beside Marie, an awkward smile covering his face, a look of radiance resting on hers.

And he had the letters.

Her letters. And one of his own, one never mailed.

He would not share the letters, or the photograph, as part of the show-and-tell of the reunion celebration. He had them for his own need.

On the drive, he thought of Marie's lamentation about her unplanned return to Overton, done on a whim, without reason. She had been sorrowful about not having had a permanent home in her childhood, had said, *If I had a hometown, I think I might enjoy visiting it. Going home must be wonderful.*

Marie's dreamy wish for a home, a place to visit, had greatly affected him. It was a revealing confession, one of the few times she ever permitted him to glimpse into the sealed-off soul of the little girl she must have been.

Yet, for Cole, going home had never been easy, the guilt of each visit settling on him like a shroud. He had broken his promise that his move to Vermont would be temporary, that he would not lose touch with his heritage. It had been done to calm the fretting of his mother. He had told her jokingly that in the modern age of the twentieth century airplanes actually flew in and out of Vermont and he had vowed to make use of them. Don't worry, he had said. You'll see more of me than you think.

It had been a lie—or Marie Fitzpatrick's mendacity at work. Not an intentional lie, but a lie still. He had seldom returned to Georgia after settling in Vermont.

His sister, Amy, reminded him of his failure. She said, How many times have you been home in the last ten years, Cole? Three by my count. A funeral each time—Mama, Daddy, Toby.

Her words were painful for him.

You're wrong, he countered. Four times. The Christmas after Mama died, I was here. Remember? It was in 1994, right before Holly and I separated for good. She went on that skiing vacation to Denver with a couple of her friends, which should have given me some clue about what was going on with her, since we were ass-deep in snow in Vermont.

I don't want to talk about Holly, Amy said.

Cole reached across the space separating their lounge chairs and patted her hand. She had never liked his ex-wife.

We were all here, he added. Rachel and Wally came down from Virginia. You and Jake had just moved back to Atlanta from Arizona. All the kids were here. I liked that Christmas. It was good. I'm glad Holly had other plans.

Yes, Amy said softly.

He could see the sheen of tears in her eyes. I miss them, she added. Mama, Daddy, Toby. I can't tell you how much I miss Toby.

Me, too, he replied.

They sat for a moment in silence. The patio, screened-in and added to the family home by Amy and her husband, Jake, was cool in the afternoon. Amy had called it a playroom for their grandchildren, but mostly it was said as a wish. Her only child, a daughter, lived in Tucson, and she seldom saw her two grandsons.

I still can't believe the timing of it, she said. October. Why did they all die in October, three years apart? What is it about October and bad hearts? Every October I go to the doctor. After Daddy died, I tried to get Toby to do the same thing, but he only laughed it off. Well, I can tell you one thing, after the scare you gave us over Christmas, when October rolls around this year, I'm going to be wherever you are and I'm going to drag you to the doctor. Do you undestand me?

I understand, he said, knowing an argument was useless.

Do you hear from Karen? he asked, wanting to change the subject. Karen was Toby's widow. She had remarried a man named Ted Goodlove and had moved to Athens.

A card now and then, she answered. Christmas. Easter. My birthday. I see her about twice a year.

Too bad they didn't have children, he said.

She couldn't, Amy replied.

I know, he said. But it didn't seem to bother Toby. He was a practical man, I guess. Sometimes I used to think we were from different families, practical as he was, and the dreamer that I was.

Amy's look was surprise and disappointment. What do you mean? He was a dreamer, too, as much a dreamer as you ever were.

Toby? he said. Our Toby? Toby of the tractor?

My God, Cole, sometimes you amaze me, she sighed. Do you think there's only one kind of dreamer?

I just—

She interrupted with a wave of her hand. Do you know those things you can buy at gift shops? What do you call them? You put them above your bed. Dream-catchers. That's it. An Indian thing, or maybe it's not. Maybe it was something invented by a Polish immigrant with a good eye for merchandising. It doesn't matter. It's like a little hoop with some kind of net attached to it. Beads and feathers to give it a touch.

Anyway, I like them, she added emphatically. Or the idea of them. Let me tell you the difference between you and Toby. Your dream-catcher would look like the net of a shrimper—this big, unrolling thing with holes in it large enough to let small fish swim free. That's the kind of dream-catcher you'd want, Cole, a dream-catcher for big dreams. That wasn't Toby. His dream-catcher would have been the size of a tea strainer. He loved the small dreams, little everyday things, like plants that bloomed, the way dirt smelled, a smile from somebody on the street.

She shook her head gravely. Oh, no, Cole, you're wrong. Toby was a wonderful dreamer, a great dreamer.

You're right, he said shamefully after a moment.

Let's talk about something else, she whispered. I'll have nightmares about Toby all night.

All right, he said.

Do you remember Art Crews? she asked. You were in school with him. At least he said you were.

He settled against his chair and thought of the writing he had done about Art and his other classmates. He remembered also that Art had not spoken to him after the incident at the prom.

Sure, he said. We were good friends at one time. You know him?

We go to church together, she replied. He's in construction, building houses. I don't think the church could get along without him. He does all the up-keep.

Art? he said with surprise.

That's the great thing about religion, Cole. It doesn't care when you find it, she said. He won't rub your face in it, but Art's one of the most Christian people I know. He's always helping the down-and-out.

Still married to Sally? he asked.

She laughed. Oh, my Lord, that ended twenty years ago, or longer. She ran off with a man she met in Anderson, South Carolina, on one of her shopping trips—a policeman who stopped her for speeding. Art's been a bachelor ever since, but he does have a lady friend, as we politely call her. He just doesn't know how desperate she is to move past friendship.

She paused and laughed again. Anyway, he said he'd like to see you before the reunion.

He knows I'm already here?

She looked at him regretfully. I'm sorry. I let it slip you were coming home early.

It's all right, he said. I'll see him, but later. I just got here, and all I'm going to do is to plant my toes in the dirt of this farm, and see if a little bit of what I used to be will sprout. I don't want to go anywhere or see anyone for a while.

Then, don't, Amy said.

He dropped back in his chair and looked through the opened door to the kitchen. He could sense the presence of his mother standing by the counter, rolling out dough for biscuits. It's been a long time, he said. I feel like a stranger.

You won't, Amy promised. Not after a few days. You just think you shook the South. You didn't. It'll all come back.

His sister knew him well. Over the next few days, Cole began to remember the place of his childhood like a recovering amnesiac—in fragments, in sudden shocks of recognition, in spurts of exhilarating surprise. The feel of the ground under his feet healed him. And the fogcap of the creek and river. And the dark scabs of caved-in, tarpaper-and-tin sharecropper houses. And the empty, unused milking stalls in the empty, unused barn. And the hand plows retired under shelters, their plow points nailed to walls like artifacts of another era in roadside antique shops. And the apple trees in the orchard rows, and the chinaberry at the yard's edge, and the carvings of names on the white, wounded trunk of the ancient beech tree. All those things healed him. His amnesia—self-inflicted—was cured by sight and by touch, by the soft, lyrical codes of a language he heard from his sister, a language that returned to him like familiar, but nameless music.

Because her husband, Jake, was away, teaching a certified public accountant's workshop in Charlotte, Amy was with him like a home nurse, leading him daily back into his history. They fished above the beaver dams, picked wildflowers from swamp mounds, found pitcher plants in damp patches, walked to a place called Ruth's Spring and sipped its cold, sweet water from their palms, visited the gravesites of their parents and of Toby, stopped by the falling-in structure that had been Dodd's General Store and the great stage of his theater of youth. One day they sliced open a cardboard box and rode it down the slick cushion of pine needles on Pilgrim's Ridge, as they had done as children. The ridge was not so high and the ride not so grand as it had been fifty-five years earlier.

Old people ought not do such things, Amy said on the painful walk back up the hill.

Two nights before the reunion, again relaxing on the patio, Amy said, I'm glad you're here, Cole. I keep expecting to wake up and find you gone.

I'm glad I'm here, too, he told her, and he meant it. He was at his homeplace and he liked being there, liked being with her. The look of peace was in her eyes, in the soft flesh of her lips, in the spider's web of gray in her hair. From his birth, Amy had been his surrogate mother, an embrace to hide in when his real mother simmered with despair over his impulsive behavior. Amy had always been witty and caring. And she had always known herself. Always. Completely.

What are you doing? she asked.

Doing?

Staring at me like that.

I was thinking that I love you, he told her simply. I guess I don't say it very often, but I do.

She blushed. Why?

I don't know. I like it when you forget yourself and cuss. I tell some of my students in Vermont that the most expressive word in a southerner's vocabulary is shit. You say it beautifully. You make profanity sound like poetry.

And you, Cole, make poetry sound like profanity, she said. Remember, I've read your stuff.

He barked a lazy, sarcastic laugh. To understand what I write, you must be a sensitive, thinking person, and you obviously do not qualify.

Oh, shit, Amy said. Then: Art Crews called this afternoon while you were wandering around outside. I told him we'd see him in the morning.

All right, he surrendered. It's probably time I met some ghosts.

What does that mean? she asked.

The past, he said. The past.

That night, in the privacy of his room, he unlocked his briefcase, took out another of Marie's letters and sat on the bedside and read it.

Dear Cole,

I saw something today that reminded me of you. It was the picture of a basketball player—his name was Larry Bird, I think—and I remembered how sad you looked in a basketball uniform, although I lied to you and told you how sexy you were. How can anyone as skinny as you were look sexy? (The girls used to giggle about the bulge we could see in those basketball shorts—you know, where the penis would be if you had one large enough to cause a bulge. You didn't, by the way.)

Still, it was a good memory, and if I close my eyes and concentrate, I can transport myself back to those nights when you were running around in some gymnasium, preening like a peacock, thinking you were a fearless, near-nude knight from some ancient kingdom. I can't tell you how many times I screamed in laughter when you would strut up the court after scoring a basket.

But don't get me wrong, my sweet friend. I love those memories. I love thinking of you as a little boy having adventures in the body of a teenager flirting with manhood. That's what you were, you know: a little boy.

And maybe you still are that person, that little boy. Maybe you have him hidden, put away in some drawer or closet like a genie that brings you secret pleasure from time to time.

I was never a little girl, was I, Cole?

Not really.

I wanted to be one, but it was impossible. That's what my mother was, and she was magnificent at it. I think I knew from my first toddling steps that someone had to be the woman in the house and since the little-girl role was already taken, I became a woman while still wearing diapers.

Oh, Cole, I am in such a restless, self-pitying mood. Forgive me.

Do you know where I would like to be tonight? I would like to be at that old cemetery—the one you took me to see on our first date, the Breedlove Cemetery, where three-year-old Daniel Breedlove sleeps forever on the bosom of God. There is no reason for you to know it, but it became my favorite place. I used to go there a lot—by myself, of course; you would have been an aggravation, or at least a distraction—and I always felt great peace among those deserted people. If I were there tonight, this is what I would do: I would read the names and the birth-and-death dates of the people buried there. I would give them such wonderful histories, they would rise up from the clay and dance in jubiliation over being reborn in my imagination.

And I would make certain each one of them had a childhood.

Write to me. Tell me you are ready to commit yourself to an institution because you can no longer live without me.

He put away the letter and, remembering his promise to Tanya Berry, he opened his laptop and began to write:

April 14, 2005

There were times when I believed Marie Fitzpatrick had cast a spell on me. Every moment of shock—pure shock—I have experienced, I thought first and immediately of Marie. Quirky memories, quirkily profound.

Marie believed every boyhood sport was barbaric and silly and that I was hopelessly miscast as an athlete, though she pretended to enjoy the melodrama of my over-blown heroism. It was part of our game, and she played it well. Gushy worship, swooning declarations.

"I hope our boys will want to play football, just like their daddy," she cooed openly in class one day. "I can't wait to see them all dressed out like little warriors. That's something their daddy can do for them—teach them football. He won't be able to teach them much of anything else, with me as their mother, but he can do that."

"Oh, Marie, that's wonderful," other girls sighed.

"Marie, I'm not about to marry you," I protested.

And Marie blinked her eyes like a seductive actress and whispered, "It's all right, Cole. Everybody knows you've got to say that. We'll have beautiful little quarterbacks. They'll be born with ducktails."

Privately, Marie berated me. "You look like the polio poster child out there. You're not big enough to play marbles, much less football. You're just plain stupid, Cole Bishop. You'll have a permanent limp by the time you're thirty and when you do, don't come to me for painkillers."

She did not like sports, but she attended games because it was part of the far more intriguing game she and I were playing. It was a dating ritual and she had responsibilities, and she would not forego them. She assumed a queen's role in the stands and even learned the trick of flicking her hair proudly whenever my name was called.

Yet, she could not resist the opportunity to instruct me in matters far more important than pubescent posturing.

Once, during a basketball game, I was injured when a player from the opposing team shoved me into a brick wall only a few feet from the backboard. As my teammates pumped breath back into my lungs, I looked up to see Marie leaning over me.

"Are you hurt?" she asked fretfully.

"Get out of here, Marie," I ordered in a gasping voice.

"Shut up, Cole Bishop."

"Coach is gonna have a fit."

"Let him. I don't give a damn."

My teammates snickered and stepped away.

"Marie, you're not supposed to be down on the court."

"I'm here, so shut up. What happened?"

"I got hit."

"I know that, fool. Why?"

"I didn't see it coming."

"What does that mean?"

"I don't know," I answered in desperation.

"You fool, you don't ever see anything coming. And quit talking like a hick. You've got me doing it."

"Marie, go away."

"I swear, Cole Bishop," she said angrily. "I can't teach you a thing."

a.

He lay in his bed and let the memory of Marie quarreling with him on a basketball court rewind and play again, rewind and play again. The moment was something he had forgot in his earlier writing, and he was glad reading her letter had jarred it loose. Being home, he believed there would be other such memories.

Through the opened window, he heard an owl, low-hooting in the woods, and the monotonous sound of frogs from the pond made by beaver with their stick-dams. Night bugs chirped bravely, cheerfully. All sounds of his childhood and different from the sounds of Vermont.

He touched his chest, let his fingers rest on the rhythmic beat of his repaired heart, and his heartbeat and the night sounds of Georgia lulled him to sleep.

NINETEEN

Art Crews had moved from Overton to a farm in Crossover. In Amy's description of it, he had rebuilt the farmhouse, bricking it, and had added a sunroom and expanded the kitchen. A showcase, she called it.

Yet, the road to Art's showcase home was a washboard road, humped slightly in the center by roadscrapers. It had been graveled and hard-packed by traffic and a skim of heat—summer in April—flowed up from it like a simmering liquid. The heat was another thing Cole remembered. Heat that seared the ground. Heat too thick to breathe.

You should come to Vermont, he said to Amy. It's not like this. You can breathe water straight out of the ground.

It's not home, she replied.

He wanted to tell her she was wrong. He wanted to say that Vermont was now his home, yet he knew she would lecture him on the difference between the home of heritage and the home of choosing, arguing that the home of heritage was the rightful place, the only place that mattered, and she would use as example her own mis-placed life in Arizona and Atlanta as proof.

You've got a point, he conceded.

Art had changed more than Cole expected. He was at least seventy pounds heavier than he had been in high school. His face told stories in the heiroglyphics of deep age lines. He was bald on top of his head and the sidehair he did have was white as cotton. The only recognizable thing about him was his smile, hingled by the dimples that had mesmerized Sally Dylan.

He said in a soft, yet glad, voice, It's been a long time, Cole, a long time.

It has, Cole replied.

Come on in, he urged. I've got some sun tea made. We got a lot of catching up to do.

They stayed at Art's home for more than an hour, sitting in his living room, drinking the sun tea he had made and refrigerated the day before. His home was neat, well-kept. On one wall was a plaque acknowledging him as Northeast Georgia Builder of the Year for 1993, and photographs with Little League teams he had coached. He confessed the cleanness of the house was the work of a woman named Brenda Moss, who had her eyes fixed on him as a late-life catch. She was a couple of grades behind us, he said. Married Luther Moss. He died of cancer a few years ago.

He asked if Cole remembered Luther. Cole confessed he did not.

He played quarterback three or four years after you did, Art said. Took over from David Crane, if I remember it right. He was pretty good. In fact, I think he was quarterback of the last winning team they had before they consolidated the schools.

Amy sat quietly, listening to the talk, the back-and-forth test of memory. She was amused, Cole thought, over his failure to connect dots of people and events.

Art told of their football teammates and of familiar teachers. Wormy, a career soldier, had been killed in Vietnam. Lamar, now an attorney, lived in Toccoa and owned huge tracts of mountain property. Corey, the father of six children, two of them serving time for selling drugs, worked for a car dealership in Monroe.

Cone Bailey had died in an institution.

Marilyn Pender had died of breast cancer.

Unbelievably, O. L. Mayfield was still alive, but in a home, ancient and mindless.

He talked openly, almost happily, of his divorce from Sally. She got out of control, Cole. Spent money like it was growing on kudzu. I hear the old boy she's with now is working two jobs just to keep her in face-lifts. Our kids—two girls—take the grandchildren to see her once in a while. But I don't have nothing to do with her, and, tell you the truth, Cole, I don't want to. Last time I saw her, she looked like a blimp. Some things turn out for the best, I guess.

And then he asked the question Cole knew he would ask: What's Marie up to these days?

Cole forced a smile, paused before saying, Your guess is as good as mine.

Alyse said you couldn't get in touch with her, Art said.

No, Cole replied.

Art's smile spread across his face. I always wondered if there was anything to all that talk abut the two of you getting married.

Me, too, Amy added. I remember how upset Mama and Daddy got over that. I got letters every other day from Mama about it.

It was a joke, Cole said. Something she made up just to toy with everybody. We had fun with it. Everyone did, as I recall. But I have to admit I admired her, even if she was a little over-board at times.

Art laughed heartily. Over-board? Cole, that girl was a one-woman assault force. I'm surprised she's not running the country. Maybe she ought to be. Maybe we could get out of that mess in Iraq.

Cole could feel a muscle twitch in his face and he forced a smile to cover it. You've got to remember, there was just one of her and a lot of us, he said, sounding more defensive than he had intended.

Art's smile stayed fixed. Cole, he drawled, if there'd been two of her, none of us would have made it through the year. Lord, she was the strangest one person I ever met. Remember her speech at graduation?

I do, Cole said.

I thought she'd gone off her rocker, Art added. But, you know what? She sort of knew what she was talking about. Everything she said would happen, happened, and then some. I would of bet my life we'd never see integration over here. Never. But I was wrong. It's worked out all right, and you know why?

No, Cole replied. Why?

Football, Art said. When blacks got on the team, we started winning. All it took, Cole. Football paved the way. All you got to do is look around at what jersey number the kids around here are wearing, and that tells the tale. Number seven. Michael Vick's number. Atlanta Falcons. And I'm talking about white kids as well as black kids. That's who they want to be—Michael Vick. You think something like that would of happened when we was growing up,

Cole? Lord, no. He chuckled. Of course, we'd of been better off if we'd had some blacks on the team, I guess.

We might have been sitting on the bench, Cole suggested.

Art's head bobbed in agreement. Cole could see a glaze in his eyes and he knew it was a glaze of memory, of being young, of Friday nights on the grassless field of Overton High School. It was the same sense of flashback he had had in his writing.

And then Art turned to Amy. Would you do me a favor? he asked.

Of course, Amy replied.

Leave Cole with me for a little while. I'll bring him home later.

That's up to him, she said. Just don't tax him. I told you about that little scare he gave us last Christmas.

I'll be fine, as long as he doesn't keep me out all day, Cole offered. I'm a senior citizen now. Have to get my afternoon nap.

Art's smile became a laugh, robust and happy. Don't worry, I'll get you back, or we'll both be falling asleep in the car. I take a little siesta, too, and I like it so much I think I must be part Mexican. Just thought we'd drive around a little bit, let you see some of the old sights. Maybe even some of the new ones.

❧

Before leaving for Georgia, Cole had had dinner with Tanya and Mark Berry at their home, a casual, enjoyable evening. He liked Mark Berry. Mark was a construction engineer specializing in large commercial projects. He was personable and bright-minded, a good conversationalist. His only apparent social failing—one Cole had never noticed until hearing about it from Tanya—was his tendency to drift to his work, his thoughts curled around some problem that needed attention. You can see it in his eyes if you look closely, Tanya had revealed. They glass over. Nothing else about him changes; only his eyes. What amazes me is that he can continue a conversation with his mouth while his mind is on the concrete foundation of some building a hundred miles away.

Their dinner had been spontaneous, a call from Tanya saying Mark had bought tuna for grilling and there was enough to feed the multitudes, but Jesus was off at a revival somewhere in the Midwest. They had eaten informally at the kitchen table and their talk had been as comfortable as the environment, prompted by a house rule strictly enforced by Tanya and known by every visitor to her home: no shop talk. Shop talk, whatever it was, was for the shop, wherever it was. Cole had always suspected it was her way of telling people not to unburden themselves to her without an appointment.

As he was preparing to leave, Mark had asked, Are you looking forward to your trip to Georgia?

I am, he had answered. And he had repeated, Yes, I am. The answer had tasted good in his mouth.

You think you're going to recognize anyone? Mark had asked.

He had laughed easily at the question. I doubt it. But I also doubt anyone will recognize me.

They'll be testing you, Mark had advised. Don't let them con you. If you come back with Confederate money, I'll know you've been taken.

As they drove away from Art's home, traveling in the direction of Overton, Cole remembered Mark's advice about being conned and he wondered if it was the reason for the visit with Art—a maneuver to bring him back to his childhood by omitting the chapter of the killing of Etta Hemsley and the burning of Jovita's home. Art had said nothing of Etta Hemsley, or of the gossip about Etta Hemsley being a girlfriend. And maybe it was all forgotten, swept away by the heroics of young black boys and young white boys winning football games. It was best to leave it alone, he decided. He would soon be back in Vermont. In Vermont, only Tanya Berry knew of the house-burning.

Art talked as they rode, reliving moments of humor.

You remember that crazy play Coach put in before we played Wrens? he said, laughing. The Hoo-Doo Voo-Doo? The one that started out like a punt and then the ball got handed off three times in the backfield before it was lateraled back to you?

Cole admitted he did remember the play. It had been like a routine by the Keystone Kops. The first time Cone Bailey called it, the Panthers had a first down on the twenty yard line of the Wrens team. He had called a timeout, had questioned Cone Bailey: Coach, do you really think they're going to believe we're going to punt on first down on their twenty yard line? Coach had replied in a bullying fashion, Listen, pissant, I'm the coach. You run the play. And they had. Three times in a row. They had lost forty-five yards.

Way I remember it, he called it again, with us being fourth and fifty-five, Art said. You just had Wormy punt the ball and Coach thought it had worked.

He laughed in a bellowing, warm outburst, then added, Lord, Cole, Coach was crazy as a loon. I guess you remember when he was put in an institution two years after we graduated. Like I said earlier, that's where he died.

Two years? Was it that soon? Cole asked.

There was a beat of silence, then Art said, Well, you were gone by then.

That's right, Cole replied.

Another beat of silence fell between them.

Town looks pretty much the same, Art said finally. But, like they say, what you see is not always what you get. Tell you the truth, Cole, things seem be going from bad to worse. They closed the last textile plant we had last year, moved everything to Mexico or China or some other place. It put over three hundred people out of work, and that's a lot of jobs for some place like Overton. We've got a couple of plants coming in to take their place, and that should help, but right now there's not much house-building going on, I can tell you that. Right now, I don't do much but repair work—new decks, painting, that sort of thing.

He paused, shook his head in distress, then added, Town's like a lot of little places. Got a lot of empty buildings now. Anybody wants anything big, they drive over to Athens or Anderson, where they can get it cheaper at one of them chain stores. You'll see what I'm talking about. The old drugstore—Bell's—has been everything but a garage. It's a beauty shop now, run by Jennifer Mobley—well, Jennifer Reese now. You remember her?

Wasn't she a cheerleader? Cole asked.

That's her, Art replied. Dated Wormy some. Went off somewhere to study being a hairdresser and now she's got her own place. From what I hear, she's got a booming business. Nice woman, too. Her grandson's on the football team now. You want to stop in and say hello to her?

You're the guide, Cole told him.

Well, why don't we skip it for now, Art said. We'll see her on Saturday night. I know she'll be there since she's on the committee. I got somebody else I want you to see.

Who? asked Cole.

You'll find out, Art answered. A soft smile covered his face.

Overton was as Art had described it. There was a sameness about it, yet it was not the same. The closed-up buildings on Main Street, dark behind the windows, had a ghost-like appearance to them—the gaiety of life turned cold and somber. Cole did not recognize many of the names where businesses still operated, but he was not surprised by it. In his childhood, most had been family-owned, family-operated. Over fifty years, death would have closed as many businesses as chain stores in other places. It was the same in Raemar.

One of the places keeping its name was Hendley's, and he asked about it, saying to Art that he was surprised it still existed.

They passed it on to their son, Joe, Art explained. You might not remember him. His name was Joe. He was four or five years behind us. Went off to Clemson and came back with the prettiest woman anybody has ever seen around here. Her name's Tiffany. Still pretty and probably the reason the store stays open. Joe got to be a bad drunk. She puts up with it, but nobody knows why.

It's where I bought my first suit, Cole said.

It's where all of us bought our first suit, Art offered. And it's where I bought my last one. Dark blue. Much as it cost, I'm going to keep it to be buried in. He chuckled, tapped the steering wheel of his car with the heel of his hand.

It could be threads by then, Cole said.

Art smiled, but did not reply.

They passed the service station that had belonged to Earl Cartwright. It was still operating, but the signage was Texaco. Cole remembered it as something else—maybe Pure Oil, though he was not certain. As Texaco, it seemed cleaner, modernized. A group of men were standing outside the front door and seeing them caused him remember the last day he had been in Overton, more than forty years past. He could see Toby again, standing in his fight posture, daring the taunters who were gathered there. A pulse of sadness surged through him. He looked away, fought to push the memory from his thinking. He saw two boys on bicycles, baseball gloves hanging from the handlebars.

We're almost there, Art said. He braked his car in front of the Overton Community Hospital, switched on his left turn signal, waited for an on-coming truck, then drove into the parking lot and parked.

The hospital? Cole said when they got out of the car.

Not the hospital, the assisted living quarters next to it, Art answered. Come on. He began a strong stride across the parking lot.

The assisted living facility of Overton County Hosptial was small, having a waiting room at the entry door and a long corridor leading to a sunroom, where patients were transported daily to break the monotony of being isolated in their quarters, though many of them had no awareness of where they were, or even who they were. The quarters were behind numbered doors along the corridor.

Art stopped at number 11 and knocked lightly on the door. He waited a moment, then opened it, leaned inside, said, You not naked, are you? He turned to Cole, winked, beckoned with his head, then stepped into the room. Cole followed.

Inside, Cole saw a pale, emaciated man sitting lean-back in a cushioned chair. He was wearing white pajamas and a loose-fitting green robe. A plasic breathing apparatus covered his nose and mouth. He turned his head slightly as Art and Cole approached him.

You're looking perky today, Art said in a chcerful voice, leaning to the man. If I didn't know better, I'd say you were ready to go dancing.

The man's head bobbed. He blinked his small eyes. Cole could see a weak smile growing underneath the breathing apparatus.

I brought a friend along to say hello, Art continued. Somebody you haven't seen in a long time.

The man's eyes moved slowly to Cole.

You know who this is, Cole? Art asked gently.

I'm afraid not, Cole answered in a polite manner.

Sidney, Art said after a moment. Sidney Witherspoon.

Cole could feel his body recoil in shock. He thought of his writing of Sidney, telling the story of Cone Bailey's rambling nonsense about Sidney being the quiet one, the one having more sex than the braggarts who talked about it. That Sidney had been broad-shouldered, muscular, wearing a bowed-down face to cover his embarrassment over stuttering. The man before him had no resemblence to the boy Cole had known. The man before him was small, bird-like.

Sidney, Art said quietly, this is Cole Bishop. You remember Cole, don't you? He was the quarterback on our football team. Remember when we played football?

Sidney's eyes moved from Cole to Art, then back to Cole. He dipped his head once. He lifted one hand weakly, let it fall back across his lap.

He knows you, Art said happily. I knew he would. Praise God for it. He turned to Cole. Talk to him, Cole. He knows you.

Cole stepped closer to Sidney, bent to him. He said, Sidney, it's been a long time. I'm glad to see you.

Sidney made his nod.

I didn't know you were still in Overton, Cole added. But like Art said, I've been away for a long time. I've lost touch.

But you're back, Art said. That's what matters, Cole. You're back.

The visit with Sidney Witherspoon was brief. He sleeps most to the time, Art said on the walk back to the car. I try to drop in to see him two or three times a week, and I think he enjoys it, but it always tires him out.

Cole asked what had happened to him.

A stroke, Art answered. About five years ago. He's been here ever since. His wife died about ten years ago of lung cancer and his children live away. Got a daugher in California and a son in Atlanta. The boy got rich in real estate out there and he provides for Sidney, but he don't get over this way very much. I just think Sidney needs to know somebody's thinking about him.

He never left Overton? Cole asked.

Stayed right here, Art replied. Got a job as a mailman. Married a girl named Claire Washington, but you wouldn't know her. She moved here a couple of years after we graduated. Her father worked for the power company.

They reached the car, got inside.

I'm glad we saw him, Cole said. It means a lot to me. He was a good person, one of the best in our class. Just sorry to see him like that.

Art nodded agreement. He started his car.

It's good of you to visit him, Cole added. I know it must help his spirits.

For a moment, Art did not reply. He sat, both hands on the steering wheel, and listened to the idling of the motor. Then: I owe it to him, Cole. When we were growing up, I aggravated him a lot about his stuttering. He paused, shook his head regretfully. I did a lot of things I need to atone for, a lot of things that rested heavy on my heart for a long time. Just glad the Lord made me see my ways.

He turned to Cole, smiled. Got one other place to take you, then we'll get a bite of lunch and I'll get you home before Amy sends out the national guard to find us.

All right, Cole replied.

The drive was a short one, a block away and across Highway 78 to a large brick building Cole had never seen. The sign in front of it read: Overton County Library.

The library? he said. This is new—to me, at least.

Been here twenty-five years, or longer, Art said.

I'm sure my mother must have written about it, but if she did, I don't remember it, Cole admitted. He added, It sure beats that little upstairs place they used to have.

They've got a lot going on here, Art told him. A lot of programs for kids.

Is this where Alyse works? asked Cole.

That's right, Art answered. She's great at it. People love her. But I ought to warn you that she's as silly as a teenager over you coming back for the reunion. She called me the day she got your letter.

Wanted to know if I had any old pictures of the football team. Said she wanted to have some to put out for people to see. He paused, grinned. But more than anything, she talked about you. Told me she'd had a crush on you at one time. She's still a fine-looking woman, Cole. You better watch out while you're here.

The memory of Alyse kissing him on the night of a dance fifty years earlier strobe-flashed for Cole, and in the memory—the strobe-flash of it—he could feel her mouth against his mouth.

Like you said, some things turn out for the best, he said.

Art laughed. Like me and Sally. He wagged his head. I hope she don't decide to show up, but Alyse said she'd be there.

You'll handle it, Cole told him.

Yeah, I guess so, Art mumbled. I'm just glad we're doing it. We're on the down-slope, Cole. If you're like me, you like to think back to when we was on the other side of it. Makes being here now all that much better.

I can't disagree, Cole said. I think it'll be an interesting night.

Art chuckled. It'll be different, he offered.

They entered the front door and turned right into a large, brightly lighted area lined with bookcases. Cole could see a number of people browsing through the maze of shelves. A group of children—black and white, kindergarten age, he guessed—were sitting around a short, circular table, talking in animated whispers to a young woman sitting with them.

Kind of nice, don't you think? Art said.

It is, Cole replied.

A long checkout counter was on their left, and behind it a glass-enclosed office with cubicles. A young, heavy woman with a round, cheerful face was behind the counter. She looked up, saw Art, flashed a smile, then turned to Cole.

You're a man of your word, Art, the woman said. This must be Dr. Bishop.

In the flesh, Art said, grinning broadly.

The woman extended her hand. Dr. Bishop, I'm Linda Hendon. It's an honor to meet you, sir. I loved your book on Joel Chandler Harris. In fact, I did a paper on it for a class at the university.

You did? Cole said.

You sound surprised, Linda Hendon replied. You shouldn't be. It's a wonderful, compassionate biography. All of us in Overton are proud of you.

Cole knew his expression was one of a person taken off-guard. He said, Well, that's—kind of you to say.

Linda Hendon beamed. Let me call Alyse, she offered. She picked up a telephone, pushed a button, waited a moment, then said, They're here.

Through the window behind the checkout counter, Cole saw a trim, blonde woman step out from a cubicle, saw her pause to look through the window, saw a smile leap into her face, could read his name on her lips: Cole.

Her embrace was warm, strong. She told him in a happy voice that she was glad to see him, and then she stepped back, inspected him, and said, You're as handsome as ever, Cole. You look wonderful. We've missed you. It's been far too long.

I'm glad to know you still have kindness in you, Cole replied. No one's called me handsome since I was twenty years old, and if I recall that occasion, it turned out she was ridiculing me, only I didn't know it.

Art laughed. Hey, you've still got some hair, he said. That's more than some of us can say.

Both of you, hush, Alyse commanded playfully. There won't be any talk about age, not around me. I have to live with that awful fact every minute of the day.

I think you're as beautiful as you were when you were a teenager, Cole told her, and, to him, it was not a lie. The age-lines of her face were gracefully placed, as though an artist had put them on her. Her eyes were bright, the green of their color soft against her skin. She had the look of serenity.

Stop it, Cole, she said giddily. You're going to make me blush. She turned to Art. Did you show him? she asked.

Not yet. Not without you, he said.

Show me what? Cole asked.

Follow me, Alyse said.

She turned and walked into the main room of the library, to an impressive waist-high mahogany table, up-tilted slightly in the back, and glass-covered. She stood to one side, but said nothing. Art stood beside her, a grin lodged on his face.

Cole stepped close to the table. He saw a thin plate of brass attached to the back of the table. Engraved in it was: *In Honor of Dr. Cole Bishop, One of Our Own.* Under the glass top, resting on velvet the color of dark purple, was a copy of *Briar Patch*, and beside it were copies of his three chapbook volumes of poetry. A card, written in calligraphy, read:

> *These Documents are Placed*
> *Here in Honor of*
> *Dr. Cole Bishop,*
> *A Native of Overton County,*
> *Whose Writings Remind*
> *All of Us that Our Heritage*
> *Is Worthy of*
> *Celebration*

He stood at the table, staring at the display. After a moment, Art said, What do you think?

I'm stunned, Cole whispered. He turned to look at Alyse and Art. But, why?

Because, Cole, we wanted to do it, Alyse said softly. That's reason enough.

How long—?

Has it been here? Alyse asked. Since yesterday. That's when Art finished it. We set it up last night, after the library closed.

Cole blinked in disbelief. He said to Art, You made this?

I'm a carpenter, Cole, he replied proudly. Sure I made it. Been working on it since January. He reached out to touch the table. Pretty good job, if you'll forgive the bragging. Best piece of furniture I ever made.

It's remarkable, Cole said. Beautiful. Amy told me you were a good builder, but she didn't say anything about this kind of work. By the way, does she know about this?

She should, Alyse said. She made Jake find the wood and she gave us a new set of books. We have some, but we wanted them to stay on the shelves. I talked to her about an hour ago, and she told me she'd left you with Art. We wanted her to be here when you saw it, but she insisted that we do it this way. She said she'd come back with you tonight, after Jake got home.

I don't know what to say, Cole said quietly. I really don't. Thank you. Like I said, I'm stunned.

All right, enough of that, Art said. I'm hungry. Let's go to lunch, all of us. Alyse?

I'd love to, she replied. Where?

Corner Café, if that's all right, Art said.

It's still in business? Cole asked with surprise.

Still there, Art told him. Naturally, it's changed hands a few times over the years—even had a Chinese couple running it for a while—but nobody ever changed the name, or much of the menu, or anything else about it for that matter. Guess they all figured it was what people were used to.

Art's description of the Corner Café had not been exaggerated. In Cole's memory, it was the same as it had been in his boyhood—the same tables, the same oilcloth table coverings, the same food offerings with the same boiling-grease odor. They took a table in the back—to keep from being interrupted, as Art called it, though people did wander to the table, recognizing Art or Alyse. Some of them Cole had known from high school—Zack Morris, Ike McLanahan, Phil Woods—yet would not have recognized them without reminders. He was greeted politely, asked expected questions about where he lived and what he did, was left by each with the same rote expression: Good to see you.

He did not explain it to Alyse or Art, but he ordered country-fried steak and green beans and mashed potatoes, a side salad with French dressing—though he no longer liked it—and iced tea with sugar. He also asked for blackberry cobbler, but the waitress—whose name was Beth, not Frankie—informed him they did not have cobbler. Too bad, he said. I really had a taste for it.

He was sure Marie would have been pleased.

The lunch was spent in talk, not of their high school years, but of their families, or of Alyse's and Art's families. Alyse displayed photographs of her grandchildren, told grandmotherly stories of affection that had left her in awe. Her face was radiant in the telling, her voice soft. Art did not try to match her and Cole thought of it as a gentlemanly deference. His own descriptions of his grandchildren were humorous—how they conned him, how he was headed for poverty because of them.

You're a soft-touch, Alyse teased.

I'm a sucker, Art countered in his good-natured way. Then, with a smile: It's God's way of keeping me straight.

You never had children, did you, Cole? Alyse asked gently.

No, I didn't, Cole said. My wife—my ex-wife—wasn't overly fond of them, but I didn't know that when we married. It's one of the things I regret, especially since I spend my time with young people who still have a lot of baby in them.

Then they're your children, Alyse suggested.

You sound like my sisters, Cole replied.

They're right, Alyse said. I feel the same way with kids that come into the library. A lot of them don't have great homes and it makes me feel good to know I might be helping some of them. I think that keeps me young.

Cole smiled obligatorily. Fifty years earlier, Marie Fitzpatrick had tried to help four black children and the town of Overton had bristled at a perceived offense. Six years later, he had been photographed holding a murdered black girl at a civil rights protest, and a black woman's home in Overton had been burned, leaving one of her children with the badge of scars. Now it was different. The change that Marie had prophesied had taken place. On the surface at least.

Did you bring anything for the reunion display? asked Alyse.

My old football jacket, Cole told her. I don't know why I even kept it all these years, but I did.

So did I, Art said, and he laughed easily. Of course, I couldn't put it on with a shoehorn.

It's going to be fun, Alyse said. We've had a good response.

At least we won't need chaperones, Art added. But if Sally does show up, I may need the sheriff for protection.

You will behave yourself, Art Crews, Alyse said. I'm sure Sally will be fine.

Art made a mugging, comical face.

And then Alyse said, I'm sorry you couldn't find Marie, Cole. I wish she could be here. A lot of us owe her an apology.

For what? Cole asked.

For being wrong, Alyse answered.

TWENTY

In the afternoon, he took his nap as he had teased he would do. It was not that he was tired; he simply needed to close his eyes and consider the happenings of the day and, in so doing, he slept. In his dream, he was in Vermont, walking in the woods with Dexter Williams, going tree to tree to inspect sap buckets hanging from maples. The air was cold, making puffs of their breathing. When he awoke, he would remember only one sentence from Dexter: It's a good year.

It was a habit—or a disease—of his profession that he put stock in dreams, or in off-center remarks he heard eavesdropping on conversations. If metaphor was the heartbeat of literary interpretation—even if the writer had no sense of its meaning—then metaphor, stretched to its limits, could be anywhere. Dexter Williams saying it was a good year was, to Cole, a possible sign that his trip to Overton had been the right thing for him, a good decision in a good year. Being with Amy and with Art and with Alyse had helped to bridge the incomprehensible distance of fifty years, and the crossing of that bridge had not been as dangerous as he had feared. He had expected awkwardness in seeing Art and apprehension upon entering the city limits of Overton, yet both experiences had been good ones for the most part. The few moments of uncertainty, of anxious memories, had not lingered. Seeing Sidney Witherspoon was part of it, he believed. Also the library display of his work, which had taken him by surprise. Amy had been giddy about it, confessing she had spent days reminding herself not to give it away, but was afraid it might have been telegraphed in her mannerisms. We're going to see it tonight, after dinner, she had declared, adding that she wanted Jake to be with them. He bought the wood, so he has a right, she had added. And I think he's been more excited about it than I have. He's always bragging on you to somebody.

All in all, a good day, he thought. A good day in a good year.

Before he left his room to join Amy on the patio in her wait for Jake, he opened his laptop, coded in the access number of his internet account, and checked his emails. One was from Tanya:

Are you still alive? I've been expecting to hear something from you. Are you writing? Let me know something so I can sleep without worry. Give my love to Amy. Tell her I tried her recipe for smoked salmon and it was delicious. Mark wants to divorce me and marry her. I told him he'd have to move to Georgia, and that took the air out of his balloon. It's a sad state, Cole, when a man cares more about smoked salmon than sex.

The message caused him to smile. He touched the reply icon and wrote:

I'm fine. The weather is a little sticky for me, and it's only April, but otherwise I'm doing well. Many things to share with you when I return. Not much in the way of writing. Don't think I really need it now. And leave your husband alone. The truth is, good smoked salmon is very much the equal of sex as I remember it. Of course, good smoked salmon is not as complicated.

                              ❧

Cole had always liked his brother-in-law. Jake Gleason was animated and loud and happy-spirited, not at all the image of a successful financial officer for a large chain of grocery stores before his retirement, renowned enough in his field still to be sought as an advisor. In his early seventies—two years younger than Amy—he had a robust, healthy look, one that fooled people trying to guess his age. He attributed it to daily workouts and to avoiding alcohol and most fried food. His only frowned-upon pleasure—Amy doing the frowning—was two good cigars a day.

Their dinner had a party atmosphere, as always, with Jake offering exaggerated stories of his misadventures while traveling. Having him in the house was like having joyful music played at full-volume.

After eating, they drove into Overton, to the library, with Jake attempting to calm Amy's sudden irritation over the city not making a big to-do over the display. It was Jake's contention that no one on the city council read anything. What did you expect of them? he asked. To Cole, Jake was likely right. He also realized that few people in Overton even knew of his work, and that, too, was understandable. A scholarly book and three volumes of poetry—poems he himself had not read in many years—did not have the same public appeal of a good John Grisham novel, not even to him.

I'm glad nothing was made of it, he said. I like it being this way.

To Cole's surprise and Amy's relief, they had been wrong about the response to the display. A small crowd of people had gathered in the front of the library—Alyse and Art and a few members of the Friends of the Library organization, and a young man with a just-out-of-college appearance who was editor of the *Overton Weekly Press*. His name was Josh Richardson. He carried with him a digital camera with large zoom lenses. I hope you don't mind some pictures, Dr. Bishop, he said. I'd like them for next week's edition.

I hope it's better than the last one they had of you, Amy whispered.

There was no formal program for the introduction of the display other than Alyse's welcome, a bubbly recitation of Cole's academic accomplishments, with a personal memory of his leadership at Overton High School. She called him an inspiration, asked if he would say a few words.

Very few, he said, and a ripple of laughter rose from the gathering. Then he added: This is an honor I shall always cherish. I've spent some time thinking about it this afternoon and it still astonishes me, and I want each of you to know it touches me deeply. I regret only that my parents and my brother, Toby, are not here to share in the knowledge of this occasion. I believe they would have been pleased to know that the aggravating child they knew and tolerated, had, in some small way, amounted to something. I will return to my teaching position in Vermont with renewed vigor because you have expressed your caring. Thank you for that extraordinary gift. As to the display, I am shocked that my sister, Amy, could keep it secret from me, and the same goes for my sister,

Rachel, who knew of it, but, unfortunately, lives in Virginia and could not be here tonight. I am amazed by its beauty, and I am especially pleased to know the construction of it was done by my boyhood friend, Art Crews. He paused, looked at Art, smiled. I had no idea he was an artist. It's certainly something he's discovered since our tragic days on the football field of Overton High School.

There was a cackle of laughter. The applause was generous.

The picture-making that followed amused Cole. He did not know how long Josh Richardson had been the do-all editor of the newspaper, but it was certainly long enough to have a grasp of the politics of such occasions: everyone needed to be included in one pose or another, regardless of their put-on protests.

It was during the picture-taking that a tall black man with a distinguished look entered the library. He wore a charcoal gray suit and dark blue tie. He had a slender face with a trimmed peppered-gray beard. And for a reason Cole did not understand, he knew immediately who the man was: Moses Elder. It was not a physical recognition, not wholly. If he had seen Moses Elder on a street in Raemar, or Atlanta, or anywhere else, he would not have known him. In Overton, he knew.

He heard Alyse say, Mayor, you made it, and he felt an involuntary twitch of surprise.

I'm sorry I'm late, Moses said softly. He approached Cole.

Mayor, this is Dr. Cole Bishop, Alyse said. Cole, this is our mayor, Moses Elder.

I know Dr. Bishop, Moses said. We met a long time ago. He extended his hand.

Mr. Mayor, it's good to see you again, Cole said, accepting the hand. Thank you for coming by.

I'm glad to be here, Moses said. He paused, then added, It's a special occasion.

I don't know if it is for the town, but it is for me, Cole told him.

We need a picture of the two of you, Alyse said excitedly. She turned to Josh Richardson. Josh? Can you get a picture?

Sure, Josh replied. Be happy to. He motioned for Cole and Moses to stand beside the display. Let's make it informal, he said. Just talk to one another and don't pay any attention to me.

I've read your book and your poems, Moses said to Cole as the flash from Josh Richardson's camera blinked over them. I enjoyed them.

Thank you, Cole replied. I'm afraid you're among the few to suffer through them.

Moses smiled. Didn't do any suffering, he said. He paused, let his face turn to the display, then added, We're proud to have this in our town.

Thank you, Cole said again.

One more, Josh Richardson called. He raised his camera, aimed it. The light flashed.

I wonder if you could spare a few minutes tomorrow, Cole said quietly. There's something I'd like to ask you.

I'd be happy to, Moses replied. Why don't you call me in the morning.

&

In his room, after late-night coffee with his sister and brother-in-law—the coffee being an excuse for Amy to critique the evening, or to gossip about it—he opened his briefcase and searched for the letter that had crowded his mind since seeing Moses Elder, a letter written in 1965. Finding it, he read:

Dear Cole,

I do not often make the mistake of telling anyone that I lived for a brief time in Georgia, simply because I have a reputation to protect and such an admission would cast serious doubt on my stability as a human being. Last night, I slipped and blurted it out to a nurse who has become a friend—in a healthy way, in case you wonder, and you probably do, being Southern. She was shocked. She wanted to know if I had had any black friends, and I told her about Jovita and Jovita's children. I also told her about Moses Elder, about how he had agreed to help me teach and how Jovita had stopped us, and it brought her to tears.

Normally, I despise weeping women, with their fragile hormonal imbalances and melodramatic psyches, but I was honestly impressed by my friend's heartache, and I had this creepy feeling that Moses was there, making it all happen. Do you believe such things are possible, Cole?

Please don't be angry, or jealous (well, jealous is all right), but you need to know that I also wrote to Moses after I left Overton. More than once. Unlike you, he did not answer my letters. Do you think the post office delivered them, or did they see my name and drop them into the trash can? Or was Moses afraid of them? I hope not. There was nothing in them that would cause trouble. All my letters were meant to encourage him, not at all like the letters you receive. With you, my purpose is ridicule because, of course, you deserve it.

No, you don't. You deserve my kindness. No, my friendship. No, my protection.

I wonder what happened to Moses. Jovita told me he wanted to be an undertaker, a job I could never do, regardless of how many bodies I will slice open in an operating room. I thought he should be a teacher, like you. He was smart, really smart. He told me he bought books whenever he had extra money. I asked him why he didn't go to the library. I will never forget his look, Cole; it was the perfect physical description of incredulity. He told me blacks were not permitted in the library.

Did you know that? Did you know the library was segregated? I didn't. I never thought about it. All the hours I spent in that pitiful place, I never saw a black person, yet it never occurred to me they were not welcome.

But I got around that. I used to check out books and give them to Moses to read. I think it terrified him, having something he wasn't supposed to have because his skin was black. He hid them in an old cloth bag.

I'm sorry. I shouldn't dump all this bitterness on you. I wonder about Moses. I think, someday, he will be a great man. Not famous like you, but a great man, and that is even better than fame. What else could we expect of a man raised from the dead?

But I also wonder about Jovita and Alfred and Seba and Sarah and Littlejohn.

I feel as though I deserted them.

As you deserted me.

But I really didn't need you, did I?

Still, I love you.

In a good way.

He put the letter away and went to bed, yet he did not sleep, not immediately. He thought of Moses Elder, of posing with Moses in the library, and he wondered if being there had been a bitter reminder for Moses. Once Moses had been a timid black boy in a white-ruled town. Now he was mayor of that town, serving his second term and, according to Amy, was highly respected, a man of shrew business acumen, a man of patience, possessing a talent for fairness. There were detractors, of course, Amy had admitted. A few hard-line racists who grumbled, but were kept in line by their own ignorance. Amy's take on the personality of Moses was telling. He was more of a loner than a mingler, but was respected by movers and shakers of both races and also by Hispanics who had moved into the community.

Art had attributed the acceptable integration of schools to football, and his point had merit on the person-to-person level, yet, according to Amy and Jake, it had been the fragile economy of the area that had elected Moses as mayor. Two companies—one manufacturing tools and another printing catalogues—were preparing to move to Overton. Part of the negotiation had been for assurances that equal opportunity for employment and equal representation in government would be in place. It was the reason the white city council of Overton had drafted Moses Elder to run for mayor, all members understanding he was not the kind of person to be a figurehead, a token. And he had not been; he had been a leader. The maneuver had worked.

Marie had been right: In his way, Moses Elder, raised from the dead as a child, had become a great man.

He wondered what had happened to the letters Marie had written to Moses, wondered if Moses had them locked away, as he had locked away his own letters from her.

His mind blinked suddenly, unexpectedly, to Tanya Berry and he could hear her advice commanding him: *Write to her.*

He rolled from his bed, turned on the nightlight on the bedside table. Then he took his laptop and opened it and keyed in a new folder, and he began to write:

Dear Marie,

I have great news to share with you: Moses Elder is now the mayor of Overton, and no crosses are being burned in his front yard. From what I am told—by my sister Amy and her husband (Jake)—he is revered for his role in keeping the town alive.

Tonight, I was with him. You will find this humorous, but the library has a display of my writing, and he appeared at the presentation. Tomorrow, I am going to spend some time with him, but you should not worry; I won't talk about you unless he offers your name. However, if it does happen, and if the opportunity to work it into the conversation presents itself, I will ask him about the letters you wrote to him. After all this time, perhaps he will be willing to tell me why he never answered them. (And, no, it isn't wholly an altruistic act to assist you in solving a mystery; I am personally curious.)

It is strange being here, having been away for so many years. I see the changes you predicted, subtle on the surface, but coming from deep roiling. Today, at lunch in the Corner Café, I saw blacks and whites eating together comfortably at the same table and it occurred to me that fifty years ago, such an act would have had bricks flying through the windows. Remember when blacks were not permitted to enter the front door of Bell's Drugstore, but had to use a side entrance? Now, there is no evidence—outwardly, I mean—of such meanness.

I thought of all of this at the library with Moses. I remembered your letter about the library being segregated (I have it with me—all of your letters, in fact) and I read it again. It stuns me still that so little has been made of that sad reality in the telling of desegregation. It's as though libraries—the centerpieces of our cultural awareness—were provided immunity from criticism.

I've seen a few of our classmates, but would not have known any of them without introductions. The reverse is also true. It is so laughable, there is no embarrassment in laughing about it. Alyse (Lewis, now Pendleton) told me she was sorry you would not be here for the reunion. She said you were owed an apology, and I'm sure you can guess why—disdain for the prophet in his (or her) own land. Strange, isn't it? Time is, indeed, a great healer.

The reunion will be Saturday night at Kilmer's. Art Crews told me it had been closed for years, but one of the Kilmer children had it renovated and our reunion is the first public use of it. I believe it will be a nostalgic experience for me. I believe I will see you there as you were on our prom night, a dazzling beauty causing gasps of awe. I promise this: I will dance one dance with you, my arms and hands in the proper dance position, holding the memory of that night. I will not care if people stare at me. I now realize it is why I have returned to Overton: to dance with you.

I will write to you of all the goings-on, give you a gossip report. I think it will be memorable.

He typed his name—typed *Cole*—beneath the letter, coded the document to read *Marie: 4-15-05*, then pushed the save button and saw the letter disappear, replaced by an icon on his desktop. He opened a folder marked PERSONAL, and then he aimed the cursor at the *Marie: 4-15-05* icon, stabbed it with the cursor's arrow, like a spear fisherman stabbing a fish, and he drug it into a sub-folder titled LETTERS TO MARIE.

He closed his laptop and then took the prom night photograph from his briefcase and held it. A great aching ebbed against the wall of his chest.

When he did sleep, he dreamed of Marie.

They were sitting quietly in a library, facing one another across a table, each holding a book. In his dream, Cole could see himself as he was—a man in his late sixties, grey-bearded, slightly stooped, the finger-scratches of age showing on his face. He could see Marie only as Marie of the prom night, Marie of the photograph. Young, stunningly beautiful in her remarkable gown, the tiara she wore holding a silver light. She looked up from her book, smiled softly, whispered, I told you I would be beautiful.

TWENTY ONE

In 1995, Jack Alewine, on sabbatical from Upton University, had driven to Vermont to visit with Cole. One morning he had commandeered one of Cole's classes, telling outrageous tales about their undergraduate friendship. The students had been delighted. They had never encountered anyone as irreverent as Jack, and his playful attacks on Cole—saying he had been escorted out of the South by elite forces of the Ku Klux Klan for being both a pedophile and a womanizer—had produced such howls of laughter that professors in nearby classrooms had had to stop their lectures.

He also had told the story of a trick he and Cole had played on a young, pompous professor named Reed Fulmer. The trick involved a teenager who worked in a service station. Jack and Cole—Jack, mostly—had coaxed him into writing a poem about a flying squirrel, mimicking the style of Emily Dickinson. They had then presented the poem to Reed Fulmer, claiming it was a recent discovery among Dickinson's papers, and they had begged him to interpret it. Reed Fulmer had found it to be astonishingly profound—flying squirrels being the metaphor for angels—and had, in fact, written a lengthy paper in support of his interpretation. The teenage author had listened to the reading of the paper while sitting on a stack of used tires, enjoying a cigarette break. His response had been one of puzzlement: That poem ain't about nothing but a flying squirrel.

Cole had joined the laughter of his class, having forgot the episode, yet he had also marveled at how Jack had used it to make a point: you had to be careful with learning, or the truth could become obscured. He had watched the faces of the students in his class, how their faces had absorbed Jack's lesson, mesmerized by the power of his presence, by the magic of his spirit.

And he had realized on that day what it meant to him to be in the classroom as a teacher.

He had always had a romantic vision about the campus of a college or university. For him, it was where life bristled, where men and women broke through the last transparent membrane of their childhood and realized they had a right to be themselves. It was like colorful photographs of swimmers springing up from the bottom of a pool, pushing off on one strong leg, splitting the water, a launched human missile breaking the glass of the surface, erupting up, up, with curls of water spilling away. He liked the faces of those swimmers, swallowing air with open, glad mouths, their eyes shining in the rinse of the water. Walking across the campus of a college or university, he had always looked for those faces, and he had always seen them. It was his blind spot that he did not see the dissidents or the apathetic or the angry or the drug-takers—the misfits he heard about constantly from colleagues. He saw only the hopeful, even in those who had the look of a misfit. He had friends who thought he was humorous. They called him a fossil, a card-carrying member of the Era of Ozzie and Harriet. They accused him of taking a detour in the late fifties, of wandering into some valley of illusion and never finding his way back into the flow of things. They told him he could not survive out of the classroom, where—they charged—he had formed himself into a protected being, like a god kneading its own image from a lump of clay, or from Silly Putty. They openly scoffed at him, saying he could not cope in the real world, the larger world, and he had wondered why they insisted on calling it a larger world. His answer to them had always been couched in a comeback intended to be forgiveably clever, but was honest: I pray you're right, if you're an example of what I would become in that larger world of yours.

And he had believed that Jack Alewine felt the same about the magic of colleges and universities.

For Cole, Jack's visit had always been a good memory. Coming shortly after his divorce, it had been a way for Cole to reconnect with his history and he had reasoned it was why Jack had made the long drive from Atlanta: to be a comforter-friend.

It had been the opposite: it was Jack who needed the comforting.

On the night before he was scheduled to leave for Atlanta, Jack had become inebriated and the anxieties he carried like a disease had spilled from him in melancholy and in fear.

Three years ago, I was considered the best goddamn teacher they had, he had lamented. I had more testimonial letters coming in than Billy Graham gets. But that's changed, Cole. It's not like an English department anymore, not to me. It's like a corporation, with witty little clichés plastered to the bathroom walls to bolster morale. But they've got it all wrong, Cole. The reason morale suffers in the first place is the insane list of policies and procedures that spell out everything from when to say good morning to when to take a leak. I swear it started with Moses leading the Jews out of Egypt. Had to have a law a minute just to keep that unruly herd on the march, and God didn't mean it that way, Cole. He meant to have some spirit in things. Spirit, Cole. That's what I've lost.

His breathing had been labored and a bead of perspiration had lined a furrow on his forehead. He had pulled a cigarette from his shirt pocket and rolled it in his fingers.

Maybe you should use this sabbatical for doing nothing more than getting away from everything, Cole had suggested.

Jack had looked up, his eyes red. Get away from it? he had said irritably. Does that work?

I'm not sure I'm the right person to ask, Cole had replied.

Of course you are. You're the perfect person. You got away, Jack had countered. Why do you think I came up here? I wanted to see if you'd found Camelot.

Cole had laughed easily. Camelot? he had said. I thought Camelot was at Upton. That's what Wade Hart used to call it.

For a moment, Jack had looked away, shaking his head, and then he had turned back to Cole. Do you have any idea what's going on in your beloved Southland? he had asked softly. My God, Cole, we're as polarized now as we were forty years ago, maybe more so. In a lot of ways we are, ways we never thought about.

I don't believe that, Cole had said.

Of course you don't. Up here you wouldn't see it , Jack had argued. There's a mood, Cole, a bad one. I see it all the time, especially in young white students, kids that grew up in integration. They leave the comforts of home and suddenly find themselves face-to-face with what they consider indignant bitching. It's that whole ridculous retribution argument, and God knows, maybe there's a point in some of that chest-beating rhetoric for everybody, but these white kids don't have the foggiest idea what they're talking about. All they know is that blacks seem to separate themselves and get away with it. Do you think a White Student Coalition would last five minutes at Upton? No way, Brer Rabbit. No way. But we've got a Black Student Coalition. Can you imagine White History Month? Or, for that matter, Red History Month or Yellow History Month? Not a chance. So what happens? Everybody gets pissed off, but they're far too politically correct to say anything about it. But the fact is, all that building resentment is hurting blacks a lot and they don't seem to know it.

He had wiggled from his chair and begun pacing, waving his cigarette like a wand.

The worse word in the world is *nigger*, he had said in a low voice. God, what an awful word. Worse than spic or kite or wop. Worse than fag. And it's too damn bad the slang destroyed a beautiful word: Negro. Listen to how it sounds, Cole. *Neee-gro.* I like Negro better than black, and I despise African-American. That, to me, is posturing. It's like Irish-American, or Italian-American or Spanish-American or Polish-American. Damn it, American is the word. He had paused, fighting for breath, then had continued. I mean it, Cole: Negro is a great word. Did you ever hear King say it? *Neee-gro.* It'd bring shivers down the spine the way he rolled it out. It wasn't a word with him, Cole, it was a pronouncement. *Neee-gro.* It's a majestic word, a poetic word, a much better word than Caucasian. Caucasian sounds like a Japanese car, or some medical procedure they perform only on women.

He had sucked from the unlit cigarette and had blown imaginary smoke from his mouth. Here's what I think, he had said. If you're a minority, and I don't care what it happens to be—black, Indian, Asian, Hispanic, harelip, amputee, drunk, whore, teacher—you're going to get shit on by somebody, even from the people who claim to be helping you. You can stand around screaming about it, but if you've got just a little bit of sense, you're going to dodge all the droppings you can.

You really believe that? Cole had asked.

Cole, I know it, he had answered quietly. That's what's been wrong with me, old friend. I'm a worthless minority with the profile of a gnat's tiny ass, and I haven't learned how to live with that sad fact, or with the sadder fact that I could scream until hell freezes over, and nobody will ever listen. And if you take a good look at me, you'll see that I'm covered in bureaucratic diarrhea.

He had looked at Cole, had smiled a nervous smile, and then he added, I've got to learn to start dodging.

Jack Alewine had died of a heart attack in his classroom at Upton University in 1998. The students who witnessed it said he paused in mid-sentence of his lecture, said the expression on his face was the expression of someone who has had a sudden, jolting realization. They said he touched his chest lightly, smiled at them, and then reached into his pocket and pulled out a package of cigarettes. He staggered to a wastebasket beside his desk, dropped the cigarettes into it, touched his chest again, mumbled, "Damn," and then he fell dead.

 махм

He had awakened with the memory of Jack, not understanding why it was there, yet accepting it, and the memory had stayed with him like a sticky aura through breakfast with Amy and Jake, and was still with him on his drive into Overton to see Moses Elder. Age, he reasoned. Hearing of so many who had died, and sensing that each had claimed part of him to take as a souvenir on their journey to the Great Out There, as Marie Fitzpatrick had mockingly called the mystery of death.

Tanya Berry had cautioned him about confronting memory long put-away. She had said the mind held memory like microscopic seeds, and he had found her description of it to be true—a random thought springing up, growing in the rapid blinking of time-lapse photograph, until the seeds became a garden.

His memory of being a student was part of the garden. He had loved that pretentious, skittish period of his life, when liberation was as cherished as education. He had belonged to a generaion addicted to liberation, a generation peeling away at bigotry like the stripping of dead, sunbaked skin. All of them—himself, Jack Alewine, Wade Hart, Marian Shinholster, Henry Fain, and all the others—had hypnotized themselves with the drone of their own rhetoric, and had adjusted their blinders to shut out anything that seemed, to them, unnecessary complaint. They had imagined themselves to be the most sophisticated, the most patient, the most righteous human beings who had ever lived, and, yet, they had been incredibly unprepared for experiences that would explode around them like miniature home wars. There was only one thing about them that had been truly commendable: *They believed.* And the world—for the sake of its quintessential humanity, if for no other reason—desperately needed believers.

The thin, fragile face of Henry Fain bloomed in his garden of memory.

Henry Fain had killed himself in 1967. Marian Shinholster had informed Cole of his death in a letter, saying that Henry had pinned to his shirt a page from a novel he was writing, and he had underlined one sentence:

He sucked the barrel of the pistol into his mouth, its cool steel on his tongue like a communion wafer, and then he pulled the trigger.

The underlined sentence had been a description of Henry's death, and his family had not understood it. He was demented, they had wailed. But Cole had understood, and he believed Marian also had understood: Henry Fain had been writing a paperback murder mystery; he was not writing of quintessential humanity.

៛

Higginbottom's Funeral Home was now Elder's Funeral Home. As a young man, Cole had driven past it many times and remembered it as a large, two-story house with a classic dignity, like an elderly lady posing in elderly clothing, still regal, still proud. Now it had a refurbished look with expanding wings. The paint of its siding was a gleaming white. A dozen cars, maybe more, were in the parking lot, suggesting to Cole that someone had died and family and friends had gathered for mourning.

He wondered if he would be intruding. He had called Moses Elder and Moses had set the time at ten o'clock and it was now ten. Still, he wondered. He did not want to interfer with the delicate negotiation of sadness.

Moses answered the door and dismissed Cole's concern. It's fine, he said. Everything I can do, I've done, and I've got good people. They know to handle things.

He led Cole to his upstairs office, a large room having large, yet simple furniture. A single, distinctive painting was hanging from one of the walls—a montage of people constructing buildings, from mud-and-grass huts to skyscrapers. The painting was rich, vivid, dramatic, its colors sizzling on the canvas. The people of the painting had proud, powerful faces. Their faces were looking up, toward roof lines that jutted into a milky blue sky off the border of the canvas. The people were black.

That's impressive, Cole said of the painting.

Moses smiled, invited Cole to sit in a leather armchair, asked if he would like coffee.

No, thank you, Cole told him.

Moses settled in a matching armchair facing Cole. His dark blue suit seemed tailored to the angular shape of his body and it occurred to Cole that he had the look of a model posing as a quiet, yet confident businessman, someone who knew answers before questions were asked.

It's good to have you back in town, he said to Cole. As I said last night, I liked your book—and the poetry. Wish I had the gift for putting words down on paper. I don't. I just like reading them.

I lean more to that preference myself, Cole replied. I always found reading to be a pleasure. Writing, for me, is labor. I wouldn't do it if it didn't come with the job. That young fellow who's the editor of the paper asked me last night if I'd wanted to be a writer when I was in high school. I told him it never entered my mind back then. He didn't seem to believe me.

Moses bobbed his head and the manner of it suggested to Cole that it was a habit, a wordless way of saying many things. He touched his hands together, fingertip to fingertip. There was something you wanted to ask me, he said calmly.

The comment surprised Cole, coming so directly, so quickly, into their exchange. He thought: Cut to the chase. And maybe that was the way of Moses, the reason he was successful; he did not become mired in babble. I do, he replied, but you might not want to address it. If you don't, I understand.

Moses said nothing. He made his head-bob.

Do you know who started the fire that burned Jovita's home? Cole asked.

Moses did not move in his chair. His eyes did not leave Cole's face. After a moment, he said, You sure you want to bring all that back up?

A long beat of silence held in the room. From below, there was a muted sound of weeping. It's personal, Cole told him. I have no wish to make anything public, but I hope you understand how that single incident has affected my life. I've carried a lot of guilt over it, and there's no reason to tell you why that's so; you know why.

Again, Moses offered his head-bob. I've learned it's sometimes best to let things lie where they fall, he said. There's been a lot of change since then.

It was a put-off remark and Cole knew it. Moses Elder did not want to pick at the scab of old wounds. It was better to talk about change.

Yes, Cole replied. Thank God. We were standing still fifty years ago. He paused, then added, I'm sorry. I've put you on the spot, and I didn't want to do that.

Moses blinked once, a slow blink showing relief. He said, That day you were here after his mama's house was set on fire, you wanted to see Littlejohn, but he was burned too bad. Would you still like to see him?

Cole had always had a haunting image of Littlejohn Curry after the fire—an image exaggerated by his sense of guilt. It was a face grotesquely scarred from seared skin, the burned side shrunk in size, leaving him with a hideous reminder of a night of terror. The image flashed again in his seeing before he replied, I would. I've often wondered about him.

He's managed, Moses said. Still lives in Milltown.

Milltown was both familiar and unrecognizable to Cole, the chilling, *déjà vu* sense of having been in a place never before visited. The neighborhood did not seem as congested as he remembered, leaving him to believe many of the homes had been bulldozed away, and the changes of the landscape were enough to confuse him. He could not remember where Jovita's house had been and had to ask Moses about it. Moses pointed to a spot between two homes, a narrow strip of land that had the look of a place where boys played their own version of baseball. It was there, he said. Took them a few years to clean it up, but they finally got around to it.

People still live here, I see, Cole said.

Mostly old people, Moses told him. Don't know what's going to happen when they die off, unless some young folks come in and try to fix things up. They do, they'd get what's standing at a good price. We been talking about it at the council. Some of the ladies want to turn it into a historic area, tying it in with the mills that used to be around here. They think they can get some federal funds for it. He paused. I hope it works out, he added, but there was no confidence for it in his voice.

What happened to Jovita and the rest of the family? Cole asked.

The explanation from Moses was brief: Jovita had died in the late 1990s, Albert was retired from the army and lived in Florida, Seba and Sarah, both married, lived in Atlanta with their families.

They come back once in a while to see Littlejohn, he said. They all wanted him to move in with them after their mother died, but he wouldn't. Said he would stay here where he felt comfortable.

What does he do for a living? Cole said.

A smile, barely visible, crossed Moses' face. He used to paint houses for Art Crews, he said softly, but he gave that up a few years ago when he hurt his back. You'll see what he's up to now, but he'll want you to keep it to yourself.

Sounds mysterious, Cole said.

I guess you could say it is, Moses replied.

There was nothing unusual about Littlejohn's Milltown home, other than an addition to the back of it that seemed out of place, seeing it from the street. Cole guessed it had been the doing of Jovita's away-children, an add-on to make things more comfortbable for their mother in her late life and when he asked about it, Moses confirmed the guess, saying it had been built by Art Crews, with no cost for labor, to honor all the years Littlejohn had worked with him. The sideboarding of the house was white, its trim forest green. Flowers bloomed in small islands of flower beds near neatly trimmed shrubbery crowding close to the house.

You sure it's all right to drop in on him? Cole asked quietly, hearing jitters in his voice.

I called him this morning to tell him I might be coming by with somebody, Moses said. Just didn't tell him who it was.

I doubt if he'll remember me, Cole suggested.

He will, Moses said confidently. But I guess I better tell you he still acts like a little boy sometimes, still gets excited. Some people just never grow up all the way.

He knocked on the door.

In a moment, the door opened and a small man, bent slightly forward at the shoulders, stood behind the archway, in the shadows of the room. He was dressed in brown work pants and a white oversized t-shirt displaying a picture of an eagle in flight. Underneath the eagle was the word *Soar*. He wore an Atlanta Braves baseball cap. The disfiguring of his face was noticeable, but not as severe as Cole had imagined. Where he had been burned had the look of thin, delicate paper that had been crinkled in a fist. Only his right ear was shocking to the sight. It was small, folded, discolored, more nub than ear. He offered a smile to Moses, a look of curiosity to Cole.

Littlejohn, you know this man, Moses said, but you haven't seen him in a few years.

Littlejohn did not respond. His gaze stayed on Cole.

This is Dr. Cole Bishop, Moses added. You remember him, don't you?

Littlejohn's eyes narrowed on Cole's face and the look of curiosity became confusion. Cole knew he was struggling to fit face with name.

Hello, Littlejohn, Cole said softly. But it's not Dr. Cole Bishop. It's just Cole.

Suddenly, a startled expression flashed in Littlejohn's face. He stepped back, lifted his hands, clapped them together once, like a boy catching a firefly. His mouth opened, but he did not speak.

Moses laughed softly. You remember, don't you?

The orange turtle, Littlejohn whispered in delight.

That's right, Cole said.

Littlejohn extended both hands to Cole and Cole received both.

I'm glad to see you, Cole said.

The orange turtle, Littlejohn said again, his voice rising in excitement. He added, Miss—Miss Marie.

Moses smiled, chuckled. I should have guessed, he said. Then, to Littlejohn: He wanted to know what you were doing. You want to show him?

Littlejohn nodded vigorously. He turned sprightly and began to rush-walk toward the back of the house. He pushed open a door to the add-on room and stepped inside. Cole and Moses followed.

The room was no longer used as living space, as it had been during the lifetime of Jovita; it was a gallery, its walls covered with paintings, majestically done. Landscapes and portraits in bold explosions of colors, as though the colors had muscle.

Cole was stunned. He stood in the doorway scanning the room, painting to painting. My God, he whispered. This is unbelievable.

Near him, Littlejohn giggled joyfully and rubbed his hands together.

That's what he does, Moses said. His sisters sell them in Atlanta. They tell me he's getting a name for himself.

Cole turned to Moses. The painting in your office? He did it?

Moses nodded.

Here, see this, Littlejohn said happily. He caught Cole by the arm and began to guide him across the room to the far wall.

Cole was not prepared for the painting.

It was a large portrait of Marie Fitzpatrick, shoulder-length. She was wearing her prom dress and Cole knew immediately that Littlejohn had taken the painting from the photograph of prom night made by George Fitzpatrick. Its likeness was startling, yet also different. The background was a faded blue, like morning sunlight on a cloudless day. Littlejohn had given her face a slight downward tilt, as though observing the world from some place private to her. Her eyes held a radiance not seen in the photograph. The expression on her face was an expression of tenderness, having the look of someone far older than the girl of the photograph.

Cole did not speak. He could feel the hard pumping of his heart, the welling of sadness.

It's Miss Marie, Littlejohn said, his voice having the glee of a child's voice.

Yes, I see, Cole whispered.

My mama had the picture, Littlejohn added. She said Miss Marie gave it to her.

It's—remarkable, Cole told him. He swallowed hard.

It's my favorite, Littlejohn said joyfully.

Mine, too, Moses said. Mine, too.

TWENTY TWO

The home Marie Fitzpatrick had lived in—the Bailey house on Church Street—was still standing, though part of its wraparound porch had been removed and replaced with what appeared to be a greenhouse room with panels of glass. The garage was still as it had been when Marie used it as a classroom, giving him the thought that there should be a plaque on it, one reading, *In this place, Overton County began to change.*

He let the words play again in his mind. No, he decided, the plaque should read, *In this place, the artist Littlejohn Curry received his first lessons from Marie Fitzpatrick.*

Such landscapes in history deserved to be marked, he thought.

He remembered a visit he had taken to Europe, a desultory driving tour through France and Germany and Austria, carefree and golden and enrapturing, and he remembered being fascinated by off-road gardens where wars had been fought and the blood of men had drained from curled, pained bodies and had congealed and blotted into the soil, turning it black. Flowers grew in rich, vivid colors in those gardens, fed by the blood-fertilizer of dead men. Small, bronze plaques told their stories of horror in postcard brevity and the messages were always the same, regardless of the language: *In this place history was planted and harvested.*

The garage of the Bailey house, the house where Marie Jean Fitzpatrick had lived for a year, needed such a proclamation.

He had parked his car on the street and had got out and was standing on the sidewalk, not far from the garage, when a woman—middle-aged, he guessed—came out of the house. Even from the distance, he could see a look of concern worm its way across her face, causing her mouth to tighten in a small O.

You looking for somebody? the woman asked suspiciously.

No, ma'am, he answered in a pleasant manner. I used to have a friend who lived here and I have some good memories of that time. I just stopped to see the place.

Who was it? the woman asked.

The Fitzpatrick family, he said. But I'm sure you wouldn't know of them. It was fifty years ago.

Never heard the name, the woman said, relaxing. She stepped off the porch to the yard. My husband and I have been living here for about fifteen years now. We bought the place from the Reinharts.

He offered a smile, said, And that's a name I don't know. A lot changes in fifty years.

You're welcome to see the place if you want to, said the woman.

No, that's all right, he told her. I was taking a little nostalgic drive through town and remembered it. I always thought it was the prettiest house in Overton.

The woman's face brightened. We think so, too. We're the Powells. I'm Linda. My husband's named Dewey. He's an accountant.

I'm Cole Bishop, he said. I grew up near here.

Bishop? Linda Powell replied. That name's familiar. Seems like I just saw it somewhere.

I have a sister who lives in Crossover, he said. But her married name is Gleason.

The library, she said suddenly. I saw it at the library this morning when I took back some books. That new display case they've got. You're that Cole Bishop?

I'm afraid I am, he admitted. I'm flattered by what they did.

Well, Mr. Bishop, I'm flattered to meet you, she chirped. I can't wait to tell Dewey that you have fond memories of our home. I'm sure he'd like to meet you.

That would be a pleasure, he said. Please give him my regards, and forgive me for intruding on your day. It was good meeting you.

You, too, Mr. Bishop, she said. I'm going to read your books soon.

He nodded, smiled, returned to his car and drove away. In the rearview mirror, he looked again at the garage and a thought came to him about the lettering on his imaginary plaque: *In this place, Cole Bishop became a different person.*

ಎ

That afternoon, in his room, he wrote another letter to Marie Fitzpatrick:

Dear Marie,

I did not know I would be writing to you again so soon, but to borrow from an overused Southern colloquialism, your ears must have been burning today.

In short, you were talked about, praised to the hilt, and there wasn't a word of exaggeration in any of it. Not much, at least. Not from my judgment.

This is what happened:

I wrote to you that I had plans to visit with Moses Elder. We went to see Littlejohn. Yes, Littlejohn. He still lives here, still in the Milltown area, and, Marie, you would be stunned, as I was, by what has happened to him. He has become an accomplished artist, gaining a considerable reputation in Atlanta, yet he prefers to stay in the background as a kind of happy recluse. From what I gather, he has a small circle of friends such as Moses, but I do not believe many people in Overton have any idea who he is, or what he does.

You would be in awe of his talent. His use of color would make you wonder if he dipped his brush in rainbows. I cannot describe his style because his style ranges from primitive to portrait. He is both miniaturist and mammothist (if there is such a word). He works with particle board and canvas, with tin cans and old tires. He is like the piano prodigy who can hear a tune—from Mozart to Madonna—and reproduce it instantly.

And here is the news that left me weak with wonder: he has a portrait of you. It was painted from the photograph taken of us by your father on prom night. I wept when I saw it. Not outwardly, not to show tears, but inwardly, where the aching resides. I would buy it from him if I thought he would sell it, but I know he will never part with it.

And we talked of you—Littlejohn, Moses, and I.

We sat for more than an hour and cobbled together fragments of our memory of you. Much of what we said was about the teaching. It is still vivid to Littlejohn, even as small as he was at the time. He called it the happiest period of his life, said he worshiped you. He loved telling the story of our prom-night visit to his home and of my tale about the orange turtle. Moses had never heard the story. He found it amusing.

I did not ask Moses about your letters. I decided against it. That's a private matter. Yet, I believe in my soul he still has them and I would guess he occasionally reads them—the way I read my letters from you. On impulse, or out of some need. One thing he said gave me an indication of it: "She was a force, one you could never quite get away from." The way he said it—gently—gave me the thought that he has been in love with you all these years, and there may be some truth in it. He has never married.

Don't you think that's a revealing statement, Marie? What he said about you being a force?

But, of course, it's true.

I did not tell them about writing to you yesterday. There are some things I am not prepared to share.

I do not think I will see Moses or Littlejohn again before I return to Vermont. We made no plans for it. Still, knowing how they have succeeded has been the best part of this journey into what I consider the lost years. Both are extraordinary men, in great part because of you.

Yes, you are a force.

One other thing: Moses told me that Julian Overstreet is dead. You remember him, don't you? He was the Overton policeman who stopped us that night we were leaving Jovita's home. He ran for county sheriff and was elected, but I suppose he never changed. Someone shot him one night as he was parked in his patrol car not far from Milltown. Moses said they never found the killer. The avenger in me—as benign as he is—would like to think Moses or Littlejohn did the deed, Godfather-style. Change, helped along.

It was a good day, Marie. A very good day. I feel at peace, yet it is not closure. A friend has taught me that closure is a poor description for settling with things. She calls it a beginning, and I think that is what is happening. Today, driving back to my homeplace—now Amy's home—I had a longing to be in Vermont. I am learning it is more than the location of my runaway; it is where I now belong.

The reunion looms, and as promised, I will write to you about it, which
will likely include a detailed account of my heroic act of survival.

ஒ

For dinner, Jake insisted on going to McDowell's Barbecue in
Crossover, swearing it featured the finest ribs not only in Georgia, or
the South, but the world. Finishes them off with orange juice and
honey, Jake said. Hard to imagine hog meat melting in your mouth
like cotton candy, but that's what it's like. You take one bite, Cole,
and you'll have everything you own in Vermont crated up and
shipped down here to you; you'll never go back.

Jake's boasting was closer to truth than fiction. The ribs were
tender, succulent, cooked to perfection, and the brunswick stew
served with them reminded Cole of the stew his mother had made on
the cold days of hog killing. Almost ceremonial, the hog killing—the
single shot in the head, the cut throat for the blood-letting, the
barrels of scalding water to peel off hair, the hoisting chain to pull the
hog up for eviscerating, the flashing knives, the cutting table, the
slabs of meat. As a boy, it had been one of his duties to keep the fire
burning under the large cast-iron pot for the rendering of lard, taken
from cubes of fat in the trimming of the meat. It had been a
fascinating thing, watching the pot fill with the soupy, tea-colored
liquid that would cool to a silky white. He had marveled at his
mother's timing in scooping the floating crackling out of the liquid
before it turned black. Nothing was as good-tasting as a thumb-sized
piece of crackling, still hot, and the crackling cornbread his mother
made from it would have caused war among gods.

He was overjoyed to find that McDowell's Barbecue also had
crackling cornbread.

Tell me if you've got anything in Vermont as good as this, Jake
crowed, making a smacking noise as he licked his fingers of the sweet
grease, causing Amy to roll her eyes in despair.

Well, we don't have this, Cole admitted.

Maybe you ought to franchise it, Jake suggested. Build a shack
on the side of the road up there, sell pork sandwiches, maybe boiled
peanuts. Have a NASCAR line of premiums. I've got a friend who

knows Jeff Gordon. Maybe he can get a few autographed posters. I hear they love that boy up north. He laughed heartily.

It was a comfortable dinner for Cole. The dining area of McDowell's was a single large room with long tables having centerpieces of paper towels, mild-to-hot sauce bottles, salt and pepper shakers, split-open loaves of white bread, paper cups holding plastic forks and knives and spoons. Its walls were decorated in farming implements going back a century, and it pleased Jake to tease Cole about them, asking, What was that? And that? And that?

Cole was surprised he knew the implements, or most of them at least. Plow points and singletrees and fenders, crosscut saws, augers, planes used for smoothing down wood, steelyards for weighing cotton, notched seed plates wrenched from the buckets of mule-drawn planters. Each had its history—*was* history. Each had been used by some person long dead, and in his way of letting imagination take over, Cole found himself fashioning fragments of stories of those people as he had done as a child, yet he did not share the stories. He was no longer a child: the jabberer had learned to stop his jabbering.

He also accepted that the stories dancing through his mind could not compete with Jake's glad ramblings. Jake seemed to know everyone in McDowell's, from server to customer, and corralled each with some rememebered something edged in humor. Cole was introduced, or re-introduced, to each person, with Jake repeating the same line: He's our *distant* relative, emphasizing the word distant, laughing each time over his cleverness.

It was a pleasing time that would be uncomfortably interrupted.

As they were finishing their dinner—a dessert of banana pudding—a man entered the dining room and the diners became suddenly quiet, even Jake. The man was large, had a rough look about it. His face was covered in an unkempt beard, gray-splotched, and his eyes had the bleary, dull expression of a heavy drinker. His clothing was dingy, the cap he wore, bearing the image of the Confederate flag, was oil stained.

He stood near the cash register, leaned one hand on the counter, and let his eyes sweep over the diners. A grin broke on his face, showing yellowed teeth. He said in a loud voice, Well, damn, people. What y'all looking at? He laughed, shifted his weight, turned to a woman who had appeared behind the counter. The woman was squat and heafty. She had an annoyed look in her face.

Don't go causing trouble, the woman warned.

The man laughed again and when he did, spittle flew from his mouth. I just come in to get me some supper, he said.

You can't eat in here, the woman told him. You been drinking. We told you about that. You want something, you got to take it with you, and you got to wait outside for it. We got families in here.

The man turned again to the diners. I reckon I know everybody in here almost, he said, grinning. His face scanned the room, stopped at Cole's table. Everybody except that fellow, he added. He took a step forward, his head cocked to one side. Who you got with you there, Jake?

Jake stood. His face was coloring with anger. He's my brother-in-law, he said, the merriment in his voice gone, command replacing it. Now, why don't you do like Caroline said and go on outside.

The man comically threw up his hands to feign fear, like a boxer backing away from assault, then he laughed again. He turned as though to leave, stopped abuptly, turned back. Brother-in-law? he said with curiosity. Cole Bishop? That's Cole? He leaned forward at his waist, peered at Cole. I'll be damned, he added. Cole, you old son of a bitch, it's me—Hugh. Hugh Cooper.

Cole stood slowly, hesitantly, knowing he was being watched. He said, Hello, Hugh.

Hugh hooted. Wouldn't of knowed you in a hundred years, Cole. You look like you got one foot in the grave and the other'n on a banana peel. How you doing, boy?

Well enough, I guess, Cole told him.

Last time I seen you, you was dating a colored girl, Hugh said in his loud voice. The grin across his face was deep and taunting.

Cole glanced at a black couple with three children sitting along the far wall. They were cowering, their arms embracing their children, protecting them.

Why don't we step outside and catch up on things, Cole suggested.

Hugh snickered. Word I heard, you married that girl and moved up north. That right?

No, Hugh, I just moved up north, that's all, Cole said. Come on, let's go outside and talk. He began to move toward Hugh.

Stay in here, Cole, warned Jake.

It's all right, Cole told him.

The grin fell from Hugh's face and a scowl replaced it. He said, Aw, shit, Cole, stay in here. I got nothing to say to you. You never was much of a white man anyhow, and I got to tell you, I don't waste my time on nigger-lovers. He let his face scan the diners, paused on the black couple with their three children. What you looking at, boy? he snarled.

The man began to rise from his seat. His wife reached to touch his arm and he sat again.

You better keep your ass right where it is, Hugh hissed.

And then a man—middle-aged, tall, his face red from kitchen heat—came from a door leading to the kitchen. He was wearing a stained apron bearing the face of a smiling pink pig and in his hands he had a baseball bat.

Hugh, get out of here, the man growled. He held the bat up in one hand.

What you gonna do, Judd? Hit me? Hugh said arrogantly.

You push me to it, you damn right I am, the man named Judd said. He stepped closer to Hugh. You get out of here right now, and don't you never let me see you come back through them doors. I've had all I'm gonna take off you. I opened this place for decent folks, not redneck drunks like you.

For a moment, Hugh did not move. He swiveled his face to Cole. I'll be seeing you later, he said in a low, threatening voice. Yessir, I'll be seeing you. He turned and jerked open the door and staggered outside, slamming the door viciously behind him.

The man named Judd turned to the diners. Sorry about that, folks, he said. We still got a few people around here that don't know when to let go of things. Hope y'all enjoy your supper. He forced a weak smile and went back into the kitchen.

Judd McDowell, Jake said to Cole. He owns the place. Used to be a state patrolman, and I guess Hugh remembered it. Otherwise, there's no telling what might have happened. He's got a mean streak in him that gets worse the older he gets. I'm surprised somebody hasn't killed him already.

Cole remembered the night of Hugh's touchdown, how Hugh had been surrounded by teammates and townspeople, by cheerleaders flinging their arms around his neck. On that night, he had been celebrated, his name shouted. On that night, he had been heroic.

I suppose the alcohol got to him, Cole said.

Something did, Jake replied. Then: Worries me, what he said about seeing you later.

Doesn't bother me, Cole said. I'll probably be gone before he sobers up.

Cole, that's the kind of man who doesn't get sober, Jake countered.

༄

The call from Alyse Pendleton came at ten o'clock on Saturday morning. She said, in a merry voice, that she was checking on him, making certain he had not developed a case of cold feet, and was still planning on being at the reunion.

I drove a long way to get here, he told her. Of course I'm going to be there.

You won't be as late as you were for the prom, I hope, she said.

Was I late for that?

You know you were.

My memory's feeble.

Don't pull that old-man act on me. You know what I'm talking about.

Okay, so we were a little late. Wasn't my doing.

She laughed. Oh, we all knew that, Cole.

Anything I can do in preparation? he asked.

Nothing, she replied. The decoration committee is probably already there. Do you remember Greer Maxey?

Greer Maxey? he said. I think so. She was shy, wasn't she?

That's Greer, or who she used to be. Didn't say a word in high school, but she's a dynamo now. Chatters all the time. She went to Georgia Tech and became an engineer. She and her husband moved back to Overton three or four years ago. Anyway, she's in charge of decorating. I told her just to make sure the jukebox was working.

So there's going to be dancing? he asked.

Of course, and you're my partner for the evening, she said brightly. Or did I fail to tell you that?

I don't remember, he answered. Along with being old, I'm hard of hearing.

Stop it, Cole.

Well, if I'm supposed to be your dance partner, it seems I should also be your escort, he said.

Why, Cole, are you asking me for a date? she teased.

I'm too old to date. I'm offering you a ride, he countered. You can think of me as your designated driver, which will leave you free to partake of the spiked punch. But if you have other arrangements, I understand.

Arrangements? What does that mean?

Maybe you already have transportation, he said. Maybe with Art.

Her laughter was sudden, joyful. That's funny. Me and Art Crews. That's really funny. I'm not sure his lady friend would appreciate that.

I forgot about her, he said. I haven't met her.

Well, you won't tonight, either, she replied. Art's coming solo. I just hope he avoids Sally. Oh, God, Cole, she looks hideous. She's overweight by forty pounds at least, her hair's bleached to the roots, and her face looks like it's been coated in wax, she's had so many lifts. I just hope she and Art stay away from one another. I don't want any trouble.

He thought of his encounter with Hugh Cooper. I ran into Hugh last night, he said, but I didn't ask him if he would be there.

I hope not, she replied firmly. Between the two of us, I didn't mail him an invitation. He's horrible. There's not a meaner man in north Georgia. It's sad what happened to him, but that's no excuse for treating people the way he does.

What do you mean? Cole asked.

You wouldn't have any reason to know, she said. He got married not long out of high school to Nancy White—something that started on our senior class trip—and she died a year or so later in childbirth.

So did the child. He never got over it. That's when his drinking started, and he's never stopped. It's a wonder he still has a liver.

In McDowell's, Hugh had had the wasted look of a wasted man. Hearing the reason, Cole felt a jab of sadness.

Six o'clock, Alyse said.

Six o'clock? he asked.

I expect you at my home at six o'clock. And don't be late. I do have to get there in time to check on things.

Look, I shouldn't have suggested driving you, he said. I know you've got a lot to do.

Cole, why do you think I called? she asked. Just don't expect me to look like Marie.

He thought of Littlejohn's painting of Marie. And don't expect me to look like Cary Grant, he said.

ॐ

The day was bright, warm, an outside kind of day. He volunteered to cut the lawn, but Amy adamantly refused to let him, saying he was not used to the heat. Besides, she added, that's Jake's job. He likes it.

Jake's older than I am, he protested.

Jake's never had a heart attack, she countered.

Jake's a damn slave, Jake said.

You wanted to take some pictures before you left, Amy reminded him. It's a perfect day for it.

And it was the way he spent the morning—walking the farm with his digital camera, taking the photographs he knew he would later print and place into an album to be displayed on the coffee table of his home in Vermont. He knew the album would seldom be viewed, even by himself. It was one of the deceptions people exercised—the pretending of never being far away from the place of their beginning. He knew many people in Raemar who had migrated from other regions of the nation, or from foreign countries, and had gradually reformed their lives, seldom speaking of their homeplaces. It was like a dimming of history.

He had been that way.

Gradually—day by day—he had found replacements in Vermont for everything that once had crowded his living. Places. People. Events. Gradually—day by day—he had reformed himself. Not consciously, still it had happened. Until the letter arrived from Alyse Pendleton announcing their reunion, his only powerful remaining attachment to the South had been his sisters.

The letter had changed things.

The letter had reminded him there were questions still needing answers.

He remembered the party for Grace Webster, and the game of fortunes. Grace's description of him had been: *The destination you seek is waiting for you at the start of your journey.*

And perhaps there had been accidental prophecy in the game.

❧

He dressed casually for the reunion, as Alyse had instructed him. No business suit, she had said. No wingtip shoes.

It's not a banker's convention, she had added. And it's not a funeral. So look relaxed and lively.

He wore light brown slacks, a blue oxford shirt with a crimson tie patterned with yellow dots, a dark tan jacket. His shoes were brown loafers.

Amy pronounced him presentable.

Don't stay out all night, she said.

Don't listen to the woman, Jake advised. Come on. I'll walk you out to the car.

Why? asked Amy.

I've got something to give him, Jake said, offering a grin.

What?

A condom, Jake said.

Oh, shit, Jake, Amy muttered. Then, to Cole: Have fun.

I hope there's some of that, Cole said.

Outside, at his car, Jake reached into his pocket and pulled out a small handgun. Take this, he said.

A gun? Cole asked, puzzled. Why do I need a gun?

I hope you don't, Jake said seriously. But I'd feel better if you had it. I don't trust Hugh Cooper.

I don't even know how to use one, Cole told him.

It's real simple, Jake said. You thumb back the hammer and pull the trigger. Take it, Cole. Put it under the car seat. Make me feel better, all right?

Cole did not want to have the weapon with him, but accepted it and pushed it underneath the front seat of his car, hoping it would not slide out in the presence of Alyse. He was uncomfortable, yet moved by his brother-in-law's concern.

One piece of advice, Jake added. Look around when you're outside.

Jake, do you know something I don't? Cole asked.

For a moment, Jake did not respond. Then he said, It's a feeling, Cole. Just a feeling. Truth is, that man scares the hell out of me.

I'll be careful, Cole promised.

And like Amy said, have fun.

Yeah, sure, Cole said. I think it's going to be low-key, just a group of aging teenagers trying to remember when they were the cock of the walk. It's my guess everyone will be worn out by nine o'clock.

Cole?

Yes.

I'm glad you came back for this, Jake said softly. Amy needed to see you, and I mean here, on this farm, not in Vermont.

It's been a good visit for me, too, Cole replied. I needed it more than I thought.

He had believed the reunion would be awkward and perhaps regrettable, yet, on the drive to Alyse Pendleton's home, he had a good feeling about it. It had been fifty years. There would be humor, and humor had a way of easing tension.

The handgun under his car seat would, one day, be part of that humor, he thought.

And if there wasn't enough humor to do the trick, he would resort to advice that his brother Toby had given him in his youth concerning moments of dread: All you got to do is put it in your mind that it's not gonna last forever. Just say to yourself that in twenty-four hours you'll be somewhere else, doing something else.

It was comforting advice.

In twenty-four hours he would be driving toward Vermont.

TWENTY THREE

Later, when it slipped into his thinking, he would remember the reunion as a night of disjointed scenes from an improvised drama, with players wandering aimlessly across the stage of Kilmer's Recreation Hall, stopping to say their made-up lines, then moving on.

Scenes dissolving into other scenes.

And there had been a rhythm to it, a kind of easy-dance rhythm. Or maybe it was the way he saw it in memory: in the trickery of slow-motion movement. The good of it and the bad of it.

Alyse. Alyse at her home. Alyse dressed in a lime green pants suit, with a simple white blouse, her hair having a new-blonde sheen, her makeup so subtle she did not appear to be wearing any, giving her the appearance of a mature Doris Day from a mature Doris Day movie. Alyse chattering happily, her energy at high-level, girlish.

Kilmer's Recreation Hall. Refurbished in such accuracy of detail, it was chilling to see, and he had thought of himself as being in a mystic story of science fiction travel, where a colony of ancients had been transported for the purpose of renewing their lives by selecting options not taken fifty years earlier.

The people there early, busy in preparation—Art and Greer and Connie Long and Caroline Scott and Leo Rankin and Charlie Slaughter—all in merry moods, all greeting him warmly, loudly, having some remembered nonsense to share.

The decorations. Streamers of twisted crepe-paper in school colors of purple and white. The display table of photographs and annuals and tattered football jackets and report cards and fashion from the period. Old newspapers offering the history of 1955—Eisenhower's heart attack, the boycott of city buses in Montgomery, Einstein's death, the Brooklyn Dodgers winning the World Series over the New York Yankees, four games to three.

The music from the jukebox. Old tunes salvaged from shelves of collectors, played softly for background, later turned up for dancing. *Rock around the Clock, The Yellow Rose of Texas, Sixteen Tons, Whatever Lola Wants, Ebb Tide, Stranger in Paradise, I Believe.* The old tunes had hypnotic power. The old tunes said, *Remember when, remember when, remember when...*

The arrival of the crowd. In groups, as couples, as individuals, gathering at the sign-in table, pinning big-print nametags on their clothing, making jest with one another, laughing over the way time had mistreated them with applications of wrinkles and heft. Old girlfriends having fun with old boyfriends, and vice versa, with their spouses looking on solemnly, squeamish about being there.

He would remember watching the gathering with the odd sensation of being suspended, floating ghost-like, and of thinking the room, itself, was crowded with ghosts—the youth of those who were there, the gray nothingness of those not there.

It had been a curious thing, the meeting of classmates last seen a half-century past. Some were standoffish, not knowing what to say to him. Others teased he had lost his Southern accent and probably his Southern heritage. Way it is when you stay around Yankees, they said behind grins. You start sounding like they do and nobody below the Mason-Dixon knows what you're saying.

There were pictures made of members of the football team—Corey and Lamar and Art and Cole and Vic Walton and Donny Cummings—all touching a football with the 1954 season record painted on it in white liquid shoe polish: 6-4.

It's a wonder we didn't get killed, Lamar had said, laughing. I still ache from it.

Art had talked again of the Hoo-Doo, Voo-Doo, demonstrating it, and his pantomime of the play attracted a half-circle of onlookers, amused by his histronics.

In his memory of the night, he would think of the aura of gentleness that seemed to cling to Art, an aura that not even Sally— as hideously overdressed as Alyse had predicted—could destroy. Art had simply nodded to her, the way a gentleman would greet a lady on a street, and then had turned away.

Cole had not been so fortunate.

Well, look who's here, Sally had said loudly. Big man on campus. You decide to see how the lowlife gets along without you, Cole?

He had refused the bait of argument, had said to her, How are you, Sally?

Better, now that I got rid of big Art, she had answered, smiling smugly. Wish my husband was here to piss him off, but he wouldn't come. Said he couldn't care less about anybody here.

Cole had smelled the scent of alcohol on her breath. He had returned her smile and walked away. She had laughed a cackling laugh behind his back.

Still, most of the exchanges had been friendly and he had been relieved. From the time he had received Alyse's letter of invitation, he had harbored uneasy feelings about how he would be received, believing there would be questions about Marie.

To his surprise, no one spoke her name. It was as though Marie Fitzpatrick had never existed.

He would remember the dinner—a buffet of surprisingly tasty offerings, far different than hundreds of occasions he had attended—and the discordant music of silverware clicking against plates, of glasses tapped in the ceremony of toasts, of the muted babble of voices colliding across tables, peels of laughter—bass to soprano—and, in the background, turned low, the jukebox music of another time.

And after the dinner, the formalities, Alyse presiding.

Self-introductions by each class member—who they were, where they lived, what they did, how many children, grandchildren. Art speaking for Sidney Witherspoon, saying that Sidney sent greetings. You ought to go by and see Sidney if you can, he added. Lamar standing, raising his tea glass, saying, To Sidney. Glasses lifted, Sidney's name echoed.

Prizes.

Stephen Willis with the most children—eight—and the most grandchildren—seventeen—awarded a blank photo album for his prolific accomplishment, and Lamar objecting, saying the committee should have been more generous, saying a vasectomy seemed more appropriate, and Stephen responding in a comic drawl, Been there, done that. Laughter exploding. Applause.

Deborah Clark traveling the longest distance to attend—from Bellingham, Washington—receiving a laminated map of the United States, with a drawn-on line from a red felt-tip marker streaking across the map to connect Overton to Bellingham. Deborah Clark, so different in appearance, there were doubters that she was who she said she was. Didn't have that chest in high school, Corey later confiding quietly among the men, taking a glance across the room—for safety-sake—at his once-pretty, now-pudgy wife. Lamar asking, How do you know? Corey answering, We went out a time or two. I just never talked about it.

Remembrances.

Art reciting names of the deceased—Wormy, Craig Gibson, Emily Murray, Oscar Thornton, Joyce Hill. Art asking for a pause of silence—a sacrifice of time offered by the living for those suspended in the eternity of death—and after the pause, Art saying, Dear God, thank you for accepting our friends and classmates into your kingdom. We remember them with love.

The prayer had impressed Cole with its simplicity.

The dance.

Love Is a Many-Splendored Thing, Alyse's choice for the lead-off tune.

Reluctant couples—men especially—moving like old people awakening from sleep, cautiously stretching muscles, and the humor of it lodged in grinning faces, in whispers, in feigned expressions of pain.

Alyse taking his hand, pulling him from his chair, directing him to the dance floor, her body fitting close to his body, close enough to cause a blush, and around them, the teasing:

Good moves, Cole.

Where's Corey? someone had asked, reminding everyone of the dances when Corey and Alyse were inseparable.

With his wife, Corey's once-pretty, now-pudgy wife had countered good-naturedly.

They're juveniles, Alyse had said to him. Don't listen.

I'm not, he had replied.

Did we ever dance when we were in high school? Alyse had asked.

I don't remember. Probably, he had answered.

I loved those days, she had said. I loved being young.

He would remember that she had placed her face against his shoulder and had whispered, I'm glad you're here.

And he would remember answering, Me, too.

He would remember the groupings, the women with the women, the men with the men—the women sharing photographs of children and grandchildren, the men swapping tales of their ailments, from enlarged prostates to arthritis. Standing among the men, he knew the tales were meant as a one-upmanship of humor, and if there had been a prize for it, Roger Carter would have won hands down with the accounting of his two-year-old heart surgery, describing how the doctors had instructed him to stay away from sexual activity until he could climb two flights of stairs. Roger saying, I got to where I could do that walking on my hands. All a man needs is a little motivation.

Roger's story had caused a smile, remembering his own doctor's advice about having sex after implanting the stent, his own doctor telling him, Just don't over-do it. He had been grateful the advice had been private and not offered in the presence of his sisters or Tanya Berry—especially Tanya.

He would remember how the smokers drifted outside to smoke, returning to the room with the lingering scent of cigarettes on their faces and clothing, the same as fifty years earlier.

Jukebox music played.

He had danced again with Alyse, and in his memory—as he had promised in his letter—once with Marie. The song was *I Believe.* Another dance was with Greer and another with Deborah Clark, who had seemed jittery and eager to leave, saying to him, I wish I hadn't come back. I don't remember anybody, and they don't remember me. I thought it would be different.

We're the strangers now, he had told her.

I was a stranger when I was here, she had said bitterly. I don't know why I thought time would change that.

And he would remember the assault of ugliness.

The door opening and Hugh Cooper stepping inside, dressed in his rough clothing, wearing his Confederate flag cap, a lopsided grin on his face, holding a bottle of bourbon in his hand.

The room falling suddenly silent. Only the music playing. *Ebb Tide.*

Well, goddamn, Hugh had said merrily.

Lamar, who was near the door, had stepped to Hugh, taking him by the arm, saying, Come on, Hugh, let's go outside.

Hugh had jerked away. You go, he had snapped. I just got here. He had turned to the staring, nervous crowd. Mailman must of lost my invite, he had said in a loud voice. Good thing I heard talk of it.

And then he had lifted his bottle high over his head, and had called out, Anybody want a little drink for old time's sake?

Come on, Hugh, put the bottle down, Lamar had said quietly. You're gonna scare people, acting like that.

Hugh's grin had stayed on his face. His eyes had wandered from Lamar to Art. There's Art, he had said. Hey, boy, how you doing? He had stepped back, a stumble step. Where's our quarterback? Where's Cole?

Cole would remember the quick touch of Alyse's hand on his arm, a warning, a begging.

I'm here, he had said.

Well, damn, Hugh had replied, laughing. Told you I'd be seeing you, didn't I?

You did, yes.

You got your colored girl with you?

He would remember the rush of anger, the hard heartstroke of it. He would remember pulling away from Alyse's hand and crossing the floor toward Hugh. He would remember the look of surprise that flickered in Hugh's face.

I have no idea what you're talking about, Hugh, he had said. But you seem determined to make an issue of it. If you've got something that upsets you about me, you and I should talk about it.

Hugh had shifted his weight for balance, narrowing his eyes on Cole. Everybody in here knows you a nigger-lover, he had said. We got the picture to prove it. Remember that, boy. We got the picture.

Cole would remember thinking of The Photograph, of the blood of Etta Hemsley dripping from his face. In her letter to him about the killing of Etta Hemsley, Marie had written, *There are still many things in your path, still many surprises, before this is finished.*

The finishing time had arrived, and he was calm in knowing it.

I'm know you've got it, he had said to Hugh, and he had heard exhuberance rising in his voice, the same exhuberance of being in a classroom. It used to bother me that it was such a big issue here, but now I'm glad it was. Everything I said about that day was true. I was just there, just watching. It was nothing more than that. I used to think it was the worse moment of my life—what happened there and what happened here. But, Hugh, the newspaper story Ben Colquitt wrote was wrong. It was wrong, and it was irresponsible. It caused a woman's house to be burned. It left her son with scars. And it caused me and my family a lot of pain. One story did that, Hugh. Yet, I would guess that almost everyone who read that story, believed it, and that includes a lot of people who are here tonight. I do understand it, though. I do. I've been hiding from it for years, but when I go home—back to Vermont—I'm going to have a copy of that photograph framed and I'm going to hang it in my bedroom. And when I look at it, Hugh, I'm going to think of you. I'm going to remember how wrong you are.

He had paused, waiting for a response, but no one had spoken. The grin in Hugh's face had curled to a snarl.

Then he had said, You remember Marie Fitzpatrick, don't you, Hugh?

Hugh had forced the grin to return. The Kotex Queen? he had said.

That's right, Cole replied. Remember what she said at our graduation? Look around you, Hugh. It's happened. All of it. That picture was just part of it.

Hugh had held his grin, had let his eyes wander over the crowd. She here? he asked.

No, Cole had answered. She couldn't make it.

What's she doing? Off somewhere teaching little niggers? Hugh had said smugly.

No, Hugh, Cole had replied after a moment. She's dead.

He would remember the ending of the reunion.

Lamar and Art leading Hugh away, outside, Art driving him home.

The silent wandering away of the crowd, some speaking to him, expressing regret over the way Hugh had behaved; most avoiding him, not knowing what to say.

The quiet ride to Alyse's home, and his understanding that she had questions to ask of Marie, yet was reluctant to ask them.

In her home, she had made coffee, had talked of Hugh, taking the blame on herself for what had happened.

I should have sent him an invitation, she had said. Maybe Art could have talked to him. Maybe he could have kept him sober for one night. It terrified me, seeing him like that. I had no idea what he would do. He's always got guns in his truck and from what I've heard, he brags about using them.

Cole had thought of Jake's handgun underneath the seat of his car and realized Jake had heard the same stories.

It's all right, Cole had told her. It was a good night. I'm glad I was here.

It'll be the talk of the town, she had said. In a week, there won't be a shred of truth to any of it.

At his leaving, standing at the door of her home, she said, Before you go, I want to know something.

What? he asked.

Do you remember our kiss?

He thought of his writing about the kiss.

Yes, he answered.

She smiled. I've thought about it since I got your letter that you'd be coming to the reunion. It's one of the best memories I have. If Corey and I hadn't made up the next day, I would have been following you around like a puppy, even with Marie occupying your life.

It's a good memory for me, too, he said.

She stepped close to him, embraced him, placed her head against his chest.

Do you know what I miss most about my husband? she said. I miss being touched. I miss the feel of someone holding me. She moved her face on his chest, and she laughed softly. I read in a magazine that senior citizens miss being touched more than anything in their life. It's what kills some of them. Not being touched. They die from need.

It makes some sense, he said quietly.

She tightened her embrace. I'm adding years right now, she said in whisper. She lifted her face to look at him. But I want a new memory. I want you to kiss me, Cole. Would you mind that? Would you mind kissing a senior citizen?

He did not answer. He leaned to her, touched her lips with his. Her hand moved to the back of his neck as it had fifty years earlier, pulling him to her, her fingers kneading him. Her mouth parted and her tongue touched his lips, moved between them. Her body shuddered against him. She held the kiss and he could feel a bloodrush surging in him. And then she pulled back, looked at him, moved her hand from his neck to touch his face.

I hope you don't regret that, she said.

No, he replied. No, I don't.

When are you leaving? she asked.

Tomorrow, he told her.

Do you mind if I write to you?

I'd like that, he said. I was going to ask the same question.

Will you tell me about Marie? Not now, but one day, she said.

He paused before answering: There's very little to tell. I never saw her after we were graduated. We corresponded occasionally, but that was all.

A smile crossed Alyse's face. I don't believe you, Cole, she said gently. If that were true, you would have told me about her death when I wrote to you. When a person can't admit someone has died, that person wants to hold on. Whatever your reason, it's fine with me. But I don't want to talk about that now. I just want you to know I've never forgotten her. What she said at our graduation changed my life. I knew she was right, but I was too afraid to admit it. I even have her speech in a vault at the library.

You do? he said in surprise. How?

Marilyn Pender gave it to me when I came to work at the library, she said. Marie left it on the podium that night and Marilyn took it. She said she thought it needed to be preserved for historical purposes.

He thought of the copy of the speech Marie had sent to him in one of her letters. He had read it many times, had marveled over her courage and wisdom. That Marilyn Pender had thought it important was, to him, stunning.

You're the only person I've ever told about it, Alyse said. Someday, I'm going to display it. Before they force me out at the library, I'm going to make it public again.

I think you should, he said quietly.

But I won't do it unless you're here to see it, she added.

I would like that, he said.

ða

It was late when he returned to his sister's home, and his sister and brother-in-law were asleep. He went quietly into his room and removed a remembered letter from his Marie collection, one dated June 10, 1963.

Dear Cole,

Last night I attended a lecture by a woman with the arrogant name of Ebony Neismith (a change from Sissy Williams). She's a black woman from Louisiana, and because of her name and because of my cynical nature, I half-suspected a comedy routine by someone who works strip joints for spending money, but I was wrong. She's a smart lady, Cole. She has her doctorate in philosophy and it's more than a piece of paper to her. She has spirit, a fire raging in her soul. She may be the only person I've ever met that I would gladly swap lives with, given the chance.

You know what she talked about, Cole? She talked about Tennessee Williams's play, "The Glass Menagerie," and, of course, I thought of my mother and of you. Do you remember how you used to scold me for making fun of my mother's love of the theater? The truth is, I was a little envious of her, I suppose, and I do remember being in awe of her when I saw her perform the role of Amanda in that play (I was very young, maybe twelve, but I never forgot it). It's a magical play, really, a little dated now, but still magical. Of all the lines in that play, it was Tom's closing monologue that got to me, Tom calling out to the memory of his sister, Laura, saying, "Blow out your candles, Laura. For nowadays, the world is lit by lightning...." You had no reason to know it, but that was the line that inspired the speech I made at our graduation, the speech that embarrassed you and my parents, and surely made me an enemy of the people.

And that was what Ebony Neismith talked about—that line. If she had been a real, pulpit, seminary-trained preacher, it would have been her scripture selection. Isn't that strange, Cole? Isn't it?

Her message? Wake up, people! The world's lit by lightning!

I think that line was written for you, Cole Bishop.

I look at the photograph of you holding Etta Hemsley and I can almost see the sky behind you streaked with lightning.

Do you know how that makes me feel?

It makes me want to be with you again—back then, I mean, back when we were the talk of the town, the main players in that sorry little melodrama of our youth, back before the lightning came flashing out of nowhere.

Blow out your candles, Cole.

For nowadays—well, you know, don't you? You've been struck by it.

TWENTY FOUR

On Sunday morning, Jake volunteered to cook breakfast, a Southern feast, he boasted. Spend time with your sister, he said to Cole. Tell her about last night. If you don't and you get away from here, she'll drive me crazy.

Cole's description of the evening was guarded. A good time, he said, keeping the details that Amy wanted to himself—particularly his time with Alyse Pendleton. It was enough to name names of people who had attended and to tell stories of innocence that had a hint of gossip about them. He did not say anything about Hugh Cooper's appearance, knowing Amy and Jake would learn of it soon enough.

The breakfast was as Jake had promised—French toast, eggs, bacon, sausage biscuits, milk gravy, orange juice, strong coffee. Artery-clogging, Jake declared proudly. Everything you don't need, but your soul begs for.

After breakfast, he put his belongings into his car with Jake's help, and he gave the handgun under his front seat back to Jake, saying, Glad I didn't need it.

Me, too, Jake told him. That son-of-a-bitch is walking trouble.

I hated to see him that way, Cole said. I remember him in a different light. In high school, he was a good friend, well-liked by everybody.

Things go sour for some people, I guess, Jake said. You can feel sorry for them, but that doesn't change the way they are. After a while, pity gets old.

It was, as Cole expected, a tearful leaving, the tears being Amy's. She again begged him to consider retirement and a move back to Georgia.

I'll think about it, he promised, knowing it was only a placating comment. In the poetic metaphor that Marie Fitzpatrick had discovered in Tennessee Williams' *The Glass Menagerie*, he had blown out the candles of his past, and that was enough. For him, the world lit by lightning was in the classrooms of Raemar University. He would stand in that electrified environment as long as possible.

The drive-away from the home of his childhood was melancholy, a sweet-sad sensation. He thought of his mother and father and of his brother, Toby. The land was infused with them, and the greening of spring resurrected them, gave them shape and form. He could hear the glad melodies of their voices, could see the waving of their hands from the arms of trees.

He wondered if he would ever again see his homeplace.

He passed the turnoff to Breedlove Cemetery and suddenly, inexplicably, he thought of the letter from Marie about going there on her only return to Overton. On impulse, he slowed his car to a stop and sat for a moment looking back through the rearview mirror at the cluster of trees covering the gravesites, then he pushed the gear handle to reverse, guiding his car back to the turnoff, and drove over the washed-down road leading to the trees.

He got out of his car and went into the cemetery and stood for a moment, remembering the sundown time with Marie Fitzpatrick on their first date and remembering also her letter about the cemetery being her favorite place in Overton.

And then he thought of a walk he had taken with his father through a similar cemetery when his father—playing to his imagination—had whispered that if he listened carefully, he could hear the voices of the dead seeping up from the ground. His father had said it was possible to feel the ground vibrating with their voices if you stopped and stood still. Absolutely still. Not-breathing still. And if you listened intently enough—put your ear to the ground—you could understand their words. There in Breedlove's Cemtery, he believed his father. He could hear voices. Plaintive, humming voices. And the earth—overgrown with weeds, the humps of burial mounds leveled by time—vibrated.

He thought of teaching Edgar Lee Masters's *Spoon River Anthology*, where voices of the dead told revealing, sometimes-desperate stories, and of Thornton Wilder's *Our Town*, where residents of the cemetery in Grover's Corner, New Hampshire, still offered opinions about the world around—and above—them.

In Vermont, near Raemar, was a cemetery having majestic tombstones. If he again taught *Spoon River Anthology*, he would have a session in that cemetery, he thought. He would ask his students to read the headstones and to create tales, fashioned in Masters' style, of those who had been buried there.

He turned to leave, then recognized the stone bearing the name of Daniel Breedlove, a name only faintly recognizable, a name worn away by rain and wind and mold. He kneeled to read its obscured epitaph: *N w esting on th bo om of od.*

He stood, stepped back, and then he saw it. At the foot of the grave of Daniel Breedlove, partly covered by the debris of leaves and grass, he saw a block of marble, no larger than the size of a shoebox.

The name chiseled into it was *Marie*.

ॐ

There was only one car in the parking lot of Elder's Funeral Home, giving it a look of abandonment. He knew, being Sunday, there was a chance no one was there, still he rang the doorbell and waited. After a few moments, he heard footsteps and then Moses Elder opened the door. He was dressed as Cole had seen him at the library and again on the visit with Littlejohn—a tailored suit, the ensemble of shirt and tie giving him a distinguished manner. A look of surprise rose in his face.

Dr. Bishop, he said.

It's Cole, Cole told him. Am I interrupting anything?

Not at all. No business today. I skipped church to do some book work, but that can wait, Moses replied.

Can we sit on the porch for a minute? Cole asked.

Of course, Moses said.

They took seats in rockers placed for mourners.

You headed back to Vermont? Moses asked.

Yes, Cole told him. Yes, I am.

Thought that's what you said the other day.

But I wanted to see you before I left.

What can I do for you? Moses asked.

Tell me about Marie, Cole said.

The expression on Moses' face did not change. He crossed one leg over his knee and folded his hands in his lap. What about her?

Her burial, Cole replied.

For a moment, Moses did not speak, or move. His gaze stayed on Cole's face, yet Cole could see his eyes go soft. You saw it? he said.

I did, Cole told him. I stopped by the cemetery on the way out. I haven't been there in a long time.

I should have told you.

I wish you had.

I thought it was too dangerous, Moses said quietly. Don't know if what I did was legal. You just can't bury people's ashes anywhere you want to.

But that's where she wanted to be, Cole said. Am I right?

Moses nodded his nod of habit. She had her ashes sent to me. Wanted to be put at the foot of the tombstone that had Daniel Breedlove's name on it. Said she wanted it to stay between us.

The stone?

I did that on my own, Moses confessed. Didn't seem right not having something.

Just her first name, though. Why that?

I thought her first name wouldn't say much, Moses answered. He paused. Except for you. I guess I knew there was a chance you'd find it. And I guess I hoped you would. Someday.

What about the letters she wrote to you? Cole asked.

I burned them, Moses replied.

Why?

Again there was a pause—long, heavy, holding grief. Finally, he said, You have to remember how it was fifty years ago. I'm black. Anybody found those letters, it would have been trouble for me.

Were they that personal?

Nothing more personal than telling me I was smart enough to get away from here, but it didn't matter. Her name was like poison in those days, Moses said. Mailman asked me about it one time. Wanted to know why I was getting letters from her. I told him she was writing something for her school about colored people.

But you never wrote to her, did you?

Once, but I didn't mail it, Moses admitted. Guess I didn't have the nerve. After a while, I quit hearing from her. Then she called me when she was dying, telling me what she wanted.

She disliked the South, Cole said. Did she say why she wanted her ashes to be buried here?

Moses smiled, a shadow of movement across his face. She told me this was where she learned the most about herself, and she guessed that's where her homegoing ought to be from. He paused, then added, That's what she called it: her homegoing.

Cole thought of Marie's fascination with the word. It was right for her.

She never knew about Jovita's house burning down, did she? Moses asked.

I'm sure she didn't, Cole said. She would have written to me about it, or she would have returned here with her own torch and she might have burned the town—fire for fire. It's part of the reason I didn't tell her. There was nothing she could have done other than make matters worse.

You probably right, Moses said.

The two men sat motionless, without speaking. A car rolled slowly along the street in front of the funeral home—an old car, having a rattling motor and a smoking contrail of exhaust, the oily scent of it drifting to the porch.

I know you don't want to answer and I won't ask you for a name, but you do know who started the fire, don't you? Cole asked.

Moses moved in his chair, rooting his shoulders into the slats. He again touched his fingertips together, licked his lips. I do, he said after a moment.

He got away with it, Cole said.

No, Moses said. No, he didn't. Truth is, he paid for it in a lot of ways. Still does, but it turned out all right for him and for a lot of other people. He's made his amends.

You sure you know the right person? asked Cole.

Moses dipped his head once. He came to me about it a few years ago, he answered. Said he needed to get it off his chest, or the weight of it was going to crush him.

A sudden chill struck Cole. He thought, My God: Art Crews. He could sense a wave of astonishment, of sadness, blink across his face. *Art.* He did not have to hear the name to know. It was a fit, all of it. It had to be Art. Art, acting impulsively, with the kind of temporary bravado that had existed in their youth, lashing out at something he did not understand. On the day of the visit with Sidney Witherspoon, Art had said, *I did a lot of things I need to atone for, a lot of things that rested heavy on my heart.* Chest-heavy, his mother had called such moments. With Art, the burning of Jovita's home would have been chest-heavy enough for him to make his confession, to do his deeds of redemption, to become the giver, the caretaker, the speaker of prayers.

Cole leaned his head against the back of the rocker and gazed at the tongue-and-groove ceiling above him, painted blue to keep away wasps. In a near-by tree, a mockingbird sang a spirited melody in a piercing soprano. The warmth of the day moved on a breeze and for a moment he believed he could smell the watery richness of a plowed field and could hear the clacking of his brother's tractor. Age, he thought. Age, mixing memory and imagination. Or maybe it was nothing more than being in the South, where memory and imagination were as similar as identical twins wearing matching outfits.

Before he left the reunion with Hugh, Art Crews had said to him, I'm sorry, Cole.

For what? Cole had asked.

For what we put you through, Art had replied with sadness.

Art, he thought again. *Art.*

He rocked forward and stood. I should be leaving, he said. I've got a long drive ahead of me.

I don't envy you, Moses told him, also standing.

Glad you were here this morning, Cole said. I appreciate all that you shared with me.

Moses again made his head-nod. He extended his hand and Cole accepted it.

I want to send some flowers here, to you, Cole said. Would you put them on her grave for me?

Be glad to, Moses said. He added, Hope we stay in touch.

We will, Cole promised. We will.

TWENTY FIVE

In 1975, he had received a letter from Marie, a ten-page diatribe about a suitor who had lied to her—*I never really liked the son of a bitch, Cole, but he had no right to lie to me.*—and he had responded in defense of the suitor, knowing that whoever he was, he would wither helplessly before the onslaught of Marie's vengeance.

He had suggested it was possible that psychologists had it wrong in their contention that truth relieved guilt and therefore set things right for victims of deceit. Truth, he had written, was a tricky thing. Truth could be more damaging than lying, if lying avoided hurting someone, or kept one from being hurt. Truth could never be absolute. It begged to be interpreted, to become perception. Truth was not entirely instinctive, he had written; lying was. Lying—gentle lying, at least—was elastic, flexible. It could be as soothing as a cooling skin creme. It forgave and kept alive dreams so cherished they were concealed secret into secret into secret, like extraordinary gifts wrapped box into box into box. If truth sets man free, he had pronounced in his advice to Marie, then lying—gentle lying—could help keep him free.

An irritated Marie had fired back a three-sentence reply: *The truth is this, Cole: What you wrote is pure bullshit. No lie. The son of a bitch is history—scalded history.*

Now, when he thought about it—when he took her letter from its safekeeping and again read her reply—he realized he had been writing about himself. He, too, had always been a liar—a gentle liar, he hoped, but still a liar.

He had lied to myself. He had lied to students who wanted to become grand writers, or teachers, but would not. He had lied to friends who unwrapped their dreams before him—secret from secret from secret—and asked in thin, hopeful voices, What do you think? He had lied to strangers who needed assurance. But he had not lied to hurt or to destroy. He had lied to see a flash of relief in eyes, to hear a sigh of worth in throats. To him, it had been a small compromise for people who would find surrender inviting. Henry Fain. If he could have been with Henry Fain, could have lied to him by praising his work, Henry Fain might still be alive. If he was wrong, then he was wrong.

Yet, he knew he was not alone.

Everyone on earth lied in some degree—great or small.

Moses Elder had lied.

Moses Elder had contended that his sole purpose in obeying Marie's deathwishes about her ashes being buried at the foot of the ancient grave of Daniel Breedlove, was professional.

Awkward, yes, but professional, a matter of business.

Cole knew there was more to it, could sense the cover-up of it in the way Moses had talked about Marie. Awe in his tone, a memory made gentle by time. He had said again—as he had said in Littlejohn Curry's home—that Marie was a force. Hard to say no to that woman, was his statement, offered with a head-shake signifying surrender. It was a gesture Cole had recognized, one he had used many times in his consideration of Marie.

Moses had talked of the day that he met with Marie and the Curry children in the garage of the rented house on Church Street.

Scared me to death, he had said, and he had recalled walking through the neighborhood to go to the house. Had remembered a white woman working in her yard glaring at him as he walked past her home. It was a glare he had never been able to dismiss—mean, arrogant, threatening.

Don't know to this day why I even went over there, he had admitted. There was just something about her.

What he did not say—the lie of it—was how profoundly Marie had affected him. Had hinted at it. Had said, Guess it was the first time I saw a white person caring about anybody with colored skin. It was a good lesson to learn.

And Marie had lied. Or had ranted to him out of habit. She had vowed never to return to Overton after her impulsive visit in 1976, yet she had willed her remains to be shipped to Moses Elder with instructions for him to put them in an urn and to then bury them in a forgotten, untended cemetery. She had chosen the land she ridiculed to be the land of her resting—if resting came with death.

Still, it did not matter. He knew where she was.

ॐ

Tanya was already seated in Arnie's Place of Gathering when he arrived, reading from a paperback book with the pretentious title of *Living a Life of Routine: How Habits Rule Us.* She quickly closed it.

So, she said. How are you?

Good, he told her. You?

Do you know we always use the same greeting for one another? she said.

He smiled, reached for the book, held it up. It's our routine.

She shrugged. All right, you caught me. But it's true. Sit down. I ordered coffee for you.

You always do, he said. You can't help it. Routine, you know.

That's enough, Cole, she said.

He sat across from her, picked up the cup of coffee still steaming in front of him, tasted it. Strong, good.

Did you do it? she asked. Did you finally finish? It's been long enough.

He handed her a manila envelope.

This is it?

He nodded.

Do you mind if I read it now?

I'd rather you wait, he said.

All right, she replied. Then: Are you really glad to be back?

I am, he told her. Yes.

I was afraid we'd lost you, she confessed.

And who would I have to irritate me if I'd stayed in Georgia? he teased.

Amy, she said.

Amy's a sister. Sisters are sweet, kind people. At least, mine are.

You're saying I'm not?

He laughed easily.

Mark wants to know if you'd like to go fishing with him this weekend, she said.

Sure, he replied. Are you going?

I don't do worms, she said. She smiled, added, Not those kind.

See? he countered. My sisters—my sweet, kind sisters—would never make such a remark. They're clean-minded, as all Southern ladies are.

Oh, now I understand, she said.

Understand what?

Why you're here, in Vermont, she replied. By your hypothesis, if Southern ladies are clean-minded, then Northern ladies—and that would include me—must be dirty-minded. Thus, I conclude you prefer the latter.

You've got me, he said.

Fine. At least we have an understanding and that could lead to almost anything, couldn't it?

He smiled, drank again from his coffee, then stood. I have to go, he said.

Where? she asked.

To my office, he answered. I'm working on a course on Edgar Lee Masters's *Spoon River Anthology*.

Good idea, she said. Maybe I'll audit it. Now get out of here. I want to read.

He stood for a moment without speaking, then said, When you read it, I want you to destroy it. I want you to destroy everything. And, Tanya, I don't think I want to talk about what I've just given you.

That's your choice, she told him.

I know, he said.

She watched through the window of Arnie's until she saw him drive away, and then she opened the envelope and began to read.

May 20, 2005, morning

There is, in my office, a magnificent new painting of an orange turtle. It was sent to me by Moses Elder as a gift from Littlejohn Curry. At my death, it is to be donated to the library of Overton, to hang with the display of Marie Fitzpatrick's graduation speech.

The painting is in my office because I want it to remind me of those gifts that may be slumbering in students who come to me for counsel, gifts that could be opened by a small tug of the bow that wraps them. I am also reminded of Marie when I look at it. And that is good, because Tanya was right in her disdain for the expression *closure.*

How can anyone have closure with someone who spent her life looking only for openings?

I realize now that I needed to write about those years and those experiences that fashioned my life, and I also needed the warm deception of writing to Marie again, as if I could put the letters into an envelope and send them to her. I do not know if the exercise of the writing was healing, but I do know it was revealing, and here is what I have learned from it: the good of living is in the sweetness of memory.

Here, then, is my last entry in what I have now named The Book of Marie.

Though I have been married and divorced, and was twice engaged before my marriage, and though I have a deep and joyful affection for the women who are my friends, I do not think I have ever truly loved any woman other than Marie Jean Fitzpatrick. To me, it is the great regret of my life that I never again saw her after we were graduated from Overton High School. We corresponded, yes. Years of letters, rushed off in frantic spurts of catch-up, separated by long, long gaps of time. I have never destroyed any of those letters. The last one I received was written in September of 1988. It came to me as a posthumous delivery. She had died of ovarian cancer. Among the papers left in her estate was the letter, composed in the last, narcotic-dull days of her life. It had been addressed to: *Cole Bishop, Town Talker.*

The letter read:

Dearest Cole Bishop,

Remember when I wrote to you about my life line? It was little more than a scratch, and now it has disappeared, vanished. Or maybe the scratch has healed. Still, I was right about my reading. Because you hold this letter, you will know that is true. I was also right about something else, something

I told you that last night we were together, swinging where first-graders played. I did regret not making love to you. We would have been wonderful lovers. In my fantasies, we have been. In my fantasies, you were both savage and gentle and our love sessions under quilts of dreams left my body exhausted and sore and my soul saturated with joy. Be careful without me, my dreamer, my famous friend. I love you. Whoever you were, whoever you are, whoever you will become, I love you. If I can, I will protect you from the other side. If I cannot—not knowing how willing they are to take instruction—I pray that your memory of me will ward off some pain.

Oh, yes, Cole.

We were wonderful. We really were.

I am tired now. I am so tired.

I beg of you one thing: Do not think of me in sorrow. Do not mourn. We had a grand, beautiful friendship, a friendship more wonderful than I ever expected or could ever imagine.

These are the last words I will ever put on paper.

I love you.

I wept for hours after reading the letter. I took the photograph of our night at the Junior-Senior Prom and propped it against a desk lamp and surrendered to my memory of us, and then I sat at my desk and tediously replied to her. It was the writing of a child laboring to find the right words to say the right thing, and now, when I read it, I see the excesses of it—the spilling-over of grief, words uncaged to fly about like freed canaries. Still, it is what I wrote and I will never edit it. When I finished it, I folded it into an envelope and put it away in a lining of my briefcase, where it has always remained.

These are the words of that letter:

Dear Marie,

You love me, you said. Whoever I was, whoever I am, whoever I am to become, you love me.

I should have written this years ago. Maybe you would not have worried so much. Maybe you would have understood me. Or maybe I would have understood myself.

I am a runaway, Marie. Child and man, I have always been a runaway.

I have run away to places you know nothing about—to Pilgrim's Ridge, to the Split Creek bottomlands, to the hay barn on the Grill place. I ran away to you, to college, to graduate school, to classrooms in South Carolina and Vermont. I ran away through inviting doors of books, traveled to lands as exotic as the names of their cities and their people. I have followed obediently—eagerly—the sweet, Circean song of words, surrendering myself to the sorcery of language welling up from alphabet-letter voices heard only by men and women who know the succor, and the torment, of isolating themselves in dreams.

I am a runaway, Marie.

But it is what I have always wanted to be.

When I was a child, I practiced transformations. I became what I read, what I heard from radio, what I saw at the movie theater. It was an easy trick. You saw me do it, ridiculed me for it. But it was easy. So easy. Strike the pose, speak the word, imagine, become.

I liked becoming, Marie. I still do.

I think it is why I teach. As a teacher, with a captive audience, I tell stories that other people—the men and women who isolate themselves in dreams—have created, and I become, by the power of wishing it, those intriguing adventurers—some bold, some fragile—who rise up from turning pages like resurrected bodies. I'm sure you will understand this, Marie: My students tell me I often assume the personalities of those resurrected bodies, that my face changes in mimicry, that my voice plays a scale of off-key accents. I am not aware of any of this. I am aware only of the faces of my students. I know by their faces if they are hearing and wondering.

Forgive the above. I should remember it's you to whom I'm writing. You would rip me to shreds for being so dreamy.

I just heard your ghost-laugh from that good world, that Out There place.

This is so hard to do, Marie, the writing of this letter. I ache from the touch of each word.

I am a runaway, Marie. Teaching helps me to be a runaway. You wrote to me of your fantasies about us—the lovers we never became. I am glad we were such lovers in your dreaming of us. Those dreams perfectly matched mine, so perfectly I wonder if we were lost in the same dreams on the same nights.

To me, teaching is an act of fantasizing, as well as an act of becoming.

Yes, I like that word: fantasizing.

You know better than anyone about my fantasizing.

I fantasize in bits and pieces, in dots and dashes, in all fragments of my life. I am as muscular as an athlete, graceful as a dancer, brilliant as a philosopher, wise as a god. I am an assassin. I touch the blind and heal them. I make love to the world's most beautiful women. I write poetry that will be quoted a thousand years from now. I soar above the earth in spaceships sailing on butterfly wings, discover lost cities of purest gold beneath pearl beds in the oceans. I speak the languages of the world with the voice of the lute. I can read the ballooning thoughts of people around me, gaze into their souls.

Runaways are always fantasizing.

But, Marie, my strange, dear friend, my almost-mate, you have never let me forget what I could not escape: reality is a story hard-earned, while dreamers always lose themselves in following after dreams.

Wait for me in that good world, that Out There place.

We will end the regrets.

And I will never again run away. I promise.